FRAN

NO ANGELS WEPT

FRANK SPINELLI

NO ANGELS WEPT

Deerfield Press

No Angels Wept
By Frank Spinelli

Published by Deerfield Press

Edited by Nicole Kimberling

Copyedit by Dianne Thies

Cover design by: Reese Dante
reesedante.com

First edition December 2023
Print ISBN-13: 979-8-9896367-0-9
ebook ISBN-13: 979-8-9896367-1-6

Printed in the United States of America

To Larry Higgins, my best friend.
I don't know what I would do without you

Chapter One

After surviving a murder attempt, a malpractice lawsuit, and nearly losing his license to practice medicine, thirty-three-year-old Dr. Angelo Perrotta sat strapped in a seat as the huge 737 descended through the dense pink clouds on approach to LAX.

Hours earlier, he kissed his boyfriend Jason Murphy good-bye. This would be the first time since they began dating two years ago that they were physically apart for more than a day. Immediately, Angelo regretted his decision to appear on the satellite radio show, *A Thorny Mess*, in Los Angeles. Jason, his left arm suspended in a sling, had been recovering from an injury he sustained at work during a fall while chasing a perp who had robbed a liquor store for drug money. Jason had slipped on the slick sidewalk and fallen flat on his back. The wide-eyed robber returned to stomp on Jason's forearm, nearly crushing his ulna, before fleeing the scene. "Are you sure you don't want to come?" Angelo had asked though he knew Jason's response even as the words escaped his lips.

Minutes after the plane landed, the ding of a bell alerted the passengers they had arrived at the gate. By habit, everyone reached for their cellphones. People began unlatching their seat belts and clicking open overhead compartments. Cellphones were powered on. Bags were retrieved. All the while, Angelo sat still. Seated nearly in the last row by a window, he had plenty of time. Staring at the busy tarmac, the sun streaking through the California smog lent everything the dreamy air of a Van Gogh painting: The ground crew in orange vests and matching caps. Everyone wearing aviator sunglasses. The scene distorted by fuel vapor floating in the air.

What was I thinking? A Thorny Mess!

The thought of coming face-to-face with the radio host, Rachel "Rocky" Thorndyke, caused his heart to release a spate of palpitations. Up until that moment, Angelo had only heard about the shock jock who stoked her listeners' insatiable appetite for conspiracy theories and infuriated journalists who criticized her for using alternative facts. With each controversial episode, Rocky's ratings exploded like a Roman candle, propelling her into the spotlight. She had become a social media star with two million followers. Her Wikipedia page offered a fascinating snapshot of Rocky as a person and artist—obsessive and eccentric, if not a bit too caustic, and yet also inspiring and daring—while considering her crucial place in radio.

Angelo bent forward. Face in his hands to keep his head from cracking open. *Three deep breaths. Serenity now.*

A flight attendant surprised him and asked if he was ill. "No," Angelo replied, "just tired." It was then Angelo realized most of the passengers had disembarked.

"Okay, but whenever you're ready..."

Three deep breaths. Serenity now. This was the basis of the mindfulness exercises he had begun months back when he first started experiencing panic attacks. His therapist encouraged him to download an app called SRNiTY. Angelo practiced the exercises three times a day and whenever he felt a bout of anxiety coming on. "Our lives are interwoven in ways we don't understand," she had explained. "Take three deep breaths and say, 'serenity now.' Call in the forces of peace, otherwise the forces of doom will line up against you. The world is vicious and illogical. Happiness is only a matter of framing. Look for opportunities by disrupting norms."

He lasted two months with her despite Jason's concerns. "You need to work out the root cause for these panic attacks," his boyfriend had said. But Angelo had been stubborn. He decided he would return to therapy when the time was right. Meanwhile, he would continue the mindfulness exercises. Deep down, they both knew Angelo's panic attacks had coincided with his obsession with the No Angels Wept Killer—the name the press had given a serial killer who had perpetrated a series of murders against young gay men in Los Angeles.

Angelo released his seat belt and maneuvered his way out of the row. He collected his bags and walked up the aisle. The same flight attendant now stood at the door, smiling. Young, Angelo thought. It was like looking at his twentysomething self.

"Thank you for flying with us." The flight attendant gently brushed his hand against Angelo's arm as he passed. "Try to have a good day."

Angelo paused momentarily. Seduced by the young man's innocent forwardness. Beard scarcely visible on his chin. "I will and thank you again."

In his twenties Angelo had been entrenched in the world of medical school. Days absorbed by lectures in vast auditoriums and evenings spent studying in a tiny library cubicle. A blurring of days so that his recollection of them, like the scene outside the plane window, was a dreamy Van Gogh landscape. Round shapes and swirling lines of color. Nothing felt sharp or focused. That was until Demetre Kostas killed Mia Garcia during Angelo's first year in private practice and buried her still living body under a cement slab in his own New Jersey garage.

Over two years had gone by, and Angelo could conjure every detail of that first year after residency. He had just landed a dream job in a private practice off Park Avenue.

Soon after, he was introduced to Demetre Kostas—the owner of an aesthetic practice called Skindom. Demetre with his darky wavy hair, intense gaze, and tan, buttery forearms. The man who befriended Angelo and beguiled him into thinking they were more than friends. Batman and Robin, Demetre had called them, but Angelo came to learn they were never friends at all. He had been merely a pawn for Demetre to subjugate, betray, and deceive. In the end, Angelo realized he had gotten off easy. It was poor Mia Garcia who paid the ultimate price.

Once he stepped off the plane, he powered on his cellphone. Angelo texted Jason as he walked:

Landed. Call U later. XO

Once inside LAX the clamor and cacophony felt like an assault. He moved quickly and with haste. Angelo had to get a taxi, check into the hotel, and meet the show's producer, Wes Plagen, before this evening's broadcast. Riding the moving walkway, Angelo passed gate after gate. A television monitor on mute showed a news reporter speaking with a grave expression. Angelo read the breaking news banner: No Angels Wept Killer Claims Third Victim.

Three deep breaths. Cellphone!

Angelo scrolled his newsfeed, confirming what he hoped wasn't true. The LA serial killer dubbed the No Angels Wept Killer had struck again. His third victim in six months. Stepping through the sliding glass doors, the sun hit Angelo like a spotlight. The heat enveloped him with unexpected intensity. So unexpected since New York had been experiencing an unusual chilly October. Angelo hurried to the section reserved for app-based car services. Mopping his brow, he read the article while he waited for his ride.

> SERIAL KILLER CLAIMS THIRD VICTIM
> Los Angeles, CA—LA County police identified

> the man who was found in his Encino apartment on Wednesday. Twenty-four-year-old Trevon Bolden's body was discovered by the Mancito Arm's superintendent after neighbors complained of a foul smell coming from inside Bolden's apartment. Taped to the medicine cabinet was a note that read, *No Angels Wept*. This is the third murder at the hands of a killer who has left his calling card now at three separate crime scenes. Police have yet to comment on whether the two previous murders with the same calling card are linked. No other information is available at this time, including suspect information.

There was footage of the body being transported from the crime scene. Photos of the first two victims. Another clip showed the first victim's mother, Mabel Knight, rushing into her apartment to avoid an onslaught by news reporters asking her thoughts about the latest murder victim.

Angelo recalled the weeks and months after Mia Garcia died. He had been hounded by reporters and turned down countless interviews asking him to recount the awful string of nightmarish events. They had all wanted the same thing: the salacious story of a cocaine addict who portrayed himself as a physician. The former go-go dancer who entertained gay men after office hours, exchanging sex for drugs he acquired through stolen prescription pads. And of course the vampires wanted to hear about Mia Garcia, the poor executive with a harelip scar. Rabbit girl. La Coneja. The perfect flaw that brought her endless grief.

And now Angelo was in LA. Hours away from his first appearance on a wildly popular radio show where he would be expected to discuss the very case he had only wanted to forget. To think Angelo had accepted an invitation to review the events that led up to Mia Garcia's death and his peripheral involvement on live radio seemed idiotic when he had wanted nothing more than to distance himself from Demetre's crimes. Yet, his sister Camille had encouraged him to consider the consequences of burying the past. "Maybe it's time you started speaking about what happened," she had said after he informed her about the interview request. "You could really help people understand the gaps in the criminal justice system when it comes to drug addiction." Camille had a point, but it took two weeks and a lot of begging from Wes before Angelo accepted the offer.

Over the course of three weeks, Angelo and Wes spoke on the phone several times and once via Zoom. Wes had Demetre's slow, measured tone. A voice that coaxed the real story from within Angelo. A version that identified gaps in the justice system. An empathetic view of the devil's grip of drug addiction. "That," Wes had said, "that's the story I want you to tell."

A black SUV pulled up to the curb. Angelo got in, resting his head against the back seat. *What are you afraid of?* Demetre was tucked away safely in prison. The malpractice case had been settled, and the Office of Professional Medical Conduct had found no evidence that Angelo had done anything unethical; therefore, his license to practice medicine remained active.

Just then, his cellphone rang. "Welcome to LA," Wes announced. "How was your flight?"

"Good," Angelo replied. "I'm on my way to the hotel."

"Do you have a minute?"

Angelo sensed something was wrong. "What's up?"

Wes cleared his throat. "Did you hear the news?"

Outside, palm tree shadows bowed as they drove south on the 110. The SUV slowed down to meet the encroaching traffic. In the distance, the storied smog so thick that the tops of skyscrapers were obscured was as recognizable to Angelo as the Hollywood Sign.

"You mean the news about the latest No Angels Wept murder?" Angelo ventured.

"Yeah, unbelievable, right?"

Unbelievable? Not to Angelo. "Clearly, every three months is a pattern."

"No, I mean, it's unbelievable that this story broke today. The day you're supposed to be on *A Thorny Mess*."

An imaginary hot poker blazed against Angelo's lower back. "Why do I sense you're about to tell me bad news?"

Wes offered an overexaggerated laugh. "Oh boy, you New Yorkers. You guys don't beat around the bush."

The car came to a full stop. Angelo couldn't catch his breath. Head between his knees to modulate his breathing, he experienced a familiar reaction. Anxiety. Panic. Annoying roommates that took up space in his body.

"Angelo," Wes called. "Are you there?"

"Just tell me the problem, Wes."

"There's no problem," Wes drawled in a strange singsong. "Well, maybe there's a slight problem. It's not a problem necessarily. More of a nuisance."

Thankfully, the SUV began to accelerate. Angelo sat up, his breathing less labored. "Wes, I just flew over five hours. What's the problem?"

Angelo imagined Wes running his hand through his sun-streaked hair. A tell Angelo had picked up during their Zoom call. Wes combed his fingers through his jaw-length hair when he struggled to find his words. The type of person who couldn't sit still when there was a conflict.

"Remember I told you Rocky is obsessed with these No Angels Wept murders?"

"Of course, I remember," Angelo said. "I told you that I've been following these murders from day one."

"So, like you, she's really, really into this case so..."

"So, she really, really wants to focus on the new murder tonight instead of interviewing me."

Exuberant laughter followed. "You're killing me man. I'm telling you. You New Yorkers do not disappoint."

"Can't say the same about you Angelenos."

"Ouch," Wes grumbled with playful woundedness. "Remember I said it wasn't a problem, but more of a nuisance."

The SUV pulled up to the hotel. Angelo grabbed his duffle bag. "I'm listening." He nodded thankfully at the driver and proceeded through the hotel entrance.

"Rocky has decided to focus tonight's show exclusively on the latest murder," Wes explained. "Instead of interviewing you, Rocky would like you to sit for the entire show to offer your expert medical opinion. You said it yourself; you've been following this case from day one. What do you say? It'll be fun."

Angelo approached the front desk. A Hispanic woman with warm dark eyes and a smile that took up much of her face greeted him. A dead ringer for Mia Garcia. "Fun, huh?"

"Angelo." Wes's tone was nothing less than serious. "I know you're disappointed, but sometimes we make creative decisions for the benefit of the show. You're already in LA. Check in, get settled, and be at the station by three."

Angelo stood frozen as the Hispanic receptionist stared back at him. Her inviting eyes and warm smile never wavered. "Okay, see you later."

After checking in, Angelo lay on the bed in his hotel room wondering when exactly he became fascinated with the No Angels Wept murders. He supposed it was just after the shocking first murder six months ago. A masseur named Keith Knight was found dead near Venice Beach. His right hand had been severed and stolen. Angelo recalled reading the article on the subway. Was cutting off a masseur's hand the killer's attempt at irony? That hadn't been the only detail that caught Angelo's attention. No, it was the calling card—No Angels Wept—hand-printed on a cream-colored dinner place card. Did the killer plan on eating Keith Knight's hand? A copycat of the famous fictitious cannibal serial killer featured in a series of books Angelo himself had devoured?

With each new victim, Angelo experienced a rush of blood like lust, an intense yearning to know the truth. The faces of those young gay men paraded across his mind on a loop. Day after day, night after night, bleeding into weeks and then months. But after the initial reports, the faces of the first two dead men receded from headline news. They had one thing in common: they were gay sex workers. Boys who had come from poor, broken homes. Unwanted. Abused. Shamed. Not the kind of people that pulled on the heartstrings of the American public.

Since the murders began, Angelo experienced a new form of anxiety. Unlike the internally combustive obsidian. The No Angels Wept murders brought on an external fear. A fear of tight spaces, of long dark hallways. Spaces and corridors with walls that felt as if they were contracting and swallowing him like a peristaltic throat. And yet, every day Angelo searched online for updates but once the initial reports were posted, those boys rarely made another appearance. That was, until today.

Outside the windows, the smog hovered like the city was wrapped in gray gauze illuminated by the intense sunlight. The Los Angeles skyline through the dark-tinted hotel windows appeared like a city after a bombing.

His watch read one 1:00pm. He could turn on the television. Drink a cup of coffee and try to stay awake. A huge clock on top of a building just outside his window displayed the temperature. 93 degrees Fahrenheit. What did he know about Los Angeles other than what he had read in magazines. The city where the sun never quit, and the sky never rained. An atmospheric anomaly: unburned hydrocarbon and oxides of nitrogen from car exhaust. Los Angeles, with millions of cars, suffered the most of all California cities because it existed in a basin. Balmy breezes that stirred up that brown cloud made eyes itchy and tearful.

Thinking allowed the time to slip, he surrendered to drowsiness. Soon he'd have to leave for the studio, but he was too tired to get up just yet. It had been a long morning of travel, and for what? To sit and listen to an adrenaline junkie spit vitriol into a microphone. In a way, Angelo felt fortunate he no longer had to relive the worst experience of his adult life. And there it was, the silver lining he needed to propel him through the rest of this day.

He only meant to close his eyes for a few moments. Instead, he passed out. When Angelo woke up, the clock read 2:45pm.

Chapter Two

If anyone had told Angelo that LA traffic rivaled New York's, he would have recommended a CT scan of their brain. Unfortunately, he learned this truth at the worst possible time. Though the radio station was a mere five miles from his hotel, it took over a half hour to get there.

Panicked, sweaty, breathless, Angelo stood before security, presenting his driver's license. "I'm going to be on *A Thorny Mess*," he told a disinterested security guard who handed him a pass. Angelo sprinted for the elevators.

He had texted Wes in the car. "Don't sweat it," Wes had replied. But Angelo, the punctuality-obsessed New Yorker, believed arriving on the dot was akin to being ten minutes late.

As the mirrored elevator doors shut, he dared to glance at his watch. It read 3:15pm. "Calm down," he said. "This is a radio show, not a surgical procedure." He caught a glimpse of his reflection: dark wavy hair, wide-set brown eyes, and the scar that ran two inches along his right cheek like a second smile. Not bad, considering inside he felt like a wrecking ball was demolishing the contents of his chest.

The doors opened moments later to a brightly lit lobby. Glass windows. Posters showcasing musicians. KLM Satellite Radio banners. A woman with black and pink hair cut into a mullet winked at him from behind the reception desk. Wes stood off to the side, leaning against the desktop like it was bar. "Dr. Angelo Perrotta." Wes grinned. "In the flesh."

Angelo wiped his sweaty palm against his slacks before he shook Wes's hand. Surprisingly, Wes seemed smaller in real life. A hazard of Zoom meetings where everyone's head appeared the size of a circus balloon. In person, Wes had those hypnotic steel-blue eyes that took up most of his overblown Zoom face. Loose sandy-brown hair curled under his prominent chin. A single sun-streaked strand flopped over his right eye. A denim shirt with sleeves rolled up to his elbows exposed tanned, muscular forearms. Low-rise blue skinny jeans completed the look. So casual, so LA, but Angelo suspected hours of preparation went into Wes's carefree appearance.

"I'm so sorry I'm late."

Wes offered a chuckle. The kind that suggested no one in LA was ever on time. "Let's head over to the studio. The show's about to start."

"But I thought…"

"The show started at 3:00pm?" Wes offered a sideways glance. "That's a trick I learned years ago. Having folks believe the show starts earlier saves me a lot of headaches."

Angelo hurried after Wes who careened through the maze of hallways flanked by glass studios and offices on either side. Meetings packed with Gen Zers, appearing disinterested and insouciant. Others displayed hosts wearing headsets. Lips pressed against microphones, shouting at an invisible audience. Every scene appeared to be set on mute. Even their footsteps on the carpeted floor were muffled. One last turn, and Wes opened a studio door. A whoosh from inside hit Angelo's face like lowering a car window. The soundproof studio absorbed everyone's voices. Angelo never heard the woman shouting until he stepped inside.

She had her back to him, but Angelo knew this had to be Rocky Thorn. Short, cropped black hair, black leather pants, and a white tank top exposing tattooed sleeves of Chinese imagery. Not anime. A hand reached to scratch her lower back, exposing a skull and crossbones tramp stamp. She spun around as if she felt Angelo's eyes boring into her. "I refuse to talk to you when you're like this, Fitz," she said right before she shoved the phone in her back pocket.

"Rocky," Wes called. "I want to introduce you to Angelo Perrotta."

She observed Angelo without speaking. Turquoise eyes sharpened. "The doctor!" she said with sudden recognition. Her grip was like a used car salesman meeting a prospective client. "Thanks for coming all this way." She bit her thumbnail. Eyes veered over to Wes. "You got him up to speed, right?"

"Don't worry, Rocky." Wes motioned for Angelo to sit at one of the two guest seats. A frat bro intern came over to speak with him as Wes and Rocky huddled. "Here's the Volume knob. Speak into the microphone. Press this red button if you need to cough."

"You mean the one labeled, cough?" Angelo asked.

The frat bro walked off hurriedly. Just then, Rocky clapped her hands once. "All right people. Everyone who doesn't need to be here, get the fuck out now."

"Remember," Wes whispered in Angelo's ear, "she's all bark." His warm breath sent a tingle down Angelo's back.

Just as Rocky's theme music blasted into Angelo's ears—a combination of heavy metal and explosive sound effects—he thought, *for the love of God what did I get myself into*? For a brief second, he even considered rushing for the exit but suspected it was locked from the outside. Trapped in a cage with a Bengal tiger.

An unexpected roar rattled him from his thoughts. Rocky howled into the microphone. Angelo glanced at the glass partition where Wes sat on the other side with twin frat bros. They all seemed amused. Avid sycophants. "Welcome to *A Thorny Mess*. I'm your fucking host, Rocky Thorn, and tonight my Thorny Messes, you are in for a treat."

Here it comes, Angelo grimaced internally. The moment where Rocky segued into his introduction, but he was wrong. Rocky carried on like she was the only person in the room. Angelo had become invisible. The only people she cared about were those driving in their cars, sitting in their living rooms, or scrolling their Instagram feeds. Her fans. Her Thorny Messes.

Another glance at the glass partition. Wes and the frat bros seemed rapt. Wide-eyed fans themselves, mesmerized by their rockstar goddess. After several minutes listening to Rocky engage with her audience, Angelo caught his reflection in the glass. Dark hair, dark eyes, and that innocent expression told him everything he should have known already. *This isn't about you. This is a show. Strap yourself in and enjoy the ride.* Just as he turned to focus on Rocky, Wes stole a peek. His expression turned concerned, but Angelo smiled to assure him that he had received the memo. Angelo was on Rocky's turf.

"All right," Rocky shouted. "I've been champing at the bit to get on the air tonight. I need to be around my peeps. That's because tonight, I'm dedicating this entire fucking show to the latest victim of the No Angels Wept Killer, Trevon Bolden aka Blaze. Now for all you vampires who just climbed out of your coffins, N.A.W. claimed his third victim. Tuesday, police found Blaze's naked dead body in his empty bathtub after neighbors complained of a super foul, super fishy smell emanating from his apartment. A poor unfortunate shlub named Carlos Munoz, the superintendent of the lovely Mancito Arms apartment complex, found Blaze. Poor bastard probably thought he was going to scrape a dead maggot-infested rodent off the kitchen floor. Instead, Munoz found the twenty-four-year-old naked in a tub minus the bathwater and one tongue."

Rocky's swagger didn't surprise Angelo, who had listened to several of her shows online. What surprised him was how Rocky knew more about Blaze's death than what had been reported in the news. He hadn't remembered reading anything about a tongue being cut out of the victim's mouth. Though it made sense considering the killer had taken body parts from the previous two victims.

"That's right," Rocky continued. "You heard me. We know N.A.W. loves his trophies like my producer loves dick." Angelo's eyes veered to Wes, who offered Rocky the middle finger. "Well, this time it wasn't the cat that got Blaze's tongue. It was the sick fucker who preys upon gay sex workers. The kind of people who live at the lovely Mancito Arms. The kind of folks no one cares about. That is except for my Thorny Messes and your patron saint of the invisible LGBTQ+ community. I'm your host Rocky Thorn and tonight you are in for one hot thorny mess. Stay tuned."

Once the commercial started, Rocky sat back in her ergonomic executive chair and fist-pumped the ceiling. Angelo stared at her expectantly, waiting for her to engage him, but she didn't know he was there. At least that's the way she acted. Angelo shot a glance at Wes through the glass partition. He offered Angelo a reassuring nod. Rocky drummed her palms against the desk marred with tiny dents just as the commercial wrapped up.

Showtime.

Angelo assured himself that Rocky's hyperbolic intro was meant to capture her fans' attention. Now that she had them in her grip, the show would proceed at a normal pace. One that was less sensational, more fact driven. *Who am I kidding?*

"So, I was driving here in my car when it occurred to me," Rocky began, "that if N.A.W. hadn't left his calling card no one would care he was plucking off fags like ducks in a shooting gallery."

Suddenly Angelo's stomach somersaulted like he was in the first car of a roller coaster making its initial descent. Rocky proceeded to speak in a manner that was equal parts offensive and empathetic. The more she spoke, the more he realized this was a huge mistake. His only saving grace was that Rocky spoke incessantly and endlessly and without punctuation. A hamster on a wheel. There was a good chance she might not even invite him into the conversation. She hadn't even introduced him yet.

"Okay, now it's time for me to shut my trap," Rocky announced as she wiped her forearm across her mouth. "I want to hear from somebody else."

Cold sweat broke out all over Angelo's body. *Relax. What was it Michelle Obama said? They go low, you…run out of the room.*

"I want to hear from you, my Thorny Messes." Rocky stared at the control panel where red lights blinked on and off like a pulse. "Caller, you're on with Rocky."

"Whoa," a male stuttered. "Rocky, you're a fuckin' rockstar!"

"Gee, I haven't heard that one before," she replied sarcastically as she dramatically clicked to the next caller. "Let's try that again. Caller, you're on and please prove to me that I'm not speaking to the president of the *Bill & Ted's Excellent Adventure* fan club."

"I don't know who they are," a girl moaned giddily.

"Fuck you!"

Just as Rocky was about to snuff out another caller, the girl intervened. "I do know the detective in charge of the No Angels Wept murders has been taken off the case."

"Is this a tip?" Rocky asked, her voice lilting playfully. "Come on girl. This is Rocky Thorn. I need more than the tip. Slip everything you got inside me now."

A little squeal. "Something about medical leave, but word is, the mayor was unhappy with how long it was taking Detective Hong Lee to find this freak."

"Hmmm," Rocky moaned. "That feels good. Come on. Work my hole some more. My ears are open." Rocky's eyes darted toward Wes. She stabbed a finger at him. "And where, pray tell, did you taste this delicious oyster mignonette?"

Wes scribbled a note and planted it against the glass. It read: confirming now.

The caller cooed like the high school quarterback had dropped her a wink. "I'm not s'posed to say."

"Don't be a tease."

The frat bros exchanged titillated reactions. Angelo felt like he was spying on naked men in a locker room. They were chest bumping and manhandling each other with varsity comradery. Wes, meanwhile, was simultaneously on the phone and typing on his laptop.

"I am *so* not a tease."

"Sure you are," Rocky drawled. "I can hear you dripping, you dirty whore." She glanced at Wes. He gave her the thumbs-up. "Okay, pussycat. You win. How about mama gives you something sweet in return for that tasty mother of pearl?"

"Really!"

Rocky gestured like she was playing with her nipples as the frat bros slapped each other on the back. "I'm gonna hand you over to my producer. He's superhot but he's super allergic to seafood. Get my drift? He's gonna send you a T-shirt. Wear it in good health."

Rocky transferred the call just as the girl was about to thank her. She took a bunch more calls. Each one she treated with her brand of dismissive, dry-witted sarcasm that Angelo imagined would have turned off most people, but not Rocky Thorn's Thorny Messes. They craved it. Lapped it up like starving feral cats.

An hour and a half later Angelo remained silent and ignored. He settled back for the last twenty minutes, convinced Rocky had no plans of engaging him in conversation. He felt momentarily at ease when suddenly, Rocky curled her lip in a semblance of a half-smile.

"By the way Messes," she said. "I forgot I have a guest waiting in the wings. A New Yorker if you can believe it. Not sure what my producer promised him, but the guy is sitting right here. Flew in all the way from Manhattan. Not bad looking either, but keep your legs crossed ladies, he plays for the other team. So, without further ado let me introduce Dr. Angelo Perrotta." Rocky smiled. Lots of bleached teeth. A shark winking at a minnow before devouring it. "Oh, I forgot. You may remember his name. A year ago, or was it two, he was famously splashed all over the news after he aided a psychopathic quack named Demetre Kostas, who buried a young woman named Mia Garcia alive in a concrete coffin. Isn't that right, Dr. Angelo?"

Something was different in her face, in her voice. It reminded Angelo of the way boys in grammar school used to ask Angelo if he was gay. The taunt of a bully, and it was then, Angelo realized, he wanted no part in this charade orchestrated by a narcissistic, mean-spirited radio host. Angelo summoned every bit of courage he had and stood up to leave. In a split second, Wes met Angelo's gaze. He saw the disappointment reflected in Wes's eyes. They had an agreement. Say what you want about Demetre Kostas, but Mia Garcia was off-limits. Wes had promised him that, but it was clear Rocky had made no such promise.

The flash of a blade caught Angelo's eye. He spun around just as Rocky produced a knife from inside her Doc Martens boot. This woman wasn't acting like a psycho; she was certifiably insane. Rocky reared the knife overhead and stabbed it into the desk, the knife handle quavering from the sheer force. By the pockmarked desktop it seemed Rocky, the knife-wielding shock jock, had done this many times before. She pointed her finger at Angelo and motioned for him to sit. Like an obedient dog, Angelo did so.

"I said, 'Isn't that right, Dr. Angelo?'" Her eyes crackled with playful malevolence.

Angelo felt a lump of acid rising in his throat. "Right?" He swallowed down hard. "There's nothing right about you or your show...*Rachel*."

She smiled stiffly. It was clear Rocky had been offended.

"Oh, I'm sorry," Angelo said, returning the playful malevolence. "I forgot. You don't go by Rachel Thorndyke. You hide behind this persona you created. Rocky Thorn. But you know what, *Rachel.* After listening to you spew bullshit for the past three hours, I realized you're not the patron saint of the invisible LGBTQ+ community."

Quietly, Wes entered the studio. Rocky raised her hand to pause him. Baring her teeth at Angelo, she urged him to go on.

"You don't speak for me or for the LGBTQ+ victims whose deaths are minimized and swept under the carpet. Because in order to do that, you'd have to be a rockstar. But you're no rockstar, Rachel *Thorn*dyke. What you are is a first-class bully. And do you know who I despise more than bullies? People who submit to them. Now if you don't mind, I want to get as far away from you as humanly possible."

Rocky and Wes stood in silence, digesting the scene. Only the blinking lights from the control panel pierced this diorama of disaster. Suddenly, Rocky poised a single finger over the red button gleaming with such intensity Angelo expected it to burn her flesh when she pressed it.

"Caller, you're on *A Thorny Mess.*" For half a second it appeared the three of them were holding their collective breaths. A charged triangulation formed around them like an electric fence.

"Holy fuckin' shit. Who is this fucker?"

Rocky's head jerked puppet-like toward Angelo. "How many times do I have to introduce him? His name is Dr. Angelo Perrotta." Click. Next caller. "You're on with Rocky."

"Where did you find this doctor, Rocky?" another caller asked. "Please tell me he's coming back. The show can't end like this."

"He's a real pistol, right?"

Adrenaline surged through Angelo's body, igniting his blood with radiant heat. Suddenly, he was swept up in the squall of *A Thorny Mess.*

"What the fuck. I mean, what the actual fuck? This doctor is dope."

The calls kept coming. A tidal wave of condemnation, adulation, and suspicion as if all this had been planned. Wes exited the studio to observe from behind the glass.

Rocky turned to face Angelo head-on. "A little birdie told me you're obsessed with our friend, the No Angels Wept Killer?"

Angelo laughed. A hard sound. "Obsessed is an understatement."

"You're from New York," she said, her voice urbane, easy. "You have your fair share of murderers. Why this one? Why N.A.W.?"

Angelo scrutinized her. "People kill all the time. They kill their husbands, their wives, their bosses. Some even kill their kids. What makes the No Angels Wept Killer different is because I believe he is murdering young gay men with a sense of urgency. Like he's doing the Lord's work."

"Urgency?" Rocky repeated with pessimism. "Doc, he killed three people in six months. I don't get a sense of urgency."

Angelo scooted forward. "That's where you're wrong." Hearing his voice in the headset had him wondering if he had ever sounded so self-assured in his life.

The year that followed Mia Garcia's death, Angelo endured the abuse of social media trolls who called him a simp, an idiot, and a fool. And for a long time, he agreed with them. But sitting in that KLM Studio, talking to Rocky, Angelo experienced an odd sensation. His skin felt like it was shedding, a molting snake, and a new, self-assured Angelo emerged. "This killer is reeking with urgency, but he's also completely in control. I'm not an expert, but like you, I follow the habits of serial killers. Call it a hobby."

"I said the same thing to my girl once. You know what she said? Take up basket weaving!"

"Can't you do both?" Angelo kidded. "But seriously. N.A.W. isn't slowing down. In fact, I believe he's ratcheting things up. He's killed three people, with each murder three months apart. What's the significance of three. The more important question is…can he maintain his restraint?"

Rocky turned to the microphone. "That's our show for tonight. I want to thank my guest, Dr. Angelo Perrotta. And contrary to what my guest said earlier, I am and always will be your patron saint of the invisible LGBTQ+ community. Until next time. Sniff the rose but beware the messy thorns."

Chapter Three

"I wish you could have been there, Jason." Angelo kicked off his shoes and pulled off his polo. "It was so exciting."

"I can hear it in your voice," Jason replied. "What's she like in person?"

Angelo wrestled with his jeans and flopped on the bed. "That's better."

"What are you doing?" Jason asked. "All this huffing and puffing. Did Wes come back to the room with you?"

"Wes?" Angelo repeated. "God no. What made you think…on second thought. Let's not go there. You have no idea how hot it is in LA. Between sweating my ass off in that studio with Rocky, the patron saint of narcissism, and the unseasonably warm weather, all I want is to be naked and alone."

Jason murmured sexily, "Now we're talking. What do you say we FaceTime and get freaky?"

Seconds later, Jason appeared on-screen wearing a white T-shirt. His prick surging over the waistband of his boxer briefs had Angelo's pulse galloping. He loved feeling so desired from someone he loved so much. "Well, someone is horned up."

Jason licked his lips. "Taking care of business on my own hasn't been easy with a broken forearm." He pulled the phone back far enough to remind Angelo of the splint on his left forearm.

"It's only temporary," Angelo offered. "Besides, you're right-handed."

It took a few seconds for them to set up their phones so they could see each other masturbating. "So, tell me again how it made you feel, talking to Rocky?" Jason panted impatiently.

Angelo stroked his cock, recalling the events of the show. "I can't describe it other than to say it felt like electricity. That is…when she finally got around to actually speaking with me. After that, it was like we were the only two people in the world."

The intensity and immediacy of what they were doing… Angelo knew they were allowing themselves to explore the outer contours of their sexual relationship. Jason stretched his muscular body on wanton display as the cone of the yellow bedside lamp glistened against his pale, smooth body. "Electricity, huh?"

"Yeah, it wasn't so exciting at first, but once people started calling in…I realized thousands maybe millions of people were listening." Angelo rolled his hips to expose the pink dimple of his anus.

A hunger wiped across Jason's face. "You're so sexy. You know that?" Jason's eyes were searing with intensity. "What else?"

Angelo could almost feel Jason's breathing in his ear. Objectively, he knew this was ridiculous, but at that moment, having phone sex for the first time felt like a confirmation of their love. "To be honest, I found most of the show boring and derivative. It was only after she referred to me as the physician who aided a psychopathic quack—"

Jason cut in, "She said what?"

"Which part?" Angelo asked, but he hadn't realized the smile on Jason's face had dropped. "That's not important because I—"

"Not important!" The question had put a brake on the proceedings. "She alleged you aided a criminal, Angelo."

"Alleged?" Angelo growled. "Sounds like someone has been studying for the LSAT."

Angelo watched as Jason's urgent swell lazily deflated, drained of its previous hungry blood. "Hey, my arm is bothering me."

"Wait." Angelo sat up, reaching for the phone. "What's the matter?"

Then understanding hit Angelo; he had broken the mood by mentioning the law school admission test (LSAT).

After Jason's injury, Angelo had been on a mission to get his boyfriend to quit the force. It had begun weeks earlier, after Jason had been attacked as his partner questioned a man whom they suspected was dealing drugs outside a liquor store. But even before that, Angelo's attitude toward his lover's profession waned. The hot cop he fell in love with, the muscular man in the fitted blue uniform, no longer sent a wellspring of excitement through is body but rather a widening of the crack of fear and worry that Jason might not make it home each night. It had become a chasm so wide they had become emotionally distant due to the cold, foreboding truth that Jason's life would always be in peril if he remained a police officer. So, Angelo, the healer, the fixer, came up with a plan: law school. What a great transition for someone like Jason who admired law and order. A career defending the righteous that didn't require him to wear a gun or patrol the crime-infested streets of New York.

But like most dreams, they were only as lofty and inspiring as the person who conjured them. Jason hadn't thought of becoming a lawyer until Angelo had presented him with this dream job. They didn't argue about it at first. More like debated the reasons. Angelo presented his rationale while Jason simply explained it had always been his true dream to be a police officer for as long as he could remember and in sharing his childhood dream, Jason had shed his armor at the feet of his beautiful boyfriend, a man he cared for enough to do whatever it took to keep him in his life. But once Angelo heard Jason out, he felt obliged to accept his decision, though he did so begrudgingly. Lurking in the shadows of their relationship was the speck of doubt that Angelo would ever be satisfied or proud that his partner was simply a cop.

After Jason was attacked and injured, the incident reignited Angelo's case. The two agreed that while Jason was on leave, he would study for the LSAT. It felt like a victory to Angelo though he knew that Jason had only agreed to take the test to make him happy…and did so begrudgingly.

"Talk to me," Angelo pleaded.

By now, Jason had hastily tucked himself back in his boxers. Their moment of shared ecstasy had been tainted by the toxic topic of law school.

Angelo's phone dinged. It was a text from Wes.

"I'm gonna go," Jason said with evident disappointment. "I'll listen to the show online tomorrow. I'm really happy for you Angelo."

"Jason, don't go like this."

A second text from Wes chimed in. "You better answer that. It might be important. I love you."

"I love you too…" But Angelo's phone had already gone black.

Wes's text read:

Meet me in your hotel bar for a drink. I have a proposition for you.

A proposition? It must be something important for Wes to have driven all the way to his hotel.

Angelo wrote back:

Okay, but only one drink.

The lobby lounge was located on the seventieth floor of the Intercontinental Hotel. At this elevation the view of downtown Los Angeles stretched in three directions, the city illuminated with gold lights. In the distance the vaporous mountains rose, lending the entire scene the dreamy quality of an impressionist painting.

Wes waved him over. As Angelo made his way through the crowd, he told himself he had no interest in the blue-eyed producer with the come-hither stare nestled in the face of an angel. He had accepted Wes's invite purely out of curiosity. "How was dinner?" Angelo asked.

"It was fun." Wes signaled the bartender. "You should have come."

Angelo shirked with playful irksomeness. "After the show, I thought it might be uncomfortable. Plus, what's the old saying: leave them wanting more." Angelo ordered a glass of Chardonnay when the bartender presented himself.

"Well, you're very intuitive," Wes said. "The entire meal Rocky raved about you. You were all she talked about."

"That's nice of you to say, but I'm a hundred percent sure you're exaggerating."

"I'm not!" Wes insisted. "Did I do something to make you distrust me or is that a New York thing?"

In his mind's eye, Angelo could see Wes as clearly as if he were studying a Hollywood script: Sexy, young producer, trying to make it big in satellite radio. Has his sights set on films. Schmoozes everyone he meets with hyperbolic compliments, and ultimately, loses all touch with reality.

Wes raised his glass. "Let's toast."

"Okay." Angelo clinked his glass. "What are we toasting?"

Wes raised his martini to his lips, paused for dramatic emphasis. "To you, the new co-host of *A Thorny Mess*."

Angelo offered a wry smile. "And you want to know why I don't trust you."

"I swear. It's the truth."

For Angelo to imagine for one second that Rocky Thorn wanted a co-host, let alone someone who had no experience, was inconceivable. Though the show ended amicably, Angelo felt a guilty antipathy toward her, and he certainly assumed she felt a lingering resentment toward him. But for Wes to have driven downtown at this hour had him wondering if he had an ulterior motive. "I hope you didn't come all this way thinking I was going to invite you up to my room?" Angelo asked.

Wes clasped both hands to his left pec in playful woundedness. "That hurt." Another dramatic pause. "Truth is, I find you a very attractive man. Totally my type, but I don't hit on men with boyfriends."

Angelo took a long sip of wine, smacked his lips, and planted the glass down on the bar. "So, you're asking me to believe that after a twenty-minute conversation on the radio. Wait. Conversation would imply both parties were listening. You mean, after a twenty-minute exchange of thorny barbs with Rocky Thorn, she asked you to come all the way downtown to offer me a job as her co-host? No, I don't believe you, Wesley Plagen."

Wes chuckled. "Angelo, you're the match to Rocky's gasoline. Trust me. She's right. She's always right."

The only reason Angelo didn't turn on his heel, march back up to his room, and throw his clothes into his suitcase so that he could leave this godforsaken experience behind him had only to do with the self-assured smile on Wes's face. *Maybe this isn't a prank?*

Regardless of how exciting it had been for Angelo, Rocky had crossed the line mentioning Mia Garcia. What if her parents heard the show? Thinking he had taken part in dredging up the memory of her death made him shudder.

"It's only for two weeks." Wes swirled his glass before he drained it. "Angelo, I believe you have the potential to host your own show. Imagine an LGBTQ+ true crime podcast hosted by Dr. Angelo Perrotta."

A hoarse whisper from behind Angelo said, "He's not pulling your leg." When Angelo turned around, no one was there. The voice was in his head.

"What do you say?" Wes urged. "It's only two weeks. What do you have to lose?"

"I have a job!" Angelo said. "I have a life. I can't just press pause."

Wes, unable to control himself, burst into laughter. He stood up and threw his arm over Angelo's shoulder. "Do you see everyone in this bar?" Wes whispered in his ear.

"What about them?"

"What about them?" Wes repeated. "Well, for starters, everyone in this bar would leap off this building for the chance of co-hosting a hit radio show like *A Thorny Mess*. Do you understand the opportunity I'm offering you?"

Wes returned to his seat, motioning to the bartender for another round.

"I don't mean to sound ungrateful."

Wes's steel-blue eyes narrowed. "Show me you're not."

Wes exuded such confidence. It was as if he operated on a hard-sell internal factory setting. He was being completely serious, and this caused a release of adrenaline so potent it made Angelo blush. "I… I don't know what to say." Angelo stuttered. "I'm still in shock."

Wes clasped a hand on Angelo's shoulder. "Say yes."

Another round or maybe two, Angelo couldn't be sure. He was reeling from the shock and excitement. Riding up the elevator, he contemplated reason after reason for him not to accept Wes's offer. The thought of working with Rocky Thorn seemed akin to working as a crash test dummy. Every day he would have to submit himself to her histrionic outbursts, her wild accusations, and all of it now directed at him. Back in his room, Angelo looked out the window. Los Angeles stretching out before him now held a promise he hadn't even dreamed about earlier, and for this opportunity, this one chance in a lifetime, for it to come out of the blue seemed too good to pass up. The glittering, gold city lights faded. In their place, Angelo saw his reflection in the glass. Turning away, he collapsed on the bed. For a moment, he lay silent, knowing what he had to do next.

"Hello," Jason answered groggily.

"Sorry to wake you, but it's important."

Jason was now fully awake, his voice filled with alarm. "What is it? What's the matter?"

Angelo hesitated a moment. "I've been invited to co-host *A Thorny Mess*."

"What?" Angelo's phone began ringing. Jason had converted the call to video. "What's all this about co-hosting? I thought you were coming home tomorrow."

Angelo sat up. "It's only for two weeks. Wes said he thought Rocky and I had real chemistry, and if things work out, he believes I have the potential to host my own podcast."

"When do you have to decide?" After a long pause, Jason added, "Oh, wait. You already have."

"They want me to begin on Monday," Angelo explained. "We'll need to prep over the weekend, so it makes no sense to fly back to New York tomorrow."

"Oh, so you're not coming home?" Jason asked, his disappointment evident.

"Are you mad?"

"Mad?" Jason chuckled. "Angelo, I love you. Not seeing you for two weeks is going to suck big-time but hearing how excited you were earlier warmed my heart. I'm not going to stand in your way. This is a huge opportunity, and if this guy Wes thinks you have potential, then you need to make me one promise."

"What's that?"

"You need to bring it every day. Show them what I see. Don't back down. Don't let anyone push you around, especially Rocky Thorn. The old Angelo that let Dr. Stanzione and Demetre Kostas use and bamboozle him is gone. You left him in New York. Promise me you will shine in Los Angeles. Promise?"

Angelo tried to speak, though his heart had lodged in his throat. "I hate being away from you, what with your injured arm."

"What am I, five?" Jason laughed. "I can manage. Trust me. Plus, I have three sisters who call me every day, not to mention yours."

Angelo suspected Jason sounded more flippant than he felt. "Why don't you come here and stay with me for two weeks?"

"Listen to me." Jason held the phone close to his face. His eyes fastened on Angelo's. "The one thing I hate more than hotels is pity. Now, stop feeling guilty. We've survived worse than being apart for two weeks. Plus, I have physical therapy, and I want to be close by in case Mary has an update on the kid who died outside that homeless shelter."

For weeks Jason had been investigating the suspicious death of a young gay runaway discovered slain outside a shelter in Manhattan. Police were called to the scene after the boy walked in front of an oncoming car. Onlookers said the boy appeared distracted. Others described him as the walking dead. Days later, Jason got injured and had to take medical leave.

"You're still hung up on that case?" Angelo asked. "I thought it was ruled an accident."

"Yeah…well," Jason offered. "Here's the thing. Once I get stuck on something, I don't give up so easily. Get it?"

Staring into Jason's eyes, Angelo experienced a sudden surge of love. For two years they had developed a bond so strong Angelo realized how much he had taken it for granted. "I love you so much Jason Murphy."

"I love you too," he whispered. "Now get some rest… and don't forget our promise."

"Okay."

"Wait until I tell everyone my boyfriend is going to be guest co-host on *A Thorny Mess*."

Angelo hung up, feeling relieved they hadn't gone to bed angry. He began to unpack, hanging up his shirts, tucking his socks and underwear in a drawer, and setting his sneakers on the rack. He hadn't packed enough clothes to last two weeks, but certainly he had overpacked for a one-night stay. A shopping spree? What a fortunate unintended consequence.

Something in his loafers rattled. Angelo retrieved the left shoe and looked inside. He found a small wooden heart. The center had been hollowed out where a rolled-up note had been inserted.

> I carry your heart with me.
> I carry it in my heart.
> I am never without it.
> Anywhere I go, you go, my dear.

Jason had remembered Angelo's favorite poem by E. E. Cummings. Clutching the wooden heart, Angelo squeezed his eyes shut, believing he was the luckiest person alive. He had found the love of his life. And yes, they had been through worse, but with Jason, Angelo felt stronger. *Yes, I am becoming stronger.*

Chapter Four

The next morning, Angelo texted his boss to ask if he could have the next two weeks off. That prompted an uncomfortable phone call, which thankfully ended with only a slap on the wrist. Angelo apologized effusively and hung up, sighing heavily with relief. He spent the rest of the morning reading everything he could find online about the No Angels Wept murders, though he had read most everything published already. Eating room service breakfast while wearing the white terrycloth hotel bathrobe, Angelo felt like the famous fictional character from the children's book, *Eloise at the Plaza*. Chewing on toast triangles with butter and marmalade, Angelo scoured articles to confirm what Rocky had told her audience the night before about the latest victim. That Trevon "Blaze" Bolden's tongue had been taken as a trophy. But Angelo found nothing to confirm this.

After working out at the hotel gym, Angelo set out to explore Downtown LA, but the streets were empty, like he was a survivor after a nuclear bomb. He texted Jason often, feeling lost without him but resisting the temptation to complain. Angelo purchased a bottle of wine to bring to Wes's house that evening and returned to the hotel.

As he dressed, the television played in the background. "Are you lost, frightened or confused?" A series of images flashed on the screen. A black and white montage that told the story of a handsome young man stepping off a bus. A runaway, walking down a filthy street where rangy looking men offered him drugs and money for sex. "You're not alone." An older man, identified as Reverend James Jarrett, appeared on-screen: round black glasses, white goatee, and pleading blue eyes. "We're here for you at the Seven Spirits Church." The camera panned back as Jarrett extended his hands beatifically. He wore a black cassock with gold-filigree-trimmed cuffs. Cut back to the young man huddled in a dark corner, sleeping outside. A hand appeared. The boy took it, and suddenly the entire commercial became saturated in color like Dorothy stepping into Oz. The final shot showed a close-up of Reverend Jarrett. "Call us. Spirits on high." Angelo clicked off the television just as the 1-800 number popped up on the screen.

He was running late. Again.

It was just before sunset when he stepped outside the hotel. The sky boasted streaks of pink and purple. In the far distance the sun blazed a golden yellow, casting sharp lines against the gorge as the Uber drove up Laurel Canyon. Wes owned a 1930s bungalow with a long driveway that provided a separation from the street, evoking a sense of privacy and tranquility. A house tucked into the lush greenery with a dirt trail that ran along the right side and down the canyon. This was exactly the type of house Angelo imagined Wes lived in.

"*Bienvenida a mia casa*," Wes announced. In the dimming gold light, his steel-blue eyes and perfect smile gleamed. Staring at him, Angelo was momentarily stunned. Wes wore a very sheer floral-print shirt that was unbuttoned to just above his navel, baggy jeans with cut knees, and bare feet. "Come in." Angelo hesitated for a second. "Don't worry. Rocky isn't here yet."

"Is it that obvious?"

Wes grabbed his arm and pulled him inside. "Only around the edges."

They entered the open living room. A vaulted ceiling, Saltillo tile floors, and a brick fireplace made the room appear very cozy, very sexy, very Wes.

"Let's get you a drink," Wes suggested. "I assume that's for us." He jutted his chin at the wine bottle still in Angelo's hand.

"Where are my manners?" Angelo handed over the wine. "I guess my edges are rougher than I thought."

Wes walked up to Angelo and hooked his arm around his neck like they were best buddies in grammar school. "You have no reason to be worried. Outside the studio she's a completely different person." They entered a large, light-filled kitchen. Glancing around, Angelo assessed the rich, russet Mexican tile, the fading sunlight reflecting on the copper pans displayed like art against a white brick wall. Wes opened the bottle after inspecting the label and poured two glasses. "Here." He handed one to Angelo. "To rough edges and new beginnings."

Angelo took a gulp and allowed the warm Cabernet to sooth him. This moment of quiet bliss was pierced by the rattling of the kitchen windows as the roar of a supercharged car engine pulled into the driveway. "What the hell is that?"

Wes offered a sly smile. "That would be Rocky and her Dodge Charger."

Angelo stole a glimpse out the kitchen window. A matte black Dodge Charger sat in the driveway. Seconds later, the front door swung open. "Mommy's home!"

Angelo's back straightened.

"Come on." Wes grabbed the bottle. "Remember, she's a completely different person outside the studio."

Rocky had brought takeaway and was unpacking the bags when they entered the living room. She was dressed in a white sports bra and denim shorts exposing her muscular legs and more tattoos. A cobra spiraled up each thigh. Their heads appeared to meet in the center; tongues flickered obscenely at her groin from either side. She did a double take once her gaze fell upon Angelo. "Well, look who it is...Dr.

Angelo." Rocky threw her arms around his neck in a wrestler-style chokehold. "You fuckin' rockstar."

"I see you brought the snakes and the pythons," Wes chided.

Rocky stood back and offered a side-chest bodybuilder pose. "I figured the good doctor here should know what he's getting himself into."

"So, we're good?" Angelo asked her.

"Good?" Rocky jerked her head. "We're better than good. You and me"—she socked him in the shoulder —"we're gonna blow the audience's mind."

Wes handed her his glass of wine. "I tried to tell him you're a pussycat outside the studio."

"Pussycat?" Rocky repeated. She cocked her head from side to side as if she was deciding whether or not that assessment was true. "More like a pussycat with fangs and claws." She bared her teeth at Angelo and hissed.

◆◆◆

They dined on Thai food as they talked through the upcoming radio shows. "We're going to work backward," Wes explained. "First, we'll focus on Blaze."

"Oh shit!" Rocky shot up from her seat. "I forgot the big scoop." She took a moment to deliver what Angelo imagined was her happy dance. Marching in place. Pumping fists. "The newspapers got it wrong. The bathtub wasn't empty. It was full of cold water."

Angelo stopped in midchew. "Really?"

"Fingers and toes showed evidence of frostbite," Rocky added.

"Which means the killer filled the tub with ice," Angelo reasoned. "To slow down body decomposition."

It was just as he had suspected. The killer's sense of urgency was ratcheting up. Odds were he killed Blaze before the three-month anniversary, and in order to postpone the body from being found, he put it on ice. "The first two murders were three months apart. N.A.W. must have zeroed in on Blaze and couldn't wait any longer."

"You called it, Doc," Rocky said. "I didn't see that one coming."

Wes clapped his hands and stood up. "Do you hear what I'm hearing? You two are naturals together. These next two weeks are going to be epic."

"My source confirmed what the caller told us on yesterday's show," Rocky continued. "Detective Hong Lee is out on medical leave." She sat down and resumed eating. It was as if sharing the news had suddenly made her famished. She piled dumplings and pad thai on her plate. "They appointed a new lead investigator."

"What happened to Lee?" Wes asked.

Rocky shook her head, sucking up noodles until she coughed.

"Take it easy there, pussycat," Wes urged. "We don't want you to go out on medical leave too."

She took a swig of wine and wiped her mouth with the back of her hand. "Wes, please don't lecture me. Just because you can deep throat better than Linda Lovelace doesn't mean you're the only expert."

The banter was amusing, but like hearing a comic trying out new material, Angelo was getting frustrated. "Can we focus on the case?"

"Apologies, Angelo," Wes said. "Rocky and I argue like brother and sister."

Angelo raised an eyebrow. "My sister and I never argued over who gives the best blow job."

Rocky spat up a piece of dumpling. "You were so right about this one, Wes. Between the two of us, next week is going to be hotter than a California wildfire."

Picking up where the conversation left off, Rocky explained that her LAPD source said the investigation had been assigned to Detective Robert Town.

"Do we know anything about this guy?" Wes asked.

Rocky narrowed her eyes. "My source described him as an arrogant asshole with a chip on his shoulder the size of Gibraltar."

"Any chance he's an LGBTQ+ ally?" Wes asked, his voice rising in hope.

"That would be a no," Rocky replied. "Just the opposite. Apparently, he's very religious."

Wes's jaw clenched before he eked out, "Oh, then we don't want to piss him off."

Rocky bit her lip. Simultaneously, Wes and Angelo cut their eyes to her. "Don't look at me like that," she blustered. "It's my job."

Rising from the table, Wes headed for the kitchen. "It's not your job to piss off a new, very religious lead detective. Chances are he was brought on for a reason. None of which likely made him happy to take over the murder investigation of three gay sex workers."

"All I did was call his office," Rocky shouted.

Wes returned with wine and topped off everyone's glass. "Yeah, how'd that go?"

Rocky offered a thumbs-down. Slowly, Wes sat, eyeing Rocky with such urgency Angelo thought they were about to draw revolvers.

Wes slammed his hand on the table. "What happened?"

Pushing away her plate, Rocky said, "I received a message warning me to stay out of his way or else."

Wes took a long pull of wine. "You know what this means, don't you?"

Angelo shook his head. "No, what does it mean?"

"It means Town will try to find a gay scapegoat for the murders," Wes said. "Anyone else will force the LAPD to consider these murders hate crimes, but not if it's one of our own."

Wes's observation caused a palpable shift of pressure in Angelo, now faced with playing a part in telling these victims' stories. "Shit suddenly just got real."

"Help me clean up." Wes stood. "There's something I want to show you."

After the leftovers had been packed, the garbage thrown out, and the dishes stacked in the dishwasher, Wes invited them into the spare bedroom. On the far side of the room was a freestanding corkboard. Across the top, a white banner read: THE NO ANGELS WEPT MURDERS. Below it was a faceless silhouette labeled: N.A.W. Beneath that were the three photos of the murdered victims.

Rocky stepped forward, marveling at it. "You made a fucking evidence board. This is so rad."

Each victim had a description card. The first read:

Name: Keith Knight, 24 years old

Birthplace: Paw Paw, Michigan

Job: Masseur

Murdered: April 22, body found by a jogger near Venice Beach, hand amputated

Wes instructed them to sit on the bed as he stood beside the evidence board like he was a college math professor ready to explain a new theorem.

"So, the first victim was Keith Knight." Wes pointed to the photo of a young Black man. Lips smooshed to one side. Almond-shaped eyes turned up in feigned embarrassment. "Six months ago, his body was found near the beach next to a pile of trash." Wes's finger followed the red string that stretched along a large map of Los Angeles to a pin that marked the location of where Keith's body had been found. "His right hand had been amputated, but the police never found it. Toxicology revealed Keith had alcohol and multiple drugs in his system, including benzos, fentanyl, and opioids."

Rocky stood up, assuming the role of co-presenter. "The theory is that the killer hired Keith for a massage. They party, get a little freaky, but then"—Rocky punched her palm—"bam, he winds up swimming with the fishes in Venice."

Wes turned to the center photo. "Next we have Gabriel Menendez." Angelo silently read the accompanying description card.

Name: Gabriel Menendez, 25 years old

Birthplace: Aspen, Colorado

Job: Go-go dancer

Murdered: July 15, body found in dumpster by sanitation workers behind Peak, a gay club in West Hollywood, right leg mutilated.

"Gabriel's toxicology, like Keith's, showed alcohol and multiple drugs," Wes explained as he tapped the photo of the smiling young man with dark, wavy hair and a flat nose. "What makes Menendez's case slightly different is that unlike Keith Knight, where the murderer took one of his hands, Menendez's leg was mutilated, not amputated."

"Yeah, but my source said parts of the leg were missing," Rocky added.

Again, Wes's finger followed the red string that led from Gabriel's photo to the location where his body was found outside Peak.

"Do we know whether Menendez had been murdered somewhere else?" Angelo asked.

"Good question." Rocky winked with pride. "Considering the amount of blood found in the dumpster, the police believe the killer mutilated the body there."

Odd, Angelo thought. Mutilating a body outside a gay bar. The killer had taken such a risk. "It appears as if N.A.W. drugs his victims before he kills them," Angelo opined, "which is odd to me." By the confused looks on their faces, Angelo decided to explain. "Serial killers typically enjoy the killing part. It gives them a sense of control and empowerment over their victims. Now, he may have cut off Keith Knight's hand while he was still semiconscious. That doesn't seem to be the case with Gabriel Menendez. You said it yourself. Too much blood found in the dumpster. As for Blaze…well, we know the body was found in his apartment on ice, likely to delay the discovery. There's no way N.A.W. cut out his tongue while Blaze was conscious. Too many people live at the lovely Mancito Arms."

"I like the way you think, Doc." Wes gripped Angelo's shoulder.

Meanwhile, Rocky had become bored or curious because she had begun to inspect the room. Looking over the desk, checking inside drawers, but when she opened the closet door, she made a sound like a detective discovering the secret identity of a killer. "Aha!" She spun around with a manic expression. "You stuffed all your games in the closet?"

"What was I supposed to do with them?" Wes explained, sounding somewhat annoyed she wasn't taking this more seriously. "I needed to clear the room for Angelo."

"Me?"

"Angelo," Rocky said, "you have no idea, but our boy Wes loves to play games. He's a real aficionado." When Rocky's cellphone rang, she exited the room. "Hey Fitz, what's up?"

"Let me explain," Wes began. "You're going to be working on a radio show with a…how shall I say this delicately? A very temperamental, narcissistic, and hyperactive person."

"That's putting it delicately?" Angelo chortled.

"Angelo, it doesn't make sense for you to stay in a hotel for two weeks when I have a spare room. You'll go crazy there. Plus, it'll give us a chance to work on the show. You'll need all the prep time you can get."

"I don't know," Angelo said. "I don't want to put you out. Besides, I should talk it over with Jason."

Rocky returned, hanging off the door threshold like she was about to do pull-ups. "Okay, amigos, I have to bounce. Fitz is having one of her meltdowns. I need to go over there and pretend to be nice."

"Good luck with that," Wes laughed. "Glad I don't have to report to anyone. You and Angelo aren't in relationships; you're on parole."

"Says the sad, single man who can't find a husband," Rocky sang as she headed out. "Love the evidence board, Wes, and Angelo, enjoy your day off tomorrow. Don't be late for our team meeting Monday before the show."

"Team meeting?" Angelo muttered.

Wes waved a dismissive hand. "I'll explain later."

Once Rocky had gone, Angelo experienced an immediate calm. It was as if her presence threw everything in her orbit into entropy, and now that she had physically extracted herself, the chaos subsided. It had to be the key to why she was so wildly popular with her audience. Their insatiable desire for conspiracy theories were stoked by the blue flame of Rocky's perpetual pilot light.

A gentle voice stirred Angelo from his existential musings. "Excuse me?"

"You survived Hurricane Rocky," Wes said. "Come on. Let's go back into the living room. I could use another drink."

Without realizing, Angelo had, in fact, accepted Wes's invitation to stay with him instead of at the hotel. "I really should go back and check out."

"It's too late to check out," Wes reasoned. "Relax. Drink some wine. Tomorrow, I'll drive you to the hotel so you can get your things and check out."

Well, that's settled.

They convened in the living room. It didn't take long before Wes began talking about himself, recounting his journey from small-town boy growing up in Michigan with a single mom to his decision to move to Los Angeles after graduating college; a decision that he regretted now since his mother passed away that year. She had been secretly battling cancer and died a few months after he landed an entry-level position with KLM. Stretched out on the sofa, Wes unloaded personal details of his life as if he was confessing to a therapist.

"My mom died when I was young," Angelo offered. "Her death is something I still struggle with even after all these years."

"I'm sorry."

"Thanks." Angelo's thoughts wandered back to Staten Island: The tiny clapboard bungalow in South Beach, the bedroom he shared with Camille, and the beach with the swim-at-your-own-risk sign. A perfectly contented life until the summer before he began high school. Angelo's mother developed back pain. She died ten months later from metastatic lymphoma. The decision to assist their mother's suicide was the most difficult decision Angelo had ever made in his life.

Wes sat up. "Can I ask you a personal question?"

"You can ask," Angelo said. "Not sure if I'll answer."

"How did you get that scar?"

To this day, the story about the scar on Angelo's right cheek would remain a secret he would share with no one. Having grown up believing a dog had bitten him as a baby, Angelo learned by sheer coincidence that his drunken father had attacked him. The two-inch sliver served as a permanent reminder that evil existed in the world.

"Oh, it's not a story worth telling," Angelo said. "A dog bit me when I was two."

Silence blanketed the room. "For what it's worth"—Wes stood—"it looks damn sexy." He offered his hand. "It's late. Let's get you settled in for the night."

Wes pulled him to his feet so promptly, Angelo literally fell into his arms. "Excuse me," Angelo said with a quick withering look. "Too much wine, I guess."

Another short, shocked silence followed as the two stood face-to-face. "Guess I don't know my own strength."

They made their way into the spare bedroom. "Nice job with the evidence board," Angelo said hastily, to cover up the uncomfortable silence.

They gazed at it briefly. "Will you be able to sleep?"

"You mean with the faces of three dead boys staring at me?" Angelo asked. "Probably not."

"How about we turn it around."

Angelo darted a glance at the board. "I noticed you have no suspects."

"As a matter of fact, I do." Wes referred to a stack of white notecards. The top one bore the name, Dino Sosano. Wes claimed it and pinned it on the map. "Dino is the manager of Peak. A real rangy guy with a sordid past. There's a good chance he knew all three murder victims. In fact, we know Gabriel danced at Peak the night before he was found dead. I'm trying to book him for the show."

"If Dino is a suspect what makes you think he'll agree to an interview?" Neither spoke again. Angelo glanced at Wes, caught him staring. "Well?" Wes raised his hand and made like he was about to touch Angelo's scar, but he stopped midway, caught himself when Angelo took a step back. "It's getting late." Angelo turned Wes around and hurried him out the door. "Good night."

"Jeez, you New Yorkers are so pushy. I mean, literally."

Once Angelo was alone, he wondered what would have happened if he had allowed Wes to touch his cheek. And what, if anything, had he done to make Wes believe he was open to that sort of contact. Angelo opened the closet door, staring at the stack of games on the top shelf. What was it Rocky had said? "Wes loves to play games."

He certainly does.

Angelo stared at the evidence board, gazing at the

young faces of the No Angels Wept victims and thought, putting Wes aside for now, he had made the right decision to stay in Los Angeles.

Now, he had to turn the evidence board around if he was going to get any sleep.

CHAPTER FIVE

Of course, Angelo decided to disregard all the empirical evidence that Rocky was the same self-absorbed person he had met that fateful day in the KLM studio—the same one possessed with a malevolent demon the likes of which no exorcism could exorcise—instead of the fast friend he had communed with over Thai food at Wes's house on Saturday night. *Don't let down your guard*, a quiet voice whispered in his ear as he sat in *A Thorny Mess*'s weekly staff meeting Monday afternoon.

"Angelo!" He looked up, meeting Rocky's gaze. She wore a Plasmatics T-shirt and black pleather pants. In her hand, she held a rolled copy of the *LA Times*.

"Sorry," he replied. "What was the question?"

"We'd like Rocky and you to start with your personal take on the meaning of No Angels Wept," Wes said.

"Great," Angelo replied. "So, we're sticking to the plan. No, surprises, right?"

"You don't like surprises, Dr. Angelo?" Rocky baited him. Her hand ran over the rolled-up newspaper in a salacious gesture. "The show is like walking a tightrope. Even I don't know if my next step is going to be my last. Get it?"

"Just keep Mia Garcia's name out of your mouth," Angelo warned. *"Get it?"*

She held his stare briefly. The match had been struck behind her eyes. The blue pilot light flared. "Where the fuck did you get this guy?" she asked Wes as they began howling with laughter. Not too long after, Angelo joined in too. It felt like they were eating Thai food at Wes's house again. The three amigos. But Rocky's vacillating temperament had

Angelo wondering if she had a personality disorder. At the very least, she exhibited all the traits of a bullying older brother.

They moved into the studio where Angelo experienced a momentary wave of post-traumatic stress. A windshield wiper swept the mist from his mind, bringing into sharp focus the memory of that day he first met Rocky: the Doc Martens boots, the tattoos, and the knife.

Who carries a knife?

Rocky sat, manspreading. She rolled her seat, pressing her body against the desktop marred with knife punctures. Behind the glass partition, Wes pantomimed for Angelo to put on his headset. "Take a deep breath," Wes encouraged in his ears. His soothing tone relaxed Angelo. "Clear your mind." Then, he began counting down. "Five, four, three, two, showtime."

An unexpected howl caused Angelo to lurch back. Rocky had come to life like a feral beast from behind a tree. Rabid. Ravenous. Rapacious. "That's right Messes," Rocky shouted. "This is your patron saint of the invisible LGBTQ, L, M, N, O, P and any other fucking letter, number or symbol you want to include. All are welcome here. I'm Rocky Thorn and you're listening to *A Thorny Mess*." She swiveled so she faced Angelo. Pressing her lips against the microphone like it was her lover's mouth, she added, "You kids are in for a treat because for the next two weeks, *A Thorny Mess* is going to focus on nothing but the No Angels Wept Murders." Within seconds, blinking red lights lit up the control panel. "Well, that was a quick response. I see you Messes already have a lot to say." Rocky shot Angelo a look crackling with mischief. "But before I get started, I need to introduce you to someone. You may remember this badass bitch from last week. He's a *dac-tah* as my beloved mother would say. That's right. He's here with me now. Welcome back, the one, the only, Dr. Angelo Perrotta. How's it hanging, Doc?"

A part of Angelo's mind understood that none of this was real, but the prescient part of his brain told him that this was more than real. It was hyperreal.

"Doc?"

"Say something," Wes whispered in his headset.

It had been two years of pushing forward past the memory of Mia Garcia's tragic death. Always an effort to push against gravity, time, and guilt. Ducking in the shadows to avoid judgmental recognition from strangers on the street, and now here he was, centerstage, on a radio show that sensationalized perpetrators and exploited victims.

Victims like Mia Garcia.

"Earth to Angelo!" Rocky kicked his leg. The jolt shook him back to the present.

"I'm sorry, Rocky," he uttered. "I was just thinking, what the actual fuck am I doing here?"

"Trust me," Rocky chided. "I was asking myself the very same thing."

"No, seriously," he continued, "I mean, why would I expose myself to more ridicule and scorn after all I've been through, and do you want to know why?"

"I'm sure you're going to tell us."

Angelo swallowed down hard. It was becoming difficult for him to find his words because the reason he had agreed to be part of this show had nothing to do with the prospect of hosting his own podcast. He realized with stunning clarity that had it not been for people like Rocky, the deaths of the three gay sex workers would only be swept under the carpet. Gone. Forgotten.

"As I sat here, listening to you, I had a moment of clarity."

"A vision you say?"

"I guess you could call it that. I mean you are Rocky Thorn, the patron saint of the invisible LGBTQ+ community, and whether or not I agree with everything you say, I see it clearly now that if it wasn't for you, no one would be talking about the No Angels Wept victims. So, thank you in advance for this opportunity."

She dropped him a wink. "Well, you heard the man. That's Dr. Angelo Perrotta, my co-host for the next two weeks, where we will be diving deep into the No Angels Wept murders. Strap on your strap-ons, Messes. We'll be right back."

"Well played, Doctor," Wes whispered in Angelo's ears. "Well played."

For the next hour, Rocky and Angelo sparred like swordsmen, defending their arguments with such tenacity, Angelo at times felt like someone had turned up the thermostat.

"There is no doubt. No Angels Wept is a biblical reference," Angelo stated.

"And yet, no one has been able to find this so-called reference," Rocky argued. "You think you can waltz onto my show and tell me what time it is? I've been covering this story for months."

"Okay," Angelo said. "What do you think it means?"

"I've already shared my thoughts on this subject, Doctor," Rocky said with a caustic edge. "I guess you haven't been listening to my show."

"Apologies." Angelo chuckled. "Won't you please share your thoughts with me now?"

Rocky puffed out her cheeks, exhaling slowly. "I believe No Angels Wept is a reference to the poem 'The Angel' by William Blake."

Angelo feigned a yawn.

Rocky did a double take. "Are you mocking me?"

Angelo stretched his arms, pretending he hadn't been listening, which only infuriated Rocky more.

She stood up and began reciting:

I dreamt a dream! What can it mean?

And that I was a maiden Queen
Guarded by an Angel mild:
Witless woe was ne'er beguiled!
And I *wept* both night and day,
And he wiped my tears away;
And I wept both day and night,
And hid from him my heart's delight.

Rocky had gotten so swept up in reciting the poem, eyes closed as she spoke passionately and dramatically, she was startled by Angelo's raucous applause. "Brava!"

She curtsied and sat down. "Thank you."

"That was beautiful," Angelo said. "You still haven't convinced me of its relevance, but beautiful nonetheless."

"You're a dick," she replied. "How's that for relevance."

"Is this the sweet talk that lands you the pretty blonds?"

Rocky didn't seem fazed by this comment. "As I was saying, 'The Angel' is a poem that speaks about innocence and corruption. Young, gay, innocent sex workers like Keith Knight and the men who corrupt and defile them. Throughout the poem, the angel declines to comfort the narrator's false fears, which reminds me of children believing in something as illogical as Santa Claus. Over the course of the poem, these beliefs slowly crumble to be replaced by the cold harsh reality of adulthood. Our killer is a guardian angel who protects his victims by snuffing them out before adulthood finally settles in."

"So, the killer is the angel," Angelo confirmed. "Interesting. Crazy, but interesting."

"Did I mention you're still a dick."

As Wes predicted, the audience went wild with the show's focus on the No Angels Wept murders and Angelo as co-host. Only a few diehard Messes criticized Rocky for selling out though she was quick to eviscerate them. On the whole, Angelo had done considerably better than expected.

Jason would be proud. Angelo had held his own with the patron saint, knowing when to step in and when to hold back to give Rocky her space. After all, it was her show.

When Rocky finally got around to asking Angelo why he believed No Angels Wept was a biblical reference, he exploded with enthusiasm with a theory he had researched for months. "You see, Rocky," he began, "there are multiple passages within the Bible that reference angels. Take Judges 2:4 for example"—Angelo reached for his phone and read—"as soon as the angel of the Lord spoke these words to all the people of Israel, the people lifted up their voices and wept."

Rocky was doing it again: displaying that bored head-rolling posture. "Yeah, so?"

"Okay, so you're not impressed," Angelo conceded. "I get it, but what do we know about angels?"

Rocky glowered. "The only angels I know are the ones prancing down the catwalk in their panties."

Angelo ignored that comment and studied his phone again. "We know that God created angels, and not the Victoria's Secret kind, and he created a lot of them. Millions if not more. They have superpowers like the X-Men. They're considered warriors like the angel Michael. Sometimes they take on human form and deliver messages like the angel Gabriel."

"Gabriel?"

Angelo nodded self-assuredly, knowing the mention of Gabriel had snared Rocky's attention and likely the attention of the entire listening audience. "To prepare for the birth of Christ, the angel Gabriel, one of God's most mighty angels, announced to the Virgin Mary that she was with child and that her son wasn't the son of her husband, Joseph, but the son of God. The Messiah."

Rocky grabbed the microphone and pressed it to her lips. "I don't know about you Messes, but there's a tsunami in my panties."

"In fact," Angelo said, the pitch of his voice rising, "an angel appeared to Mary's husband, Joseph, in a dream three times."

Rocky regarded him with keen appraisal. "Did you say three?" They stared at each other for several long seconds.

Wes had to prompt them. "Someone speak...now!"

"So, let's recap," Rocky began. "Angels are everywhere in the Bible. The angel Gabriel, which is the same name of the second No Angels Wept victim, tells the Virgin Mary she's knocked up by God, not her husband. An angel visits her husband, Joseph, *three* times to warn him not to stone the bitch because, well, she is carrying God's son. Three as in the number of months our boy N.A.W. has spaced apart his murders." Rocky sat back, setting her boots on the desk, grinning. "Pretty interesting stuff you laid on us, Doc. One problem, not once did you mention an angel fucking weeping!" Rocky sat up abruptly. "That's all for now, my Thorny Messes. I'll be back tomorrow with my co-host, Dr. Angelo Perrotta. Until next time. Sniff the rose but beware the messy thorns."

Wes gave them two enthusiastic thumbs-up. There was no denying it; their chemistry was electric. The red lights on the console never stopped blinking throughout the entire show. It was as if they were a perfect combination. Angelo's credibility as a physician played nicely against Rocky's balls-to-the-wall candor.

"Great show," Wes said in their ears.

Just then, Angelo noticed the control room had filled up. In addition to Wes, there were the two frat bros plus two young, wide-eyed female interns, and a pair of men wearing suits.

The whoosh from the door opening sounded like a nor'easter humming outside a window. "Rocky," the suits sang in unison as they entered.

"Excellent show," said the taller of the two.

"Yeah, just amazing," said the other. "Really amazing."

Angelo found it amusing the way they competed for her attention.

"Thank you so much," Rocky said in a patronizing tone, "but who the fuck are you two?"

Boisterous laughter was followed by overlapping conversation.

"...she really is hilarious..."

"...for sure..."

"I mean, what you see is what you get..."

"...no pretense. Totally refreshing..."

They tossed out effusive remarks like pennies flung to a street urchin. Rocky wanted none of it. "Guys, guys, guys," she interrupted. "May I introduce you to my co-host, Dr. Angelo Perrotta." Suddenly, all eyes were on Angelo, followed by competing hands to shake and hyperbolic compliments.

"You're such a natural..."

"...are you really a doctor?"

"...you wouldn't happen to have your prescription pad handy..."

More laughter, followed by even more overlapping conversations.

Out of the corner of his eye, Angelo saw Wes listening intently to the receptionist with the black and pink mullet. She handed Wes a message. He read it and entered the studio. "Great show tonight."

"What's that in your hand?" Rocky crossed her arms over her chest. "Please, don't tell me another parental control group is boycotting the show." Wes handed her the note. "Well, I'll be a horse's ass." She handed the note to Angelo and fist-pumped the ceiling. "Motherfucker, I don't believe it!"

The suits eyed Angelo expectantly. They shared the crazed expression of spectators watching a man on a ledge. "Who wrote this?" Angelo asked.

The receptionist clenched her teeth. "It was a voice message. The phones have been ringing off the hook."

"Read it out loud," Rocky urged.

Angelo held up the slip of paper. "It says, Revelation 5."

"What does that mean?" the taller suit asked.

Just then, frat bro two entered the studio holding his cellphone. "I found it, Wes. It's a passage from the Bible."

Rocky's eyes latched on to Angelo's. "Give it to Dr. Perrotta. Let him read the Bible passage. It only seems fitting."

Frat bro two handed Angelo his phone. At first, Angelo wasn't sure how he felt about this but unexpectedly, he experienced a sudden surge of excitement.

Angelo read: "And I saw a mighty angel proclaiming in a loud voice, 'Who is worthy to break the seals and open the scroll?'

But no one in heaven or on earth or under the earth could open the scroll or even look inside it.

I wept and wept because no one was found who was worthy to open the scroll or look inside."

"Who's weeping?" Wes asked.

Frat bro one entered on cue. "The person weeping is John the Apostle. I just looked it up."

"We have to call the police," Angelo said. "Right?"

The two suits stepped in immediately. "Hang on just a second," said the taller one. "Let's not rush into this. The less people who know about this, the better."

The second one agreed but added, "What if we use it to tease tomorrow's show?"

Angelo's entire body jerked. "Are you insane? This could be a clue. We need to contact the police. Rocky, what do you think?"

"You want to know what I think?" Rocky eyes scanned each of their faces, a self-satisfied grin plastered on her face. "I think our boy N.A.W. is a fan of my fucking show."

CHAPTER SIX

In the early hours of the following day, Angelo lay in bed, wide awake and ridiculously exhausted. He closed his eyes and allowed himself to revisit the string of events from the night before. To allow the vivid memories of the show to play back on a loop. He lay there and experienced the thrill, the excitement, and the worry until at last he flung back the sheets and got up.

The smell of coffee hit him once he stepped outside the spare bedroom. Wes was on the phone when he entered the kitchen. He wore his go-to faded jeans with cutout knees but with no shirt. Propped against the kitchen island, his golden skin stretched over his sinewy torso, revealing the striations in his chest and arms. Wes smiled once he saw Angelo in the doorway. He covered the phone with his hand. "There's coffee. Help yourself."

Angelo found a clean mug in the cupboard and poured a cup. He stepped outside. The ground was damp from the morning dew, but no rain fell. It hardly ever rained in California, or so Angelo had been told. The air had a sweet smell. There was no denying that waking up every day to this weather would soften even the most cantankerous of demeanors, but Angelo was a New Yorker at heart. LA was fun to visit but living here…it wasn't for him.

"Morning." Angelo spun around just as Wes enveloped him with his bare arms. Suddenly, Angelo felt trapped, off-balance. "I have good news. Come inside, I'll make breakfast."

"You cook?" Angelo asked.

"How about some scrambled eggs and toast?" Angelo sat at the island as Wes cracked and scrambled eggs in a bowl. "I just got off the phone with Mabel Knight."

"Who?"

"Keith Knight's mother," Wes clarified. "I thought you were an N.A.W. expert?"

"Right," Angelo offered. "The caffeine hasn't hit me yet."

Butter melted in the frying pan as Wes recapped the conversation. "She agreed to call into the show tonight to discuss her son, but there's one stipulation." Wes's jeans kept sliding down, exposing his bare ass.

No shirt. No underwear. This guy lives dangerously. "You really should put on an apron," Angelo suggested.

Wes looked over his shoulder, grinning. "Why?"

"I mean you are frying eggs in melted butter, wearing hardly any clothes," Angelo replied. "Aren't you worried about splatter?" Not to mention Angelo was finding it difficult to focus.

Wes popped two slices of bread in the toaster. "Whatever you say..." He pulled a black apron from a drawer and donned it. "Happy now?"

"What's the stipulation?" Angelo asked. He juggled the conversations in his head, ignoring the one that centered on Wes's semi-naked body.

Wes set a plate of scrambled eggs and buttered toast in front of Angelo. "Mabel agreed to call in as long as no one mentions anything about her son being a sex worker."

"So, you lied to a grieving mother."

Wes snorted. "I'll speak to Rocky. Don't worry."

Angelo sipped coffee, sensing Wes's fixed attention on him. He looked up, and their gazes locked for what seemed like a long time. Too long for it to feel comfortable. "The eggs are delicious," Angelo finally said. He plastered a smile on his face to hide his awkwardness. *Is he flirting with me?* It felt to him as if Wes was flirting: The undivided attention, the semi-naked body, the way too cheerful disposition this early in the morning. Not to mention the doting scrambled eggs-making host. *Focus.* Not on Wes's jeans sliding off the round hump of his ass, but on Mabel Knight. Wes said something, but Angelo was lost in his thoughts. "I'm sorry, what did you say?"

Wes's phone ringing cut through the moment. He snatched it off the island and stared at the number. "I'm going to take this and grab a shower."

Angelo nodded absently.

"Hey," Wes asked him. "Everything okay?"

Angelo frowned up at him. "It's nothing. I'm just not a morning person. Answer your phone before it goes to voicemail."

Wes crossed his tanned arms over his chest. "Angelo, talk to me."

"Do you really think N.A.W. was listening to last night's broadcast or do you think some overzealous Thorny Mess called that message in?"

Wes dropped his head, hair dangling over his face. "Rocky is more than a shock jock. She's more than just the patron saint of the invisible X, Y, and Z. She's a business-woman."

Angelo managed a weak smile. "Oh, so she only said that N.A.W. was listening for the radio executives' benefit."

Wes offered an appeasing smile. "I stopped making sense of Rocky's decision-making process a long time ago. She didn't get to this point in her career without creating a sense of excitement. That's what she does best: she gets people excited. Whether they're her Thorny Messes or radio executives, Rocky knows how to push people's buttons and she does it well."

Wes's phone started up again. He glanced at the number and heaved a frustrated sigh. "Let me take this." He walked into his bedroom and shut the door. Wes's voice was lower, nearly inaudible through the door, but Angelo heard that he was furious. He walked over slowly to listen.

"...absolutely not..."

"...I'm not having this conversation..."

Angelo backed away quickly before Wes opened the door and found him standing there. "Is everything okay?"

Wes chuckled. Quite unexpectedly, he grabbed Angelo's face with both hands. "Okay? Tell me. When are things ever okay in life?" A quick but tense shake. If this had been a gangster movie, Angelo would have thought he was about to have his neck snapped. "I'm going to take a shower. Finish your breakfast."

Angelo sat at the island and ate, mesmerized by Wes's life, apart from what he had shown Angelo. Never would he have imagined Wes as someone who had a temper. He always appeared even-keeled, unfettered, but even the most unflappable of demeanors hit a breaking point. That, or they hid behind impassive exteriors to avoid showing their true identities.

Another call. This one, Wes made himself. This time, Wes spoke softly. Whomever Wes had called was someone to whom he had something to say, his voice lower, urgent. Angelo listened, but he couldn't decipher any of his words.

What am I doing?

Angelo walked into the spare bedroom and turned the evidence board around to study it. Chewing on his lip for a few seconds, he reviewed the facts. The killer had chosen three gay sex workers. Moreover, two boys were Black—Keith Knight and Trevon "Blaze" Bolden—and one Latino, Gabriel Menendez. Angelo wondered if this was intentional.

"See anything?"

Angelo spun around to find Wes standing very close behind him.

"You scared me," Angelo said, slightly out of breath. "I thought you were taking a shower?"

"Sorry about that," Wes offered. "I thought you heard me. Guess you were too wrapped up in my amazing evidence board."

"It just occurred to me that all three victims are men of color. Clearly, it's a pattern, but only the first victim, Keith Knight, had family in Los Angeles."

Wes nodded, moving to inspect the photos more closely. "What about it?"

They continued to stare at the board, not each other. "You don't find that interesting?" Angelo asked.

Wes nudged Angelo with his shoulder. "I didn't say I didn't find it interesting. I'm asking you what you think. What's the story? Tell me."

Angelo cleared his throat, understanding now he was being asked to rehearse for tonight's episode. "I believe N.A.W. is a gay white man, probably late thirties to early fifties. I believe he struggles with his sexual identity. He has for a long time. Then, one day, he meets someone." Angelo tapped the photo of Keith Knight. "Maybe someone he knows. Someone who fits his profile. Someone he likely sees with a degree of regularity."

Wes turned to Angelo. "Like a neighbor?"

"Bingo."

"You're good, Dr. Perrotta." Wes cupped Angelo's face with his hands and planted a kiss on his lips. Angelo didn't move a muscle in reaction. It lasted only a second, maybe two, before Angelo pulled away. "You're *really* good. You know that?"

"Thank you," Angelo barely managed to say. He was still somewhat in shock.

"I'm going to hit the shower," Wes called on his way out of the guest bedroom.

Thank God. Angelo needed a moment to recover. The semi-naked chef making eggs was one thing. But a kiss. Wes had crossed a boundary, but Angelo quickly reasoned that being away from Jason and staying with someone who was essentially a stranger—an incredibly good looking and sexy stranger—had him on edge. Wes had only kissed him out of excitement. Nothing more. Besides, what was a little peck between friends?

He laughed then. Laughed at himself for being so prudish. He sat down on the bed, still staring at the evidence board and chuckling to himself. It felt foreign to have another man's lips on his. For the past two years, Angelo had only tasted the same lips. Jason's lips, and those lips were the only lips he wanted or desired. What felt foreign to him, maybe slightly forward, was actually very innocent when he thought about it more. Certainly nothing untoward. Wes and he were friends now. This was Hollywood after all. Angelo was sure everyone in LA kissed each other on the lips.

He felt at ease, then, believing he and Wes were friends settling into each other's company with no pretenses, no inhibitions, so Angelo pushed aside a harmless kiss and willed himself to focus only on the case. *From this point on*, that's *all that matters.*

◆◆◆

Hours later, Angelo and Rocky were back in the studio. The room felt charged. Electric. Primed for an unexpected explosion. Like walking through a minefield.

"So, yesterday," she spoke into her microphone. "Toward the end of the show, you may recall, my co-host and I were debating whether No Angels Wept is a biblical reference or a literary one, but we ran out of time."

"Lucky for you," Angelo piped in.

Rocky coughed, "Bitch." She seemed to be urging Angelo to join in, to stop being so buttoned up even though they were discussing the murders of three young men. "*But* and I'm not talking about the non-existent butt my producer has; I'm talking about the message I received right after the show. Am I right, Dr. Angelo?"

"You bet your butt you are."

Angelo knew she was teasing the audience. How else could she fill three hours? Building the suspense was one of her gifts. More than being shocking, Rocky could draw out a story to the point where even Angelo was tempted to beg for mercy. End the agony. But this was show business. Stretch the story. Build the suspense. These were all things they had discussed at their daily meetings.

"After the show yesterday," she continued, "I received a message and it read, Revelation 5."

"And what a revelation it was."

Rocky's eyes widened comically. "You're killing me, Doc. More on Revelation 5 and John after the break."

Wes entered the studio. "Rocky, Mabel Knight is on the line. I don't know how long she'll remain on hold. You have to take her call as soon as we get back on air."

Rocky stood up, stretched. Angelo couldn't read her at all; couldn't tell if she heard Wes or was ignoring him. "Why are you still standing there, Wes?" she asked finally. "I heard you. We all heard you. Now go back into your little room and let me do my show."

Her order silenced Wes as abruptly as a slap across the face. Wes smirked at Angelo. An expression that conveyed, *welcome to my world.*

Angelo thought Rocky sounded bitter, and it got him wondering if there was something underlying, some argument they hadn't fully resolved. *Was Rocky the person Wes was arguing with earlier on the phone?*

"Is everything okay?" Angelo asked Rocky. "Is there anything I can do?"

"Yeah," Rocky said. "Mind your own fucking business."

Angelo sat in silence, counting down the seconds until they were back on air and wondering how he was going to turn this awkward moment around. When he thought about it in a theoretical way, Angelo wondered if Rocky and Wes were entangled in a co-dependent relationship that swerved recklessly from bosom buddies to sworn enemies in the span of a nanosecond. And yes, their relationship was none of his business. Up until then he had answered when spoken to, engaged when appropriate, knowing that any minute Rocky could turn on a dime. That was the price anyone paid who dared to venture into her soundproof beehive. Everyone was a worker bee here to serve the queen.

"My first guest tonight," Rocky said, turning serious. "Is the mother of Keith Knight. On the line may I welcome, Mabel Knight. How are you, Mrs. Knight?"

Dead silence followed. Rocky glared at Wes, her arms flailing, but Wes rolled his hand in a gesture for her to continue. Mabel Knight was on the line.

"Hello, Mrs. Knight," she continued with a forced lightness in her voice. "You're on the air."

In the world of radio, a few seconds of dead air heralded an impending disaster. An iceberg in the near distance, and Angelo was a passenger on the SS *Thorny Mess*. He had never witnessed such nail-biting apprehension.

"Hello?" Mrs. Knight's voice was tremulous, rickety. "Can you hear me?"

Rocky squeezed shut her eyes with the excruciating frustration of a home-health aide tending to a senile patient. "Yes, Mrs. Knight. We can hear you fine. This is Rocky Thorn. You're on live radio."

More dead air followed.

Rocky's mood jacked up. She was losing patience. "Mrs. Knight, are you there?"

"Hello, Miss Thorn," Mabel said, talking over her. "Are you there?"

"Yes, I'm here, but call me Rocky, and I'll call you Mabel? How does that sound, dear?"

"Well, that sounds all right," Mabel replied. "Are we on the radio?"

Clamping a hand over her mouth, Rocky appeared to be holding back a scream of frustration. "Yes Mabel," Rocky shouted. "We're live. On the air. Are you with me, dear?"

"I'm here," Mabel said, sounding more at ease. "I've never been on the radio before."

"First time for everything, right," Rocky snorted with sarcasm. She reached to press the Cough button and cleared her throat. "Mabel, how are you holding up since your son's murder?"

"Well, if I'm being honest, it hasn't been easy. I miss my gentle son."

"I'm sure you do," Rocky said. "What can you tell us about Keith that hasn't been reported already? Describe your son to us."

Like most mothers, Mabel Knight gushed over her son, but only in the way a loving mother can. Highlighting his good traits and minimizing his bad ones. Rocky and Mabel talked for a short while. Interviewing a grieving mother clearly wasn't something Rocky enjoyed. In order to do that, Rocky had to show restraint and empathy, characteristics Angelo didn't think came to top of mind when describing Rocky Thorn. Soon he heard Rocky wrapping up the interview.

But something happened.

Mabel Knight was prattling on about Keith's kindness and how everyone that knew him thought he was the sweetest, gentlest person they had ever met, when Rocky dropped her head and clasped her hands behind her neck. She froze in that position for several seconds, allowing the woman to speak endlessly until finally, Rocky interrupted her.

"Mrs. Knight," Rocky said, her frustration evident. "I'm curious to understand how much you knew about your son's line of work. Specifically, the sex work."

Angelo jerked his head toward Wes who had stood up, waving his hand frantically for Rocky to stop this line of questioning. Keith Knight's history as a sex worker was a topic they had agreed was off-limits. Except Mabel Knight had made that deal with Wes. Rocky apparently hadn't gotten that memo, or more likely, she had crumpled it into a ball and shot it in the garbage. It seemed to be a pattern with Rocky.

"I…I don't know anything about that," Mabel Knight stammered.

"Mabel, honey, please." The warmth in Rocky's voice had been replaced by a familiar chilliness. "You know as well as I do that your son was turning tricks as a masseur."

"I don't know what you're talking about," she insisted.

A tap on the glass partition. Wes's steely, ice pick eyes pierced the tinted glass but Rocky ignored him.

"I know you don't want to believe your gentle son was providing happy endings"—Rocky's tongue glided across her front teeth—"I mean, what mother would? It's just that if you accepted this…you might be able to help solve your son's murder instead of enabling his killer by sticking your head in the sand."

The red call buttons gleamed with such intensity they reflected off Rocky's face, turning her fair complexion crimson. Wes stormed in, cutting a finger across his neck. "Stop it! Stop it," he mouthed, but Rocky waved a dismissive hand at him.

While they argued, arms flailing like two characters in a silent film, Angelo listened to Mabel Knight sobbing.

"Mrs. Knight," he said in a low voice. "I can't imagine what this has been like for you. To lose a child. Your only child. It must be devastating."

"Who…who is this?" she asked.

"I'm Dr. Angelo Perrotta."

There was a pause where all Angelo heard was sniffling and sobbing. "Pleasure to meet you, Doctor."

The hopelessness he experienced moments earlier gave way to a glimmer of faith, but still he felt like shit, running interference for Rocky. "What do you remember most about Keith?"

"He had a beautiful voice," she said. "Even the church thought so. On occasion, he sang with the choir."

"Oh, for the love of Christ," Rocky groaned. "What the fuck do you think you're doing Dr. Perrotta. This is *A Thorny Mess* not the Oprah fucking Winfrey show."

Angelo cut in. "I can tell you are a religious woman. Is that right, Mrs. Knight?"

"I wasn't always," she admitted, "but once I found Jesus, He spared me."

"Spare me," Rocky said, reeking with disgust. Wes raised a finger to his lips, his expression pleading with Rocky to stay quiet.

"I don't want to speak to that woman anymore," Mabel Knight said in a harsh voice. "I don't know what kind of game you're playing, but I didn't come on this show to listen to her mock my gentle son. She has no right saying those ugly things about him."

"Mrs. Knight," Angelo pleaded. "This is not a game."

"No, it's not," Rocky shouted. "It's a goddamn joke."

A gasp escaped Mabel Knight's lips. Rocky had already insulted her son when she referred to him as a masseur who provided happy endings. By the sharp intake of breath, Angelo suspected the God-fearing woman believed taking the Lord's name in vain was the final straw.

And Angelo was right. Mabel Knight had hung up.

"Well, that my Messes," Rocky said, "is Mabel Knight's version of a mic drop." Rocky turned her attention to the control board. "Caller, you're on with Rocky Thorn."

"You are no patron saint," said a gravelly-voiced male. "You are a psychotic bitch. How could you talk to that poor woman like that?"

"The same way I talk to assholes like you," Rocky shouted. "It's my show, and if you don't like it, guess what? Don't listen." When Rocky glanced at Angelo, she had a manic look in her eyes. "Caller, you're on with Rocky Thorn, as in host of *A Thorny Mess*, in case anyone fucking forgot."

"Talk about good cop, bad cop," said a woman. "You two are dynamite. I don't want the next two weeks to end."

"Darling," Rocky chuckled. "It's only just begun. Am I right, Doc?"

Angelo hung his head, refusing to answer.

Rocky turned away and clicked on another caller. "You're on with Rocky Thorn."

The voice that spoke sounded synthetic, robotic, like someone speaking through a distortion device. "Well done, Rocky. I love that you're focusing on N.A.W."

"Is this Stephen fucking Hawking," Rocky joked, not feeling unnerved by the creepy-voiced caller. "I mean, what an honor, sir."

"Ha, ha," said the mechanical voice. "You should be in show business. In the meantime, if you want to learn more about the N.A.W. victims, may I suggest you search online, specifically the website RentAGuy.com."

Angelo shot a look at Wes who had gone back into the control room. The frat bros frantically typed on their phones.

"Look up the profile, Black Knight," the caller went on. "You may find exactly what you're looking for."

"*Domo arigato, Mr. Roboto*," Rocky sang. "Now why don't you tell us who you are?"

"Another time," the voice said in a taunting, lyrical way. "Just remember, it's not the thorns you should beware of; it's the invisible worm."

"Invisible worm, huh." Rocky offered a sarcastic grunt and disengaged the call. "The only worms I enjoy are at the bottom of a tequila bottle." She glared at Angelo, but he remained silent. "I guess you really never know what's going to happen from one minute to the next on this show. I want to thank my co-host, Dr. Angelo Perrotta and my special guest, Mrs. Mabel Knight. That's all for now. I'm your host, Rocky Thorn, and remember...sniff the rose but beware of the messy thorns." Before she finished delivering her sign-off, Angelo stood up. He bolted for the door just as Wes entered. He held up his hand, freezing Angelo. Rocky threw off her headset and marched up to Angelo. "What the fuck is your problem?"

Angelo stood in silence, shaking his head. "You went too far, Rocky. Mabel Knight is still mourning the loss of her son. She didn't deserve that."

"It's called show business," Rocky spat. She bumped her chest against Angelo's. He was pressed right up against the door. There was nowhere for him to go. "Wes, tell your buddy we're not here to play nice-nice in the sandbox."

Wes maneuvered his arm in between them until Rocky backed off. "Let's just take a deep breath."

"You two are pathetic," Rocky gritted. "I guess you really didn't mean it when you said if it weren't for me no one would be talking about the No Angels Wept victims? Huh, Angelo? Guess you were just blowing smoke up my skirt. Well, no thank you. I don't need your compliments. I know what I'm doing. I'm a professional, and I deserve respect!"

Rocky turned away, caught up in the swell of emotion, she kicked the trash pail by her desk, hurling it against the glass wall. This wasn't the first time Angelo had witnessed her violent outbursts, and instead of shrugging it off as just another one of Rocky's tantrums, he wrestled with the cold hard truth that she often became unhinged when she felt disrespected.

The frat bros entered the studio. "Just so you know," frat bro one said, "gentle son is trending on social media."

Rocky glanced over at Angelo with a told-you-so glare. "Trending, huh?"

"You know what else is trending?" Frat bro two scrolled his phone. "Rockgelo."

"What does that that mean?" Angelo asked.

"It means you and Rocky have your own portmanteau," he replied. "Like Brangelina and Bennifer."

Wes grabbed the cellphone from him, eyes scanning. "I don't believe it."

"This is next-level shit!" The bros high-fived.

Looking up from the phone, Wes stared directly at Rocky. "It's true. It's all true."

Slowly, Rocky strolled over to Wes, eyes glimpsing the screen but not to read it. Smug, tight-lipped, she only flashed her turquoise eyes at him. "Guess this means I actually know what the fuck I'm doing."

Wes handed over the phone for Angelo to read it for himself.

Rocky sucked her teeth. "Now, can we go to Wanda's? Mamma needs a tequila shot."

Chapter Seven

Angelo felt exhausted of the entire human race by the time they sat at a table in the half-empty Mexican restaurant on South La Brea. A duo of bikers pounded shots at the bar. A gay couple toggled between feeding themselves and their twins.

Before Rocky even sat down, she ordered a round of tequila shots. The thought made Angelo's stomach churn. Outside it was dark and miserably hot. Since he had arrived in Los Angeles, the weather had been atypical. Every day someone felt compelled to talk with him about it as if his arrival on the West Coast had somehow impacted the forecast.

Though they had left the radio station with a small sense of validation that what they were doing was having an impact, what kind of impact depended on whom you asked. Without a doubt Angelo felt uneasy with the way Rocky handled Mabel Knight, and if the indicator for success was to trend on social media, then Angelo thought it might be time for him to bow out.

Rocky raised a shot glass. "To Rockgelo!"

"Cheers." Angelo managed to sound mildly amused, but his gut felt hollow. He wondered what Mabel Knight was doing at that moment. While they shot back tequila and prepared to feast on tacos, on chips, and on guacamole, he couldn't help but imagine Mabel Knight sitting alone in a dark room, clutching a photo of her son, sobbing. As he stared absently out the window—at the cars, at a woman pushing a shopping cart—Angelo forced himself to think about the three victims.

A stray dog strolled unbothered past the restaurant neither wearing a collar nor accompanied by an owner. The dog sat in front of the restaurant and began licking its paw for a few moments before disappearing round the corner.

"Is everything all right?" Wes asked just after Rocky stepped away to take a call.

"All right?" He could hardly imagine Wes asking such a question. Out of nowhere a thought careened into his mind. The killer had cut off Keith's hand because he was a masseur, but in recalling that Keith had come from Paw Paw, Michigan, he wondered if the connection of punishing a sex worker who used their hands for a living was too obvious. What if the killer knew Keith was born in Paw Paw?

Once Rocky returned to the table, Angelo shared his theory. His heartbeat quickened with a burst of excitement watching Rocky's eyes glaze over with stunned amazement. "That is an interesting thought," she said. "Except Gabriel Menendez was from Aspen, Colorado."

"And Blaze," Wes added, "was from LA."

"You know what bothers me," Rocky went on, "why did N.A.W. cut out Blaze's tongue? I mean, I get cutting off Keith's hand since he was a masseur, and mutilating Gabriel's leg because he was a go-go dancer, but why Blaze's tongue and not his dick?"

Behind him, Angelo heard the indelicate murmur of the biker duo snickering. Rocky's eyes swerved to look at something over Angelo's shoulder. "Hey baby," she said to a tall, slender woman. Long blue-black hair framed an oval face with mascaraed blue eyes and maroon-colored lips. This had to be Fitz. She wore black leather pants and a torso-tight tattered Iron Maiden T-shirt that revealed tattooed sleeves up both arms. *A dead ringer for Rocky. They could be sisters, in fact.*

"You must be Angelo," Fitz said. "Rocky was right. You are cute. By the way, she hasn't stopped talking about you since you arrived in LA." Angelo's cheeks burned with embarrassment as Fitz shook his hand.

Wes said, "We were just talking about—"

"Let me guess," Fitz jumped in with an exaggerated eye roll. "N.A.W. is all Rocky talks about."

Fitz could hardly muster the same sense of euphoria describing Rocky's nightly one-way conversations about the No Angels Wept Killer. Yet, listening to her play back the case, Angelo heard it imbued with religious pessimism.

"So, you agree No Angels Wept is a biblical reference?" Angelo couldn't contain his grin. "You hear that, Rocky?"

"I believe the killer is targeting gay sex workers," Fitz clarified, "and whoever they are, certainly they subscribe to an evangelical, right-wing Christian ideology. Whether their calling card is a biblical reference is not the point."

"Then what is the point of a No Angels Wept calling card?" Rocky asked impatiently, as if they had had this conversation many times before without any resolution.

Momentarily, Angelo was distracted by crude sexual laughter. The bikers were making kissy noises accompanied by ribald remarks toward Fitz. Rocky could not contain her annoyance. Calmly, Fitz placed her hand on Rocky's, offering a gently squeeze.

"Listen," Fitz continued, commandeering the conversation back to the case. "I'm sure No Angels Wept means something. I'm simply saying it doesn't matter. At the very least the killer is offering a commentary that no one cares when gay sex workers die. Not even angels weep."

"Hey sweetheart."

Fitz could not maintain her focus. Distracted by the bikers' obvious jeers, she clenched her hands into fists. Angelo knew from the sudden silence around the rest of the table that everyone had noticed it too. Angelo stole a glance. One look at the bikers' faces, a kind of dopey-excited expression like two teenage boys flipping through a lingerie catalogue, caused a sinking sensation of despair within Angelo, rising from his feet through his belly until he experienced a roar of blood in his ears.

Angelo made the choice to press Fitz further. "So, you think the killer is a religious nut of some kind?"

"I'll go even further." Fitz forced a grin. "My guess is that the killer is a self-hating homosexual who clings to his Christian doctrine and kills gay men to repent for having sexual thoughts about them. It's the classic Christian conundrum, and for the record, Jesus said nothing about homosexuality in the Bible. Only his apostle Paul does, but Paul doesn't condemn homosexuality because sexual orientation didn't exist back then. Paul's condemnation is toward sodomy and any other deviant sexual manifestations those crazy Romans cooked up. Some argue that Paul's condemnation of homoerotic acts may have arisen from Paul's own feelings of guilt and shame with being a homosexual himself. And this produced in him such self-loathing, he condemned homosexuals in retaliation."

Angelo sat back, chuckling. "I'm impressed. You certainly know your religious history."

"I grew up the child of a Baptist minister." Fitz paused to smirk. "You heard the saying, 'the ones that preach the loudest often have the most to hide'?"

Rocky laughed lightly. "My baby is so smart."

"Oh," Fitz interjected, "bet you anything N.A.W. grew up without a father."

Fitz's laser-sharp assessment had stunned Angelo into silence. Rocky and Wes exchanged irksome glances. "Angelo grew up without a dad," Wes offered.

"Well, who didn't?" Fitz reached to pat the back of Angelo's hand. "Bet it still stings, huh?"

"Hey, sweetheart," one of the bikers called out. "Can you settle a bet? We'll buy you a drink." Fitz paused to take a sip of water, but Angelo felt the exquisite tension. A sphincter of anger tightening around them. "Come on. We only want to know how it's hanging."

"Or if it's still hanging," the other chimed in.

The sound of their guttural laughter set off an ice pick of annoyance in Angelo's ears. Fitz slammed her hands on the table, rattling the silverware. "How about I come over there and shove my fist in your mouth!"

"Fitz," Angelo started. "It's not worth it." Seeing their aggrieved faces, heavy-lidded eyes brimming with amusement and contempt, Angelo knew where this was headed. "I say we call it a night," he offered. As much as he felt Fitz was being harassed, no good would come from a physical altercation.

It took a second for Angelo to process, a millisecond to realize he hadn't said the right thing, and suddenly he saw the expression on Fitz's face. Self-recrimination. Self-loathing. It seemed to wash over her as if these bikers' comments had detonated a bomb. Obliterating a dam that held back long-suppressed emotions that now swelled like a tidal wave about to crash on the shore. She looked Angelo dead in the eye. "I've been fighting assholes like them my whole life. If you want to scuttle into a dark crack like a cockroach, be my guest, but I refuse to back down."

"I'm sorry," Angelo said. "I have a thing about violence."

Fitz smiled. "Me too, but sometimes there's no getting around it."

The squeezing knot in Angelo's gut twisted once Fitz stood up. She turned around to face the bikers, but the manager came bursting through the kitchen doors. "Fitz, are these men bothering you?"

As Angelo couldn't have predicted, given no point of reference to feed off, Fitz exuded a self-assured yet calming, confrontational manner. She stood in front of the two bikers. A silent standoff. In the distance, Angelo heard a baby crying.

"Fitz," the manager pleaded. "Don't..."

Rocky rose from her seat, setting her boot on the chair. *Was she going to reach for her knife?* Angelo could hardly catch his breath.

One of the bikers stood up too, tugging at his leather vest. "Relax," he said to the manager. "We were just having a little fun with her...er, I mean him...I mean, he/she."

Without saying a word, Fitz struck the man squarely in the throat. He dropped to his knees, emitting a high-pitched wheeze. Paralyzed, Angelo couldn't believe what he had just witnessed. The precision. The force. Fitz obviously had combat skills.

Before the other biker had a chance to intervene, Rocky pulled her knife. "Why don't you take your friend home before someone really gets hurt."

The biker helped his buddy to his feet. Glaring confusedly, the two stumbled out of the restaurant. Fitz dug into her back pocket and peeled a couple of twenties from a roll of cash. "Here," she said to the manager. "Let me know if this doesn't cover their bill."

The manager took the money and retreated hastily back into the kitchen. Crisis diverted.

Rocky and Fitz rejoined the boys. "Are you all right?" Angelo asked.

Glancing at her knuckles, Fitz shrugged. "I'm fine." She slung her arm around Rocky's neck and pulled her in for a kiss. "You ever heard of Switchblade Sally? Well, meet Rocky the Ripper. She'll cut your heart out." Rocky nuzzled her nose against Fitz's ear.

"You two are a couple of bad asses," Angelo said.

Fitz nodded, and Angelo understood that she didn't want to elaborate. Though the enormity of this conflict, the sheer velocity with which Fitz and Rocky had snatched control of it, hadn't fully registered with Angelo, he understood it was time to move on. “Rocky,” he began, “I’ve been meaning to ask you if you knew what the caller meant by the invisible worm?”

Rocky dropped her head back, shaking her hair. “What a dick.” Turning to Fitz, she explained, “Some asshole using a device to distort his voice called into the show tonight suggesting we check out the profile Dark Knight on RentAGuy.”

Fitz fixed her gaze on Rocky. “Interesting.”

“So, I checked the site before I got here,” Rocky continued. “Dark Knight was Keith Knight’s handle. In fact, his profile is still up.”

“Why do you think the caller suggested you check out his profile?” Angelo asked.

“I’m not sure.” Rocky frowned with the effort to think. “My hunch is that all three victims had profiles on RentAGuy.”

“I checked earlier too,” Wes said. “I couldn’t find the other two victims, but that’s because they don’t use their real names. It’ll take a while to scan all those profiles.”

“I’ll check tonight when we get home,” Rocky said and turning to Fitz asked, “you want to help me do some investigative work, babe?”

Fitz bristled. “Nah ah. Not tonight. You’re taking the night off from the No Angels Wept murders.” Rocky’s expression deflated. Abruptly, Fitz stood up, yawning. “I think I’m gonna call it a night. Quit while I’m ahead.” She extended her hand across the table. “Pleasure to meet you, Angelo.”

Angelo smiled warmly, but he turned concerned when he saw her hand was red and swollen. “You should put ice on that tonight.”

“Will do, Doc.”

It occurred to Angelo that Fitz was distancing herself from the conversation. He couldn’t quite pin down whether it was the mention of RentAGuy or the residual concern she had assaulted someone that made her want to leave so quickly.

Rocky smiled at last, tentatively. "*Manana amigos.*"

Watching Rocky acquiesce to Fitz, Angelo felt he'd been given a peephole into their private life. "Wait," he said. "You never explained what the invisible worm means."

Rocky offered a flinching sort of smile. "We'll talk more tomorrow." She jerked her head toward the door where Fitz was waiting. "Duty calls. Oh, and Angelo, one more thing. What happens among the three of us stays with the three of us. No secrets. That's the three amigos code. Okay?"

Angelo glanced at Wes, who nodded. "Sure," he replied to Rocky. "I'm down with the T.A.C."

She laughed. "You're killing me, Doc."

As Wes paid the check, Angelo's mind gyred over certain aspects of the case. Pieces that didn't quite fit together. The evening had wrapped up too quickly and thankfully they had avoided any further physical confrontation, but Angelo still had so many questions.

In the car, Angelo stared fixedly at the road, thinking. "I'm still kind of freaked out by that caller."

"The one using the distortion device?" Wes asked. "Don't be. Fans are constantly doing crazy shit like that to impress Rocky."

"But they knew Keith Knight's profile handle," Angelo offered. "I wonder if the caller knew Keith personally."

"Or maybe the caller did what all the other Thorny Messes do," Wes said over him, "troll people's lives online because they don't have one of their own. It's not that big a leap to assume a gay guy who offers massages has a profile on RentAGuy."

A short while later, they found themselves back at Wes's home, staring at the evidence board. If only Rocky had explained the significance of the invisible worm maybe Angelo would have a chance at getting a few hours of sleep, but his mind churned these unanswered questions over and over, attempting to piece them together. He had been so preoccupied he hadn't realized Wes had written RentAGuy on a notecard and pinned it to the board.

"I'm just saying for the sake of arguing," Wes conceded, "that if all three victims have RentAGuy profiles that would be another link they share."

Angelo smirked with validation. Instead of gloating, he simply said, "You're right."

"Come on." Wes turned Angelo around and escorted him into the kitchen. "Let's have a drink." Alcohol, it seemed, had become the answer to everything. The lubricant that greased their gyring minds.

"What's Fitz's story?" Angelo asked. "She's fabulous."

Wes poured them each a hefty glass of wine. "She's kind of a big deal around here."

"Tell me everything."

Wes inhaled and exhaled slowly. "Full transparency. What I'm about to tell you is in the public domain. So, I'm not betraying any confidences."

"You?" Angelo kidded. "Never."

"Fitz is a trans woman. She's a former intravenous drug user, ex-sex worker, and a person living with HIV. Legend has it that after she kicked heroin, she became an HIV warrior." The title seemed perfect to Angelo. They moved into the living room where Angelo flopped on the couch, and Wes took a seat in his oversized armchair. "A few years ago, Fitz began doing outreach to get boys in the biz tested, but many of them refused. They claimed they felt stigmatized going to the HIV clinic and the university hospital. So, Fitz bought a mobile van and began offering testing outside gay clubs and bars…like Peak."

"She *is* a warrior." Angelo lifted his glass. "Fighting HIV stigma by using a mobile van. Genius."

"The local news did a profile on her, though we had to drag her kicking and screaming. Fitz is pretty tight-lipped when it comes to privacy."

Angelo sat up. "Come to think of it, she shut down once Rocky mentioned RentAGuy."

"Like I said, Fitz is an ex-sex worker. A long time ago, she had a profile on RentAGuy to support her habit. Lots of guys paid lots of money for her. Now, she doesn't like to talk about it. Not that she's ashamed. It's more about moving on for her. Paying it forward. I imagine the reason she reacted that way earlier had to do with the fact that sex workers deserve their privacy even though their profiles are public. Does that make sense?"

Wes's words, spoken casually, brought a wave of satisfaction over Angelo. "It does. Thanks for explaining."

As they relaxed in each other's company, a long lull of silence followed. Suddenly, Angelo realized he hadn't called Jason. "Shit!"

"What's the matter?"

Angelo glanced at the clock. It was too late to call him now. "I'm slacking off on my responsibilities as a boyfriend."

"Isn't love grand!" Wes mocked him mercilessly. "What's the point of a relationship if you're bound to certain rules?"

"I'm not bound to rules," Angelo corrected him sharply. "We're in love, and with that comes a certain degree of responsibility to let the other person know you're thinking of them when you're on the other side of the country. At the very least, I should have called to say good night."

"I'm only busting your chops." Wes swung his legs over the chair's armrest. "It's very sweet listening to you talk about Jason."

"When was the last time you were in a relationship?" Angelo asked.

Wes stared into his wineglass. "I had a boyfriend a very long time ago. A photographer who fucked all his male models. I broke it off after my third bout with syphilis." Wes met Angelo's gaze and winked.

Something dug at Angelo. Maybe it was Wes's fatalistic view. "Have you thought about getting back on that horse?"

"Why is it gay guys in relationships believe single gay guys aren't happy unless they're in relationships?" Wes asked. "You say you're happy, but here you are stressing out over slacking off on your responsibilities as a boyfriend."

"You're deflecting," Angelo said, which had him wondering if there was something more to Wes's past than he was letting on. "You mentioned your mother died the year you moved to Los Angeles. What about your father?"

Wes dropped his head back, sighing exhaustedly. "Here we go ladies and gentlemen. In our next segment, Dr. Angelo Perrotta will delve into Wes's absent-father syndrome."

"I didn't mean to…"

"Stop!" Wes held up a hand. "Prepare to be embarrassed. I never knew my father. Mamma was a whore. Plain and simple." The shock of this disclosure jolted Angelo. "Any other questions, Doc?" His eyes widened like a maniac.

Angelo looked down at his hands, away from those eyes. "I'm sorry, Wes. I didn't mean to pry."

Wes stood up, holding out his hand. "One thing I won't do with you is commiserate over daddy issues." His eyes locked with Angelo's, and the manic eyes had been replaced by cheerful ones. "Hey, I have an idea. Why don't you text Jason now. That way when he wakes up it will be the first thing he reads."

Angelo blinked at this buoyant solution. An unexpected and somewhat romantic suggestion from a sworn bachelor. "I just might do that." He took Wes's hand to stand up. "I'm off to bed." Stopping just outside the spare bedroom, Angelo turned back. “What would you say if I told you I was going to call Mabel Knight tomorrow and apologize?”

Wes thought about it. “I’d say you were wasting your time.”

“I guess you’re right.”

“You didn’t let me finish,” Wes added. “Why call her when you can visit her in person tomorrow?”

Angelo didn’t say anything in reply. He waited, wondering if Mrs. Knight would find his unexpected appearance on her doorstep an aggressive violation of her privacy. “I don’t want to scare her.”

“We won’t. Not if we don’t bring Rocky.”

Chapter Eight

Mabel Knight lived in a one-family beige stucco house in Compton. Angelo and Wes arrived in the early morning. The front lawn was mostly brown except for sparse patches of green. Rusted black bars protected the windows and front door. A chain-link fence surrounded the property. The neighbor's two pit bulls growled as they walked up the front path. Once Wes rang the bell, heavy feet padded toward the window. A woman peeked from behind faded lace curtains. "What do you want?"

"Mrs. Knight," Wes began. "My name is Wes Plagen. I'm the producer of the radio show, *A Thorny Mess*. We spoke on the phone."

The woman shook her head violently. "I have nothing to say to you."

"I completely understand why you don't want to speak with us," Wes continued. "We came here to apologize."

"Then you made the trip for nothing."

Angelo heard the quaver in her voice. He regretted bothering the woman so soon after her call to the show. It was obvious she was still traumatized by the experience. "Mrs. Knight, I'm Dr. Angelo Perrotta. I was—"

"I remember you," she interrupted. "For the life of me I can't understand why you, a doctor, would take part in a show like that, and with that awful woman. You should be helping people, not hurting them."

Angelo hung his head, nodding. "I'm very sorry, Mrs. Knight. Like Wes said, we only came here to apologize."

"What do you people want from me?" she begged. "I've lost my son, my only baby. News reporters have turned my son into a horrible person just to get higher ratings. I only agreed to come on your show to finally tell people who Keith really was. Boy was I wrong. That horrible woman only turned out to be just like all the other nasty reporters. You people are evil."

"We're so sorry," Angelo said.

"Do you know I even found one going through my trash can," she added. "He found a pill bottle and had the nerve to ring my bell and ask me if Keith had HIV. Can you believe someone would ask that to a mother who had just lost her only child!"

Angelo willed himself not to break eye contact with the woman. At the very least, she deserved to be heard. "I'm so sorry," Angelo said again. "I didn't know your son was ill."

"There was nothing wrong with my son!"

Angelo took a step back, surprised by the woman's reaction. "I only assumed he was ill because you said he was on medication."

She scoffed, drew the drapes closed and stomped away.

"Well, that was an epic fail," Wes muttered.

"When did I become a parasite?" Angelo turned away in defeat, but paused, hearing footsteps approaching the door. It swung open.

"You see these?" Mabel rattled a pill bottle at Angelo. "You're a doctor. Tell me. What are these for?"

Trembling, the woman standing before him was tall and curvy with pleading eyes and a flat nose. Someone whose loss had sanded away any joy, warmth, or optimism, revealing underneath a knotty and splintered persona.

Wes said, "Mrs. Knight, won't you let us come inside so we can talk about this in private?"

She stared at them. Angelo saw a woman struggling with trust and seeking answers. A deeply wounded person who had no business trusting them. *Please*, he thought to himself, listening to the din of his own labored breath as he stood on her sunny porch, *give me a second chance.*

"All right." She stepped aside. "Come in."

Mabel led them into a quaintly wallpapered room, stiflingly warm with a faint odor of rosewater. A fan rattled on the floor facing a navy recliner. The seat cushion and armrests were faded and worn. Mabel turned down the television and offered them a seat on the couch. Coupons littered the coffee table. Apparently, she had been cutting them out of the weekly circular while watching a religious sermon on television. She offered them a drink, but they refused.

"May I see the pill bottle?" Angelo asked. He inspected the white bottle. The label had no patient name, no expiration date. Nothing to suggest this medication had been prescribed for Keith Knight. "Did Keith have any medical problems that you were aware of?"

She shook her head. "As far as I know, there was nothing wrong with my son."

"It's possible these pills didn't belong to Keith," Angelo reasoned.

"Then why were they in his nightstand?"

Angelo shrugged. "I don't know, but the bottle doesn't have Keith's name on it." Angelo opened it and shook a few pills into his palm. Each one bore the letters, PLX.

"Can't you tell what they are by looking at them?" Mabel asked.

"Wish I could." This wasn't the first time Angelo had been asked that question. "They are labeled, but I don't know what these letters mean." Mabel massaged the nape of her neck, listening. Angelo returned the pills to the bottle and handed it back to her. "I see you were reading." Angelo gestured toward the Bible on the end table.

"Every day," she admitted proudly. "It gives me comfort."

Angelo glanced at Wes. A thought transmuted between them, an idea to probe the woman about the Bible. "Are you familiar with Revelation 5?"

Her head jerked, a quick twitch indicating she was seemingly surprised by the question. "Well, funny you should ask. It was just two weeks ago. No, maybe it was last week. The reverend spoke about Revelation. I'm not entirely familiar with the specifics of Revelation 5, but I do know that the Book of Revelation is about the prophecy."

"What prophecy?" Angelo asked.

"That Christ will triumph over Satan," she said with an emphatic optimism. "It's about hope, Dr. Perrotta, and the second coming of our Lord Jesus Christ."

Angelo decided this moment was as good as any to ask what he really wanted to know. "Yesterday, you said that once you found Jesus, He spared you. May I ask what He spared you from?"

Mabel, to Angelo's dismay, sighed. "Oh, that. Well, it's true."

It was a risk, Angelo knew, asking such a personal question so soon after being invited into her house, but Angelo didn't want to waste time. For a moment, the conversation halted. Wes's cellphone rang. He glanced at the caller ID. "I'm going to take this outside."

Perfect timing! Once Wes was outside, Angelo pressed Mabel. "Would you mind telling me what you were spared from?"

Mabel leveled her eyes at him. "You know, Doctor, everyone's journey to salvation is personal and private. What makes you think I'm going to bare my soul to you?"

"I'm sorry," Angelo asked. "I hope you're not offended."

"I know you're probably a very nice person, but I already have a reverend who hears my confessions. I will say, that for many years, I was lost. It wasn't until Keith had come into my life that I found the Lord and He spared me. Unfortunately, I couldn't save my son."

It was clear Angelo had outstayed his welcome. Time to leave the woman in peace. "I'm sure you did everything you could."

Mabel looked at him. She held his gaze for a bit too long. "Would you like to see his bedroom?"

This invitation seemed almost a divine intervention. Naturally, he was delighted but he contained his enthusiasm. "Yes, I would." Angelo followed her down the beige-carpeted hallway. Family photos hung on the walls, mostly of Keith at various stages of childhood. A sprawling narrative that conveyed a beautiful boy with wonderous eyes. A boy who grew into a tall, sinewy man with a cunning awareness of his beauty.

The room at the end of the hall was small. A single bed was made up with blue-and-white checkered sheets. A poster of Frank Ocean and Rihanna hung by the bed. Angelo went straight to the photos on the dresser. There was one of Keith posing with a young man—smooth diaphanous skin and pretty, his hair in blond waves like a cherub, his eyes the color of indigo—outside a stark white building with three spires. "How recent is this one?"

"That was taken just weeks before he died. Keith had gone to a retreat organized by the Seven Spirits Church. I thought he would have found salvation there, but something wasn't right with my boy when he came back."

"What do you mean?"

Mabel shook her head and shut her eyes. How Angelo hated himself for pressing the woman, again. He dared to lay bare her woundedness, her vulnerability. He ignored her protests and allowed the stifling silence to pack the room like they were wrapped in gauze. Mabel lifted the pill bottle. "I believe it was these that did that to my son. Whatever they are didn't agree with Keith. For days after he came back, it was like he wasn't himself. Drugged up is the only way I can describe it."

Angelo could not help staring at her. Were they not discussing the woman's murdered son, he would have probed further. There was still so much to understand, but Wes entered the house. "We have to leave," he called from the front door.

"Thank you, Mrs. Knight," Angelo said.

"Spirits on high," was the last thing she said before he exited her house.

◆◆◆

Without a doubt, Wes seemed on edge. Whomever he had spoken with, their conversation was weighing heavily on his mind. And almost as if Wes had read Angelo's mind he turned and said, "Listen, when we get to the station don't tell anyone we visited Mabel Knight."

"Is everything okay?"

Wes seemed to require a moment to get his bearings or think about what he was going to say. "Mabel Knight is a member of the Seven Spirits Church."

"I know," Angelo said. "She mentioned that Keith had gone on a retreat with the Seven Spirits Church right before he was murdered."

"When did she say that?" At this point Angelo wanted Wes to slow down. The car careened around the bend with such speed, Angelo heard very little of what came out of Wes's mouth.

"You're going too fast." Angelo reached for the wheel but stopped himself. "What's wrong?"

"If anyone asks"—Wes combed his hand through his hair—"say we didn't know she was a member of the Seven Spirits Church."

The truth was that they didn't know, but Angelo felt it didn't matter at this point. He wanted Wes to focus on the road. Wes's knuckles were white on the steering wheel. For the rest of the drive, he seemed preoccupied. They had stopped talking by the time the car swung into the parking lot on North Sycamore Avenue. He turned off the engine and slowly turned to Angelo. "Reverend James Jarrett runs the Seven Spirits Church. Today he called the station to complain that Rocky and I misled a grieving woman in order to get her to appear on *A Thorny Mess* only to exploit her son's murder."

"But that wasn't our intention—"

"I know, but Reverend James Jarrett has a lot of connections in this town, particularly with the LA County District Attorney's Office, the mayor's office, and the LAPD."

"What does that mean?"

"Hopefully only a slap on the wrist." But Wes's doleful expression told Angelo otherwise.

They hurried into the station, up the elevator and down the hall where they ran into Rocky. "Wes," she shouted. "Mabel Knight is a member of the Seven Spirits Church?"

"I just found out."

"Jesus Christ, Wes." Rocky's voice quavered with such uncharacteristic fear, Angelo almost didn't recognize it. "Seven Spirits! Of all the churches, why that one?" Her body bent in half. Wes attempted to pull her upright. She remained hunched forward, shaking her head like a petulant child.

"We'll get through this," Wes urged. "Where are they?"

"In Femi's office."

Standing outside the station manager's door, Wes said, "Deep breaths everyone," but Angelo was too confused. Smiling, they entered Femi Adebayo's office. The half Nigerian, half British station manager began her career in broadcasting by hosting an overnight show on BBC Radio 5 before she accepted a position in Los Angeles managing content and programming. Femi stood up to greet them. She had dark crescent-shaped eyes, full lips, and short-cropped hair. "Come in," Femi said with a smile and a sigh. "I'd like to introduce Detectives Town and Boniface."

Town's eyes locked on Rocky, scanning her from head to toe, taking in her pink combat boots, camo jumpsuit, and barbed wire necklace. His eyes rolled toward Boniface, who sat with a neutral smile plastered to his face. Angelo thought he was more old school—short, paunchy, wearing an ill-fitted suit and a wide tie.

When Town stood up, Angelo was impressed by his height. Six feet five inches, he guessed. Pale skin with the chiseled features of a graphic novel villain and a torso to match. Except his shoulders were rounded. A sign of bad posture, Angelo decided. That or an old injury. Instantly, he commanded everyone's attention with his loud booming voice. "As you know," he began, "I was brought on to oversee the No Angels Wept murders after Detective Hong Lee went out on medical leave." Town focused on Rocky, who was leaning against the door with her arms folded across her chest. Her frown and posture evidently offended Town, who thought to stand intimidatingly close to her. "We take these murders very seriously."

Rocky gave an outraged laugh. "Then why hasn't anyone been charged?"

"Rocky," Femi intervened. "Let's hear what the detective has to say."

Town snickered, observing Rocky with condescending amusement. "Miss Thorndyke, I understand your frustration. Trust me. We're all frustrated, but the previous investigation was inept. Town shot a look at Boniface who stared at his shoes. "That's why I'm here"—he turned to stare at Rocky again—"but, that's not why I'm here today."

"The suspense is killing me," Rocky muttered.

Town tore his gaze away from Rocky and sighed with frustration at Femi. "I assume you condone this kind of behavior."

Femi's eyes sharpened. "Detective…"

"Disruptive behavior might be condoned here," Town continued, "but not when it affects a woman like Mabel Knight. An upstanding member of the Seven Spirits Church." He fell silent, staring off into space, and then found himself, focusing his intense gaze back at the three of them. "I'm not sure what went through your mind when you decided to torture Mrs. Knight—"

"Torture!" Wes countered. "Come on!"

"Yes, torture," Town shouted over him. His voice cold and firm. "I couldn't believe what I heard, particularly from you, Miss Thorndyke!"

"Detective Town," Angelo intervened calmly. "For what it's worth, Wes and I went by Mabel Knight's house earlier today to apologize."

Seeing Wes squeeze his eyes shut, Angelo forgot they had agreed he would keep their visit a secret, especially when he saw the muscles in Rocky's jaw tighten.

Town took several menacing steps forward. "Stay away from Mabel Knight. You hear me?" Gazing around the room, he added, "I won't have you interfering with my investigation. Have I made myself clear?"

Rocky turned her eyes toward the window; Wes and Angelo froze. The air coagulating around Town's threat until Femi cleared her throat. "It won't happen again, Detective."

"As for you." Town stood inches away from Rocky's face. "There's a new sheriff in town."

Rocky huffed a laugh. "A new sheriff?"

"That's right," he said, matching her amused condescension. The tension between them crackled with such conductivity, Angelo could see it. "I wonder what happened to you as a child that turned you into such a nasty bitch."

"Don't talk to her like that," Wes shouted.

"It's a shame really," Town continued as if he hadn't heard Wes. "A pretty face like yours doesn't deserve such a disgusting mouth. I'm watching you. I heard all about the fight you started last night. It seems you and your"—he craned his head back to look at Boniface—"is it boyfriend or girlfriend, Sal? I'm not sure which."

"Fuck you," Rocky hissed.

Town's face beamed with satisfaction. Turning to Femi, he barked, "Keep your people in line. This is your final warning."

It had been an abrupt, terrifying meeting that ended with the detectives storming out of the office like a tempest had blown through. An experience that triggered panic and fear, brought on by a shit storm Angelo never wanted to encounter again. But something told him this wasn't the last time he'd see Detective Town and his minion, Boniface.

Femi leaned on her desk, heaving a long sigh. "Thank God that's over."

Without warning Angelo was assaulted by a flurry of punches, almost too fast for his brain to comprehend he was under attack. Falling to the floor, still in shock, Rocky straddled him. "You fucking rat," she spat. "You went to Mabel Knight's house behind my back!"

Wes and Femi attempted to pull Rocky off him, but she continued unfettered, landing blow after blow until Wes dragged her into a corner. Femi crouched beside Angelo. "Are you all right?"

He held a blank expression for no more than two seconds. "What did I do?"

But just as everyone was recovering from the shock, Rocky jumped up and began kicking Wes. "And you! You're supposed to be my best friend. You fucking snake!"

Femi ran into the hall and called for help. It took three interns to restrain Rocky. When it was all over—Rocky storming out of the station and threatening never to come back—Angelo felt both confused and ashamed. And yet, simmering beneath it all was fear, a familiar sense that Rocky's temper could be ignited by the slightest spark. Warning voices echoed resoundingly in his head. One of the loudest shouted for him to return to New York immediately.

Femi helped Angelo up. He sat in a chair, head between his knees, heaving. *Three deep breaths. Serenity now.*

Wes began pacing, brushing a shaky hand through his hair. "It's this case. It's this damn case. It's getting to her."

"You think?" Femi asked.

Wes reached for his phone. "I'll call her."

Femi marched toward him, grabbing his hand. "Leave her alone. She needs to cool off. Besides, you're the last person she wants to speak to right now."

Angelo sat back contemplatively in the chair. He watched with a sense of detachment as Femi spoke to Wes. He was aware now that his participation as co-host of *A Thorny Mess* had breached beyond the three hours they spent in that studio with its padded, soundproof walls, microphones, and Cough buttons. Well beyond any of that. The decision to visit Mabel Knight's home had crossed an ethical boundary. He was no longer a spectator obsessed with a salacious serial killer. He had become a parasite, feeding off the families of the murdered victims. *When had this happened,* he asked himself. *And for what?*

Wes extended his hand. "Amigo?"

A hundred things went through Angelo's mind. An image of Mabel Knight's face appeared. Dark, confused eyes. Troubled eyes that begged for an answer. And then there was Rocky. The outrage she displayed moments earlier seemed overblown, displaced. What was it about the Seven Spirits Church that spurred such anxiety in Wes and such fury in Rocky? Suddenly, Angelo found himself sliding toward something bigger than he could have imagined.

Go back to New York. Leave now.

"Amigo?"

Angelo observed Wes with the keen sense that if he took his hand, there would be no turning back.

"Come on. I'll buy you lunch." Wes pulled him to his feet.

Again, Angelo's thoughts drifted back to the faces of the three victims no one cared about. Angelo didn't know how this would all end or what he'd find when it was over, but he refused to quit because it was the right thing to do. The only thing to do.

Chapter Nine

Outside, the sun felt intense on Angelo's neck. He was still somewhat in shock, never anticipating that the worst part about being called to Femi's office to meet with the lead detective on the No Angels Wept case was not the verbal tongue-lashing Detective Town enacted, but the physical assault from Rocky Thorn.

These tantrums and outbursts seemed expected and contained in the soundproof KLM studio, but Angelo had realized in a short period how much they bled into everyday life. Except everyone in Rocky's orbit seemed to tolerate these off-air attacks with the kind of understanding that if you chose to domesticate a tiger, it might eat you one day.

Angelo believed violence was never the answer. Yet, once again, he found himself the target of someone's violence. Angelo swore he wouldn't be a victim again. Not after suffering from the physical and emotional abuse perpetrated against him by his alcoholic ex-boyfriend, Miles. Enduring the brunt of abusive men was something he had in common with his mother and sister. After he broke up with Miles, and Camille divorced her abusive husband, Trace, Angelo swore he would never be someone's punching bag. *No, never again.*

Rocky's behavior toward him, and toward Wes, was unacceptable. Explaining her actions as the consequence of having too much passion was a poor excuse. Being the patron saint of the forgotten LGBTQ+ community didn't give her the right to hurt people, and if Angelo was going to remain one of the three amigos, he had to set boundaries. Violence was his line in the sand that could never be crossed again.

"My jaw hurts." Angelo massaged the angle of his mandible.

Wes lifted Angelo's chin and inspected his face. "I don't see a bruise."

"Why do you put up with it?"

Looking down, shaking his head, Wes said, "I don't know. Maybe it's because I know where she's coming from."

"You mean the psych ward?"

"Don't look now." Wes nudged his head toward a gray Ford Crown Victoria parked across the street with a conspicuous Detective Town behind the wheel. Heavy-lidded eyes, narrow and sharp like the eyes of a hawk.

"The intimidation continues," Angelo said.

Wes huffed. "Just smile and wave."

Baiting Town seemed like an awful idea. The man looked like he collected Hitler memorabilia.

They walked across the street to a diner on Santa Monica Boulevard called Café '50s. A large neon sign in the shape of a clock read: Time to Play. The red and white striped entrance reminded Angelo of a circus tent. They sat in a maroon booth in the back. Vintage celebrity headshots lined the wall behind the counter just above a sign displaying the specials of the day. The walls and the ceiling were a collage of memorabilia: the American flag, *Life* magazine covers, I Like Ike posters, and advertisements for Camel and Chesterfield cigarettes. Angelo glanced at the menu, but he wasn't hungry. Who could eat after the morning they'd had?

"I'm having a cheeseburger," Wes announced. That answered Angelo's question. "What about you?"

Angelo pulled his eyebrows together with such intensity, they twitched. "Are we seriously going to ignore the thorny elephant in the room?"

Wes reached for Angelo's hand, but he pulled away. "I get it. She overreacted."

"That wasn't an overreaction," Angelo jumped in. "That was a physical assault."

"You're right," Wes whispered. "Rocky's behavior was unacceptable, but understandable if you only knew her past."

A waitress wearing a red uniform with a white Peter Pan collar and capped sleeves appeared. "Hello, gentlemen," she said in a cheery voice. "What can I get you?"

"Two coffees for now," Wes replied.

Once she was out of earshot, Angelo started in. "Please, enlighten me with Rocky's history that gives her the right to assault people."

Wes explained that a year ago, Rocky had insisted on dedicating an entire episode to Reverend James Jarrett, the spiritual leader of the Seven Spirits congregation, after the *LA Times* ran an exposé about the former researcher turned pastor. "The article claimed Jarrett and his congregation were targeting young gay men," Wes whispered. "To convert them."

"To Christianity?" Without realizing it, Angelo had begun to whisper too.

"No." Wes hushed once the server returned with their coffees. Forcing a smile, Wes ordered a cheeseburger, but Angelo's stomach was in knots. He was too eager for the server to leave them so Wes could finish telling him the rest of the story. "Reverend Jarrett is a so-called renowned expert in gay conversion therapy."

"You've got to be kidding me."

Recounting these events had set Wes's blood to boil. "If only I had known Mabel Knight was a member of the Seven Spirits Church," his voice quaked with rage. "I wouldn't have booked her on the show." He pounded his fist on the linoleum table. Angelo flinched. Heads turned in their direction, sideways glances from an elderly couple. Angelo suppressed his outrage, suspecting there was more to this story, but a '50s inspired diner where the special of the day was called Aunt Liz's Golden Fried Chicken wasn't the place to hear it.

"Okay," Angelo said in a singsong voice meant to lighten the mood, "but you didn't know Mabel Knight was a member of the Seven Spirits Church. Town warned us not to interfere with his investigation, and that's that."

Wes arched his back like a bow being pulled tight. A long exhale followed. "You're right. Town warned us, and that's that."

"Is everything all right here, gentlemen?" The server set a cheeseburger down in front of Wes.

Like a spangle of sunshine, Wes assured the woman everything was more than all right. It was perfect.

"You sure I can't get you anything?" she asked Angelo, but someone had caught his eye. A young man had entered the diner: Thin framed, blond ringlets, and indigo eyes. He moved about as though he had just gotten up from a deep sleep. It was the boy in the picture with Keith Knight.

"Hold that thought." He scuttled out of the booth. A glass of water crashed to the floor. The young man's eyes locked on Angelo. *Yes, it's him.* But there was something off about him. His eyes were dull. His movements sleepy. "Excuse me," Angelo called out to him. "I don't mean to trouble you, but do you know—"

The young man bolted out the door. Angelo took chase. *What am I doing!* But he was running just as the young man opened his car door. Throwing his body against it, Angelo watched the young man stagger back, horrified. "Dude, what is your fucking problem?"

Panting, body surging with adrenaline, Angelo apologized. "I don't know what just came over me. I am so sorry."

The car keys trembled in the young man's hand. "I don't have much money."

"No, no, no," Angelo pleaded. "I just want to ask you a question. If it makes you feel better, I'm a doctor."

The jittery boy surveyed him. God only knows what he saw, staring into Angelo's crazed eyes. What kind of doctor is he, Angelo imagined the young man was thinking. "Just back off. I'm not interested in whatever it is you want."

"You knew Keith Knight," Angelo blurted. "I saw you in a photo in Keith's bedroom."

Stuttering, the boy tried to deny it, but Angelo knew this was the same person in that photo. He would have known him anywhere, at any distance. The indigo eyes were a dead giveaway. Except up close, they were dulled. Vacant. Anxious red blotches appeared on the boy's face like bee stings. "Just step away from my car," the young man said, his voice cracking.

"Please," Angelo begged. "I just want to ask you a few questions about Keith Knight. I'm investigating his death." This was not helping. The blotches. The trembling. Clear signs indicating Angelo had only confused the anxious boy. "I'll buy you lunch." Angelo turned to point at the diner but found Wes standing outside. A beefy cook in a white T-shirt and matching pants blocked the doorway.

Distracted, Angelo didn't notice the young man had slipped into his car. When the engine roared to life, he stumbled back in shock, tires shrieking and churning up gravel that sprayed him. Before the car sped away, Angelo yanked his phone from his pocket. He snapped a photo of the license plate just as Wes came up from behind him. "Apparently we're too rowdy for the lunchtime regulars."

Angelo spun around, staring at Wes confusedly, but then he saw the large cook still standing in the entrance with his Popeye-arms folded over his chest. The waitress and a pair of old folks gawked at them through the window. Observing this scene now, Angelo cringed inwardly. *My God, I have turned into such a parasite.*

◆◆◆

Nobody had heard from Rocky. Her violent reaction to learning Wes and Angelo had visited Mabel Knight without informing her first, coupled with the fact that Mabel was a member of the Seven Spirits Church—the organization led by the powerful Reverend James Jarrett who nearly got Rocky fired after she profiled him on *A Thorny Mess*—had more than set her teeth on edge. Wes described it best as a severe allergic reaction.

But Wes assured Angelo that Rocky didn't hold grudges. "Why don't I believe you," Angelo said to him as they got ready to leave for the studio. Wes had just tried Rocky again, but she didn't answer her phone. "What do we do if she doesn't show?"

"She'll show." Wes's fingers had twisted in his hair so that when he tugged them free, loose strands were tangled around his knuckles.

"Wes," Angelo insisted. "There's a really good chance she won't show. We have to entertain that fact. I just want to know—"

"You don't know her like I do!" Wes exploded again like he had at the diner. This dark side had broken free twice in such a short while; Angelo wondered if Wes was losing control. Withering roots unable to support the solid trunk he presented to everyone. Wes raked both hands through his hair again. His breathing slowed down. "She'll be there," he assured Angelo. "Rocky has never missed a show. There's a reason for that."

"What's the reason?" Angelo pressed.

Wes scoffed at Angelo's insistence, his dogged determination for answers. "Because."

Angelo sensed his reluctance. Nervous, he stood in front of Wes, poised like a high diver on the edge of the board. "Please, I have to know."

"Because!" Wes shouted. This time, the outburst seemed to shake him, as though the anger unsettled him. "Because," he repeated softly. "She wouldn't do that to Rands."

"Rands?"

"Miranda," Wes clarified. "Miranda Rose Thorndyke. Rocky's little sister."

Little sister?

Wes explained that Rocky had a younger sibling identified as female at birth, but Miranda disclosed to Rocky that he was a boy, Rands, when he was eleven, and from that day on Rocky staunchly defended her little brother against their parents' concerns, recriminations, and objections. It was this responsibility as the older sister, Wes explained, that produced Rocky's ferocious protectiveness over all things LGBTQ+.

Angelo was captivated by the intensity with which Wes spoke. His dark side had been wrangled, stuffed back where Wes kept it in check. He never raised his voice, every sentence had a measured, introspective quality, and whenever he concentrated on offering a new disclosure, his left eye twitched.

"Yes," Wes chuckled. "Rocky was a big old softy for Rands. She used to let him get away with anything.

"Rands began wearing clothes that made him feel more comfortable in his body, opting for baggy jeans, oversized sweatshirts, and baseball caps. If anyone said anything derogatory to him, Rocky annihilated them.

"When Rocky entered high school, Rands had to fend for himself in middle school. He often came home and locked himself in his bedroom. Rands began cutting himself to deal with the bullying. Kids made photos of his head superimposed on torsos of naked women and taped them to his locker. They filmed him getting beat up in the boys' rooms and posting the videos on YouTube."

"That's awful," Angelo said. "What happened to Rands?"

Wes froze, struck by an invisible lightning bolt. "Rands came home one afternoon and locked himself in the bathroom. He had cut his wrists and bled out in the tub. Rocky believes he may have been raped. The detectives said there was trauma"—Wes made a circular motion over his groin—"down there."

Angelo wanted to hug him, but he could tell that Wes didn't want to. He sensed his anxiety, and some resentment, anger, and sadness.

"The worst part…" Wes heaved a long sigh. "The school's superintendent had known about the bullying and torture, but he did nothing to stop it."

This sad story, unfortunately, had become more common of late. Certainly, social media added a complexity to the torture LGBTQ+ youths experience. Angelo couldn't imagine what it must be like for trans kids. Cyberbullying was fortunately something he didn't have to contend with. The thought that bullying continued after school, in your own bedroom where you were supposed to feel safe… Your computer now a portal to an endless cesspool of hate.

"I guess that's when Rocky became the patron saint of the invisible LGBTQ+ community."

"That was precisely the moment," Wes confirmed. "She takes that role very, very seriously."

Angelo thought back to the first time he met Rocky. Frustrated by her rudeness toward her audience, her dismissiveness toward him, Angelo had lashed out. Called her a bully of all things and questioned what authority she had to ordain herself the patron saint of the invisible LGBTQ+ community. "This explains a lot. Thank you for telling me."

"Shit." Wes glanced at his watch. "We're going to be late."

Chapter Ten

Coming off the elevator, Angelo and Wes were greeted by a tense looking Femi. "There you are!"

"Is she here?" Wes asked.

Femi turned back toward the receptionist with the black and pink mullet. "I've called her a gazillion times. No answer."

Wes held Femi's shoulders. "She'll be here."

Femi inhaled sharply through her nose. "I hope you're right."

They walked toward the studio. Angelo maintained a safe distance behind them as Femi discussed what they would do in the unlikely event Rocky didn't show up. How unlikely? Angelo was unsure, especially since the show went live in less than thirty minutes. In the control room, the frat bros stood up when Femi entered. "We have a choice between a best of Rocky's rants or the classic episode where Rocky interviewed the guy who inspired the play about marrying a goat."

The receptionist rushed up to them, breathless. "Wes, there's a guy named Dino here. He said Rocky is supposed to interview him today." Her head bobbled as she waited for further instruction.

"Shit," Wes said under his breath. "I forgot about Dino Sosano."

"You deal with Dino," Femi ordered. "I'll choose which episode we'll play if we don't go live."

Wes began taking step after step backward. "We *will* go live."

Nothing had unfolded this day as Angelo had anticipated. The events hurtled in time like a vessel shot into space. *Maybe it would be best if Rocky took the night off.* But after hearing about Rands, Angelo knew deep down she wouldn't. It sickened him to wonder how their reunion would play out. What were the chances Rocky had calmed down, realized she had crossed a line, and was rushing to the studio with her tail between her legs?

Zero point zero zero. We're talking about Rocky fucking Thorn.

He dipped into the men's room, feeling the tension settling around his bladder. He stepped up to a urinal and relieved himself. Staring ahead at the robin's egg blue tile, he took three deep breaths. Faint whiff of bleach and urinal cake. He winced at the shock of the pungent smell up his nostrils. It'll be all right, he made himself believe. What else could go wrong?

Behind him, he heard someone in the stall, a strange high-pitched screech like a whining kitten. "I can see you, Doc."

Angelo spun around, leaking urine on his sneakers. "What the… Rocky, is that you?" A stab of fear. Rocky began laughing, and Angelo experienced a palpable threat of punishment. "What are you doing in here?"

"What do you think I'm doing," she said with luxuriant sarcasm. "I'm taking a piss."

The stall door kicked open. Rocky sat on the toilet, not pissing. In fact, she was fully dressed, wearing a motorcycle jacket, black jeans, and fingerless black leather gloves. She held her knife in her right hand. Angelo noticed that she had carved words into the stall wall: Snake. Rat. Men suck. Thick black eyeliner circled her turquoise eyes like a child had taken a magic marker to her face.

"I know you're upset." Angelo zipped up his jeans, reclaiming what was left of his dignity. "I apologize for not telling you we were going to Mabel Knight's house. Had we known she was a member of the Seven Spirits Church, we wouldn't have gone."

Rocky groaned, pulling her right knee to her chest and then her left. She stood up and swaggered to stand in front of Angelo. "You're sorry, huh?"

"Yes, but there's something else I need to say."

Rocky cocked her head, inspecting Angelo's ears, his eyes, and finally his mouth. "Oh yeah, and what's that?"

Clearing his throat twice, Angelo began, "Regardless of whether or not we did anything wrong—"

"Wrong," Rocky summoned a defiant tone, but her teasing turquoise eyes seemed to proffer their own goad. "This isn't about right or wrong. This is about the three amigos code. T.A.C. Remember? First being, we don't keep secrets. *Comprende*?"

Angelo understood loud and clear. Visiting Mabel Knight without informing Rocky was high on his list of stupid things to do while in Los Angeles, but it was necessary. He felt a convulsion of self-loathing at what his betrayal had cost him.

"Regardless of that fact," Angelo recited in a voice meant to instill confidence but when echoed back to him against the tile sounded quavering and tremulous. "Violence is never the answer."

God, how he wished Wes would burst through the door...or anyone for that matter. Even a frat bro would do. Someone whose presence would pierce this expanding orb of awkwardness.

"Violence," Rocky repeated. She raised the knife to Angelo's face. The tip just millimeters from his nose. "You mean…when I attacked you in Femi's office?"

"Yes," Angelo replied. "But I get it now. You felt betrayed, and that's a trigger for you."

Surprised, she gaped at him with mocking amusement. "Oh, you had a light bulb moment. I'm so happy you understand me now."

"I know about Rands."

An icy stillness overcame Rocky's expression. "You know about Rands too. Who told you…wait, I know who told you. My best friend. Wes must have told you."

"I'm so sorry, Rocky. Now I get it. I understand where you're coming from."

Rocky assumed an introspective demeanor. He suspected this disclosure had flooded her with emotion, recalling Rands. "I'm actually relieved you know."

He sighed, delighted with Rocky's reaction. "So, we're good?"

"For sure," she assured him. "We're totally good."

Still, the good fortune of this conversation having landed softly buoyed Angelo to confide in Rocky about the events that took place earlier that day at the diner. Staring at him with a yearning ferocity, Rocky listened to Angelo explain the sheer luck he had running into the very boy he had seen in a photo with Keith Knight.

"That's incredible." She returned the knife to her boot. "Did you get his name?"

"No, I freaked him out, but I did get a photo of his car."

Her face, shuttered, sprang open with excitement. "Look at you," Rocky teased. "Snapping photos of a getaway car. Quick thinking, Sherlock. Let me see it."

Angelo felt only a wisp of suspicion; was it possible that Rocky had an ulterior motive? Reluctantly, he took out his phone and showed her the photo of the car pulling away with a clear view of the license plate. Rocky gazed at it intently, muttering the license plate number to herself.

The bathroom door swung open. "Jesus Christ," Wes said. "You're here."

Rocky looked at him strangely. "Of course, I'm here. We have a show to do."

She glanced at Angelo. "Good talk. No more secrets, right?'

"Cross my heart."

"See you on the other side." Rocky exited the men's room, pounding gently on Wes's chest as she passed him.

Wes hung back, eyeing Angelo cautiously. "Everything good?"

"Yeah, we talked it out. We're good."

"Really?" he asked suspiciously.

Angelo swung his arm over Wes's shoulder. "Come on. You heard the patron saint. We have a show to do."

♦♦♦

Angelo's impression of Dino Sosano was of a man about fifty, possibly younger, roughened skin like used sandpaper, untrimmed hair, and yellow tinged eyes behind blue-tinted glasses. "My first guest tonight," Rocky announced to her listeners, "is a man at the epicenter of the No Angels Wept murders. I'd like to welcome the manager of Peak, Dino Sosano, to the show."

Rocky wasted no time asking Dino whether he had a sexual relationship with any of the victims. Chuckling, he brushed off the question with an emphatic no regarding all three dead men. He seemed more than mildly amused by Rocky. It was obvious to Angelo he was a fan of the show or, at least, he knew enough about Rocky to anticipate the types of questions she'd ask him.

"Of all three victims," she continued, "is it accurate to say you were the closest to Gabriel Menendez?"

"Yeah," Dino replied. "That would be accurate. I liked Gabe. He was a real sweetheart. Always polite. Always respectful and very humble."

"Not so tough on the eyes either," Rocky kidded.

Dino broke into a wheezy laugh. The brown stains on his teeth and burn marks between his index and middle finger told Angelo that Dino was at least a pack a day smoker. Maybe more. The yellow tinge of his sclerae had

Angelo wondering if Dino had a chronic liver disease. Viral hepatitis.

"Gabe was a cutie," Dino admitted. "Without a doubt."

She held up a photo of Gabriel dancing. "I mean look at that body. What did he have, a nine-pack." More wheezy laughter from Dino. "You mean to tell me, you never tried to hit this?"

From the start, the overall tone of this interview had rubbed Angelo the wrong way. Obviously, he knew Rocky was attempting to gain Dino's trust, engage him in some friendly banter mixed in with a tinge of provocative sexual imagery both to humor Dino and titillate her audience. She had to find an in while performing this balancing act. Yet, something didn't seem right.

"Come on," Dino said. "Gabe could have been my son."

Here, Rocky sat back grinning. "You mean to tell me Gabe never fooled around with older men?"

"For money, sure," Dino confirmed, "but not to date."

"Was he close to Keith Knight?"

"Yes, Keith was like an older brother to Gabe, not that they were very far apart in age. It's just that Keith had been turning tricks longer."

Rocky smiled broadly. "Turning tricks. God, I love this guy. Isn't Dino a hoot, Dr. Angelo?"

"Yeah, he's a real throwback to the '70s." The studio light struck Dino's face in such a way that Angelo thought it aged him. Sallow skin. Yellow eyes behind blue-tinted glasses, and that wheezy smoker's laugh. What was he thinking, appearing on *A Thorny Mess*?

"What was Gabe's reaction to Keith's murder?" Rocky asked.

"What was Gabe's reaction?" Dino repeated as if that was the dumbest question he'd ever heard. "Not good. It shocked everyone because it seemed like things were on their way up for Keith."

"What do you mean, on their way up?"

"Gabe said he had a new boyfriend, but he had to keep it under lock and key because the guy was some bigwig whose life would be ruined if their relationship became public."

Rocky groaned seductively. "Thanks for spillin' the tea, D. Any chance you know the identity of this bigwig?"

Dino began laughing a gassy, husky laugh. "Can't help you there. If anything, Gabe was loyal. Whatever Keith told him, he took to the grave." Angelo heard an imaginary rimshot. "Boys in their line of work tend to be loyal." Dino leaned in. "But I don't have to tell you. I'm sure your girlfriend spills all their tea."

Rocky didn't take the bait. Instead, she surprised them with a new line of questioning. "Where did Gabe pick up men?" she asked. "At Peak?"

Dino flicked his gaze to Angelo. "I know what's she doing. She's trying to trap me. Get me to admit something that ain't true."

"Me?" Rocky feigned innocence.

"You know very well no one turns tricks at Peak," Dino said. "Gabe, like Keith and Blaze, were on that RentAGuy site. Don't you know someone who had a profile on RentAGuy?"

Again, Rocky refused to bring Fitz into the conversation. "Do you know Gabe's profile handle?"

"Sure I do." Dino tugged at the collar of his T-shirt. "Can I get a glass of water or something? It's hot in here." Rocky signaled Wes. Seconds later, one of the frat bros entered with a bottle of water. "Thank you."

"Gabe's handle," Rocky prompted him. "You were going to tell us."

Dino chuckled, thinking. "It was cute. Gabe went by the handle Amigo-go."

"Amigo-go!" Rocky howled. "Now that's funny."

Angelo shot a glance at Wes. He seemed just as unnerved. It wasn't as though there was something wrong. In fact, up until that moment, the interview was fine, but fine was not the standard to which Rocky held herself. All this forced conviviality. The hooting and howling weren't Rocky. It was all pretense to proffer something more. What that was, Angelo had no idea, and it set him on edge.

"That is really cute." Rocky dabbed her bone-dry eyes. She dragged it out a few seconds more before turning serious. "Gabe's death must have really torn you up."

His response, which he expressed by bowing his head, fist pressed against his lips, was overly dramatic in Angelo's mind. "It killed me."

"You were the last person to see Gabe alive, correct?"

Alarm registered in Dino's eyes. "I don't know about that," he replied with a slight chortle. "He was dancing that night at Peak. *Lots* of people saw him."

"You told the police that Gabe stayed after Peak closed."

And there was the trigger. "You wanna go there?" Dino warned.

Rocky grinned. "We're already there, my friend. In fact, you told the police that Gabe had gone missing for several days prior to his death. Did you file a missing person's report?"

Dino shifted uneasily. He glanced at Angelo, but he returned an unwavering stare. "Mr. Sosano, she asked you a question."

Dino nodded, chuckling under his breath like he finally caught on to the joke, but Rocky turned brutal. "Isn't it true that in 2018, you were accused of propositioning a minor while you were living in St. Petersburg?"

He smiled, but it gave way to a grimace. Then he prevaricated, realizing she already knew the answer, but he refused to reply, as if admitting the truth would make it definitive and public. "You're a real a bitch. You know that?"

"I'll take that as a compliment coming from a scumbag like you." Dino's mouth hung open. He looked humiliated, and for the first time, Angelo thought Dino didn't just look old, he looked like a dying, old man. "But forget that for now. To be fair, the boy was a go-go dancer like Gabe. He had no business dancing at a bar. Let's just say it was all a misunderstanding. Dino likes young guys. Young go-go dancers to be correct. What I want to know is why you didn't report Gabriel Menendez missing if you two were so close?"

"Boys come and go all the time!" Dino rose to his feet. "Who can keep track?"

"Weren't you curious?" Rocky pressed. "Gabe goes missing for days then shows up to dance. Out of the blue, and you didn't ask, hey friend, where have you been?"

Dino's head seemed to retract into his shoulders. "It wasn't any of my business."

"Isn't it true that after Gabe went missing for days, he returned to Peak and asked you to get him cocaine so he could dance because he was so out of it?"

"That's a lie!"

"Boys come and go," Rocky continued, "but Gabe wasn't just any boy. Isn't that right, Dino?"

"I don't know what you're getting at lady."

"That *is* what you told police after Gabe was found murdered." Clearly, Rocky had done her homework. "That you and Gabe were best friends and that you were relieved when he turned up Friday night to dance."

"I don't remember saying that."

Rocky regarded him curiously. "Well, let me refresh your memory. Gabriel Menendez, your best friend, disappeared for days, but you didn't notify police. On Friday, July 15, he showed up to dance at Peak, but he was too tired. Gabe asked you to score him some coke, and you, being his best friend, didn't think to ask him where he had been or why he was so out of it because why ladies and gentlemen...

it was none of Dino Sosano's business. Bet you still got your bestie the coke, right?"

"You bitch!"

"Funny thing is, you didn't file a missing person's report with the police. No, why would you? Wouldn't want to attract the police's suspicion. Not with your past but once Gabe was found dead you sure as shit sang like a bird to the police. And Messes, you want to know why?" She paused to catch her breath. "Because Dino was desperate to control the narrative." She locked eyes with Dino. "You knew the police were going to hear it from all the other dancers that you had the hots for Gabe, but the hot, *young* amigo-go didn't give you the time of day. Not unless he needed you to fetch him coke, and you did. Didn't you? You did whatever that hot, young Latino asked you to do because you were his bitch!"

Dino threw off his headset. "You're a fucking bitch and a liar!"

"It's all in the police report, asshole. Now get out of my studio."

He burst through the studio door, screaming as he disappeared down the hallway. *Police report.* How did Rocky get the police report when the investigation was still open?

"I want to thank my guest, Dino Sosano," Rocky said with gameshow host enthusiasm. "This is Rocky Thorn. We'll be right back."

At the break, Rocky didn't engage Angelo. She stared at her microphone unblinkingly as though remaining focused was imperative. *What does she have up her sleeve.* He'd find out soon enough. Wes began counting down from the break. As if a switch had been flipped, Rocky sat upright. Showtime. "I'm Rocky Thorn, and we're back. During the break, we cleaned up the studio. Isn't that right, Dr. Angelo?"

"Huh?" Angelo mumbled. Lost in his own thoughts, the mention of his name startled him.

"I'm talking about the two men in hazmat suits," she continued with the pretense. "The ones who fumigated the studio after that vile, flea-infested scumbag Dino Sosano tore out of here?"

"Oh, I missed them," Angelo joked weakly. "I was in the bathroom taking a Silkwood shower."

Rocky let out a quick howl. "Make sure you undress outside when you get home," she continued. "In fact, I would burn those clothes."

Laughing was expected, but Dino's brisk departure had not eased the tension in the studio. If anything, it felt like Angelo had changed seats with Dino.

"You had an interesting afternoon," Rocky chided. "Heard you ran into somebody at the diner. Isn't that right, Dr. Angelo." When Rocky turned to stare at him, he detected that sharp gaze. A look that told him he was wrong. Things between them were not *good*. "You ran into a friend of Keith Knight's."

The seat cushion felt like the coils of a stove heating up. Suddenly, he knew exactly how Dino Sosano felt. "Now Rocky, let's not go there."

"Oh, you don't want me to go there, Dino. Er, I mean, Dr. Angelo."

A swooning sensation overcame him. Angelo felt light-headed. On the verge of fainting. *Why is she doing this? I should have never mentioned Rands. What was I thinking?*

"Thorny Messes," Rocky began. "Dr. Angelo is so smart. While trying to engage with this young man whom he identified as someone he saw in a photo with Keith Knight while in his bedroom, the young man fled. But guess what kids? The quick-thinking doctor took a photo of his car, and guess what? I got his license plate digits."

"Don't do it, Rocky," Angelo warned.

The light glinted off her eyes and suddenly they glowed like sunlight reflecting the turbulent surface of the sea. "Don't do what?"

He might have gotten up. Taken Dino's lead and

stormed out of the studio, but something compelled him to stay. Instead, he flicked his gaze over at Wes, pleading, but of course Wes did not intervene. He wouldn't dare.

"Thought so." She regarded him with chill distaste. As if she had been planning this since he showed her the photo in the men's room. Waiting, like she had with Dino. Patiently waiting to find an in, and now she had found an in with Angelo. "Calling all Messes," she announced, and then without pausing, Rocky recited the make, model, and license plate number for the car that Keith's frightened friend drove off in. The response was explosive. The light-board throbbed red. "Caller, you're on with Rocky."

Angelo shook his head. Standing up, he pushed his chair away, sickened. Rocky snapped her fingers, but this time Angelo did not obey like a trained dog. He headed for the door, but Wes entered before he could leave.

"Why y'all wasting your time with the likes of that scumbag Dino," said a woman who identified herself as Helen. "Y'all should be looking into Guy Cleveland." Angelo watched Rocky and Wes connect as if this name held some meaning to them both. "He's the one who started Rent-AGuy."

"Thank you, Helen," Rocky said. "This Cleveland guy has no social media presence. Does anyone have the skinny on GC?"

Once again, the show had gone off the rails. Tightrope or no tightrope, Rocky didn't have the right to take out her anger with Angelo on-air. Certainly, she had no right abusing Dino Sosano even if he was a scumbag. Unstoppable was the only word he could think of to describe it. Kicking ass and taking names. *Poor Guy Cleveland. God help you whoever you are.*

"No social media presence!" Helen said in a high-pitched tone. "Well, if that isn't shady then I don't know what else is."

"What else you got for me Helen?"

"All I know is that Guy Cleveland sold RentAGuy after Keith Knight was murdered to an undisclosed LLC."

"Well, you know what that means," Rocky said, baiting her audience. "My guess is that Guy Cleveland sold the platform to distance himself from Keith Knight's murder. I wonder why, Guy. What, pray tell, do you have to hide?"

"Can't you stop this?" Angelo whispered to Wes, but he knew the answer. This was *A Thorny Mess* after all.

"Thanks, Helen. Caller, you're on with Rocky Thorn. You say what?"

"Hello, Rocky," the familiar mechanical voice answered. "Tonight's show has been very entertaining."

"Mr. Roboto, I was hoping you'd call."

"I really enjoyed listening to you gut that smelly fish, Dino Sosano. Nice job."

"Thank you." Rocky leaned forward and cleared her throat. "And what do you have to say tonight?"

"Don't waste your time with Guy Cleveland," the voice autotuned. "You should really be looking into the Seven Spirits Church. You remember them, don't you, Rocky? I seem to recall you highlighted Reverend James Jarrett a while back. Why don't you chase him with the same fervor you chase N.A.W.? Remember, it's not the thorns you should beware of; it's the invisible worm."

Rocky was struck uncharacteristically silent. It was as if she didn't know how to respond, or she was too afraid to speak. Angelo rushed back to his seat, donning the headphones. "Hello, this is Dr. Perrotta."

"How lovely to finally meet you, Doctor. I've been waiting patiently. We have so much in common, you and me. Won't you convince our friend Rocky to revisit her investigation into Dr. Reverend James Jarrett and the Parallax Institute?"

Wes disconnected the call. “That’s enough of that.”

Rocky stared at him pleadingly. “Why is this happening?”

“I don’t know,” Wes replied. “I really don’t.”

Chapter Eleven

"Hey, it's me. Call me. I don't care what time it is. Just call me tonight. Love you."

Once the message ended, Angelo pressed Play again. He listened to it seven times, sitting on the bed in the spare room in Wes's house. Darkness all around him. All he could see was the outline of the evidence board. The soft glow of his cellphone as it played Jason's message again and again was the only light in the house.

What have I gotten himself into? Everything had gone from bad to worse in the span of a day. An incongruous and calamitous course of events that led him here, alone in Wes's house. After the show, Rocky and Wes met with Femi to decide whether they were going to continue with the plan to focus on the No Angels Wept murders. If Femi had her way, she wanted them to move on. Wes pleaded with her to reconsider. They spoke in hushed voices inside her office while Angelo stood in the hall. What he couldn't understand was why everyone feared Reverend James Jarrett and the Seven Spirits Church. There must be more to that story. More than Wes had told him at the diner. Clearly, whatever happened rattled him to the point of losing his temper just talking about it.

Finally, he got up the nerve to call Jason. "Hey, how are you?"

"How are you, is the million-dollar question."

Angelo bit his lip. "I don't know. Honestly, I don't know how everything got so out of control."

"I'm not going to sugarcoat this," Jason said. "What you're doing is hurtful to the police investigation. Making wild allegations and exposing people's private information on-air is not what I thought you signed up for."

A long silence followed. This was the part where Angelo suspected Jason was allowing him to stew in his own juices. Of course, he knew he was right. This wasn't what Angelo had signed up for. Clearly, Rocky was only thinking about her ratings and stoking her listeners, but deep down, Angelo knew the Rocky she presented in real life was not like the person she was on-air. How those two individuals became so disparate, Angelo hadn't a clue.

"I didn't mean for it to turn out like this, Jason. Are you disappointed?"

"I would be lying if I said I wasn't." The finality of this statement was like accepting someone had died.

The tears came unbidden. Angelo wiped them away quickly though no one was at home to see him weeping. Learning he had disappointed Jason gutted Angelo. His opinion was the only one that mattered. Another long silence followed during which Jason choked back what sounded like tears. "Jason, what's wrong?"

"I feel so stupid." He hesitated before adding, "I'm not in a good place. It's that kid. I can't stop thinking about him."

That kid, Angelo knew, was the boy struck dead outside a homeless shelter in Manhattan. Jason and his partner had been investigating his death right before Jason was assaulted. "Did you find out something new?"

"His death was declared an accident," Jason croaked. "That, we expected, even though the bystanders said the kid looked like a zombie right before he was struck by the car."

"Then what is it?'

He took a jagged breath. "Mary investigated the homeless shelter. Apparently, two other boys died while staying there this past year. Both were declared accidental overdoses, but the toxicology reports are missing."

"You think these deaths are related?"

"I don't know what I think," Jason groused. "I'm just feeling sorry for myself. My arm is in a splint. My boyfriend is twenty-seven hundred miles away, and all I want to do is hold him. Have him tell me the world isn't a terrible place."

"The world isn't a terrible place," Angelo said with slow emphasis. "Not as long as we're together."

Jason dissolved into a tearful laugh. "Jeez, who knew I was such a baby. I guess it's a hazard growing up with older sisters."

"Well, you'll always be my baby."

"Okay, that's enough of this Irishman's pity party."

It broke Angelo's heart to hear Jason sound so downtrodden. Suddenly, he had a moment of clarity. *What am I doing in Los Angeles when I have a man that loves me, that needs me, in New York?* Since they first met, Jason had been by Angelo's side, protecting and loving him through the malpractice case and the OPMC investigation, not to mention, supporting him emotionally after Demetre killed Mia Garcia. And now when Jason needed him, Angelo was thousands of miles away.

"What if I come home?"

Jason responded cautiously. "Now, Angelo. Don't make any hasty decisions."

"I mean, really, what am I doing here? This was supposed to be fun, but it's time for me to come home."

"Do you mean it?"

This was the question he seemed to have been dreading. Staring at the evidence board, at the faces of those three dead gay men, Angelo hoped Jason would never ask him to come home early. Jason, being too proud, never would have, but now that the idea was in the open, Angelo found the answer came easily. "Yeah, I mean it."

"Why don't you sleep on it?" Jason suggested. "Love you."

Angelo sat in silence for a while before he got up from the bed. Walking toward the evidence board, Angelo took one of the notecards and wrote Guy Cleveland's name. He pinned it under the growing list of suspects that now included Dino Sosano.

A weight had been lifted off Angelo's shoulders. Jason's plea for him to return home had provided him with the perfect tincture of strength to escape this awful thorny mess he found himself in. Whatever happened to Rocky, to her brother Rands, none of that excused the way she treated Mabel Knight or Wes...or himself. When all was said and done, Rocky remained a deeply troubled and vindictive person. Someone who should be working out her issues with a professional in private, not on a pulpit in public. And Wes. Poor Wes. Angelo held a soft spot for him, having been a doormat himself for many close friends in the past, particularly Tammy, a colleague and an alcoholic who only came to terms with her sobriety when it was right for her. Only now did Angelo see how Wes enabled Rocky like he had enabled Tammy.

When his cellphone rang, Angelo expected it to be Jason again, but the caller ID came up unknown. He answered it anyway.

"Listen to your cop boyfriend," the caller said.

Angelo experienced a stab of fear. The voice sounded familiar but, in that moment, confusion overwhelmed him. "Who is this?"

The clatter of trash cans outside rattled him. He moved through the dark house toward the front window. Standing a few feet away, cautious not to get too close, Angelo could make out the bin. It had toppled over by the right side of the house where the path led down the canyon. Everything else was in shadow.

"Stop interfering in people's private lives, especially good, wholesome, upstanding Christians. Go back to New York...or else."

"Who is this?" Angelo shouted. "How did you get my number?"

Angelo held the phone close to his ear. Suddenly, a shadow detached itself from the others. Galvanized with fear, Angelo hurried to make sure the front door was locked. Walking tentatively back to the window, staying out of the moonlight, Angelo's heart lurched. He could make it out clearly. The figure of a large man stood about thirty feet away. At first, he didn't recognize the male voice. Only belatedly did he realize it was *his* voice. Detective Robert Town.

"I know who you are," Angelo said, deepening his voice in an attempt to conceal his fear. Silence followed, but he could still hear the caller breathing. "What do you want?"

"Go home," the caller intoned with the finality of an axe striking a log.

Silence followed again, but this time, Angelo heard no breathing. The call had been disconnected. When he glanced out the window, the figure had disappeared back in the shadows. Angelo toyed briefly with calling the police. *What good would that do*? It was the police who were trying to intimidate him. He turned on all the lights and waited for Wes to return home.

Angelo didn't know what he felt in that moment. Fear, certainly, but there was something more. Anger. Snowballing as each minute passed. An anger that consumed him because Angelo found himself at the icy center of something far bigger and more dangerous than he had ever anticipated. Jason was right. It was time for him to return to New York. Leave Los Angeles tomorrow. Detective Town had warned them and for him to show up here, tonight, meant that he had taken a personal interest in Angelo. Who was he to stand up to the lead investigator in a string of murders? He was a doctor, for Christ's sake. He knew he was out of his league. They all were. Plus, there was more. Something Wes and Rocky hadn't told him about Reverend James Jarrett and the Seven Spirits Church. *Yes, I'll leave tomorrow, but first, I need to know everything.*

At last Wes pulled into the driveway. Opening the door, he looked around before he met Angelo's worried gaze. "Why are all the lights on?"

Angelo explained it all: the noise he heard outside, the figure looming in the shadows, and the caller who threatened him if he didn't stop interfering in the private lives of upstanding Christians and return to New York. At first, Wes appeared wary, as if he didn't believe Angelo. He darted back outside. Angelo followed him as he made his way to the right side of the house where they found the trash bin lying on the ground. Wes righted it and cleaned the garbage off the lawn. "You sure it wasn't a coyote?" he asked Angelo.

"I know the difference between a man and a coyote."

Wes sighed, realizing how ridiculous a question that was to ask. "Come on. Let's go inside and have a drink."

"I don't want a drink, Wes. I want to talk. I need answers. What haven't you told me about Jarrett?"

They returned to the living room and sat in their usual places. Wes sipped wine while Angelo stared at him. "Well?"

"All right!" Wes gulped more wine and set down the glass. He stood up and began pacing. "After we did the show on Jarrett, the station received a ton of calls and emails. I mean, a ton. All of them asking for Rocky to issue an apology for slandering Jarrett's good name. There was even a petition demanding KLM fire her, but obviously that didn't happen."

"Why?"

Wes picked up his wineglass and took a sip. "Femi. Femi fought for us. In the end, we didn't issue an apology, not that Rocky had any intention of apologizing, and we were allowed to continue doing our show, on our terms. The only thing we had to promise management was that Jarrett and the Seven Spirits Church were off-limits."

Angelo remained skeptical. "And that's it?"

"What more do you need to know?" Wes poured the remainder of the bottle into his glass. "You sure you don't want any?"

Tight-lipped, Angelo resisted the urge to tell Wes he drank too much. Instead, he said, "I get the sense you're leaving something out. Rocky doesn't back down from a fight. Christ, I watched her take on two bikers. She carries a knife." Angelo stood up and loomed over Wes. "Something else happened besides a bunch of calls demanding her termination. You saw it yourself today. Rocky froze the minute that caller mentioned the Seven Spirits Church and the Parallax Institute. Now, you can drink every bottle of wine in this house, but you are not going to bed until you tell me everything."

Wes huffed. "You New Yorkers..." He walked into his bedroom and returned with a faded copy of the *LA Times*. "You want to know everything." He thrust the paper into Angelo's hands. "Read this."

The front page had a photo of Jarrett: round black glasses, white goatee, wearing a black cassock with gold-filigree cuffs. The headline read: What Is Doctor Reverend James Jarrett Hiding at the Parallax Institute?

Angelo fell back on the sofa and began reading. The article reported that after earning his MD in psychiatry and a PhD in behavioral science, Jarrett developed a psychological framework to treat post-traumatic stress disorder used in conjunction with an experimental medication developed by the biotech Ulysses Corp. Dr. James Jarrett was described as, "effusively charming" and a "psychiatric chameleon." These characteristics enabled him to shift careers after several previous failures—notably the forty-million-dollar post-traumatic stress disorder treatment that nearly bankrupted Ulysses Corp after several veterans in the program committed suicide. One killed his entire family before turning the gun on himself. During the two-year FBI investigation, Jarrett earned a third degree: Reverend.

"This guy Jarrett sounds like a peach," Angelo said once he'd finished reading the article. "What I don't understand is why the church went after KLM and Rocky when it was the *LA Times* that broke the story."

"They went after the *LA Times* too." Wes poured Angelo a glass of wine. This time he accepted it. "You know what I think? I think N.A.W. called the show tonight using that distortion device. I believe he knew about the shitstorm that happened after Rocky targeted Jarrett, and now he wants us to focus on him and the Seven Spirits Church again. To take the heat off the No Angels Wept murders."

Angelo appeared dubious. "I don't know if I believe that. Besides, it doesn't matter."

"What's that supposed to mean?"

"I spoke to Jason tonight," Angelo said. "We agreed it's time for me to return to New York."

"You can't leave now." Wes sat next to Angelo on the sofa. "Listen to me. I think we're getting close to catching him. I spoke to Rocky and Femi. They agreed to continue the show's focus on N.A.W., but only if you stay on as co-host."

"I've made up my mind," Angelo said, though that familiar tickle of intrigue began to flutter. "Jason needs me. I made him a promise. Besides, Rocky is too volatile. Take tonight for example. She had no right sharing that boy's license plate number with her audience. What if he goes to the police?"

"And says what?" Wes argued. "Rocky Thorn gave out my license plate number? It's not like she accused him of anything except being some guy in a photo with Keith Knight." Standing up, Wes took Angelo's hand and pulled him into the spare bedroom. "Everything we need to catch him is right here. I know it."

The evidence board had left Angelo with a sense memory; a dogged imperative to continue the investigation despite his fear, frustration, and exhaustion. Staring at the faces of those three dead boys, he knew returning to New York now meant that he was giving up on them. He had agreed to stay for two weeks, though Rocky had proved to be too combustible and inconsistent. But there was no denying this case compelled him, and the tug of curiosity wasn't something so flimsy he could snap himself free.

Angelo wrote down Seven Spirits Church on one card and on a second he wrote, The Parallax Institute. "Where should I pin these?" he asked.

"Does this mean you're staying?" Wes asked.

"Let me sleep on it." Angelo stared at the evidence board. He could not tear his eyes away.

Chapter Twelve

The next morning, Angelo woke up in a panic. Momentarily confused, he had to remind himself that he was in Los Angeles, sleeping in Wes's spare bedroom naked. His head was spinning, but the events of the previous day acutely sprang to life like a jack-in-the-box. It surprised him how deeply he'd slept, considering everything that had happened.

Throwing on a pair of shorts, he stared at the evidence board and reviewed the names of the persons of interest. Swarmed by the possibilities this list provided, he got out of bed and added another name to the list: Dr. Rev. James Jarrett. He stepped back to stand in the rising autumn sun, which poured through the window and saturated him in a rich, intoxicating pool of gold.

The familiar scent of coffee and something he couldn't identify drifted in, swirling around him, waking him from his residual drowsiness. He had a feeling of déjà vu, recalling the morning Wes cooked him breakfast, shirtless. Just then, a knock at the door heralded the appearance of Wes holding two mugs. "Morning sleepyhead. Thought you could use some coffee."

"What time is it?"

"Just after ten." Wes handed him a mug. Thankfully, Wes was fully dressed. Same baggy jeans with cut-out knees paired with a snug white T-shirt bearing the letters KLM. Angelo sipped the coffee, enjoying the warmth spreading in his chest.

"Come with me." Wes's eyes were kind, flirty, grayer in the sunlight rather than steel blue. "I have a surprise for you."

"What is it?"

Wes harrumphed. "Just come with me."

On the patio, just off the kitchen, Wes had set a table for two. Toast, butter, organic marmalade, and a quiche were laid out in the center of the table along with a vase of freshly picked flowers. "What's all this?" Angelo asked.

Wes arched his eyebrows—deep, mischievous—and insisted, "I'm not coming on to you. This is a bribe. No one, and I mean no one, can resist my Aunt Nina's leek and Gruyère quiche."

Angelo didn't have the heart to tell him he had already decided to stay in Los Angeles until the end of the week. He maintained that Rocky's provocative approach, though inconsistent and at times violent, kept the memory of those three murdered gay sex workers alive when all the mainstream media wanted to do was sweep them under the rug. For now, he was content with playing along with the charade since Wes had gone to all this trouble. Besides, Angelo wanted to discuss his decision with Jason before he told Rocky and Wes.

"Well, let me taste Aunt Nina's quiche," Angelo kidded, "and see if it lives up to the hype."

The sun was high, and the air was clean and breezy. Wes seemed so utterly attentive, pulling out the chair for Angelo to sit, so clever and skillful that Angelo was quite disarmed by him. Wes had woken up early and done all this in such a short time. They ate in the shaded alcove overlooking the hillside and the silent sunny rooftops of the neighbors' houses. It surprised Angelo how hungry he was and how much he ate. Without a doubt, he was charmed by Wes's efforts, but putting all this aside, there was serious business to discuss.

"You can tell your Aunt Nina that her quiche is a winner."

"Does that mean you'll stay?"

Slowly, Angelo nodded, trying as he did to contain Wes's enthusiasm. "I still have to talk with Jason, but I think he'll agree to a compromise." Wes stared at him expectantly. "I think it's only fair if I finish the rest of the week."

"That's better than nothing." Wes was unable to contain his excitement. "I envy Jason. He's lucky to have you."

Angelo smiled. "We're lucky to have each other."

"You New Yorkers…so insistent. Anyway, I can't wait to tell Rocky. She's going to be thrilled."

Once again, Angelo didn't believe Wes. He recalled his interaction with Rocky the day before in the men's room. She seemed unhinged brandishing a knife as they argued about Angelo violating the three amigos code. He would never forget the strangeness of her reaction after he mentioned the death her brother, Rands. The bleakness in her eyes forced him to shake off the clutch of fear, recalling it. "I don't know how you put up with Rocky. Come to think of it, I don't know why I'm choosing to put up with her for two more days."

"We're gluttons for punishment I guess." Wes meant to spread jam on his toast, but the marmalade plopped onto his chest, leaving an ameba-shaped orange stain on his T-shirt. "Shit!"

"You better blot that with club soda or it'll stain."

"Oh please." Wes pulled the shirt over his head. "There's plenty more KLM T-shirts at the station. Besides, on a beautiful day like today, who needs one."

A voice from inside the house, called out, "Hello, is anyone home?"

Angelo gave Wes a look of concern. "Who's that?"

"It's probably Rocky," he replied not appearing alarmed someone had entered his house unannounced. "We're in the back yard." As the figure moved through the living room, it became crystal clear this person wasn't Rocky.

"I knocked but no one answered."

"Can I help you?" Wes asked the striking blond man.

Angelo had to squeeze his eyes shut. All at once, pieces of his face,—the even features, the light blue eyes—assembled like a jigsaw puzzle. "Jason!" Angelo shouted as the dawn of recognition rose in his consciousness. "Oh my God. What are you doing here?" Stumbling to stand, Angelo hurled himself at him. He planted his mouth on Jason's lips, kissing him thoroughly. Slow, sensuous, almost dizzying kisses while Jason shouldered off his duffle bag and wrapped his arms around Angelo's waist. When Angelo pulled back, he let his forehead rest against Jason's and smiled. "Why didn't you tell me you were coming?"

"That would have ruined the surprise." Slipping his hand inside Angelo's shorts, Jason's eyes went wide. "Excuse me, Dr. Commando!"

Angelo felt the blood rushing to his cheeks. He stepped back, turned his head toward Wes who was pretending not to gawk, and realized with stunning clarity how this scene must look to Jason: Angelo, wearing a T-shirt and shorts minus underwear. A shirtless Wes in loose fitting jeans, also minus underwear. A romantic table set for two. Fresh cut flowers and…my God, a homemade quiche! "We were just having a late breakfast," Angelo added quickly.

"What's the special occasion?" Jason asked. "Pretty flowers."

"This was my idea to thank Angelo for doing such a great job." Wes extended his hand. "You must be Jason Murphy. I'm Wes." Angelo winced inwardly as Jason wrapped his thick fingers around Wes's hand, squeezing it to the point where he could see Wes straining to smile.

"We had no idea you were coming," Angelo said. "Are you hungry?"

"Nah, I ate on the plane."

A knot of apprehension formed in Angelo's gut. "I...I was just about to call you. We were just talking about you. Right Wes?"

"We actually were."

Silence followed. Suddenly, Angelo couldn't think of anything else to say. He was too mesmerized staring at Jason, who was staring at Wes. It was as if his two disparate worlds had collided. Jason stood at ease. His chest like armor. Biceps testing the limits of his polo sleeve hems. Add the splinted left forearm and Jason appeared threatening standing next to Wes's tanned, sinewy torso and loose-fitting jeans.

Wes clapped his hands together. "Would you like a cup of coffee? Or maybe you'd like to take a shower. You've had such a long flight."

"Thank you," Jason said, "but what'd I'd really like is to check into the hotel where Angelo was supposed to be staying." Angelo chuckled uneasily. Another awkward pause followed when suddenly Jason added, "I'm gonna head out. I'm sure I'll see you again, Wes. Sorry if I scared you." Jason started back inside the house and paused at the back entrance. "Angelo, are you coming?"

Angelo reacted as if someone had splashed cold water in his face. "Oh my God. Of course. Let me get my things. I'll be ready in ten minutes." Angelo caught Jason sizing up Wes. "Come Jason. You have to see the evidence board Wes made."

Inside the spare bedroom, Jason inspected the evidence board. "Nice job," he said, but Angelo seized him with hungry kisses. His erection poked through the slit in his shorts. Seeing it, Jason kicked the door shut and gave Angelo's cock a squeeze.

"What a surprise," Angelo said breathlessly as Jason stroked him. "I'm so happy to see you."

"Yeah?" Jason muttered. "Why don't you show me."

At first, Angelo didn't move or stop smiling. Not having seen Jason in days, he marveled at his beauty. Angelo slid his hands into Jason's jeans, feeling the swell of his penis pressed between his abdomen and denim. Deftly, Angelo unzipped Jason's jeans and squatted. He sighed as his lips passed along Jason's shaft, forgetting how much room his cock took up in his mouth. It felt overwhelming and erotic, as if Angelo might gag, but he refused to allow himself to pull back. In fact, he inhaled through his nose and allowed his throat to swallow Jason's entire erection, nose pressed against the tuft of blond pubic hair.

As he stroked and sucked Jason's cock, images flashed in Angelo's mind. A shirtless Wes. Angelo commando in shorts. The look on Jason's face when he saw them eating breakfast outside. He tried to lose himself in the moment, frantically stroking and sucking, but the images flashed again, slapping his mind with derision. Angelo attempted to shut them out, focusing on Jason. *I want to do this. I love doing this.* But the images assaulted him like bombs crashing from the sky. Jason guided Angelo's head up and down, grunting. Angelo gagged once and Jason stepped back, looking at Angelo's face with smiling uncertainty. "Why don't we do this later?"

Angelo shook his head, committed to the moment. "No, I want to."

"No one's saying you don't want to." Jason backed away and pulled up his jeans. "I don't want to. Not here…not in Orlando Bloom's house."

"Who?" Angelo sat on the floor, defeated, his erection deflating between his thighs.

"The guy from those pirate movies. The one with the hair."

Angelo stood up, crossing his wrists behind Jason's neck. "Don't worry about Orlando Bloom."

Jason pulled his head away. "Can we just get going? I want to relax with you in private."

"Okay, it'll only take me a few minutes to pack." Angelo regarded him cautiously. "You're not mad. Are you?" Angelo asked quickly, as if Jason had accused him of cheating. "We were just having breakfast. All that, outside, was to bribe me into staying because after we spoke last night, I told Wes I planned on returning to New York."

Jason stood in silence. He appeared stiff and in no mood to talk. "Angelo, I'm tired. Can we please go to the hotel?"

Angelo sighed and dropped his eyes. More than anything, he wanted to hear Jason say he wasn't mad. He refused to let Jason think there was anything between him and Wes.

"I have an idea," Angelo said as he threw his clothes into his duffle bag. "After we get settled in our room, why don't we check out Los Angeles. I haven't done any sightseeing since I arrived Friday."

Jason's gaze shot to meet his, and his lips curled into a smile. "Can we go to the Griffith Observatory? I've always wanted to go."

"The Griffith Observatory it is."

Falling onto the bed, Jason watched Angelo finish packing. "Hey, come here."

"Let me finish so we can leave."

"Angelo," Jason ordered. "Lie next to me for a minute." Angelo stretched out beside him. It took several seconds for his body to relax, to relent, but moments later their bodies felt like one again. Arms encircling one another like they had never spent a moment apart. He could do that with Jason; just hold him and be held. "I missed you so much," Jason whispered in his ear. "Sorry if I was a bit of a grouch earlier, and no, I don't think there is anything going on between you and Orlando Bloom." They remained in a tight embrace for a long while, listening to the synchronized beats of their hearts against their chests. “Plus, I find his artfully mussed hair so pretentious. Don’t you?”

“Oh my God,” Angelo said. “That hair is sooo pretentious.”

◆◆◆

As planned, Angelo and Jason spent the day touring Los Angeles. They hiked into the rugged hills in Griffith Park, up the trail leading from the parking lot, past coastal sage scrub, lilac, toyon, and sumac. They hiked for hours, holding hands. Jason never asked about *A Thorny Mess* or the No Angels Wept murders, and Angelo decided not to bring either up. Today was all about reconnecting.

The summit offered them spectacular views of the entire Los Angeles Basin, including Downtown Los Angeles, Hollywood, and the Pacific Ocean to the southwest. Jason took photos of the Hollywood Sign and posted them on Instagram, but it was the observatory that impressed Angelo the most. The majestic white structure, the symmetry of the five windows on either side of the main entrance, and the iconic domes that sat on top of the building like alien pods had landed long ago and fossilized on the summit of Mount Hollywood.

Though Jason denied it, Angelo suspected he was tired from the flight. He kept turning his head away to yawn. Angelo suggested they return to the hotel so he could shower and change before heading to the studio. It never occurred to him to ask Jason if he wanted to join him. He assumed he would, but as they hiked back to the parking lot, Angelo felt uneasy about introducing Rocky to him. Without a doubt she would love Jason, but Angelo wasn’t sure if he would feel the same. He hadn’t been a fan of Rocky Thorn from the start, and after last night’s show,

Jason made it clear he didn't care for the gimmicks she employed.

Angelo squinted at Jason through his sunglasses. The sun beat mercilessly on their heads. Sweat soaked their T-shirts, leaving damp stains down their backs and chests and under their arms. Angelo had an idea; what if he suggested Jason stay at the hotel? After the show, they could go out to dinner alone and catch the drag show at Peak. This idea gained momentum in his mind. *Yes, I'll suggest a date night with dinner and a drag show at Peak.* Jason would love nothing more than to be alone with him after having been apart for nearly a week. Shamelessly, Angelo knew this plan afforded him the opportunity to speak with Dino Sosano. Something Dino had said on air didn't sit well with Angelo. When Rocky confronted Dino with the statement he made to police that Gabe stayed after Peak had closed the night before he was found dead, Dino confronted her with a warning: *you wanna go there?* A threat that didn't appear to rattle Rocky but a threat, nonetheless.

The second question that burned in Angelo's mind had to do with the mystery man Keith had been dating right before he was murdered. Sitting in the hotseat, Dino shut down all of Rocky's questions, feigning ignorance, but Angelo wondered if Dino, like Mabel Knight, would feel more comfortable speaking with him outside of the studio, away from Rocky.

Unexpectedly, Jason reached for Angelo's hand. "Can I say something without you getting mad?"

"Jason Murphy," Angelo replied, squeezing his fingers, "what a stupid thing to ask a hotheaded Italian."

Jason stopped walking and turned around to face him. "But what a sexy hothead, huh?"

"Spill it."

"Would you mind if I skipped the show tonight? I'm beat as fuck and would love to just listen to your sweet voice on the radio. I promise to make it up to you by taking you out for a romantic dinner for two after."

"You don't want to come to the show with me?" Angelo asked. It was too good to be true. Angelo began laughing uncontrollably.

"What's so funny? Are you happy or mad? I can't tell either way."

But Angelo continued laughing even harder. To think he had agonized over how he was going to convince Jason not to join him at the studio, only for Jason to have made the decision for him. The entire situation seemed too funny to do anything else but laugh.

CHAPTER THIRTEEN

"This is *A Thorny Mess*, and you're joining us for day four of our No Angels Wept coverage. I'm your host, Rocky Thorn. Beside me, I have my partner in crime, Dr. Angelo Perrotta. How's it hanging, Doc?"

Angelo briefly met Rocky's gaze. "I'm hanging in there," he replied tonelessly.

It struck Angelo suddenly, what if Rocky had been a character in a book by Judy Blume—enthralling and revelatory until he had outgrown that kind of story. What if he now wanted to read something else? Having had a peek behind the curtain, the mighty Rocky Thorn ceased to exist as someone unattainable. A fault with celebrity: once you get too close, you realize they're made of the same flesh and bone as everybody else. Maybe Jason had brought into sharp focus how Rocky's tactics bordered on cruelty, certainly rogue, and his part co-hosting the show suggested a level of endorsement, being a physician.

Fortunately, this journey would come to an end tomorrow. Before going on the air, Angelo met with Femi, Rocky, and Wes to announce he would be leaving the show a week early. Wes had already tipped off Rocky. Told her that Angelo's hot cop had shown up out of the blue. A caveman reclaiming his bride, Jason intended to drag Angelo back to New York by his hair whether he wanted to go or not, which Angelo thought was an unfair characterization and meaningless sour grapes. Angelo explained he had come to this decision on his own. Femi and Rocky didn't argue. Clearly, there was no point.

"Well, Messes," Rocky said, shaking Angelo from his thoughts. "I have some bad news. It seems *A Thorny Mess*'s house physician, Dr. Angelo Perrotta, is leaving us early. Yes. I know. Shock. Gasp. Clutch your pearls. Snort a line and down your champs. The time has come to say goodbye." The lightboard began to blink red. Rocky winked at Angelo. "Caller, you're on with Rockgelo."

"Mommy. Daddy," a girl whined. "I don't want you to get divorced!" This was followed by cartoonish sobbing.

"Mother is still here," Rocky assured the caller. "I promise as long as I have a mouth, you will always have a mother."

"Besides," Angelo cut in. "I'm not being shipped off to Siberia. I loved every minute being part of this show. Truly, it has been an honor. Thank you, Rocky."

"It's been my pleasure having you." For a second, Angelo thought he saw the glint of a tear in her eye. "And like you said, it's not like you're being shipped off to Siberia. Dr. Angelo is a friend to the show. Our door is always open. Now don't let it hit your ass on the way out."

"Today is not even my last day, and already, she's showing me the door."

"Caller, you're on with Angelocky?"

Angelo choked a laugh. "Angelocky!"

They became hysterical, laughing. It felt good to Angelo to feel this light. The world around them had been consumed with converging dark clouds, shadows, and a sense that danger was just around the corner. It felt as if a crack had opened, allowing a beam of sunshine to enter their dark world. After tomorrow, Angelo was optimistic there would only be bright days ahead.

"Sorry caller." Rocky regained her composure. "You're on the air."

"I'm so sorry to hear Dr. Perrotta is leaving," the familiar electronic voice said. "There is still so much left for you to discover."

And in an instant that crack sealed up. "What more is left for me to discover?" Angelo asked.

"In due time."

"Listen, iRobot," Rocky began. "I'm growing tired of you and your cryptic messages. If you got something to say, then just say it."

"It's not the thorns you should beware; it's the invisible worm."

"That's it!" Rocky disengaged the call. "I'm over this guy. We'll be right back after the break."

Immediately, Angelo asked, "Will you now explain what this invisible worm business is all about?"

Wes entered the studio with the frat bros trailing closely behind. "It's a reference to William Blake's poem, 'The Sick Rose.'"

"I know all about the invisible worm!" Rocky lifted her hands to her face as if she was about to claw her own eyes out. "That asshole with the computer chip for vocal cords is fucking with me because on Monday I defended my theory that No Angels Wept was a reference to Blake's poem, 'The Angel.'"

Wes and Angelo exchanged confused expressions. "Then why aren't you jumping up and down?" Angelo asked. "Doesn't this validate your theory?"

"No, it does not."

On the verge of protesting, Angelo was silenced by Wes. "We don't have time for this. We're back in sixty seconds. Rocky, wrap it up and let's talk about this after the show."

◆◆◆

Rocky and Angelo sat across from Femi in her office. Wes, as usual, paced the room. The frat bros occupied themselves with their cellphones. Femi started first. "What's this business about 'The Sick Rose'?"

Rocky stood then. Angelo watched her. He had never seen her like this, so hesitant and nervous. Retrieving her phone, Rocky read aloud:

O Rose thou art sick.
The invisible worm,
That flies in the night
In the howling storm:

Has found out thy bed
Of crimson joy:
And his dark secret love
Does thy life destroy.

Femi's eyes darted around the room. "Any idea what the significance of this poem is?

Rocky bit her thumbnail, ignoring Femi. "Maybe it's about life and death," Angelo ventured. "The rose is a symbol of life and worms are often associated with decay because they feed upon dead things."

"Maybe the worm symbolizes a dick?" one frat bro said.

"Everything symbolizes dick to you," the second frat bro drawled.

"Here's the thing," Wes spoke up. "One interpretation could be life or death, but another could be masculine versus feminine. I mean, *Rose* is capitalized. Blake could be referring to a woman named Rose. And worms are kind of phallic. Maybe the worm is going to deflower Rose?"

Femi nodded slowly, waiting to see if Rocky had anything to add. "You're unusually silent, Rocky."

It was a curious poem. One Angelo had never read, but there was no doubt in Angelo's mind that it held some special meaning to Rocky. Angelo felt it, watching her, wondering if it was the poem itself or the eerie feeling the caller knew something personal and was taunting her with it.

"'The Sick Rose' has many interpretations," Rocky finally said. "One is that Rose has a fascination with the invisible worm, but in the end, this dream to have a worm cost Rose her life."

Clearly, Angelo now realized this poem wasn't about the No Angels Wept murders. *Rose has a fascination with the invisible worm. Rose.* The word, as Wes mentioned, had been capitalized. And then it hit him. Rose. Miranda Rose Thorndyke. Rocky's younger sibling. The caller was referencing Rands. "Rocky, you don't have to talk about him," Angelo said.

Angelo's phone buzzed in his pocket. A text message read:

Is date night still on?

When Angelo met Rocky's gaze, he was sure this time he detected tears. "Don't worry," she said. "After tomorrow, this won't be your problem anymore."

"Him, who?" Femi asked. "The caller?"

"No, not the caller." Rocky cleared her voice. "Somebody else. Somebody close to me."

Femi sat back, looking troubled. "Could this person be in danger?"

"No," she replied. "There's no chance of that."

A slow dawning of comprehension came over Wes. "Oh, I get it now."

Rocky began shaking her head in an obsessive manner as if by shaking it, the thoughts trapped inside might fly out. "That's enough about the damn poem. Anything else, Femi?"

"Yes," she said. "Someone is feeding us information. What I'm about to share with you relates to that little stunt Rocky played yesterday, reciting that young man's car tag."

Simultaneously, everyone leaned forward.

"This information cannot leave this room," Femi continued. She paused here to take a deep breath. "We received an anonymous tip. The car in that photo Angelo took is registered to Robert Town."

"Detective Robert Town?" Wes exclaimed.

"Do you think that boy is Detective Town's son?" Angelo's cellphone dinged again. *Shit!* Stepping outside the room, he called Jason. "Hey, sorry. Why don't we meet at the restaurant. I can take an Uber and be there in ten minutes."

"I'm already at the restaurant," Jason said. "You said seven and now it's seven thirty."

"I'm so sorry." Angelo wiped a hand down his face. "I'm leaving now."

When Angelo returned to Femi's office, everyone stared at him like mourners at a wake. A frat bro walked over and held up his phone for Angelo to see what they had already discovered. "Looks like you were right, Doc."

Angelo's eyes scanned the article:

Santa Barbara, California—Leslie Town, 52, passed away on Thursday, February 16, 2003, surrounded by her family. She is survived by her loving husband Robert Town and their son, Robert "Bobby" Town Jr.

Accompanying the article was a photo of Leslie with her husband and blond-haired son, who bore a striking resemblance to the young man in the photo Angelo saw in Keith Knight's bedroom.

Chapter Fourteen

Hours later, Angelo and Jason sat at a table by the stage at Peak. Overall, the day couldn't have gone better. Angelo didn't have to return to New York because Jason had decided to surprise him in LA. They had a romantic reunion hiking to Griffith Observatory, and afterward, Jason decided not to join Angelo for the radio show, avoiding a potentially awkward introduction between him and Rocky. Now they were both more than tipsy, having drank a bottle of wine while sharing a romantic dim sum dinner. A perfect date night. Except for the slight hiccup where Angelo was forty minutes late.

It was difficult for Angelo not to tell Jason everything that had transpired during the show: the meaning of the invisible worm and the identity of the boy he saw in the photo and at the diner. Rushing out of Femi's office, he hadn't had time to discuss what implications this revelation provided them with. If the blond boy was Detective Town's son, that meant there was a good chance Bobby was also gay. *How does an unabashed homophobe like Detective Town reconcile that his only child is queer?* Unless, of course, Detective Town didn't know.

A sleepy looking Jason was playing the bongos on the tabletop when Angelo excused himself to use the restroom. "Order me a drink," he said to Jason.

"Let me guess," he slurred. "You want a Cosmo, right?"

Angelo kissed him on the cheek and made his way to the bar. Peak was packed with skinny twinks sucking lollipops and posting photos on Instagram. Shirtless, hairy daddies hovered like bears waiting to pounce. Everyone seemed to be on Grindr. Music blared overhead. The DJ had been playing disco classics the entire night. In twenty minutes, the drag show was to begin. All in all, Angelo had managed to rescue date night. There was just the one covert operation left for him to complete.

Stepping up to the bar, Angelo addressed a shirtless Latino wearing a harness and a leather jockstrap. "I'm looking for Dino. Is he working tonight?"

The bartender took a moment to show Angelo his moves. Pec muscles thumping in time to his groin. "Yeah, he's working."

This begged the question Angelo was forced to ask. "Can you get him for me please?"

"What?" he shouted over the music.

"Can you get him for me please?"

This interaction left Angelo irrevocably cauterized from any desire to be single again. He recalled those many nights he and Tammy drank too much in lesbian bars in the West Village and how electric it had all felt to him then. Leaving this world behind, Angelo imagined a sinkhole of sadness would have collapsed in its place, but Jason's love had more than filled any emptiness that sinkhole left.

A six foot drag queen wearing a red wig like meringue peaks addressed the bartender. "Alejandro, can you get mamma a glass of sparkling water?"

"I love your outfit," Angelo said to her.

She lit up like someone had plugged in a Christmas tree. Stepping back, she offered Angelo a full view of the red and white postal service dress she was wearing. "Thank you, handsome."

"What's your name?"

"My name," she repeated with a shimmy. "My name is Anna Gramm." Alejandro handed her a glass of sparkling water. "Hope you plan on sticking around for my show."

A split second later, Angelo spotted Dino on the other side of the bar, chatting up a short go-go dancer wearing angel wings. He was unmistakable in a black leather vest worn over a *Sopranos* T-shirt and an air of seething horniness. "Dino," he shouted, but of course he didn't hear him. Angelo shouldered his way through the crowd until he stood next to Angel Wings. "Dino, remember me?"

Dino's expression fell like a soufflé. "What do you want?"

"I just want to ask you a few questions. Off the record." When Dino craned his neck to look past Angelo, he added, "Don't worry. I'm alone. Rocky's not here."

"There's a special place in hell for people like Rocky Thorn."

Angel Wings glowered at Angelo, but he returned the sentiment beset by frustration at having to compete for Dino's attention with someone who looked like they were starring in their junior high Christmas pageant. "Can I borrow him for a sec?"

At last Angel Wings got the hint and barged passed Angelo. Feathers floated in the air behind him in the squall of his hasty retreat. "Why did you have to do that?" Dino asked.

"I'm sure he'll be back for his nighttime feeding and burping."

"Ha, ha."

Angelo was at a loss for how precisely to approach Dino. He supposed it best to be direct. "Yesterday, you said that right before Keith was murdered, he was seeing someone whose life would be ruined if their relationship became public. Any idea who this mystery man is?"

"Even if I knew I wouldn't tell you."

"Why?"

This question seemed to baffle Dino, who signaled the bartender for another drink. "I don't owe you anything. Besides, if I knew who it was, I would have told the police."

Considering how much Dino had told the police about Gabe, it made sense that he would have come clean if he knew anything about Keith's relationship. "Did you ever see Keith with anyone here?"

Dino turned his head, cupping a hand to his ear. "I'm sorry. I can't hear a word you're saying," he said it with such a facetious tone, Angelo understood it to mean only one thing. He retrieved his wallet and removed a twenty. Dino's eyes lit up with a kind of childlike wonderment. "Yeah, I seen him here with a young blond boy. Crazy blue eyes. Skinny."

"You got a name?"

"Nah, but I know they gone on one of them Seven Spirits Church retreats together."

Retreat?

Angel Wings came up behind Dino, resting his chin on his shoulder, looking peevish and impatient. "Come on, Dino. You promised." He tapped his finger to his left nostril.

"One last question," Angelo pleaded. "Did members of the Seven Spirits Church come to Peak to convince boys like your friend here to join the church?"

Dino kissed the boy on the cheek. "Oh yeah, them Seven Spirits folks come here all the time wanting to get boys to come back with them, offering food and a place to stay. Lots of boys go. Not sure what happens to most of them. The ones that came back complained that the church was too strict. Sure, they gave them food and a bed, but the ones I spoke to said weird shit went on there. Not worth the trouble even if they were allowed to play video games and watch war movies all night. It's like I was trying to tell your friend Rocky before she started accusing me of not being a good friend to Gabe, boys come and go all the time in LA. Many get swept up in sex work, porn, and drugs. The lucky ones go back home before they get in too deep."

The music stopped suddenly. "Queers and queens," a baritone voice boomed over the loudspeaker. "May I introduce our first performer of the evening, Miss Anna Gramm."

Fuck. I need to get back to Jason before the show starts. "Thank you, Dino. You've been very helpful."

Dino grabbed his arm. "I didn't say it yesterday, but your friend Rocky was here the night before Gabe was found dead. I saw her talking to him with my own eyes."

"Rocky Thorn?" Angelo asked. "Are you sure?"

"I am now that I got a closer look at her under those bright studio lights. She was here that night. Not sure why she went after me the way she did. I could have said something, but I didn't think it was worth the effort."

"I thought we were on a date." Angelo spun around and found Jason teetering on the brink of a meltdown.

"Oh, Jason." Angelo swallowed down hard. "I'm so sorry. I went to the bathroom and ran into Dino on my way back." He offered stilted introductions and explained that Dino had appeared on *A Thorny Mess* the night before.

Jason eyed Dino skeptically. "Well, do you want to watch the show or not?" Jason asked Angelo.

"Yes, I was just saying good-bye. Come on." Angelo took Jason's arm. "Let's get back to our table before somebody takes it."

Jason pulled Angelo close. "I can't help but think you brought me here so that you could speak to that guy." Angelo's body stiffened as Jason spoke in his ear. "If you wanted to speak to him, all you had to do was be honest with me about it."

"Jason—"

"Now, before you say a word, think about what I just said."

A convulsion of self-loathing at having misled Jason roiled through him. Angelo couldn't bring himself to look into Jason's eyes. He could only stare at the drag performer with her thick red lips and her red and white postal service uniform. "Jason," he began, but suddenly the spotlight found them.

"I'm sorry," Anna Gramm said, "is my act getting in the way of your conversation?"

Angelo felt the strangeness of this predicament settling around them. It felt like being tied to a stake before burning.

"Let's get out of here," Jason said. "We're causing a scene."

As they turned to leave, they heard Anna Gramm's amplified voice. "Everyone, let's give it up for itchy ebb." Confused, they turned around, squinting in the yellow glow of electric light. Anna Gramm's eyes gleamed with a perverse amusement. "That's an anagram for, bye bitch."

◆◆◆

Outside Peak, it felt like falling into a pool of still, cool water. Boys were smoking in the corner. Loud shrieks and high-pitched squeals of laughter. Angelo sensed Jason's frustration but knew he wouldn't confront him. As usual, Jason played the long game. This would all be over tomorrow. Angelo knew that Jason had convinced himself that once they returned to New York, all this would be behind them. And in many ways Angelo wanted to believe that too but at his core, he wondered how long it would take before he latched on to another series of crimes perpetrated by someone with authority over innocent victims. What Jason refused to understand or chose to overlook was that in returning to New York, they were only running away from a problem that would follow them wherever they went.

"What's the situation here with taxis?" Jason asked.

Just as Angelo reached for his cellphone to call an Uber, he heard a voice call his name. "Oh my God, Fitz!" He ran to give her a hug. "I completely forgot you worked outside Peak. You have to meet my boyfriend, Jason."

Fitz's eyes locked on Jason as he walked toward them. "He is a hot cop. Good for you, honey."

After Angelo made introductions, Fitz gave them a tour of her TerraStar chassis decorated with oversized Keith

Haring art. "Wow, this looks more like a party bus instead of a mobile testing unit," Angelo said.

"That's the point," Fitz explained. "How else can anyone attempt to overcome stigma other than to normalize the testing process, though I hate the word *normal*."

Inside, there was a waiting area with blue vinyl booths, one testing room, and a lavatory. "This is really incredible," Jason said. "Every square inch is accounted for."

Angelo and Jason sat in the waiting area as Fitz spoke with them while seated behind the reception desk. "I heard tomorrow's your last day on the show." Fitz pressed out her lower lip. "I'm sad to see you go. I hope Rocky didn't drive you away."

Angelo reached for Jason's hand. "No, it all boils down to competing priorities. Still, I'm pissed Detective Town hasn't caught the bastard." A thought popped into Angelo's head. "Hey, did you happen to test any of the victims?"

Fitz looked at him curiously. "Doctor," she began in a low voice. "I would think you would know better than to ask me that. On second thought, I can't believe you just asked me if I tested them." She glanced at her nails and muttered, "Now that's fucked up."

Jason shot Angelo a look of disappointment. He slapped his knees. "We should go."

"Don't go," Fitz begged. "I'm sorry if I got shady. It's just that confidentiality is a big thing for me. I'm sure you heard all about my troubled past, but this girl"—Fitz snapped her fingers—"got her act together."

"I noticed the way you shut down the conversation the other night when Rocky brought up RentAGuy," Angelo said. "If the profiles are public, I don't understand how confidentiality plays into that."

"Truth be told, I had a very good run as a sex worker on RentAGuy." She dropped her head and glanced up at them, smirking. "Lots of cis men wanted to get with this unicorn. The reason why I shut down Rocky was because I knew those boys. They confided in me, and I didn't want to get into it with y'all. No offense, but I don't know you like that."

Laughing helped to lighten the mood. Interestingly, Fitz seemed much more open and relaxed compared to the other night. Angelo wondered if it had to do with the bikers taunting her or maybe she was more forthcoming now that Rocky wasn't around. Seizing the opportunity to verify what Dino said earlier, Angelo asked, "What do you know about the Seven Spirits Church?"

"Church," Fitz groaned. "More like a cult if you ask me." Fitz went on to confirm what Dino and Wes had told Angelo, that members of the Seven Spirits came to Peak to lure gay boys back with them, promising them food and a place to sleep, and that she didn't know what happened to most of them but that the ones who escaped described the odd circumstances they had to put up with.

"Did you know that in 2021, over 57,000 children went missing in LA?" Fitz asked. "Suicide is the third leading cause of death among Los Angeles County youths."

"I had no idea," Angelo admitted.

"Those poor lost boys of Los Angeles," Fitz said. "Some are never seen or heard from again. The smart ones go back home, but many end up dead…" She trailed off, clearly contemplating what she was about to say. "Have you read the *LA Times* article about Dr. Reverend James Jarrett?" Fitz asked. "I recommend it to every boy that passes through these doors. Most, I know, never bother. Ah youth and beauty. Often such a fatal combination."

"I read the article," Angelo said. "What I want to know is how did the authorities allow Jarrett to get away with it?"

"He continues to get away with it," Fitz said. "After those veterans committed suicide, the FBI launched an investigation. In the meantime, Jarrett became a reverend and started the Seven Spirits Church. That's when he began his gay conversion therapy program using the same methods and providing that poison drug, Parallax."

"Parallax," Angelo repeated. "I've never heard of it."

"That's because it never got FDA approval," Fitz said. "According to the article, a twenty-six-year-old soldier took a rifle and shot his wife and baby in the head before taking his own life. By the time the police finished their investigation, three other military personnel discharged from the Parallax Institute had committed suicide. All of them were enrolled in Jarrett's clinical trial."

Angelo wondered how Jarrett got away with it. It seemed so obviously criminal to him. Jarrett's shamelessness, his selfishness to do or say whatever it took to grab the fruit he wanted off the tree. Claim it for himself.

"Once Rocky read that article," Fitz continued, "something changed inside her. She met with the reporter, hoping he would appear on her show. That poor guy risked everything to go undercover."

Undercover? What courage that took.

"After Rocky profiled Jarrett on *A Thorny Mess*, those spirits-on-high fanatics terrorized her. They followed Rocky everywhere. Made death threats. It affected her so much she went to the police, but they refused to investigate Jarrett or his church since she had no proof the church was behind it all."

Rain began to patter on the roof. It almost filled up the hole of silence that suddenly gaped between them. Again, Jason slapped his knees. "Okay, now I have to insist we get going. I'm still on East Coast time."

Fitz came around the desk to kiss them good night. "Honey, wait until you're my age. You'll be in bed by nine." Just as Jason turned to leave, he stumbled into a cooler and the contents spilled onto the floor: baggies of white powder, syringes, and bottles of pills. "Whoopsie, you found my stash."

Hurriedly, Angelo and Jason began cleaning up. "I'm so sorry," Jason said. "I didn't even see it. Shows you how tired I am."

"Relax, honey," Fitz assured him. "It's my fault for keeping the cooler by the door, and before you jump to any wrong conclusions, those are not mine."

"You don't have to explain," Angelo said.

"It's from the boys who want to give them up," Fitz continued. "I also run a needle exchange program."

"You're my hero," Angelo said.

Once everything had been cleared up, Jason and Angelo said good-bye again and returned to the hotel. Inside their room, they held each other in bed for a long time, trying to make sense of it all.

Finally, Jason sat up. "I need to talk to you."

Something in the way Jason spoke, in the way his back straightened, caused a flood of alarm to wash over Angelo. "What is it?"

"I love you," he started, "you know that, right?"

What an awful way to begin a conversation. "Why do I get a sense you're about to tell me something bad."

Jason nodded absently, as if he had memorized a script. "My concern is that you still haven't gotten over the death of Mia Garcia. In my non-medical opinion, using an app is not going to cure your panic attacks."

"I gave up the show," Angelo argued. "Tomorrow is my last day. What more do you want?"

Jason rubbed a hand over his mouth as if he didn't know how to articulate his feelings. "I want you to get professional help from a therapist, not an app."

This suggestion felt like Jason had walloped Angelo in the head. "My therapist recommended the app."

"There are other therapists," Jason countered. "Why is it doctors make the worst patients?"

What happened to Jason playing the long game? Angelo was certain Jason would feel relieved once they returned to New York. *Why is he raising this concern now?*

Pre-LA, the Jason he knew was kind, nurturing, and supportive. Post-LA Jason was critical, confrontational, and judgmental. Normally a man of quiet strength, Angelo didn't recognize this version of Jason. But when he contemplated this further, he realized how much he had underestimated him. Misjudged his ability to see through the quagmire the No Angels Wept murders had created. Foresaw exactly what would happen once they returned to New York and Angelo was left to ruminate, to wrestle with his reflection in the mirror.

Angelo rolled onto his side, away from Jason's gaze. "I don't want to talk about this now. Can we please just go to sleep?"

"There's something else I need to say," Jason said. "I've been keeping a secret from you."

Angelo lifted his head from the pillow. Confused, he stared at Jason, trying to imagine what was so upsetting he had to keep it from him. "What is it?"

"Two secrets, actually," Jason admitted.

"Two!" Angelo sat up. Jason's expression was impossible for him to read. The affectionate man who'd flown across the country to surprise him was nowhere to be seen. Instead, he appeared emotionless, as if an imposter. Angelo rubbed his fingers across his aching eyes. "Tell me."

"The first is that I have been studying for the LSAT."

Who is this blond man? The Jason that Angelo knew wouldn't keep a secret like this. "Why didn't you tell me?"

"I don't know," Jason started. "No, that's a lie. I do know." He took a deep breath. "I was worried that if I took the test and didn't score high enough, you would be disappointed."

Angelo shook his head. "I'd be sad, not disappointed."

"Angelo," Jason said as if he was about to broach a difficult subject. "You're tough. In fact, you're one of the toughest people I know. Sometimes I think, who could live up to your high standards?"

Standing up, feeling momentarily light-headed, Angelo couldn't process Jason's accusation. "Yes, I'm hard on myself, but I never judge others."

Jason remained still for a long time. It was hard for Angelo not to go to him. Acquiesce. A default setting he found comforting. Admitting guilt had always been easy, and he felt such an urge to apologize, knowing that if he did, Jason would declare his love despite Angelo's faults. But not today. Angelo remained steadfast, allowing silence to fill the room until Jason spoke first. "You judge people all the time," he said. "You judged Camille, you judged Tammy, and you judged me. That's why you suggested I take the LSAT, because you judge me for being just a cop."

"That's not true." Salt stung his cheeks as he wiped tears away. "If anything, I judge myself the most."

"Yes, you do." Jason stood up and hugged him. "You are your own worst judge and jury. Sometimes it's hard to be around you when you're at your most critical, but I love you. We all do. That's why it's crushing to think my life is a disappointment to you."

Angelo tore away from Jason's embrace. *No, I'm not buying this.* Camille had married an abusive man and Tammy had been a drunk, but he didn't judge them. If anything, he had enabled them. Aside from that, Angelo considered everything that had led to this moment. "You're conflating separate issues," Angelo argued. "Camille and Tammy have nothing to do with me suggesting you take the law school entrance exam. You're the one who said you expected more from your life."

Walking across the room, shaking out his hands, Angelo spun around.

"I can admit my faults," he said, the pain burning up in his throat, "but I never judged you for being a cop. Never. You're much too perfect for me to judge. I only want what's best for you, and the only reason I recommended you take that fucking exam was because I never wanted you to look back on your life and say to yourself…if only I had done more." Angelo squatted, dissolving uncontrollably into tears. Pointing his finger at Jason, he croaked, "So don't put that on me."

Clenching his hands into fists, Jason screamed, "Fuck!"

The chill that went down Angelo's spine felt almost physical, it was so intense. He was sure the guests in the rooms that sandwiched theirs would complain to the management about Jason's keening. They had disagreed before but never like this. This was a full-throated fight. Jason's accusations had knocked the wind out of Angelo more thoroughly tonight than Miles ever had.

Jason looked away, holding a hand to shield his eyes. *It's this case,* Angelo told himself. This case had infiltrated his life and had now metastasized to their relationship. *Say something, Jason is weeping.* "You said you had two secrets," Angelo rasped. "What's the other one?"

Peering at him with bloodshot eyes, Jason said, "I've been following the No Angels Wept murders since the beginning. I just never told you because I…I didn't approve."

"Look who's passing judgement now."

"Goddamn it!" Jason shook his head impatiently. "Let me finish." He continued doggedly. "I didn't approve because I knew chasing after this murderer wasn't going to make those panic attacks magically disappear, but I also knew you always do whatever it is you set your mind on. You always have. You're thickheaded, and that's why I love you."

"Thickheaded?" Angelo repeated lightly. "I know a hot cop. He's obsessed with a case. A young man was struck by a car outside a homeless shelter. And get this. Even after this cop had his arm broken, he still won't quit thinking about that boy."

Jason smooshed his lips to one side. "I guess we both love thickheaded men."

Tears welled in Angelo's eyes. "I love him more than life itself."

Jason walked across the room to hug Angelo. "I don't want to fight."

"What do we do now?"

Jason pulled Angelo toward the bed. Make-up sex seemed inevitable, but surprisingly, that wasn't what Jason had in mind. "Let's talk through the case. I have some ideas."

"Wait. What?"

They sat on the bed. Jason took Angelo's hands. "For example, I believe the killer is cherry picking his victims. That's why he needs three months to find them."

Up until this moment, Angelo believed no one understood his fascination with the No Angels Wept murders, dismissing it as an obsession to avoid coping with Mia Garcia's murder, and even though that was partly true, the murders of these three gay sex workers had triggered something else inside him. And now, for the first time, Angelo felt validation from the person that mattered most in his life.

"I think waiting three months means something to him." Angelo tucked his feet under himself. "But knowing Blaze was found on ice makes me think he can't wait another three months."

"I agree. Like most serial killers, he's growing impatient, which means only one thing."

Without hesitation they stared into each other's eyes and came to the exact same conclusion. "He could strike again at any time."

CHAPTER FIFTEEN

The alarm woke him. Angelo's eyes sprang open. He found himself facedown, legs spread apart with Jason's face firmly planted between his buttocks. There was nothing better than waking up from a deep sleep to a warm, wet tongue. Angelo arched his back, luxuriating in the slow torment of Jason's talented mouth. *Am I dreaming?*

"Good morning," Jason groaned as he rose along Angelo's back. Now wide awake, Angelo allowed himself to bask in this pleasure mixed with residual slumber. Jason kissed the nape of his neck as he maneuvered his arms underneath Angelo's, pulling his body firmly against his. Jason's erection was situated perfectly between Angelo's buttocks. He had only to roll his hips for his cock to find the warm, wet hole, entering with a single thrust. Angelo moaned as Jason pushed himself deep inside. "I don't ever want to fight again like we did last night."

Angelo braced against the nightstand, pumping himself hard on Jason's cock. "Never again." Pressing his face into the pillow, Angelo loved the intensity. "Harder."

Jason wrenched his right arm around Angelo's neck in a vise-like grip. Thrusting faster now, their skin slapping an applause. "I mean it. I never want to fight like that again. Okay?" Every word was met with a measured thrust, an insistent pounding. "Say it!" Jason grunted.

"No, never again." Angelo liked that Jason was taking what he needed and making demands. Hooking his left arm across Angelo's belly, Jason's splint scorching his skin like a lit match, Jason pressed his face deeper into the crook of Angelo's neck, pumping into him with no other expectation than to orgasm. "Feels so good," Angelo managed, knowing he wasn't going to find release, but happy to know Jason soon would.

The pace of Jason's thrusts quickened. "I'm not going to last."

There was no one else in the quiet, dimly lit hotel room, nothing but the two of them in this moment. Jason's arm tightened around Angelo's neck. Gasping, Angelo grabbed Jason's biceps as he continued to hammer into him, snapping his hips back and forth until finally Jason let out a groan and came.

The moment felt at once strangely intimate and completely brutal, but sweet nonetheless, particularly as Jason's body shuddered as Angelo expelled his diminishing erection from his body. After Jason pulled out, he turned Angelo around and they kissed, gently and with warm affection. "Did you come?" Jason asked, still panting.

"No, I didn't have to."

◆◆◆

By now it was nearly noon. A lifetime later, Angelo thought. What ecstasy. What bliss. The ache in his butt as he walked with Jason through the hotel lobby and out the front door was a pleasant reminder of their lovemaking. No connection existed between their previous life and the life they lived now. Suffused with honesty and passion. Their sex life careened into uncharted territory with a strangeness that was as bewildering and confusing as if they had been driving in a strange country after sunset. The peril seemed at once exciting and dangerous, and erotic…like a winding road that led to who knew where.

"What do you want to do today, my love," Jason asked, kissing Angelo's knuckles as he pulled their clasped hands to his lips.

"I'm hungry," Angelo said. "I know this diner that may or may not seat us."

"Sounds like a challenge I'm up for."

Ready to face a world at odds with them, Angelo saw it, and a sinking sensation hit him. "Oh, no." The Ford Crown Victoria was parked across the street. Detective Town wasn't glaring at him from the driver's seat; he was standing beside the car as if he had been waiting for them.

"What's the matter?" Jason asked.

"We'll see." Angelo walked directly toward him. "Detective Town, how can I help you today?"

He squinted at Jason. "Is this your NYPD blue boy?"

"Officer Jason Murphy," Jason replied with a twinge of sarcasm. "At your service."

"Get in," he told them. "Let's go for a ride." Town opened the back door.

Angelo and Jason exchanged wary glances. "Do we have a choice?" Jason asked.

"Just get in the fucking car."

Boniface sat in the passenger seat but failed to acknowledge them. Town threw the car in gear and drove along 7th Street. Angelo hoped Town planned to circle the block. Within minutes, the car got on the 110. "How are you enjoying your stay in Los Angeles?"

"It's been interesting," Angelo replied. "Met some interesting people. Present company excluded."

Town quirked an eyebrow at Boniface. "What did I tell you?" He glanced at Jason in the rearview mirror. "You should teach your friend to respect authority. I don't take kindly to disruptors."

Angelo sensed the strain between Town and Boniface, whose eyes never veered from the road ahead.

"Well, you won't have to worry about either of us after today." Jason offered Town a broad smile. "We're heading back to New York tomorrow."

"Finally, someone is thinking rationally," Town said. "If only you had come earlier, Officer Murphy. Maybe things wouldn't have gotten to this place."

"Well, I'm here now," Jason said.

"I was brought on to solve this series of unfortunate murders," Town said to Jason as if he was the only person in the car. "I believe these murders were brutal and senseless, but these three young men were working in a dangerous industry. If that's what you want to call it. The circles they ran in often had them consorting with the lowest of the lows."

"Lowest of the lows," Angelo repeated. Jason gave his knee a squeeze to silence him.

"What's that, Doctor?" Town asked.

"Nothing." Town nodded at him, seemingly contented that Angelo had caught on to his rules. "Take Fitz Ranchin, for example. On the outside he portrays himself as someone helping these degenerates but he's not."

He?

"Detective Town," Angelo began in a calm voice. "Fitz transitioned a long time ago. She's a trans woman."

Town bristled. "You realize what you're saying makes sense to no one."

"I respectfully disagree."

The car, silent as a morgue, sped up. Town changed lanes recklessly, taking the Flower Street exit. Angelo braced himself against the unexpected maneuver. Catching the gleam of amusement in Town's eyes, he was cautious not to make too much out of it. Apparently, the detective was enjoying himself too much. "I don't think you really appreciate how much damage you and your friends are doing to my case," Town said. "She's using her show to divert attention away from Ranchin because he's a person of interest."

Angelo's eyes skittered toward Jason but only for a beat. This was the first Angelo had heard Fitz was a person of interest. Seeing Town's eyes staring back at him unblinkingly in the rearview, he knew this disclosure was meant to throw them off, but Angelo offered him nothing.

"Think about it," Town said. "Fitz knew all three victims. He drives a mobile van for Pete's sake. I mean, what better way for him to dispose of the bodies."

Simmering, Angelo seethed with anger, listening to Town disrespect Fitz even after Angelo had corrected him. He thought back to that night at the Mexican restaurant. Something Fitz had said to him while being taunted by those bikers: *I've been fighting assholes like them my whole life. If you want to scuttle into a dark crack like a cockroach, be my guest, but I refuse to back down.* "*She,* goddamn it! Fitz is a she!"

The car came to such an abrupt stop, Jason and Angelo lurched forward. "Get out!" Town shouted. A V-shaped vein bulged from his forehead. Angelo turned to Jason, but he was hurrying him out the door. "Stay out of my way," Town warned them. "Go back to New York." The tires screeched as the car sped away.

Made to walk back to the hotel, Angelo decided to call Wes. He felt it was important for him to know that Town considered Fitz a person of interest.

"What do you mean *A Thorny Mess* is shut down?" Angelo asked, but he only caught bits and pieces. Rocky was shouting in the background.

"Femi called us this morning," Wes explained. "*A Thorny Mess* is on pause."

"What?" Angelo stopped walking. "Don't say another word. We'll be right over."

Chapter Sixteen

Mere seconds after exiting the car, Angelo heard Rocky carrying on inside Wes's house like a preacher speaking in tongues. Angelo hesitated, petrified at the thought of engaging her in such a state. He recalled how Rocky had flown into a red-eyed rage after meeting with Town; she'd pummeled him for betraying her trust.

"Welcome to the snake pit." Wes opened the front door. His eyes flared with the beleaguered exhaustion of a mother nursing a colicky infant. "Enter at your own risk."

"Fuck Mabel Knight for complaining," Rocky shouted from inside the house. "Fuck her gentle son. Fuck Town! Fuck everyone!"

"Is she always like this?" Jason asked.

"Full disclosure," Wes whispered. "She's been drinking."

Angelo sighed. *What else could go wrong?* Fortunately, he had Jason to protect him.

Wes escorted them into the living room where Rocky sat slumped on the sofa. She turned her head back to glare at them. "Oh, look who it is. Judas Iscariot and his maimed hot cop boyfriend."

"I'm Judas?" Angelo balked.

"Yeah, you're Judas." Her voice was cold. Clipped. "If you hadn't told Town about your little visit to Mabel Knight's house, none of this would have happened."

"What happened?" Angelo asked, though he was terrified to hear the answer.

Snatching her wineglass off the coffee table, she took a long pull. "Jarrett's lawyers are threatening to sue KLM over the way I treated Mabel Knight."

“That’s not all.” Wes went on to explain that Jarrett planned to hold a press conference outside KLM studios tomorrow afternoon, accusing the station of allowing Rocky to use her platform to further orchestrate attacks on Reverend James Jarrett, the Seven Spirits Church, and traditional Christian values unless KLM fired Rocky immediately.

“I’m guessing Femi didn’t tell Jarrett’s lawyers to go to hell,” Angelo said.

Rocky kicked the coffee table. “Screw Jarrett and his church!”

Wes exhaled. “*A Thorny Mess* is on hiatus until further notice.”

“Unbelievable,” Angelo said. “So much for freedom of speech.”

“This is all your fault,” Rocky spat at Angelo, then mockingly added, “for what it’s worth, Detective Town, we went by Mabel Knight’s house earlier today to apologize. Why don’t I make it up to you too and suck your dick.” Then she pantomimed oral sex, jerking her fist to her mouth.

From the start, Angelo had been able to keep his anger in check, understanding that for some reason, Rocky projected her rage on him. With his physician’s mind he rationalized that this wasn’t personal, but today, the taunting and finger pointing had awoken the Staten Island Italian in him.

“That’s right,” Angelo hissed. “I have a big mouth. Guess we all can’t be as secretive as you.”

“Now Angelo…” Jason intervened calmly, but there was no stopping him.

“Why didn’t you tell us you were at Peak and hung out with Gabriel Menendez the night before he was found murdered?”

This disclosure, Angelo saw, took Rocky by surprise. She shot up from the couch, bumping her chest against his. “What the fuck are you talking about?”

"Dino told me you were at Peak on July 15," Angelo said, not backing down. "Did it slip your mind?"

Rocky's stare was confused and intense. "I go to Peak all the time to visit Fitz. And yeah, I like watching go-go dancers. As a matter of fact, I'm considered a big tipper, but I had no idea who Gabriel Menendez was until the news reported he was a dancer at Peak. That scumbag Dino can point fingers all he wants. I'm no killer."

"It's true," Wes added. "Just because Rocky was at Peak doesn't make her a murderer. Besides, she was with me the nights Keith and Blaze were killed."

Something soft and wounded registered in Rocky's face. His accusation, so stunning, had wacked her in the head like a mallet.

"Rocky," Angelo said. "I'm sorry. I didn't mean to insinuate—"

"That I'm a murderer," she interrupted with a half sneer. "You just did."

Wes came to her and offered a hug. It was the first time Angelo had ever seen this side of Rocky. As she trembled in Wes's arms, Angelo realized the extent to which this case had affected her, had affected him. They were all feeling the pressure. Jason rubbed Angelo's back. "I think we should go," he whispered.

"No," Angelo replied. "I need to tell Rocky what Detective Town told us just now."

"Tell me what?" Rocky and Wes were sitting close on the sofa, holding hands. Her mascara had smudged. Her eyes were bloodshot.

Angelo eased himself down on the sofa, facing them. "Detectives Town and Boniface came to our hotel earlier. Town believes Fitz is behind the No Angels Wept murders."

"What?" Rocky gripped the sofa armrest like she was about to tear it off. "If they want to fuck with me and the people I love, I'll fuck them right back." Rocky shot up from her seat. "I'll show Town. I'll get on social media and tell all my followers that Detective Robert Town, the homophobic clown, has a gay son who was fucking Keith Knight."

"You are not going to do that," Wes said, grabbing her hand so she couldn't reach for her phone. "We don't want to poke that bear."

"I agree," Jason added.

"I do too," Angelo said. "Remember, the photo I saw with Keith and Bobby Town looked like it was taken outside a church. Mabel Knight and Dino told me that Keith had gone on a Seven Spirits Church retreat right before he was murdered. There's a good chance Detective Town is a member of the Seven Spirits Church."

Tears welled in Rocky's eyes. "Wes, what are we going to do? Jarrett won't back down this time. The Seven Spirits Church is bent on destroying us."

"It'll pass," Wes assured Rocky, but she sat shaking her head and wiping her eyes.

Angelo wanted to believe Wes, but after what felt like forever sitting in his living room mired in this horrible reality, it occurred to Angelo that the situation was hopeless. Yet, something still nagged at him. "Can I ask a question?"

"Go ahead," Rocky replied tonelessly.

"Wes said the Seven Spirits Church came after you once you profiled James Jarrett on your show. I'd like to hear your side of the story."

Rocky stared at Angelo, momentarily speechless. Her eyes like a grate being yanked down over a store window. Angelo was certain she'd decline when suddenly in a rush, Rocky sat up. "After I read that article," she began, "I reached out to the reporter and met him at his apartment. He told me he had gone undercover, posing as a runaway to gain access to the Seven Spirits Church. Church members were profiling young, homeless gay boys, offering them food and a place to stay, but there were rumors something more sinister was going on at the church, and he wanted to get to the bottom of it."

"What kind of sinister rumors?" Angelo asked.

Usually, Rocky spoke to Angelo while maintaining an unwavering stare. Now, she looked away, not meeting his eyes. "Jarrett was experimenting with conversion therapy on homeless gay boys against their will."

The sentence hung in the air like a stink.

"How is that even possible?" Angelo asked.

The absurdity of his question registered so sharply in Rocky's expression that Angelo felt ridiculous for asking, but it was a question begging to be asked. How, followed by…why. Why would an esteemed researcher experiment on anyone against their will let alone homeless gay youths? Words like *incomprehensible* and *cruel* came to mind immediately.

"Did you read the article," Rocky asked. Angelo nodded. "Then you know Jarrett's research went belly-up after those veterans killed themselves. While he was being investigated, Jarrett became an ordained minister and started the Seven Spirits Church."

"Part of his ministry included gay conversion therapy," Wes added.

Rocky snorted in derision. "Yes, but he wasn't having much success. What the reporter didn't put in that article was that he had heard rumors Seven Spirits Church members were infiltrating gay clubs, preying on young gay runaways."

Angelo was lost. "For what reason?"

"To lure them to the church to perform gay conversion therapy against their will."

The conversation paused here as Angelo considered this wild accusation. It was one thing to run a clinical trial where a few participants committed suicide while on a study drug. Having participated in clinical trial research, Angelo knew fatal adverse events were typically an uncommon occurrence but occasionally happened. For a researcher like Jarrett to begin a covert study as an ordained minister, enrolling young participants against their will, seemed more akin to running a cult than a clinical trial.

"And you believe this reporter?" Angelo asked, his skepticism evident.

Rocky glanced over at Wes, who had gotten up from the sofa. He was pacing by the window, fussing with his hair in an obsessive, nervous way. He paused to meet Rocky's gaze. "No, no, no," he said. "No, we are not revisiting the past. Have you forgotten what happened last time?"

Rocky stood up, gripping Wes's forearms. "You know as well as I do that Angelo is not going to let this go," she insisted. "The genie is out of the bottle. We have to tell him."

"I don't understand why you want to drag them into this," Wes said. "They're leaving tomorrow. Let them go."

Rocky stepped away and stared out the window with her back to them. The decision to inform Angelo and Jason what else the reporter had divulged to her seemed bigger than anything Angelo could imagine. Worse, what if anything did it have to do with the No Angels Wept murders? Angelo was caught in a maelstrom of fear and apprehension. Wanting to know what else the reporter had said and concerned it might propel them further into danger.

"I want to know everything," Angelo said. "We're in this together. Remember? The three amigos."

A quick cut to Angelo and Jason, Wes's eyes were full of dread. He grabbed Rocky's wrist and pulled her back to the sofa. How fast this happened, this eruption of fear in Wes. It surprised Angelo. "Think about what you're doing," Wes insisted.

"I have thought about it," Rocky replied. "If there is one thing I know, it's that Angelo is not going to give up until he hears the truth. He's one of us. Cursed with curiosity. Except he has it worse than both of us"—she cut her eyes to him—"isn't that right, Angelo?"

Intuitively, Angelo knew exactly what she was referring to. Jason must have sensed it too because he reached out and held Angelo's hand. It was as if Angelo could no longer hide or pretend that everything he did, everything he would do, wasn't because of Mia Garcia. She had become the fulcrum of his life. The wrong to make right, though he knew on many levels that was an insurmountable obstacle. A set up for failure. There was no going back and changing the past, he knew, but he could effect change in the present.

"What did the reporter tell you, Rocky?" Angelo asked slowly, emphatically. "I want to know."

Rocky and Wes stared at him with sharp, concerned eyes. A warning as if to say once this truth is heard it cannot be unheard. And then, a snap decision. "Why don't you listen for yourself." Rocky took out her cellphone and slammed it on the coffee table. "I recorded our conversation even though I never asked him for permission."

"Is that even legal in California?" Jason asked.

"No," Rocky said quickly, "but Fitz told me to do it anyway. She thought it might come in handy one day."

"Angelo," Wes warned, "are you sure you want to do this?"

Of course, he wasn't sure. How could he be? But something nagged at him like an itchy wool sweater. Something that suggested whatever Rocky recorded would bring this case into sharper focus or plunge him deeper into an already dangerous situation. Angelo squeezed Jason's hand. They gazed into each other's eyes. An unspoken pact that they were in this together. "Yes, we want to hear it."

"Jesus Christ!" Wes crossed his arms over his chest. Lips pursed, shaking his head. "Hold on a minute." He disappeared into the kitchen. Minutes later, Wes returned holding a bottle of Cabernet and four glasses. “You’re going to need a drink for this.”

The four sat in Wes’s living room, staring at Rocky’s cellphone like it was a grenade, and in a way, Angelo knew what he was about to hear was going to blow his mind. After Wes poured them each a glass, he sat down in the leather club chair. Rocky leaned forward and pressed Play.

The conversation began with the reporter recounting the events that led to his decision to go undercover at the Seven Spirits Church. He had been looking into Jarrett’s past after reading a report about a twenty-six-year-old soldier, living near the military base in El Segundo with his wife and eighteen-month-old baby boy. One night, the soldier got up and shot his wife and baby while they slept. Then he put the gun in his mouth and killed himself.

“I discovered this veteran was taking part in a military rehabilitation program at the Parallax Institute,” the reporter said. “A program that used a behavioral framework and an experimental drug to treat veterans with PTSD.”

His investigation led him to Houston, Seattle, and Atlanta. Cities where three other veterans from the War in Afghanistan lived. All three had killed themselves within ninety days of each other.

“Soon after the fourth suicide,” the reporter said, “the Parallax Institute shut down. Ulysses Corp pulled their funding. Jarrett was out of a job, but he was also in extremely hot water. Three separate investigations had been launched: one by the FDA, the second by LA County Police, and the third by the FBI.”

The reporter assured Rocky that Jarrett and his program were not going to be held accountable. It was a military program after all, sponsored by the U.S. government. Plus, his reporting had hit a familiar snag. No one would speak with him on the record, particularly the man at the center of it all: Dr. James Jarrett.

"My understanding," the reported continued, "was that he took a sabbatical. I had a hunch he was sent to a rehab facility. Certainly, this man had to be under the influence of alcohol or some drug, but I was wrong.

"Less than a year later, Dr. James Jarrett had added the title reverend to his name. He began the Seven Spirits Church and gained notoriety in assisting men in reducing their same-sex attractions and exploring their heterosexual potential.

"Homosexuality," the reporter quoted, "is an adaptation to a deep-rooted trauma that splits the boy from his masculine nature."

"Conversion therapy," Angelo heard Rocky say to the reporter, but he corrected her.

"No, this is not your typical conversion therapy," the reporter said. "It's reparative, but whatever. You say potato..."

The reporter explained that while he was investigating Jarrett's new role as the spiritual leader of the Seven Spirits Church—building a congregation and assisting men with their unwanted sexual urges—he began hearing stories about missing gay boys from WEHO. Transients and runaways that came to Los Angeles in search of stardom. Most were escaping their family's consternation for being gay.

"It was completely arbitrary," the reporter said to Rocky. "I was eating carnitas from a taco truck off Wilshire Boulevard when I read a flyer for a missing boy stapled to a pole. A nineteen-year-old who was last seen bar-backing at Peak went missing. So, I went down to the club and spoke to the manager."

Dino fucking Sosano.

"The manager told me that he knew the missing boy," the reporter said, "and that a few others had gone M.I.A. after being lured to Seven Spirits Church."

Having been blessed or cursed with the appearance of a much younger man, the reporter decided to play the part of runaway gay boy and visited Peak later that week. The first night, he sat at the bar and caught the eye of a man who introduced himself as Gates. "He bought me a beer," the reporter said. "Gates asked me a lot of questions: how old are you, where are you from, do you have any family? Bizarre questions I thought, for a man who was supposedly trying to pick me up, but Gates had something other than sex on his mind."

On and on the conversation between the reporter and Rocky continued. With each passing minute, Angelo felt himself sinking deeper into a plot that seemed so detached from reality, he would have never believed it had he not been listening to the reporter speaking through Rocky's cellphone.

Shortly after the reporter met Gates, he was coerced into leaving with him. The promise of a hot meal and a warm bed. Enticed by cliches: *You don't belong in a place like this. You're better than these other boys. Let me help you. You're not alone.*

You're not alone. Angelo wondered where he had heard that before. *Yes, the television commercial for the Seven Spirits Church. We're here for you. Spirits on high!*

"It seemed almost too easy," the reporter said. Angelo detected a change in his tone. A faint nasal sound had infiltrated his speech. Angelo wondered if he was on the verge of tears. "So, I went with Gates to the Seven Spirits Church."

A long pause followed. "And?" Rocky asked him.

"That was that," he replied. "Not much to report at first. There were ten of us. Boys of different ages. All young. All gay. Mostly runaways. Boys whose families had thrown them out for being gay. It was just as Gates had promised, hot meals and a warm bed. We lived in the church basement, which reminded me of my high school gymnasium. Slept on cots, dormitory style. Spent days cleaning the church and tending to the grounds. Our only form of entertainment was watching war movies, which they played on a loop. Leaving the church was strongly discouraged. A few boys got bored and left. No one made a fuss. By the third day, I thought, 'Everything seems okay. Nothing going on here.' Boy, was I wrong."

Rocky hit Pause and stood up to stretch her arms. Angelo was surprised to find his glass still full of wine. Without him realizing, Wes had opened a second bottle and kept topping off their glasses. Angelo wondered how many bottles of wine they'd consume before they heard the entire story. Gallons, he imagined.

"Is everyone ready?" Rocky asked.

"I'm not." Wes pouted as he gulped more wine.

Angelo did the same and settled his head against Jason's chest. "Are you okay?"

Jason clasped his arms around Angelo's body, nuzzling his lips against his ear. "As long as I got you," he whispered. "I'm better than okay. I'm great."

Rocky pressed Play. Angelo took three deep breaths. *Serenity now.*

"On the third day," the reporter said, "five of us were selected to go on a retreat that weekend. It was located at the former site of the Parallax Institute."

"What kind of retreat?" Rocky asked him.

"I didn't know at the time," he replied. "All we were told was that we were going to take part in a type of exercise, that it was being led by Dr. Reverend Jarrett himself, and that we should be on our best behavior."

The reporter described being taken to a compound in Pasadena. An impressive set of buildings. A grand entrance with three spires. A courtyard that led to a cathedral, a dormitory and wing of offices. Upon their arrival, the boys were treated to a welcome reception. A tall woman, lithe and white-haired, served small cakes and cups of fruit punch. Gates gave the boys a tour before they were escorted to where they would be living for the next two days. A dormitory with bunkbeds and a big screen television that played old war movies on a loop. For their participation, the boys were to be paid two hundred dollars in cash at the end of the retreat.

"The next morning, after breakfast," the reporter continued, his voice shaky, "my group was led into a room overlooking the mountain side. Jarrett sat cross-legged on an oversize pillow. He was wearing a billowy white shirt with gold trim around the cuffs, linen pants, and Jesus sandals. He asked us to take off our socks and shoes. We, too, sat on cushy pillows in a circle. A nineteen-year-old boy I will call Shane sat in the center of the circle, facing Jarrett. What none of us knew at the time was that Jarrett had induced Shane into a hypnotic state."

"Hypnosis?" Angelo interrupted.

Rocky pressed the Pause button. Her eyes lingered, a little disconcertingly, on Angelo's face. "It's all part of the conversion therapy."

A ripple of fear juddered through Angelo's body. *Using hypnosis made sense.* It allowed Jarrett access to Shane's subconscious.

"I'm not following this." Jason's face contorted in confusion. "I'm still stuck on the fact that Jarrett went from researcher to preacher, but he's still experimenting on people. Only this time it's gay boys."

Rocky stared at him for a long moment, her jaw set, flinching with frustration. "Can everyone just shut the fuck up and listen." Then she snatched her phone and pressed Play again.

"Once we were assembled," the reporter continued, "Jarrett began by describing the exercise. He said that he was going to have Shane re-create the trauma that haunts him by calling on people in the room to play specific roles. He would then confront them with his anger, remorse, hatred, or confusion and they would respond in character by apologizing, forgiving, and validating his feelings."

When Rocky asked the reporter about the trauma that haunted Shane, he replied there was no such trauma. He learned later that the boy was induced into believing a trauma existed. Jarrett's conversion therapy consisted of two parts: One in which the boys were induced into believing they were veterans. The second involved taking an experimental drug.

"The Seven Spirits Church was running a clinical trial?" Angelo balked. "That's not possible."

"Are you not listening?" Rocky said. "Stop interrupting and listen."

"These *special* boys," the reporter went on, "slept in an off-site dormitory connected to the main building by an underground tunnel. That way, if anyone—reporters, police, or the FDA—came snooping around, they could shuttle the zombie boys back to the off-site dormitory and out of sight."

Underground tunnel! Angelo shuddered at the thought.

"Are you okay?" Jason asked.

Angelo pulled Jason's arms tight across his chest. "As long as I got you," he said, "I'm better than okay. I'm great."

"If you two lovebirds are finished," Rocky cut in, "I'll resume our regularly scheduled program."

"Jarrett," the reporter went on, "told the group that Shane would now re-create his traumatic experience in this safe environment. In return, we were to supplement his negative memories with an alternative narrative in which he felt supported by feelings of love and compassion. I remember Jarrett removed his spectacles and placed his hand on Shane's shoulder. He said, 'Now, tell us what happened.' But Shane became visibly distressed. It was painful to watch, and everyone became uncomfortable. That's when I realized we were trapped in that room. There were two guards posted outside the double doors. There were bars on the window. There was no way out."

Jason leaned forward and pressed Pause. He stood up and began pacing. "You mean to tell me this nutjob research guy, Jarrett, went into hiding after several vets killed themselves while taking part in his clinical trial, but then he came back as a reverend converting gay boys into being straight?"

Rocky sipped wine, her eyes on him, unblinking. "We need another bottle of wine."

Wes shot up from his seat. Angelo was still digesting what he had heard so far when Wes returned with two bottles and poured another round. Logically. Intellectually. He knew that somewhere in the back of his mind Jason was right to question the reporter's story. Yet, swirling in the front, pressing against his eyeballs, Angelo believed every word he had heard so far. Wes hadn't yet sat when Rocky pressed Play and snatched her now full glass of wine off the coffee table.

The reporter started up again. "Shane said that during his last deployment, his battalion was assigned to work alongside the Army Special Forces soldiers in a district that was considered a Taliban hotbed. I watched as that young man broke down. He covered his face with his hands and wept, but Jarrett didn't stop him. He said to Shane, 'We can see how distressed you are by this, however, the central part of this exercise hinges on you allowing us to witness your distress. Use the Frame.'"

The reporter went on to describe how Jarrett directed other members of the group to play roles in Shane's story.

"The boy to my right served as Shane's guide, helping him as he relived the trauma. The boy to my left played Shane's ideal father, whose job it was to say all the things Shane's real father never said. Then, Jarrett asked Shane, 'Who should play the role of the dead boy's mother?' That's when Shane, for the first time, broke from Jarrett's gaze. He pointed at me. 'Him,' Shane said. Jarrett then instructed me to sit in the center of the circle, facing Shane."

Jason sighed and shook his head. "Turn that thing off for a minute." Rocky complied, smirking sardonically. It was as if part of her was enjoying watching Angelo and Jason attempt to make sense of something so unconscionable.

"What dead boy?" Jason asked.

Rocky did not meet Jason's gaze, but looked past him, deep into a dim corner of the room. Angelo found himself looking squarely into Jason's eyes. "Babe, let's listen. I'm sure we'll find out soon enough."

"Babe?" Jason stared at him strangely. "We have a deal. Remember, Angelo? You only call me babe when something's wrong."

"Something *is* wrong, babe," Rocky interjected. "Now do as your boyfriend suggests. Shut up and listen."

Jason bristled and snuggled closer to Angelo.

Rocky clicked on the recording and the reporter began speaking again. "Shane said that one afternoon, he was leading an exercise through the empty streets of Kabul. 'There were no people on the streets. No stores open. No one anywhere. Suddenly, there was an explosion.' It still amazes me to think how much detail Shane provided even though this was a false memory."

The reporter's voice warbled for a few seconds. Rocky explained that she'd kept her cellphone in her pocket, not realizing that the more she listened, the more she'd shifted uneasily in her seat, covering the microphone.

"Shane described that he heard a sound like someone slaughtering a goat. He said that goats make this sound when they're frightened. It's like they're crying for their mother. Shane said that growing up on a farm, every time they slaughtered the goats he hid because he couldn't stand their cries. All you heard was *Ma! Ma*!"

Jason wriggled his entire body as though tormented by a swarm of red ants.

"Pay attention to this part," Rocky said in a hushed whisper.

"But it wasn't a goat," the reporter continued. "Shane said when he looked up, a little boy was running toward him. The boy was on fire, running, but like in slow motion. Shane said he tried to throw off his gear, as much of it as he could. He wanted to get the boy to stop running, but he kept running toward him, screaming, *Ma! Ma! Ma*!" At this point, Angelo heard Rocky on the recording expressing her disbelief. "I couldn't believe it either," the reporter said to her, "but that's what Shane said."

Angelo shook his head. If this were true, if Dr. Reverend James Jarrett performed this form of radical conversion therapy on young gay men, some of them underage, and all of them nonconsenting, then this wasn't simply illegal. It was inhumane.

The reporter proceeded to describe how Shane began to decompensate. "He could hardly speak. He was sobbing uncontrollably. He said that by the time the burning boy was just a few feet away, Shane made the decision to open fire. Then Shane started punching his head. Jarrett instructed the young man acting as his guide to stroke his back as the other, playing his ideal father, held his hand. It was the craziest shit I have ever experienced. It was like Shane wasn't merely recalling these false events; he was reliving them."

Rocky pulled her legs toward her chest, wrapping her arms around them. Angelo braced himself. Terrified of what the reporter might say next.

"Shane told us that the boy died immediately, but that the boy's mother had witnessed everything. She ran over to embrace her dead son, but he was still on fire. She lunged to hug him, but Shane said he pulled her away to avoid catching fire. That's when Jarrett stepped in again. He crouched next to Shane. 'There's the boy's mother now,' he said, pointing to me. 'What do you want to say to her?' Shane wouldn't look at me. He fixed his gaze out the barred window, tears streaming down his cheeks. Finally, Shane's eyes met mine. He said, 'I'm sorry. Please forgive me, but I only wanted to put your boy out of his misery.' Meanwhile, Jarrett kept whispering, 'Don't worry. You're safe within the Frame.' And then this is where the train went off the tracks. Jarrett looked at me and said, 'Tell Shane you forgive him. Tell him you understand. Tell him you know he spared your son a life of misery.' But I refused. I couldn't say that to Shane."

Outside it was nearing dusk. This day had passed with unnatural slowness, and then swiftness, listening to the reporter's account. Rocky pressed Pause. Everyone stared into space. No one looked at one another.

"So," Jason ventured. "The burning boy is the gay boy living in Shane, right?"

Outside was calm. No wind. Not even the treetops stirred. Everything had become still. "Power is an intoxicating drug," Angelo said in a voice no louder than a whisper. "It's so potent; the more you have, the more you want."

"This is more than just being power hungry," Rocky said tartly. "This is about the power to control people. To make impressionable young gay men believe who they really are is so evil they have to snuff out that part of themselves to live a life free of misery."

Everyone turned to her in shock. It was as if she had contextualized Jarrett's ideology so completely and concisely there was nothing more to add.

"After I spoke with the reporter from the *Los Angeles Times*, I knew I had to speak out about Jarrett and the fucked-up conversion therapy he was performing illegally on those boys. I was warned not to do it, but Wes knew no matter what, I was going to speak out." She glanced at Wes who raised his wineglass and nodded a salute. "My life changed for the worse the day after we went on the air about Jarrett. I received death threats. I was followed. They even threatened my family." Rocky paused, pressing her hand against her sternum.

"Take a deep breath," Angelo said to Rocky. He took three himself.

"Wes and I almost lost our jobs," she said, her voice cracking. "Sponsors started pulling ads."

Wes stood up and sat next to her. "But we didn't lose our jobs. We survived."

"I need to speak with this reporter," Angelo said.

Rocky sipped wine and smirked again. "Sure. You can find him at 204 North Evergreen Avenue."

Angelo typed the address into his GPS phone app. His face went ashen. "What's the matter?" Jason asked.

"That's the address for Evergreen Cemetery," Angelo replied.

Rocky grinned broadly. "Days after the *LA Times* ran the story about Jarrett, the reporter was fired. The *Times* ran a retraction, stating certain statements in the article were unsubstantiated and unsourced. Three days after I met with him, he was found hanging in his shower. His death was ruled a suicide."

Suicide? A shiver of panic rippled down Angelo's back. This story was inconceivable and yet, every word the reporter said rang true. More chilling was that Rocky had spoken to him right before he died. "You don't believe he committed suicide?" Angelo asked.

Rocky stood up to stretch again. "No, I don't."

What, if anything, this had to do with the No Angels Wept murders Angelo was unsure. Certainly, he hadn't expected this twist—a research physician gone evangelical minister performing illegal and inhumane experiments on young gay men. And suddenly, he remembered something.

Very quickly, Angelo began piecing it all together. The photo in Keith Knight's bedroom, the one taken with Keith and Detective Town's son, Bobby, had been taken outside a building with three spires. This had to be the same compound the reporter described.

"Mabel Knight told me her son had gone on a retreat with the Seven Spirits Church," Angelo said, in a kind of rush. "She said Keith wasn't the same when he returned. She described him as being drugged up." Angelo shot up from the sofa. "Wes, remember? She showed us a bottle of capsules with the letters, PLX. They had to be the same ones the reporter spoke of."

"What's PLX?" Jason asked.

"I don't know," Angelo replied. "Maybe it's an acronym for something."

"Oh my God," Rocky said. "PLX is an abbreviation for Parallax."

"Parallax," Jason confirmed. "Like the institute."

Angelo caught his breath, knees quivering like a rippling stream. "We have to speak with Jarrett."

"Hold on." Jason reached for his boyfriend's hand.

"Listen to me." Rocky looked at him squarely. "As far as Jarrett is concerned, you don't know what kind of shitstorm you're walking into. But I can tell you that if anyone even so much as takes a whiff outside that church, your life will plunge nose-first into the ground and explode."

Angelo stood there irresolute, blinking. It was Rocky's stillness, Angelo decided, that suddenly filled him with dread. She appeared so placid as to seem almost catatonic, though beneath that blank stare remained the faintest echo of fear.

"Promise me," she shouted. "Promise me you won't go poking around the Seven Spirits Church."

Angelo sat down feeling defeated. What kind of stronghold did Jarrett have that he could commandeer such power over the police, over the *LA Times*, over Rocky Thorn? Running an inhumane experimental clinical trial on nonconsenting young gay men. For what? To reverse their homosexuality. As if that were possible. Surely, Jarrett had to know that. Unless, of course, this experimental drug, PLX, could achieve the unimaginable.

For several long seconds, Angelo imagined the implications of such a drug. And the frisson produced by this preposterous, yet alluring idea comprised a homeopathic dose of intrigue. *Would I take it?* He repeated this question to himself—an odd, disquieting conundrum bubbled up inside him.

"Imagine if such a pill existed?" Angelo asked abruptly.

"A gay-away pill?" Rocky asked with a mirthless laugh. "Why? Would you take it?"

The thought had crossed Angelo's mind, recalling all those years he had been tortured in Catholic school. A young, gay adolescent so confused by the bullies that taunted him over something he hadn't yet fully understood. Something that was obvious to everyone else but himself. And then, throughout high school and college, days and months and years where he observed heterosexual couples falling in love. Displaying their affections so openly and proudly while he hid his because if he were to display his true feelings, he faced ridicule and exile. Surely, his mother had known years before he got up the courage to come out. Gently tried to coax it out of him, but Angelo, so filled with dread, so consumed with guilt, hid his identity. Suppressed it for years, like he suppressed the pain he felt over having been abandoned by his father. They coalesced, galvanizing with one another like a tumor. A black malignancy that grew inside his chest. *The obsidian.*

"Yes, I would consider taking it," Angelo said.

Jason unfurled his arms from Angelo's body. "You would?"

Almost immediately, Angelo felt Jason's affection recede with a tide of disappointment. Never had Angelo experienced such chilliness from him. Not from Jason, not once in the two years they had been together. Jason, who was optimistic, kind, and warm, had only held Angelo tighter the times he'd wanted to pull away. Jason, whose strong arms protected Angelo from the world. The same arms that were unlatching from his body now as if he had been jettisoned like some repellent piece of trash. Angelo reached for Jason's hand, desperate to reclaim it, but Jason had moved to the other end of the sofa, staring at him in utter disbelief. Quickly, Angelo attempted to explain. "I don't mean now," he stammered, "but you have to admit if such a pill existed, you would consider it. Can you imagine how your life would have turned out?"

"I can," Wes drawled. "It would be like living in a black and white movie. No color. I prefer the life I have now, thank you very much."

"Hear! Hear!" Rocky raised her glass. "Fuck the breeders."

"You say that now," Angelo argued, "but would you have considered it when you were a teenager?"

Rocky cackled. "Oh, man. You are a hoot, Doc." She rose to her feet, bent at the waist so her face was mere centimeters from Angelo's face. "Poor baby," she taunted, using a little girl voice. "Wuz you teased in that big, bad Catholic school? Did the nuns hit you with a wuler 'cause you were a flaming little homo?"

Angelo stood up, insulted. His honesty had inoculated the grave discussion with an air of alacrity. "In fact, I was teased. What gay kid wasn't, but that's not why I would have considered taking a pill to make me straight."

Rocky sat back, crossing her legs dramatically. "Please, tell us. I can't wait to hear this." "Didn't any of you want a family?" Angelo asked.

"I thought *we* were family," Jason said.

The hurt in his voice pierced Angelo like a dart. "We are, Jason," he said, attempting to correct himself. "I meant a family with a wife and kids."

"You mean, a real family." Jason stood up. "I'm gonna step outside. Get some fresh air."

What have I done? His argument, a haphazard collection of words, was broken. Any attempts at mending it were futile. A precious vase that had been shattered and inexpertly glued back together.

The sound of clapping jarred Angelo from his thoughts. "Bravo, Doctor," Rocky said with obsequious laughter. "Talk about bad bedside manner."

"Talk to Jason," Wes urged, but Angelo shook his head.

He was tired. They were all tired and punchy. *The fresh air would do Jason good.* He would talk with him later. For now, he had to focus on the matter at hand. *I need to speak with Jarrett.* Then, as if Rocky had overheard his hardheaded internal thoughts, she warned, "I don't care if Wes and I have to strap you to the bed and take away all your clothes, I'm not letting you anywhere near Jarrett."

The awkward silence that followed made Angelo feel stupid and selfish for being so transparent. What would he even ask Jarrett, and what were the chances he'd get anywhere near him without a well-vetted appointment? Angelo experienced a blast of frustration like a razor of cold in a New York winter breeze.

Just then, Jason opened the sliding glass door and entered the room. "I have an idea."

Angelo heard them collectively catch their breaths.

"What if Angelo and I paid the Parallax Institute a visit," Jason suggested. "I mean, he is a doctor. What if he asks to learn more about the conversion therapy. You said Jarrett is a renowned expert."

"He's adorable," Rocky said to Angelo. "If you don't put a ring on that hot fuck's finger, I will."

Jason ignored Rocky's sarcasm. "I'm serious."

Wes wiped a hand across his face. "We know, Jason, but the Parallax Institute closed. Remember? Ulysses Corp pulled the plug, and the institute was shut down."

"Then where are they experimenting on these gay boys?" Jason asked.

"At Savior of Saints," Wes explained. "The Parallax Institute was reopened months after Jarrett began the Seven Spirits Church. Well, the same building as the Parallax Institute. They just changed the name."

"Savior of Saints?" Jason raised a hand to his mouth. "SOS?" All at once, Angelo observed Jason shudder as though his neural synapses had reestablished contact with his nervous system. "You're not going to believe this." He stared at Angelo, his face slack with dismay. "Angelo, remember the case I was working on right before I got attacked and broke my arm?" Jason turned to Rocky and Wes, raising his splinted left forearm as proof. "I was investigating the death of a teenager who was found dead outside a homeless shelter in Manhattan. Jesus Christ." He began pacing back and forth. "Onlookers said the boy looked like the walking dead, but the toxicology report came back negative."

"Slow down," Angelo said. "What does that have to do with this?"

"Angelo," Jason said, his voice rising. "That kid. The one who died. The name of the shelter he was staying at was called Savior of Saints."

It seemed too coincidental for there to be two different Savior of Saints youth shelters. *What are the odds?*

With each day, there was a new connection which, once engaged, appeared to have been inevitable, irrevocable; yet, at that very moment Angelo juggled with each revelation. Unable to make sense of them all. It seemed to Angelo almost as if fate had led him to this very moment.

A chime indicated Angelo had received a text. Frazzled, his fumbling fingers groped for his phone. "Oh, no."

"What is it?" Jason asked.

Another chime. This time from Wes's phone. Even as perspiration broke across his brow, Angelo knew exactly what was happening. He experienced an odd, prickling anticipation. When the third chime rang, the death knell from Rocky's phone, Angelo braced himself. "Rocky," Angelo began, but it was too late.

She jumped to her feet, stumbling toward the door. "We have to get to Peak. Dear God, not Fitz!"

Chapter Seventeen

By the time they arrived at Peak, the street was mobbed with onlookers. Police held them back as EMS workers loaded a stretcher onto the ambulance. A white sheet covered the body. Rocky bolted ahead of them weaving her way through the dense crowd, urgency etched on her face. Once she learned the body belonged to Fitz, Angelo observed her wither like a collapsing tent, a puddle of fabric on the ground.

Peak's parking lot was awash with blinking blue and red police lights. The growing number of spectators encircled Rocky like a scrum as she clung to Fitz's lifeless body.

It hadn't taken long for the crowd of mostly gay men to realize the grieving woman was none other than their patron saint of the forgotten LGBTQ+ community. When she dislodged the contents of her lungs in an earsplitting howl that was part banshee scream, part lion's roar, it seemed to pierce the unguarded hearts around her like a stake. Real-time questions were raised: *Did the police use excess force? Could this be a hate crime? It took two detectives to apprehend one trans woman?*

Angelo observed Detective Town from the periphery, viewing Rocky with the laparoscopic stare of a surgeon preparing to excise a tumor. His invasive scrutiny told him what Angelo already knew. The crowd was galvanizing. Their sadness, suspicion, and despair evident. People wanted answers…and now. This prompted Town to order two officers to separate Rocky from the body, but she refused to let Fitz go. And when they used force to extract her from this evolving situation, the crowd rose against the police. The result yielded a series of physical assaults. Out of nowhere, just as the police reinforcements came to strengthen the line of defense, a bottle struck an officer in the head. More bottles and cans were thrown at the police. The response was excessive: the police employed zip ties and mace. The fanatical crowd grew, bolstered with each passing minute thanks to rallying cries on social media. More police cars arrived as backup. They arrested some of the rioters.

Sirens receded in the night like dying animals, and the red and blue lights faded in the darkness. Angelo closed his eyes in disbelief. Still, the police would not listen to Angelo or Wes as they argued for Rocky's release. Even Jason, the New York City cop, could not get the LAPD to give in. Town had seen to that. His goal had been to create a disruption so heightened it distracted everyone from what had actually happened in Fitz's van just hours earlier. They were helpless as they watched officers force Rocky into the back of a police car. She emitted one final full-throated shriek that swamped Angelo with shivering fear.

The misery of the chaos outside Peak was surpassed only by the misery of what took place after Rocky had been taken away. Angelo, Jason, and Wes culled together whatever bits of information they could glean into a narrative that concluded Fitztina "Fitz" Ranchin, formerly Fitztucker Ranchin, had been a person of interest for days after several witnesses said they saw her with all three victims. Detectives Town and Boniface had paid a visit to Fitz's mobile van to question her, she had refused to leave with them voluntarily, and an altercation ensued where Fitz allegedly pulled a knife and fatally stabbed Boniface, leaving Town with no other choice but to discharge his weapon, killing the alleged No Angels Wept Killer.

An amorphous tension grew from his accusation. News trucks arrived at the scene. In what seemed like no time at all, overly coiffed, overly made-up reporters stood in front of Peak's signage, spotlighted as they grimly recounted the events into cameras that transmitted their reports to homes throughout California and beyond.

A story so leached of truth, it was merely a hollow casing. A fired bullet like the one that had killed Fitz.

The swirling pain of the three No Angels Wept murders did not quite obliterate the fresh new anguish of Fitz's death. Wes went to the police station downtown to wait for Rocky to be released. Angelo and Jason returned to the hotel. They were tired but couldn't sleep. Hungry but couldn't eat. A feeling of catatonia set in; they moved about the room like zombies. But the real torture was watching the television news. "Last night, Detective Salvatore Boniface was murdered outside a gay bar called Peak," a television anchor reported. "The twenty-year LAPD veteran arrived with his partner Detective Robert Town to question Fitztina Ranchin about the string of murders involving gay male prostitutes."

"Prostitutes," Angelo shouted with incredulity. "They're called sex workers. I mean, who uses that word anymore?"

"It is believed Ranchin became combative with police and fatally stabbed Detective Boniface. Detective Town discharged his weapon, killing the forty-four-year-old woman. Now police are investigating evidence recovered from Fitztina Ranchin's van, which may lead investigators to conclude she was behind the No Angel Wept murders."

"You forgot the *s*," Angelo shouted. "No *Angels* Wept! What kind of reporter are you?"

The solemn newscaster concluded with, "Boniface is survived by his wife and three children."

Jason clicked off the television. He hugged his boyfriend, but Angelo had gone rigid in his arms. His anger and frustration with this case had hardened into an exoskeleton, turning stiffer with every dead end until he was barely able to move. "It's not over," Jason said.

"Isn't it?" Angelo pulled away from Jason. "Town got exactly what he wanted. He solved the No Angels Wept murders and pinned it on a member of the LGBTQ+ community." The pilot light of failure roared into a flame, and Angelo was engulfed in the blistering heat of his exhaustion. "I want to go home."

Jason kissed Angelo's right eyelid and then his left. Gently, so that it felt like a moth's wings. "What you need is a shower and something to eat," Jason reasoned.

"No," Angelo sobbed. "It's time to go home. It's time for me to face the fact that I was wrong. Finding the murderer of these three gay boys is not going to bring Mia Garcia back."

Whatever horror Angelo and Jason had stumbled into, he decided in that moment it was time for them to step away. Since Mia Garcia's death, Angelo had been ebbing away in a self-imposed purgatory that felt more dire than death itself.

"I'm not only thinking of me," he tried to say, but the words got choked up in his throat. "I'm thinking of you… my love. I'm thinking about our family."

Jason's face underwent an evolution of expression, as if he were solving a riddle. "Do you mean that?"

"I don't know what I was thinking when I said I would take a pill to make me straight," Angelo cried. Tears muddled his vision like being held underwater. "I'm sorry. You and I are a family. A real family. I don't know what I was thinking. I was… I was…"

"Shhh," Jason whispered. "Stop talking and kiss me."

Jason's tenderness filled Angelo with a deep burgeoning despair for having dragged him into this mess and for having disrespected their relationship. Confronted with the pain of failure, he blamed himself and cursed his stupidity. And all for what? A foolish notion that he could unbridle himself of guilt if only he found the courage to solve this mystery. That was the answer, and it crucified him. But if he had learned anything from all this, it was that his life was not his own. Whatever he did now and for the rest of his life belonged to Jason just as much as to himself. Angelo's actions mattered. This revelation roused in him a clear directive that tingled to life like a reanimated limb.

Like his, Jason's heart raced. Quick percussive panting, flaring nostrils—no words. Only grunting as they kicked off their sneakers and undressed. In the delirium of this moment, an indescribable lust swelled inside Angelo, conflicted that he should experience such a longing, such a craving for Jason only hours after Fitz's death. It was the improbability of these two emotions, loss and lust, that had brought on a rapturous fantasy to be with the man he loved. Disembodied from the grief and embracing the passion of his lover inside him.

With a sense of urgency that this moment would pass if they didn't act on it now, Jason spat on his hand and rubbed his palm against the soft pucker of skin between Angelo's buttocks. Angelo sucked the breath from Jason's mouth as he allowed Jason to finger him. Fitz lying dead in her van flashed before Angelo's eyes. In a convulsive desire to push the image away, he focused on Jason. "I love you. I love you so much." Pressing his face against the taut, muscular ridge between Jason's pecs, he spread his legs, readying himself. The sound of a long, drawn-out groan escaping Jason's lips fired Angelo's erection as it swelled against his abdomen.

Gripping Angelo's ankles, Jason stared down at him. The grin on Jason's face was as sexy as it was dangerous. "Tell me you want it."

"God, yeah." Jason arched his back and allowed a long stream of saliva to bathe his cock. Angelo gripped the headboard as Jason pushed the head of his cock just beyond the pink dimple and stopped.

"Say it," Jason gritted, blue eyes blazing. "Say it!"

Angelo's breath quickened, imaging Jason's cock piercing deeper inside him. "Fuck me, Jason." Fueled by lust, Jason maneuvered Angelo's left leg over his shoulder and straddled his right, plunging his erection past the ring of muscle, sending a trill of pleasure through Angelo's body. So unlike Jason to be this aggressive... Something opened inside of Angelo. Such muscle-straining, chest-tightening passion had Angelo wishing this could last forever. Deep, persistent thrusts, Angelo trembled and moaned. Sweat dripped off Jason's chest and into Angelo's mouth. "Harder."

Angelo stroked himself as Jason beat against him, skin slapping. "Can you come?" Jason groaned. Nodding, unable to speak, Angelo grabbed Jason's buttock while feverishly masturbating. "I can't hold on." Jason exploded, slamming into Angelo with such force, the bed came away from the wall. Angelo trembled and groaned under him. Waves of ecstasy as he orgasmed. Rolling tides of euphoria rendered them helpless and motionless in the moment.

"I love you, Jason. I love you so much." Jason fell on top of Angelo, bodies convulsing as they caught their breath. "Let's leave tonight," Angelo said, still panting. "We can take the red eye and be back in New York by morning."

"Are you sure?" Jason asked.

"I want us to leave tonight. Okay?"

"Okay." Jason moved close to Angelo, kissing his lips lightly. "I told you. As long as I got you, I'm better than okay. I'm great."

◆◆◆

A short while later, packing his suitcase as Jason showered, Angelo once again scolded himself for bringing his injured boyfriend into this disaster. Hadn't he suffered enough after being attacked on the streets of Manhattan?

Arm broken. Out on medical leave. Fortunately for them, Jason had agreed with his plan. The plan to return to New York brought about a cheeriness in Jason that had been notably absent since his arrival in Los Angeles. The sex had only added to his mood. Jason strutted around their hotel room with the pride of a new father doling out cigars.

It didn't concern Angelo that their sex had evolved. At one time he'd been concerned that over two years they would grow bored with each other, but just the opposite. Perhaps it was the stress. Maybe it was frustration. Whatever it was, Angelo had no complaints. And in a way, he was optimistic about where their sex life would go once they returned to New York.

After Angelo finished packing, he stared intently at his laptop, reading the *LA Times* article for the umpteenth time. There had to be someone who worked at the Parallax Institute back then who would be willing to speak with them now. A doctor, a nurse, maybe even a staff member?

The only other physician mentioned in the *LA Times* article was a psychiatrist named Scott Monroe. He had joined Jarrett's team a year before the *LA Times* article was published. Angelo searched online for published abstracts by James Jarrett during this period. One article published in the *Journal of Modern Psychi*atry was a retrospective study of suicide rates among returning veterans from Afghanistan. Dr. Scott Monroe was co-author.

A Google search showed Monroe authored several published research articles. One in particular entitled, "Implementing the Use of Artificial Intelligence to Predict Suicide Among Veterans Suffering from PTSD" caught Angelo's eye.

Jason came out of the bathroom, a towel wrapped around his waist. "What's that?"

Angelo pulled him down for a kiss. He craved affection, attention, and lots of it. Even after making love, he felt an insatiable desire to have Jason close by. "I can't imagine what Rocky's going through," Angelo said. "I don't know what I'd do if I lost you."

Wrapping himself around Jason's body, Angelo felt swathed, protected in his ample arms. "I'm not going anywhere." Angelo experienced a twinge of guilt for being so needy when Jason had only been loving, attentive, and accommodating. "Have you spoken to Wes?"

Angelo hadn't even texted him. Being connected, though peripherally, to another murder had triggered memories of the events that followed Mia Garcia's death. Without realizing, he had gone into self-preservation mode, recalling those days and weeks after Demetre Kostas was arrested. He and Dr. Stanzione subsisted in a funnel of focus. "Concentrate on the patients, save the practice" had become a mantra they focused on instead of their emotions. Fitz's death had brought on a similar sense of detachment toward Wes and Rocky. There was no other way forward than to pull back. Hearing any news about this case had the potency of reigniting Angelo's interest, and he didn't want that. He'd had enough. But lurking just below the surface, like a shark looming beneath a crop of swimmers, was his unshakeable fear the murderer was still out there.

"I'll text Wes in a minute," Angelo said. "I've been reading the *LA Times* article."

"Again?"

There was no denying the skepticism in Jason's tone. Angelo imagined that no matter what he said, Jason wouldn't believe they were going home until they boarded their flight. Until that time, any mention of the case had the potential to sabotage their plan.

"There's this physician named Scott Monroe," Angelo said with the clinical tone of a pathologist observing slides. "He works at the veterans center. Not too far from here."

"Oh yeah?"

Jason finished getting dressed. Sitting on the sofa by the desk, he seemed to be bracing himself for bad news. "Let me guess. You want to pay this Dr. Monroe a visit?"

"I was thinking about it," Angelo said not looking up to meet Jason's gaze, "but only if you agree to come with me."

On occasion, Angelo forgot Jason was a cop. Not that it would take graduating from the police academy for anyone to see past the translucent meninges to read Angelo's thoughts. "So, if I say I don't want to go…then we won't go?"

Angelo understood that Jason was on to him. That fact and the fact that it didn't matter to him, had already played out in his mind like a game of chess. Angelo was already two moves ahead. "You know you want to go just as much as I do."

"I don't want to go," Jason said, "but if you want to go, just say so. Stop playing games."

"I want to go." Jason laughed, sounding like he had won the argument but lost the bet. At any rate, it didn't matter. "Think of it as one last stone we have to overturn."

Jason leveled his eyes at Angelo. "You mean one last stone *you* have to overturn."

"Are you disappointed?" Angelo knelt by Jason's feet. "Nothing's changed. We're still leaving tonight. Promise."

"Okay," Jason replied with a sigh, "but I need coffee first."

◆◆◆

They drove to the veterans center on Redondo Beach Boulevard in Gardenia. Poverty had ravaged this part of town. A dusty orange lent the streets a somberness like passing into another world that felt dirty and less enchanted than the one they had just left behind. Streets littered with trash. Homeless people camped on the sidewalks in tents. Intoxicated bodies draped against walls, a few sprawled across the pavement singly or in pairs. They drove past abandoned buildings marred with graffiti. Jason pulled the car into the veterans center parking lot, which was surrounded by a tall, chain-link fence.

Stepping through the entrance of the dingy white and green building, Angelo experienced a flash of memory, recalling his days as a resident physician. Those long hours he spent admitting patients in the emergency room. Swaying in the trace of boredom as he listened to his attendings on rounds, and the never-ending calls from nurses, pleading with him to enter orders in the middle of the night.

Security directed them to the second floor. Angelo greeted the receptionist and explained he was a doctor who urgently needed to speak with Dr. Monroe about a mutual patient. The skeptical looking receptionist picked up the phone and spoke in a hushed whisper. "A Dr. Perrotta is here to see you. He said it's in regard to a mutual patient." She paused to listen. Turning to look at Angelo, she asked, "What's the patient's name, Dr. Perrotta?"

Angelo smiled wanly. "Tell Dr. Monroe he treated this patient at the Parallax Institute."

The woman appeared momentarily stunned. "Oh, I see."

Jason sat among the other patients in the waiting room, men mostly, wearing clothing that identified them in one way or another as veterans. He occupied himself with a newspaper. The lurid banner headline on the front page read: NAW Is DOA. Photographs of Peak's parking lot and an old mugshot of Fitz from years ago when she was arrested for prostitution appeared below it. Jason coughed to catch Angelo's attention. Reluctantly, Angelo took the newspaper from him and stared at the front page in dread.

Ten minutes later, Monroe entered the waiting room. A man about Angelo's height, with tight, curly dark hair and close-set blue eyes, looked directly at him for several seconds before his gaze swerved away as if from pain. "Dr. Perrotta?" His eyes never locked on Angelo's.

"Thank you for speaking with me on such short notice." Angelo extended his hand, but Monroe gazed at it like he was viewing a new life form through aquarium glass. Instead, Angelo motioned toward Jason. "This is Jason Murphy." Angelo felt a quiver of awareness; a sense that Monroe was assessing this encounter with mounting suspicion. A seizure of regret at having brought Jason passed through Angelo. "He's my partner," Angelo added, hoping the word partner would allay his fears. A heavy silence followed, which Angelo tried to alleviate by suggesting brightly, "He can wait out here if you like?"

"Come in." Monroe hastily escorted them both into his office.

Inside, the sun-soaked office overlooked the Hustler Casino. Angelo took a quick glance around the room. Behind Monroe's desk were floor-to-ceiling bookshelves stacked with sundry psychological textbooks. A framed photograph of Monroe standing alongside a tall, thin woman and twin girls. A vacation photo from a cruise, Angelo deduced. They were posed around a life preserver ring that bore the letters SOS. "Lovely family you have." Angelo jerked his chin at the photo.

Monroe twitched, glancing over his shoulder. "Oh, yes. Thank you."

"I'll cut to the chase," Angelo said. "We wanted to ask you about your experience working with Dr. James Jarrett at the Parallax Institute."

Monroe's eyes shot him a brief, piercing glance, but he neither refused outright to speak with them nor did he offer to comment. At least not right away.

"I read the *LA Times* article."

Monroe snickered. "Who hasn't. That article nearly cost me my career." He stared at the wall where his medical school diploma hung. "From the beginning. From the start, actually, I always suspected something was wrong with Jarrett, but I was too blinded with ambition."

Instantly, Angelo identified with him, thinking of his younger self making wrong decision after wrong decision for the sake of his career. "What's the old saying?" Angelo opined. "Ambition is vital, but dangerous."

Monroe strained to maintain eye contact, but it lasted only several seconds. "I was introduced to Dr. James Jarrett at a hospital fundraiser. He was familiar with my research involving the rising rate of suicide among veterans suffering from PTSD. Do you know more active-duty U.S. soldiers kill themselves than die in combat?"

"I didn't know that." Angelo glanced at Jason, smiling, feeling a sense of relief that Monroe was opening up to them.

"During my post-doc, I developed a word association test to measure a person's bias for being alive or dead using AI technology," Monroe added. Jason shifted uncomfortably in his seat. Monroe paused for a moment, narrowing his eyes at Jason. "You find this confusing?"

"Me?" Jason chuckled. "I just don't understand how you can predict if someone wants to live or die using a computerized test."

Monroe smirked. "I can show you." He stood up and gestured for Jason to sit in his chair, standing far enough away so that their bodies never touched. Reluctantly, Jason changed seats, offering Angelo an eye roll for being the Guinea pig. Monroe clicked on a folder that opened the test on his computer. "Sort the following words under either 'Life' or 'Death' and try to do it as quickly as you can." Random words began to appear: alive, funeral, die, thrive, breathing, suicide. Jason began dragging the words to what he believed was the appropriate bucket. "Once you establish a rhythm the test will begin to measure bias."

"I feel like I'm playing a video game," Jason said, having gotten the hang of it.

"The faster the patient and the fewer mistakes, the less likely they are to kill themselves," Monroe said. "You're doing very well."

"You mean I'm not going to kill myself?"

"Not likely," Monroe replied. "Of course, the actual test takes longer, but you get the idea. The results showed a ninety-one percent success of predictability. This met our primary endpoint and proved statistical significance."

"That's quite the accomplishment," Angelo said. "No wonder you caught Jarrett's attention."

"I don't know about that." For a strange, disjointed second, Monroe appeared to wrestle with Angelo's insinuation as if that thought had never crossed his mind. "He invited me to visit the institute."

"The Parallax Institute." Jason stood up to allow Monroe to sit down. "Funny name, no?"

"Not really," Monroe said matter-of-factly. "A parallax involves two distinct views of the same object. For example, when a driver looks at the odometer and sees the indicator directly over the number sixty, that is the speed at which he's driving. But the person in the passenger seat sees something else. To them, the indicator lies nearer the forty-five mark. It doesn't mean the car isn't traveling sixty miles per hour, but rather, the perception is based on where you are seated in the car. This represents a parallax."

"How does an odometer relate to a brain, Doc?" Jason asked.

"Considering the biology of depression, we know the complex neural circuit that becomes disordered in post-traumatic stress disorder involves the amygdala, an almond-shaped part of the brain involved in the processing of emotions and memory. Jarrett's work with veterans at the

Parallax Institute asked the question: What if there was a medication that blocked certain memories used in conjunction within a psychological framework? Would that change the patient's perception of their trauma?"

"Was the medication in the class of anti-psychotics?" Angelo asked.

"It was a first in class," Monroe corrected.

"So, what went wrong?" Angelo asked.

Monroe hesitated. His eyes stared fixedly at his diploma again. "One of life's ineffable, unpredictable details called an adverse event. Four men committed suicide while enrolled in the clinical trial."

Listening to Monroe speak with such frankness was an eerie sensation, like walking through a home that had been burgled. There was an echo of sadness and a twinge of regret under all that candor, a cavity left by his entanglement with Jarrett that if tested, would collapse under his weight. But Angelo was eager to push Monroe to his limits. "What happened?"

"I left soon after the first soldier killed his family and then took his own life. I spent years and thousands of my own money defending myself against the Office of Professional Medical Conduct even after the police had cleared me of any wrongdoing."

Angelo wrenched forward. "You don't have to tell me about the OPMC. I know them well."

"What an unfortunate commonality for us to share," Monroe laughed dryly. "Eventually, I was cleared. Dr. Jarrett, as you may know, lost his license. He began a ministry called the Seven Spirits."

Angelo found it interesting how Monroe lapsed into a vexed sort of melancholy when he wasn't speaking. It was as if the shadows of those dark memories rose in his mind, taking form like a ghost.

"He may have swapped his stethoscope for a priest collar," Jason said, "but it looks like the reverend hasn't given up on research."

"That's impossible," Monroe insisted. "In the beginning, we had substantial government support. It all came to an end during the investigation. After that, Jarrett had no credibility among researchers and academicians. None whatsoever."

"I hope you're right." Angelo stood up. Glancing at the Monroe family photo, the four of them clinging to that life preserver, Angelo wondered if this tragic experience was already behind them by the time that photo had been taken. "Thank you for speaking with us."

Monroe stood up to escort them out. "What about your patient? The one I took care of at the Parallax Institute."

Angelo glanced at his feet. "There was no patient. Listen, you've been very honest with us. So, I feel obliged to return the favor. We're looking into the No Angels Wept murders."

Monroe cocked his head. "Haven't the police apprehended the killer? I recall hearing a report about it this morning on the drive to work"—Monroe began nodding—"yes, I'm certain of it. It was a woman, I believe."

Squinting, Jason corrected Monroe. "The police haven't confirmed if the woman they killed last night is the No Angels Wept Killer."

Monroe's lips formed a grin like a gash. "You believe the police used excessive force."

"I didn't say that," Jason replied.

"But you believe it," Monroe insisted. "Otherwise, why would you say, 'the woman they *killed* last night.' Killed implies you believe the police used excessive force. If you didn't believe that you would have said something like, 'the woman that died in an altercation involving the police.'"

"I think you're twisting my words," Jason said with a dry chuckle that indicated to Angelo that he was growing impatient. "Anyway. Nice to meet you, Doc."

"Wait," Monroe said. "You don't believe Jarrett is involved in the No Angels Wept murders?"

It occurred to Angelo that he might have confused Monroe's frankness as a sign of amiability, but like his word association test, what if Jarrett's former colleague had been assessing them. Luring them into a false sense of security to earn their trust so they would confide in him? And now they had shown their bias against Jarrett, exposed themselves.

But Angelo rebuked himself. By all accounts Monroe had distanced himself from Jarrett after the first veteran killed his family and then committed suicide. Turning his back on the man who had set him up at a glittering institute rife with affluence, accolades, and approbations only to land in a weathered veterans hospital on the outskirts of town, mired in bureaucracy, budget cuts, and boredom.

Whether Jarrett was involved in the N.A.W. murders remained to be seen. Still, there was no denying what Angelo heard at Wes's house: Jarrett was experimenting on young gay men against their will and holding them captive at Savior of Saints. Suddenly this rippled with incipient clarity, like hearing the sonorous swell of eerie music in a horror movie.

It was as if his mind couldn't make room for both these competing conflicts: gay boys imprisoned against their will and Fitz's death. His mind, unable to toggle between them, focused on one and compartmentalized the other. Until now, Angelo was intent on returning to New York, and the fizz of excitement was now circumvented by the feverish desire to save those boys trapped at Savior of Saints. But he had promised Jason they would return tonight on the red eye.

"Thank you again for speaking with us," Angelo said.

Monroe moved to open the door. Angelo offered his hand but like before, Monroe glanced at it with an uncomfortable smile. "Take my advice." Monroe clasped his hands behind his back. "Don't go digging into Jarrett's past. Too many powerful people will see to it that you're stopped."

Angelo experienced a squiggle of panic. "That sounds like a warning."

"Not a warning," Monroe said. "Just some friendly advice, and by the look on your face, I see you won't be taking it. Anyway… Best of luck to you." Just as Jason passed the threshold, Monroe added, "Speaking of funny names, I always thought No Angels Wept was an absurd calling card for a serial killer."

Angelo stepped back inside. "What did you say?"

"No Angels Wept." Monroe chortled. "It's an odd name for a serial killer. Don't you think? The No Angels Wept Killer hardly rolls off the tongue like Son of Sam or The Night Stalker. I always thought it might be an anagram versus a calling card."

"Anagram for what?" Jason asked.

"I wouldn't have a clue," Monroe replied.

Chapter Eighteen

They drove in silence for a while before either of them said a word. Angelo's brain felt like it was sloshing inside his skull, as though it was dissolving. Thoughts swirled in his mind as he recalled what that now dead reporter had said to Rocky.

Funneling like a tornado was the very real belief that something more sinister was going on at Savior of Saints. He felt himself perspiring like he was raging with a fever, thinking about those boys still being held against their will. Angelo fiddled with the air conditioning. He lowered the window and stuck out his head. Closing his eyes, he let the moist air caress his cheeks. *Three deep breaths. Serenity now.*

"How are you holding up?" Jason asked.

Angelo's eyes blinked. He raised the window and sat back. "I'm better now." For much of his adult life he'd come to understand the thorny interior of his character, but since Mia Garcia's death, anxiety seemed to bubble inside him like an uncorked champagne bottle.

Jason reached across Angelo's shoulders. "Come here."

He scooted closer, resting his head on Jason's shoulder.

"What do you think about Monroe," Jason asked.

Angelo, who had been completely distracted with the images of those boys he had conjured in his head—confused, drugged, and frightened—failed to respond to Jason. His mind a deep, dank crawl space of wretched possibilities. "I'm sorry, what did you say?"

"Monroe, what did you make of him?"

"Odd," Angelo said.

"Right!" Jason's body twitched with sudden alertness. "And what was with the no hand shaking? He basically treated us like lepers."

"Not sure." Angelo stared out the window at the modest one-level homes that lined the streets, identical in every way. "Maybe he's a germaphobe or neurodivergent."

"Neuro what?"

"It's a term used to describe when someone's brain processes, learns, or behaves differently than what is considered typical."

"Monroe is different. I'll give you that. Who else would have come up with a computerized suicide test?"

Blood flashed across Angelo's face with such force it left him light-headed. "What did you call it when Monroe showed us his computerized suicide test?"

"I don't remember…wait, I said it reminded me of a video game."

Tense, Angelo felt it overwhelm him again like a bout of vertigo. Another piece of evidence added to the overstuffed file belonging to the No Angels Wept Killer. "When I spoke to Dino that night at Peak," Angelo began, "he said the boys who returned from Savior of Saints were offered room and food in exchange for completing chores. He said that in their free time they were only allowed to watch war movies and play *video games*."

"You think Jarrett made those boys take Monroe's suicide test?"

Angelo still harbored a vivid recollection of the recording Rocky had played for them. The reporter's chilling description of the Frame exercise, and Shane, that poor hypnotized boy reliving a false memory of his time spent in Afghanistan during the war. Having the boys watch war movies made them more susceptible to the idea they were veterans. The subject matter burrowed under their skin in a feinted manner. "I'm not sure if Jarrett is using Monroe's suicide test," Angelo said, trying to figure how it fit in Jarrett's bigger plan, "but I wouldn't put it past him."

"For what reason?" Jason pressed.

"Maybe Jarrett administered the test at baseline," Angelo offered, "and then again at different timepoints to assess whether the boys were progressing. A behavioral frame is not enough. It's too subjective. Monroe said the results showed a ninety-one percent success of predictability and proved to be statistically significant. By using the same test and achieving similar results, those quantitative measures would lend credibility to Jarrett's work."

They resumed their silence. Angelo's thoughts drifted to scenes he imagined of the boys trapped at Savior of Saints. His brain swirled with too many high-voltage assumptions of unspeakable horrors those boys were enduring; the war movies that played endlessly throughout the night, the paltry meals, the handcuffs that bound them to metal bunkbeds. All thoughts he could not power down.

"Angelo!"

"What?" he replied with mocked innocence.

"Don't what me. Your eyes are fixed on the windshield like you're having a vision of the Virgin Mary."

Angelo avoided Jason's eyes. They had been together long enough it was as if they could read each other's minds, particularly when Angelo was thinking of doing something that might be considered dangerous. "It's just that I can't help but think about those boys at Savior of Saints."

"The answer is no," Jason said with such insistence, Angelo shuddered. Before he had a chance to ask, *no to what*, Jason continued with, "No, you are not going to Savior of Saints to poke around."

When Angelo turned to face Jason, it was as if Jason had been speaking to a child. He bore a look of paternal consternation.

Ever since they had left the veterans center, Angelo had been racked with worry about the gay boys being held against their will at Savior of Saints. Within seconds of leaving Monroe's office, Angelo had begun plotting a way to drop subtle hints so that Jason would come up with the idea to visit Savior of Saints, as if the idea sprang from his own mind. This time, Angelo had been outmaneuvered.

"Say it," Jason barked. "I want to hear you say you're not going to go to Savior of Saints." Angelo glanced again in Jason's direction only to find him staring intently at him for several long seconds, not the road ahead.

"Jason!" Angelo shrieked. "Look where you're going."

Jason eyed him, unblinking. "Say it!"

Angelo's eyes toggled between Jason's wide eyes and the oncoming cars. "Okay. Okay. I promise."

One final mistrustful glare before Jason cut away to stare back at the road. Angelo attempted to even out his breathing as the fear of a collision subsided. Jason reached over and gave Angelo's knee a squeeze. "I'm sorry I yelled. It's just…I know how your mind works."

"I get it."

Suspended between the roaring of car engines on either side of them, the moment felt oddly still and final to Angelo. But a torque of dread returned, and Angelo wrapped his arm across Jason's abdomen, squeezing him. *Three deep breaths. Serenity now.*

One long quiet moment later, a text broke the silence. A number Angelo didn't recognize:

Can U talk?

This was followed up with:

Bobby Town. Here.

Bafflingly, this seemed only to confound the day further. "You've got to be fucking kidding me."

Jason jerked his head at Angelo. "What?"

"It's Bobby Town." Before he had a chance to text him back, his phone began ringing.

"I need to see you." Bobby sounded desperate, shaky, like he'd been sobbing. This fact brought with it an eerie chill. As if Bobby were waving to him from across a misty lake, beckoning him from the other side. Angelo set the phone on speaker so Jason could listen. "Can you come here?"

This notion gave Angelo a haunted feeling, as if they were walking into a trap, and instead of sensing the whiff of Jason's disapproval, Angelo was shocked to hear him say, "Text us your address."

Angelo jerked his head to Jason, but Jason did not meet his gaze. "Full disclosure," Angelo said to Bobby, "I'm with my boyfriend. He's a cop."

"See you soon," was the last thing Bobby said before hanging up.

Still stunned, Angelo didn't ask Jason why he agreed to meet with Bobby when moments earlier he expressed a staunch objection to visiting Savior of Saints. He suspected that Jason's investigative mind wished to hear what Bobby had to say. Another stop on this collision course they had stumbled upon. At any rate, Jason had volunteered to go, and there was no denying the zing of satisfaction Angelo experienced.

"I know you're asking yourself why I agreed to meet with Bobby," Jason said.

"I wasn't thinking…" Angelo stopped himself from lying. "Okay, yeah. I was asking myself that very question."

"Do you want to hear my answer?"

"Yes, please."

Jason shot him a serious look. "Going to Savior of Saints on our own is stupid. Detective Town would be on our asses before we got past the front door. Besides, that reporter said they kept the drugged boys off-site. So, I seriously doubt we'd find what we're looking for. At the very least, we'd get the fake tour they reserve for everybody that comes by. Bobby, on the other hand, is a completely different story. Him reaching out to you strikes me as a cry for help. We should use it to our advantage. You know... Good cop, bad cop. We don't want to come across as too desperate." A flicker of something glittering in Jason's eyes caused Angelo to jolt with manic exhilaration. There was something about Jason when he commanded a situation that brought about a swell of pride in Angelo. "What?"

Angelo beamed. "Nothing."

"Nothing, huh?" Jason shook his head. "Oh, Dr. Perrotta. Whatever you do. Don't take up poker."

◆◆◆

Twenty minutes later, they pulled up to the address Bobby had texted; a small Spanish-style hacienda in Glendale. Angelo hesitated, but Jason was already moving around the car to open the passenger side door. *He's in full cop mode.* Instantly, Angelo felt calmer. Who would be foolish enough to ambush a cop?

When the front door opened, a very tall, lean man with thinning blond hair and hazel eyes greeted them. "You must be Angelo. I'm Guy Cleveland."

Guy fucking Cleveland!

Angelo stared with blank attention, as if awaiting a cartoon bubble to materialize over Guy Cleveland's head saying, *surprise*! But this snag had failed to yield a comic resolution. Staring at the man who had eluded any online presence, Angelo's ferocious impulse to speak with him was suddenly stymied by fear. If they passed this threshold there would be no turning back.

"This day is full of surprises," Jason said as he stepped inside. "I'm the cop boyfriend, Jason Murphy."

"Come in, Officer Murphy."

"Angelo, are you coming?" Jason asked. Sensing Angelo's hesitation, he held out his hand. "It's okay. We came all this way. Let's hear what they have to say."

Cleveland led them to a room with a vaulted ceiling and dark wood floors. Two dark-brown distressed leather couches were positioned in front of sliding glass doors that overlooked the yard. A black, white, and orange Native American rug stretched across the entire floor. A chandelier of antlers hung overhead. "Please, have a seat."

"Where's Bobby Town?" Angelo asked, radiating impatience.

"I'll get him."

Once they were alone, Angelo whispered in Jason's ear. "I decided to play bad cop. Is that okay?"

Jason pinched the bridge of his nose. "God help us."

Cleveland returned. "Bobby will be here shortly."

"We can't stay long," Angelo said a tad too harshly.

Jason sidled up to him, squeezing his arm. "Easy there, tiger," he muttered.

Bobby Town entered the room, wringing his hands. The young blond man appeared thinner than Angelo recalled, if that were possible. The sallow acne-scarred skin, the glassy indigo eyes with dark lines etched beneath them—all indicated a person in fierce, headlong withdrawal of some kind.

"Bobby?" Angelo managed to retain a calm demeanor when all he wanted to do was ask if the young man was ill.

"Thank you for coming," Bobby said in a jacked-up, jittery way that felt oddly close to tears or laughter. "Thank you for coming."

Cleveland held Bobby's hand, interlacing his extraterrestrial-size fingers with Bobby's so that they looked more like father and son sitting side by side. "Did you find the house easily?" Cleveland asked.

Angelo nodded with avid accord. He willed himself not to speak, but the thudding of the pulse in his temple drove him crazy. "So, what's so important you had us drive all the way here?"

Bobby drew a nervous breath. His expression changed like a pebble tossed in a pond; it rippled with fear. "You need to stop looking into the Seven Spirits Church. Jarrett has many powerful friends in this town. You have no idea the danger you're putting yourselves in."

"Are you fucking kidding me?" Angelo said with a snort of condescension. "You had us drive all this way just so you could warn us!"

Wiping his nose, Bobby appeared visibly shaken. Immediately, Angelo regretted having raised his voice but for the life of him he couldn't understand why Bobby had them come all the way to Glendale to tell them something he could have said to them on the phone. And yet, as with so much else, he couldn't help himself from probing further. "That can't be it."

"I'm serious," Bobby said. "I'm doing you a favor. I'm sorry I made you drive all this way, but they're listening. They know your every move. Stop your investigation."

Angelo had a flash of memory, thinking back to that night he saw a dark figure outside of Wes's house and the call he received from someone who sounded like Detective Town: *Listen to your cop boyfriend. Stop interfering in people's private lives, especially good wholesome, upstanding Christians.*

Just then, Bobby's phone began ringing. The jolt, so startling, caused him to jump up from the couch. "Shit! I told you." His eyes cut to Guy. "I knew this was going to happen!"

Cleveland gripped Bobby's arms, steadying him. "Calm down."

Bobby pulled away from his embrace. He stormed into the other room like an actor going off script in the middle of a play, leaving Angelo and Jason confused. Angelo heard Bobby whispering, his voice cracking as he spoke. "Is he all right?" Angelo asked pointedly. "I mean, physically?"

"I'm taking good care of him. Don't worry," Cleveland assured him. Angelo decided not to pursue the topic further.

When Bobby returned a short while later, his cheeks were blotchy and crimson. Cleveland stood up to embrace him again, nuzzling his lips against Bobby's ear. "Is everything okay?"

"Well." Angelo stood up. "Thank you for wasting our time. We won't be taking your advice. Jarrett's people crossed the line. Now it's personal."

"What's that supposed to mean?" Bobby asked.

"May I remind you that I'm an Italian New Yorker. Once you come for my family, we don't back down." Angelo offered Jason a sly smile.

"That's right." Jason pumped his splinted arm in the air. "This is personal."

"Wait!" Bobby shook his head, presaging he had more to say. "Can I talk to you in private, Angelo?"

Angelo dropped Jason a slow wink to indicate a private chat was his plan all along. Turning back to Bobby, he said, "You get five minutes."

Bobby led him to a small room that was likely intended as a second bedroom, which Cleveland had converted into a den with an oversized couch, wide-screen television, and a circular table displaying a board game. Angelo said, "Okay, spill it."

"You New Yorkers are aggressive as fuck."

"So I've been told," Angelo said. "Now spill it, otherwise, I'm leaving."

Bobby's demeanor shifted imperceptibly. He began circling the table, running his finger along the edge like he was giving careful consideration to what he said next. "Fitz isn't the No Angels Wept Killer."

Angelo scoffed. "No shit." He held the edge of the table, hawking Bobby with an aggressiveness that suggested he might flip it over. "Who is the killer then?"

"I don't know." A frazzled looking Bobby locked eyes on Angelo with a desperate, teary expression. He took a jagged breath, attempting to even out his breathing. "All I know is that the police will announce they found evidence in Fitz's truck. Evidence that will prove she is the murderer."

Gripping the table as a kind of ballast, Angelo shouted, "Are you kidding me?"

The pause stretched as they continued to stare at each other, and now Bobby's lip quivered. "I overheard my father talking on the phone last night. He was whispering to someone. I don't know who, but I heard him say, 'I've taken care of everything.' Something about killing two birds with one stone."

"That could mean anything." Angelo's excitement deflated like a punctured helium balloon. Just moments earlier, he had arrived at the house ablaze with hope, but Bobby's persistent evasions had doused any prospects of a break in this case. Instead, Angelo's antipathy toward Bobby unleashed his acid tongue. "I shouldn't have come here. I wanted to trust you. I wanted to believe you weren't like your father, but you're just like your father."

Bobby's eyes went wide. A revulsion roiled through his body so intensely, he began to sob, groaning like a wounded animal. "I'm nothing like my father!" He squatted, gripping the table to keep from falling to the floor. "You don't understand what it's like being the gay son of Detective Robert Town. Growing up, I always felt like a loser."

Angelo crouched beside him. "I can't imagine what that must have been like, but something made you call me. What was it?"

Bobby's face was mottled and flushed, as if he had come down with a fever. He took refuge hunched under the table, knees to his chest, arms hugging his knees. "Just leave me alone."

Bobby's body began shivering almost convulsively. Angelo watched him for several long seconds before he stood up to leave. Glancing down at the table, he noticed the Scrabble board for the first time, the lettered tiles arranged in intersecting rows and columns.

"Interesting," Angelo whispered to himself. Instantly, he recalled what Scott Monroe had said to them earlier at his office. That in his opinion, No Angels Wept seemed more like an anagram instead of a calling card. *For what, though?*

Suddenly, it felt peculiar being in Guy Cleveland's house with Detective Town's son. At that moment, Angelo hated himself for being there. It was as if the totality of everything he and Jason had been through, listening to the reporter recount the gruesome facts about Savior of Saints, Fitz's tragic death, and Dr. Scott Monroe's warning to stop digging into Jarrett's past, had brought them to this final, disappointing end. He rallied his swirling, confused emotions and decided to make use of this time alone with Bobby. "You and Guy," Angelo ventured. "You two seem… close."

One corner of Bobby's mouth curled up into a vague semblance of a smile. "He's been wonderful to me. After Keith died, I had no one to talk to."

"How did you two connect?" Angelo asked. "He has no social media presence. None whatsoever."

Bobby waved his hand dismissively. "Oh, I got his info from Fitz."

"Fitz gave you Guy Cleveland's contact info?"

"Uh, yeah," Bobby remarked with the flippancy of an obnoxious teen.

Angelo recalled how tight-lipped Fitz had been when he asked her if Keith Knight or Gabriel Menendez had been her clients. Going so far as to scold him for asking her to breach patient confidentiality. Fitz wasn't the type of person who'd share contact information without asking permission first.

"Hey," Angelo started in again, matching Bobby's high school tone. "So, what's the story behind Mabel Knight's troubled past?"

Bobby sighed exaggeratedly, itching at his jawline and leaving red welts. "Mabel Knight was a heroin addict and a sex worker when she was younger. Once she got pregnant, she joined a church program to kick the habit. You know, so she could raise her baby on her own. Child Protective Services had threatened to take Keith if she didn't clean up her act. Which she did." Bobby continued to scratch and pick at his face. "Can you imagine her reaction when she found out her gentle son was not only gay but a sex worker? Talk about the apple not falling far from the tree."

"What happened?"

Bobby's expression turned rueful. "Mabel threatened to throw him out unless he got help from Reverend Jarrett."

"Is that where you two met?" Angelo asked. "At the Seven Spirits Church."

"Yes," Bobby said, sniffling.

"Are you coming down with something?" Angelo asked, feigning concern.

Here, Bobby turned guarded, his cheeks flushing. "I'm fine." He stood up. Momentarily, his knees buckled.

"Are you sure you're all right," Angelo pressed, taking Bobby's arm to steady him.

"I said I'm fine!"

"Talk about being aggressive as fuck," Angelo offered lightly. Bobby gave a choked laugh and ran his hand across his mouth. He sniffed hard. This time, Angelo ignored the symptoms. It was clear Bobby didn't want to talk about them.

Part of Angelo felt bad for him. The closeted gay son of

a homophobic detective. Alone with no mother or siblings to confide in. Yet with another part of his mind, Angelo was totally convinced Bobby knew more than he was letting on.

"You didn't happen to go on that retreat with Keith Knight at Savior of Saints?" Angelo asked with a directness that jarred Bobby.

"What retreat?"

Here was another blunder, Angelo thought, recalling the photo in Keith Knight's bedroom. The one taken of him and Bobby outside Savior of Saints. "Mabel Knight told me her son attended a retreat at Savior of Saints right before he was killed."

"You ask a lot of questions about Savior of Saints." Bobby began wringing his hands again.

"You didn't know Keith attended a retreat right before he died?" Angelo insisted. "I thought you two were close?"

"Not as close as you think," Bobby said in an anxious, querying upper register, as if every answer were a desperate lie. "I mean, he was an escort. Hello! I met him at church, and we became friendly. That's all. Do you honestly think my father would let me hang out with someone like that?"

"So, Keith never mentioned anything about a retreat?"

"I hadn't heard from Keith in weeks," Bobby said with a such exigency it led Angelo to believe this was the first time he was being straightforward. "The next thing I know he's back on RentAGuy. When I confronted him, he told me he had a rich client with a high-profile career that would be destroyed if their relationship became public."

Angelo nodded, taking a step closer toward Bobby. "Any idea who this mystery man is?"

Bobby swallowed, then bit his lip. "He never told me who it was."

Behind him, Angelo heard Jason chatting with Cleveland. "Bullshit," Angelo hissed. "Stop lying to me. I know you know more than you're letting on."

Bobby took a step back, appearing self-conscious. He looked past Angelo as if he were hoping Cleveland and Jason would enter the room and put an end to Angelo's questions.

"Tell me!"

Bobby cowered as if he expected Angelo to strike him. "All I know is the mystery man had a traumatic childhood, like Keith. Something about his mother being raped at twelve and her uber Christian parents not allowing her to get an abortion."

"What an awful story."

"Ya think!" Bobby glowered. "It gets better. When the boy turned sixteen, he told the grandparents, who by the way raised him as their son 'cause the boy's real mother hung herself, that he's gay. That day the grandparents threw the boy out. Told him not to come back until he *fixed* his problem."

"Fixed?" Angelo repeated. "What an odd thing to say."

"I know," Bobby said. "Like neutering a dog. I told Keith to be careful. This man is damaged, I told him, but Keith wouldn't listen."

Staring at the young man, Angelo was overcome again by a deep sadness. Something more than wistfulness resided in those bleary eyes. For Keith to have shared such details about his new man left Angelo to believe two things: this man was more than just a client, and Bobby had been in love with Keith Knight.

Something must have happened at that retreat. Why else would Keith take up with a new client if the purpose of the retreat was to cure him of being gay? Mabel had described her son after returning from the retreat as someone who appeared drugged. Likely a side effect of Parallax, Angelo assumed. He wondered if Keith stopped taking the medication just after meeting his new man. All the while, Bobby held a secret wish to snag Keith's affection. After Keith confided in him about the burgeoning relationship with the mystery man, the rejection must have been crushing to Bobby.

Angelo recalled that first time he met Bobby. The boy appeared frightened, with dull eyes and sleepy movements. Had he been on Parallax at the time? Clearly, he didn't resemble that boy now, and Angelo wondered if something had uprooted inside Bobby that had been buried and suppressed. Something which Bobby too seemed ready to unearth, but maybe didn't know how. "Why did you really ask me here?" Angelo asked. Bobby's lips parted to speak, but nothing came out. "Bobby, you can talk to me. I want to help you."

"It doesn't matter anymore," Bobby said, turning cold.

"It mattered enough for you to call me," Angelo insisted, and now, it struck him to take a gamble. "It had to have mattered or else why would you call into *A Thorny Mess*?"

Bobby seemed on the verge of crying again but wouldn't let himself this time, angrily wiping his eyes in the crook of his arm.

"I know it was you," Angelo said, doubling down. "You can buy a voice distortion app on iTunes for five bucks. Won't you tell me why?"

"I think you should leave now," he whispered.

Angelo grabbed him by the arm. "What was it you wanted to tell me?"

"Go back to New York before it's too late. Go back right away. That's what I wanted to tell you. You don't want to get in any deeper than you already are. Fitz is dead. The police have their serial killer." Bobby looked so anguished saying this. He couldn't look Angelo in the eyes. "You don't know my father," he said, taking a shaky breath. "Forget the No Angels Wept murders. Go back to New York and forget everything."

Stepping back, Angelo stared at the sniffling, trembling boy, imagining what kind of life he had growing up.

Exposed to such hate for being something he couldn't control. Made to feel like a loser. Something deep inside him that felt wrong at home but vibrant, colorful, and genuine everywhere else. How long did it take to break such a spirited child? Angelo didn't know. He was only grateful he grew up with such a loving mother and sister.

"Fitz is dead, Bobby," Angelo said in an even voice. "I refuse to allow your father to make her a scapegoat because of who she represented. It wouldn't be fair to her or her family, and it wouldn't change the fact that someone is still out there killing young gay men. Think about what you're asking me to do. Think about Keith Knight, Gabriel Menendez, and Trevon Bolden."

Bobby dropped his face in his hands and sobbed for several seconds before he inhaled sharply through his nose.

Standing before this trembling, shaking young man, Angelo knew that once he left Guy Cleveland's house, it would likely be the last time he ever spoke to Bobby. Though he was tired and frustrated, Angelo was equally fired up and determined. He knew in his heart Fitz wasn't the killer. *Someone had a motive. Someone who likely had something to lose. Someone with a high-profile career that would be destroyed if their relationship became public. The mystery man.*

Angelo breathed heavily. "Bobby, who is Keith Knight's mystery man?"

Shaking his head, Bobby replied, "I don't know."

Clutching Bobby by the wrist, Angelo spoke deliberately. "I think you know who it is, and I think you know why I'm asking."

"I don't know." Bobby strained to maintain eye contact, but Angelo detected the faintest of tremors. A tell that told Angelo he was lying. This moment with Bobby was perishable and fading. Angelo was losing him. Not knowing what to do next or what to say, Angelo was not surprised when

Bobby whispered, "Don't say I didn't warn you." Bobby broke away to join Jason and Cleveland in the other room. He had said all he was going to say.

It was time to leave.

Chapter Nineteen

Back in the car, Angelo wasted no time rifling through the glove compartment for a pen and something to write on. "What did you and Bobby talk about?" Jason asked. "You were in there long enough."

"What a colossal waste of time," he replied. "Damn it. There's no pen." Angelo took out his cellphone.

"What are you doing?"

"There was a Scrabble board in the room where Bobby took me," Angelo stated. "I think Monroe was right. What if No Angels Wept *is* an anagram?" A Google search provided Angelo with an anagram tracker. Immediately, he plugged in the letters.

"You mean to tell me Bobby made us drive all the way out here for nothing?"

Angelo couldn't concentrate on his phone and hold a conversation with Jason at the same time. "This is useless," Angelo said in frustration. "We have to find a store. I need to buy a Scrabble game."

"Where am I going to find a store that sells games?" Jason asked.

A second Google search located the Glendale Galleria. A short while later, Jason turned off West Colorado Street and parked in the lot across from Target. "I guess you want me to go in?" he asked with playful irritation.

"Love you, hon," Angelo said without looking up from his phone.

Alone, Angelo abandoned the tracker and typed NO ANGELS WEPT as a note on his cellphone. Mentally, he tried to use the letters to spell the names of the victims, but there was no K for Keith Knight, or M for Gabriel Menendez, or B for Trevon "Blaze" Bolden. Growing frustrated, Angelo threw himself against the seat.

Think. Think.

If No Angels Wept was an anagram, had the killer intended there to be three words? Angelo couldn't be sure, but it seemed like a good place to start. Except the letters were too fixed in his mind for Angelo to see them any other way. It was as if No Angels Wept had been branded on his brain.

Think. Think. Focus on Keith Knight.

What did he know about the first victim? Amid his mounting frustration, Angelo felt a tiny blip of possibility. Closing his eyes, he visualized words associated with Keith Knight: BLACK. MASSEUR. HAND. GAY. BOY. MAN. SEX.

Jason opened the car door with a bag tucked under his arm. "Anything?"

"You scared the shit out of me," Angelo exclaimed after having caught his breath.

"Sorry about that." Jason handed the game over and started the car. Just as he was about to back up, a horn blared as a car sped past them. "Son of a bitch," Jason shouted. "Slow down, buddy!"

Suddenly, it struck Angelo like falling through a trapdoor. "Son!"

Angelo reached for the Scrabble game, tearing off the plastic wrap. Rummaging through the tiles, he collected the twelve letters. Using the lid, he maneuvered the letters from NO ANGELS WEPT and spelled, SON. Jason watched as Angelo pushed those three tiles aside to focus on the others. That left him with: ANGELWEPT.

"Son?" Jason read out loud. "What's that?"

"Think of words that relate to the first murder victim." Angelo gazed at the tiles. "Anything come to mind?"

"Did Keith have a nickname?" Jason asked. "Something his mother called him?"

A dreamy silence overcame them, and in the trill of that silence, Angelo saw it clearly. GENTLE SON. From the remaining three tiles, he formed: PAW. Angelo rocked back and forth, overwhelmed with the giddy infusion of promise. They had broken the code. NO ANGELS WEPT when rearranged spelled, GENTLE SON PAW.

"Paw?" Jason asked. "Because the killer cut off Keith's hand?"

"Well, yeah, but Keith was from Paw Paw, Michigan. So, there's that too."

Jason threw the car in gear. "Let's get back to the hotel. I still haven't changed our plane tickets. We're still leaving tonight, right?"

Angelo nodded, but for the entire drive he was seized with the thrilling thrum of victory matched only by the perilous pull of dread, like the moment you fall forward on the rope after losing at tug of war. The question remained; what did any of this mean? Sure, they had figured out the anagram associated with the murder of Keith Knight, but there were still two more anagrams to solve.

Then what?

Angelo stared at the tiles in the lid of the Scrabble box and asked himself the question that had vexed him since leaving Dr. Scott Monroe's office: Were they really going to return to New York tonight? How could he even ask himself that when he had promised Jason they were sticking to their plan?

Angelo stole a glance at Jason, who looked straight ahead. Still guarded after nearly being clipped by that speeding maniac, Jason's eyes never veered from the road. This allowed Angelo to enjoy, in sidelong glances, Jason's stunning beauty. His strong jaw, his perfect nose. Recalling the images of Jason as a little boy. Photos his mother hung on the wall along the staircase: a ten-year-old little leaguer with a bat across his shoulders, a thirteen-year-old graduate in cap and gown, and Angelo's favorite, the gangly young man in a tuxedo, grinning at his prom date.

Any person, any sane person would clamor to return to their comforting cocoon in Manhattan. An existence they had forged together after Angelo had placed them in such peril it nearly cost them their lives. And now, like an addict searching for his next drink after suffering from the worst hangover of his life, Angelo was seriously considering not returning to New York with this beautiful man beside him.

The reason he knew, was fear.

Angelo was too frightened to return home, to his life, because then he would have to face the void when he looked in the mirror. This thought was so jarring, Angelo shuddered as if feeling the sharp edge of an envelope flap slicing into the skin between his fingers.

"What's the matter?" Jason asked.

"Nothing." He lied because he didn't want to start an argument. He chased it with a half-truth: "I'm just thinking about words associated with the second murder victim."

Only a fool would ask Jason to stay in Los Angeles. This kind, gentle, and loving man. The same man who held him in his arms after he woke up screaming Mia Garcia's name. The ghost that haunted his dreams. The spirit that triggered his panic attacks; the ones that plagued him ever since he became consumed with the No Angels Wept murders. Was it Mia's face he saw when he dared to peer into the void?

This has to stop. He berated himself silently while vowing for it to end now. Their relationship wouldn't survive another calamity. It was time he listened to the echoes of warning. Dr. Scott Monroe and Bobby Town were right. *It's time to leave Los Angeles. Return home to New York. Live your life with the beautiful man beside you.* Yes, he decided. It was time to go home. Forget about the No Angels Wept murders because none of it was important. The only thing that mattered was sitting just inches away.

Suffused with joy that he had come to realize there was no other option but to return home, Angelo vowed that returning home wasn't enough. *I will find a new therapist. I will begin the necessary work to heal myself. I will unpack the events that occurred after Demetre Kostas's incarceration. I will forgive myself for Mia Garcia's death because if I don't, my relationship won't stand a chance.*

Angelo took Jason's hand from the steering wheel, interlacing their fingers. He bent forward and kissed each of Jason's knuckles. "What's gotten into you?" Jason asked, "and don't say nothing."

He gazed into Jason's eyes. "I love you. I love you. I love you."

A smirk grew across Jason's face, reminding Angelo of another photo on the wall of his mother's house, a gem he'd decided at that moment was his favorite. An eight-year-old Jason dressed as a police officer on Halloween.

"Thank you," Angelo said, still holding Jason's hand. "Thank you for taking me to see Bobby Town. You were right. I know that now. I've been lying to myself and lying to you. I *am* obsessed with these murders, and the panic attacks started shortly after Keith was found dead. This has to end. Now. I'm just sorry the one time we go away we ended up chasing after a serial killer instead of sipping cocktails on the beach." Confiding in Jason, Angelo experienced a profound relief. Lulled with the dreamy imagining of what flying home on a plane together would be like, a blanket tossed over them, hands clenched underneath it. Free of the crippling fear someone was watching them. Free of murder. Free of anagrams. Free of death. "Let's go home."

"Where do you think we're going?" Jason chuckled.

"I mean it this time, back to New York," Angelo said. "Just like we planned."

"What about the boys?" Jason asked with caution. "Are you ready to leave behind the boys at Savior of Saints?"

Angelo felt caught off guard momentarily. "I'm not leaving them behind. I'll do what I can to help, but I'll do it from New York. I'll find another reporter. Someone who will listen to that recording. The most important thing right now is you and me. And more importantly, I've also decided it's time I return to therapy. SRNiTY is an app. I need a living person to help me with these panic attacks."

Jason pulled Angelo's hand to his lips. "That makes me so happy."

They drove back to the hotel in silence, holding hands. Cool blue sky, clouds like cappuccino froth. Angelo returned his gaze back to the Scrabble lid. At the pieces now jumbled that once spelled GENTLE SON PAW and NO ANGELS WEPT. The tug of curiosity clawed at his back. Angelo gave himself permission to continue deciphering the second anagram. He thought about Gabriel Menendez as Jason drove with a smile plastered on his face.

Think. Think. Focus on Gabriel Menendez. What did he remember about the second murder victim? Closing his eyes, he visualized words: LATINO. DANCER. GO-GO. LEG.

Leg!

Imperceptibly, so as not to disturb Jason's bliss, he maneuvered the tiles to spell LEG, leaving NOANSWEPT. Where was Gabriel from, he asked himself? Aspen. He slid the five letters over to form ASPEN LEG. That left him with the letters ONWT.

"Town," Jason said. "It has to be Aspen, Town, leg."

Angelo regarded him with guilty eyes.

"Don't worry," Jason assured him. "You think I was going to let a brand-new game of Scrabble go to waste?"

They agreed to wait until they got back to the room before they began working on the anagram for murder victim number three. By the time they parked the car, rode up the elevator in the south tower, opened their door and poured the tiles on the desk, Jason had already figured out one of the words: ANGEL. Trevon "Blaze" Bolden had been the only victim who was born in Los Angeles. "That seemed almost too easy," Angelo said.

That left, NOSWEPT. With the remaining letters, Angelo assembled: TWO and PENS. Next, he tried POET but that left NSW.

"What about PEW?" Jason asked excitedly.

"Angel, pew, snot," Angelo read out loud. "Are you kidding me?"

"Don't judge me."

"Apologies sir, I'll make sure to watch my tongue," Angelo joked, and then it hit him. The words seemed to converge on their own, as if Angelo was witness to a vision. Seconds later, he formed ANGEL SPEW NOT. "That's it," Angelo said. "Blaze had his tongue cut out."

"And you can't spew words without a tongue."

Flopping on the bed, Angelo felt depleted. "The reference to Revelation 5 was meant to throw us off when it was an anagram that tied the murdered sex workers to their city of birth and the trophy the killer took from them."

Jason fell on the bed next to him. "You realize the killer left the calling card after the murders, not so we could figure them out."

The tone of Jason's voice was chilling. "Then why did he leave it?" Angelo asked.

Jason pulled him close. "He did it to amuse himself."

Angelo considered this. Still, the suspicion persisted with increasing intensity, as if it was inevitable that they should discover all these clues on the same day. Or were they being led to draw these conclusions as part of a bigger conspiracy?

Angelo lay on the bed in silence, ruminating on the bizarre, unfolding suspicions the anagrams presented him with but also about how the life he had known—as a man with a medical career in New York, and a romance that had hit a comfortable stride—felt incalculably distant now.

A short while later he awoke to the feel of Jason's entire body pressed against his back, his instep to Angelo's heel. The ding of a text had sounded like a gong. Angelo jerked upright, his heart pounding. He grabbed his phone off the nightstand, eyes blearily reading it. Wes wrote that he had just returned home with Rocky, who had been detained by the police all night. Jason stirred beside him, still asleep. It was searingly sad to think Rocky had spent long hours in jail just after discovering Fitz had died. He imagined how her thoughts must have veered between unshakeable disbelief and a profound longing for justice.

Angelo slipped into the bathroom and called Wes. "How is she?"

"Believe it or not, she's resting now."

According to Wes, Rocky had undergone hours of questioning about her relationship with Fitz. Detective Town wanted to know how long they had been together, whether she knew about Fitz's sordid past, and the nature of her work testing sex workers and people who used drugs for HIV and hepatitis C. All the while, Wes had spent that time trying to get in touch with KLM's legal team. Femi arrived at the police station just after 5am. Together, they waited until the radio station's lawyer finally arrived. Rocky was released just after 8am.

"I've never seen her like this," Wes said. "It's like she's a husk of her former self."

Forced to answer long hours of questions while simultaneously mourning the loss of her lover had been meant to torture and punish Rocky. She was made to be an example; one that broadcast Detective Town's depth and breadth of power. Shamelessly advertising to everyone in the LGBTQ+ community like a billboard in West Hollywood that he would show no mercy to anyone who stood in his way. All the more reason for Angelo to return to New York. *Too dangerous.* Once again, he reassured himself that he could do more for those boys at Savior of Saints from the safety of his Manhattan apartment than he could from a hotel in Los Angeles. Far away from Detective Town's all-seeing eye.

"I can't imagine what you've both been through," Angelo whispered. "You must be exhausted."

"I'm happy to be home," Wes said. "Did you sleep?"

He and Jason had barely slept and what little sleep Angelo got had left him lethargic and anxious. A tingling sensation ran like a current through his body. "Not much," Angelo said. His mouth was dry, his voice hardly audible as he whispered, "You would not believe the morning we had already. Essentially, I'm operating on fumes."

If he doesn't ask, I won't tell him. But Angelo knew Wes, no matter how tired he was, would want to hear all about it. "Do tell."

Angelo went on to describe their meetings with Dr. Scott Monroe at the veterans hospital and with Bobby Town at Guy Cleveland's house.

"Are you kidding?" Wes interrupted, but Angelo continued unfettered, as though if he didn't get it out in one breath, he might forget some critical detail. Wes listened, his breathing quickening as Angelo described each encounter with the toneless inflection of a secret government informant, leading up to the final revelation that left Wes speechless.

"No Angels Wept is an anagram!"

Silence stretched out between them until Wes emitted a slow exhale. "I don't fucking believe it," Wes slurred. "You figured all this out just from a game of Scrabble?" Angelo thought Wes's words came out like his mouth was perspiring.

He sounds tipsy.

Quickly, he glanced at his phone. It was nearly one in the afternoon. He and Jason had slept for less than an hour.

Waking from such a short, deep sleep, Angelo's brain felt scrambled.

Maybe Wes is tired or maybe he is drunk. Shit. The guy deserved a drink.

"You have to come over," Wes pleaded. "Rocky is gonna want to hear all about this. Jeez! Wow! An anagram. I'll order food. What time can you be here?"

"Wes," he began, though he cringed at the thought of telling him they were planning on returning to New York tonight. "There's something I need to tell you."

"Can it wait?" he replied. "Come over. Rocky is going to shit. An anagram. Who'd a thought?

"Listen to me—"

"I knew you'd break this case…"

"Please, Wes…let me finish."

"…Rocky will die—"

Angelo cut in. "Jason and I are returning to New York tonight!" He steeled himself for the cannonade of questions he anticipated would follow, but oddly there were none. Just a deafening silence. Angelo wondered if Wes had hung up or if he'd been so blindsided, it left him stymied like a slap.

Finally, Wes said, "Oh."

Angelo launched into a longwinded explanation that filled the bathroom like hot shower steam. A haze of self-recrimination for not putting his family first. Self-loathing for thinking only of himself. He even used the example of putting the oxygen mask on himself first before he could help others. "It's all for the best," Angelo prattled on hurriedly. "I have to think of my psychological safety."

"But the killer is still out there." Wes's words cut through the fog of Angelo's self-pity.

I know, Angelo mouthed. I'm a coward. But he said nothing, believing he could offer no explanation that would satisfy Wes. Angelo was too depleted from lack of sleep. He cracked open the bathroom door and stared at Jason, still in bed. He pulled the phone away from his ear to listen to Jason's breathing, a faint wheezing sound like a snoring dog.

"Angelo!"

"I'm sorry, Wes. My mind is made up."

"What about Fitz?"

A quick jab of guilt, Angelo replayed the last conversation he had with Fitz in her mobile van. The allegations she raised against Dr. Reverend James Jarrett and the Seven Spirits Church seemed outrageous then, and he bit angrily into his lip, thinking that a short while afterward, Fitz would be dead.

With a heavy heart, Angelo shoved the image of Fitz from his mind. This was the end. The No Angels Wept roller coaster had come to a disappointing stop. The safety bar lifted. This was where Angelo got off. However unsatisfying this ending felt, it was all for the best. Whatever wrench these past two weeks had thrown at him, he still had a career, and most of all, the love of a wonderful man sleeping just a few feet away.

"Well, I guess this is it," Wes said, sounding downtrodden and defeated.

"Don't say it like that," Angelo replied. "I'll stay in touch." But even as he heard the words, Angelo knew the truth. Sure, they would make the effort to exchange emails at first. Schedule the rare Zoom or FaceTime call. Send a random text to which the other would reply with a thumbs-up emoji. Eventually, all communication would dwindle.

"Can I ask you for one last favor?" Wes begged. "Come over and say good-bye in person. It would mean a lot to me, to Rocky."

Outside, Angelo heard the rain, like cheering outside the window. He gazed at Jason's chest, rising and falling with each breath, and was seized with the desire to climb back in bed, close his eyes, and allow his body to melt into Jason's. Acquiesce his mind to untangle all the thoughts that swirled untethered and disordered there.

"Besides," Wes added. "You left some clothes here. I even washed and folded them. Please, say you'll come by. Even if it's only for a few minutes."

Guilt stirred in his soul, fluttering like the wings of an injured bird. "All right," Angelo whispered, "but I need to shower first."

"Yay," Wes said. "See you soon."

Angelo hung up feeling like he had made the right decision, even though he hadn't run it by Jason first. Considering it was still early afternoon, Angelo planned to shower, dress, and Uber to Wes's house. That would leave plenty of time to reminisce and return before their 11pm flight. Angelo imagined the whole visit wouldn't take more than three hours door-to-door. Saying good-bye in person would be the final act to this unfinished script. A scene he'd have to improvise.

Chapter Twenty

Angelo emerged from the steamy bathroom to find Jason sitting at the desk in his boxer shorts, arranging Scrabble pieces into words: WAG. NAPLES. GET. SEEN.

Jason looked up, grinning. "Hey sexy."

"Why thank you kindly, sir," Angelo offered a dramatic twirl. "Hey, would you mind if I went over to Wes's house to say good-bye?"

"Not at all. I think it will be good for you to see them. It'll bring you closure."

Angelo chuckled. "When did you become fluent in psychobabble?"

"I watch OWN," Jason replied. Angelo walked over and kissed the top of his head. He began massaging Jason's shoulders. Peering down at the words he had assembled haphazardly into meaningless trios. Not surprising. They had figured out the first three anagrams based on past murders. What did they know about the killer's next victim? Nothing, which made solving that anagram next to impossible. "How's Rocky?"

"Wes said she had a rough night."

Jason winced. "I bet." He reached back and wrapped his arm around Angelo's damp leg, caressing it. "Do you want me to come with you?"

"Only if you really want to."

"I really don't," Jason said quickly.

"It's probably for the best." Angelo walked over to the dresser. He dropped his towel and pulled on a pair of briefs. "It'll give me an excuse to leave early. You know how much I hate drawn out good-byes. Besides, Wes sounded like he'd been drinking."

"Take the rental car."

"Me?" Angelo laughed. "Drive? In LA. No thank you."

"It's up to you," Jason uttered, though Angelo saw that he had resumed fiddling with the Scrabble tiles once again.

"Have you come up with anything new?"

Jason turned to meet Angelo's gaze. He appeared suddenly mesmerized as though he was viewing Angelo for the first time. "You are so damn sexy." The shower had revived Angelo. The hot water pulsating against his body felt good. Still, it was insane, Angelo mused, ridiculous for Jason to feel such lust given everything that had happened. "Come here."

"I have to finish getting dressed," Angelo protested.

"Come here first." Jason swiveled to face him. "You're so beautiful. You know that?" He stood up and wrapped his arms around Angelo's waist, sliding his hands inside Angelo's briefs and caressing his bare buttocks.

"Gentle," Angelo said. "That splint scratches."

He drew Jason's head toward his. They kissed hungrily. The taste of Jason's mouth sent a trill to his groin. Angelo allowed himself to feel the warmth of their embrace, the persistent beating of their hearts, and debated briefly if he should break free from the protective shield his boyfriend's body provided. Jason maneuvered him toward the bed. Angelo came up for air. "Wait. If I don't go now…"

Jason heaved a long sigh. "Okay. Go. Now. Before I attack you."

Pulling himself away, Angelo finished dressing. "I won't be gone long."

Descending in the elevator, Angelo experienced a buoyancy, a lightness. *What is this?* Relief. He was relieved, not disappointed, but relieved. Tonight, he'd return to his life unscathed. But as he opened the Uber app, typed in Wes's address, and waited for his ride, it occurred to him that neither Rocky nor Wes were as fortunate. It was important for him to remember this when they were reunited. *Do not appear overly excited to return home when you see them. They might come to believe none of this mattered. When that couldn't be further from the truth.*

He focused instead on the sun. The raindrops that clung to the palm tree leaves. Most of all, he thought about Jason. *You're so beautiful. You know that?* What more did Angelo need in his life?

A black Toyota arrived. Angelo got in the back seat and greeted the driver. Half-listening to the radio, he felt refreshed, fortunate, and yes, relieved to be going home. There was a new calm coming from within. A distinct diminishing of his underlying anxiety, which would have been completely expected, riding in the back of an Uber to say good-bye to new friends after having lost one in such a tragic, senseless way. The threat of a panic attack seemed like a distant horn, a ship sailing away from him.

In this moment, a clear-minded Angelo imagined the three amigos reunion in a world where everything had gone as they had hoped: Sipping wine in Wes's living room, congratulating themselves for having solved the No Angels Wept murders, and laughing until their ribs felt like they were tearing apart. A tearful group hug. Promises to stay in touch. *Call, email, or text. Anytime. Day or night.*

As the car turned onto Laurel Canyon Boulevard and drove to West Hollywood, Angelo prepared himself for the worst. This reunion was tainted by death, disappointment, and despair. Unlike anything he'd possibly imagined. Fitz's death had changed everything, bringing with it three unavoidable stages to consciously uncouple in this time of grief: anguish, anger, and accusations of abandonment. Like a tennis match, the three would volley from uncontrollable tears to harsh exchanges of words they'd later forget followed by finger pointing and finally, terse good-byes.

Sadly, Angelo knew this was inescapable.

The Uber climbed the winding hillside road overlooking the canyon. A faint shallow sun pulsated behind clouds like a failing heart. Angelo recalled the first time he'd been to Wes's house. How long ago that seemed now. Days, but it felt more like weeks, months even. The driver's eyes latched on to Angelo's in the rearview. "You gonna answer that?"

Angelo realized his phone was ringing. "Hey, I think I found something." The urgency and excitement in Jason's voice ruffled the swathe of calmness Angelo had enshrouded himself in.

He listened, his ear tight against the phone, willing himself to hear. "What is it?"

"Guy Cleveland told me he grew up in a town called, Gnaw Bone, Indiana."

"Gnaw Bone?" Angelo repeated. "Okay."

"The letters in No Angels Wept spell SPLEEN TO GNAW."

A sensation of disgust like bile rose in Angelo's throat, choking him. After several seconds, his voice wormed through. "You think Guy Cleveland is N.A.W.'s next victim?"

"Probably not," Jason reasoned. "Although he was a sex worker once. Why don't you text me Bobby Town's number. I'll call and check in on Guy."

Angelo heard rather than felt the escape of breath from his mouth. *This isn't over.*

"Angelo?" he heard Jason say. "Are you still there?"

The car pulled over. "Give me a minute. I just arrived at Wes's house."

"Don't be long."

Waiting for Wes to answer the door, Angelo saw Rocky's car parked in the driveway. The matte black Charger, dewy from the recent rainfall, appeared like a sweaty beast, resting after a kill. Angelo texted Bobby's cellphone number to Jason. After what seemed like a long time, the door opened.

Leaning in the doorway, squinting with bloodshot, pinwheel eyes, the handsome man was so wasted he could hardly stand. "Angie!" Wes laughed, a low register, wicked laugh. "Get over here." Unexpectedly, Wes pulled Angelo in for a bear hug, sobbing what sounded like, "It's awesome to see you." Smelling of booze, but also of something like talcum overlaid on the stench of sweaty armpits. Clearly, he was in a fragile emotional state.

The elongated hug felt as much intimate as it did final. Angelo had no idea how he would break free, or what he would say, but that was no longer his greatest concern. If Wes was this drunk, he couldn't imagine the state Rocky must be in. In the Uber, Angelo had played out what this reunion would be like, and now that it was upon him, he felt completely stricken with anxiety over the unknown.

"What a night," Wes said. "Come in."

On the front porch, gazing into the darkened house, Angelo stood unmoving as if paralyzed. Wes tugged at his arm like a little boy dragging his father to an ice cream truck. It had begun to drizzle again. A light mist patted against Angelo's cheeks.

Wes glanced up at the sky. "Raining again. Well, don't just stand there. Come in."

Moving into the living room, where twenty-four hours earlier Angelo listened to that now infamous recording, he got a better look at Wes. Face as sickly white as the underbelly of a fish. Sunken eyes. Bloated cheeks. Wearing just boxer shorts and a T-shirt smeared with God knows what. The scene in the living room, once familiar, seemed bizarrely alien to him now with the absence of Jason and Rocky.

Where is Rocky?

From somewhere ahead, muted singing and thumping rhythmic bass music played. "Wine?" Wes offered.

"Is it even twelve?" Angelo kidded.

"It's twelve somewhere." Wes could hardly stand, swaying to the point he had to grip the edge of the sofa. Drunk or drugged or both, he explained somewhat incoherently that he was not in great shape. "We could use a drink."

"Looks like someone already has."

Wes stumbled into the kitchen. "Don't judge me."

Poor guy, Angelo said to himself. The past twenty-four hours must have been tough on him, on Rocky.

Where is Rocky?

Listening to Wes prattle on in the kitchen, Angelo had no idea what he was saying. He moved into the spare bedroom. Inside, the music was louder, the thumping bass more emphatic. Angelo allowed himself to be led past the threshold as if lured by a siren's song, toward the N.A.W. evidence board. The faces of the three murdered gay men stared back at him.

Wes appeared in the doorway. "Here you go."

Angelo said nothing as he accepted the wine from Wes. He could have said anything, but this moment felt solemn, like a memorial.

"Cheers," Wes said. "To Fitz."

Angelo made eye contact as they clinked glasses, but quickly averted his gaze from Wes's wild, pained expression. Angelo didn't know what else to add. Fitz was dead. Wes had lost a friend. Rocky had lost her lover.

"Where is Rocky?" Angelo sipped.

Wes exhaled exhaustedly. "Sleeping, thank God."

"I was hoping to say good-bye?"

Wes looked away. "I don't think that's going to happen."

Angelo took another sip. Gazing still at the evidence board, he felt failure pooling around him. The act of entering the spare bedroom turned forensic, as if investigating an actual crime scene. The blinds were shut tight against the sun, but it wasn't sunny. He caught a whiff of something rancid. Dirtied wineglasses, plates, and cutlery scattered on the floor along with discarded clothes and wadded tissues. Angelo located the music and turned it down. The thudding beat ended. *Thank God.*

With a groan like someone orgasming, Wes collapsed on the bed. Tears stained his bloated, fish-belly cheeks. "Goddamn Town. He never liked Fitz. Not from the minute he laid eyes on her. I knew it. I knew he'd find a way to pin these murders on her." Bawling now like a child, Wes pounded his fists against the mattress. *Stage 1: Anguish.* "You know," Wes continued, "the police are going to announce they discovered evidence in Fitz's mobile van that proves she's the killer."

Angelo recalled Bobby had said exactly that earlier. "What kind of evidence?"

Wes's face was a mask of grief and misery. "The trophies… Town told Rocky they found the trophies stolen from the victims in Fitz's van."

"In Fitz's van," Angelo asked in clarification as the implications of this discovery formed a chrysalis in his mind. If the police had discovered tangible evidence, then that would prove without a doubt that Fitz was the No Angels Wept Killer.

"Town said they discovered a decomposed hand and a tongue in a cooler."

"Fitz's cooler?" Angelo recalled the evening he and Jason visited Fitz in her van. Jason stumbled over Fitz's cooler, spilling the contents on the floor. She explained, as they retrieved everything from the floor, that this was where she stored drugs the boys gave her when they wanted to quit using. "Jason and I looked inside that cooler. There weren't any body parts in there."

"Fucking Town. I hope he rots in hell." *Stage 2: Anger.*

The rain began pelting at the window. Angelo's exhaustion flooded him, and he thought longingly of his hotel room, craving the warmth of Jason's body with a heady, physical intensity. Another sip of wine. *Think! Say something to lighten the mood.* "I forgot how much work you put into this evidence board."

"Thanks." Wes sat up, stared into his wineglass, and sipped. "A lot of good it did Fitz." Wes's eyes, usually bright and cheerful, were sulky, dull, and opaque. Angelo sat next to him, drew his arm across Wes's shoulders and pulled him close. They sat quietly for several long seconds before Wes asked, "So, how did you do it? How did you figure out No Angels Wept is an anagram?"

"I told you. It occurred to me while we were at Guy Cleveland's house." Angelo scrutinized the evidence board. At the faces of the three victims.

"Tell me again how you ended up at Guy Cleveland's house?"

Angelo heard himself chuckle. "Bobby Town called me."

"So, Bobby Town calls you out of the blue, and you agreed to meet him at Guy Cleveland's house?"

"I didn't know he was at Guy Cleveland's house." Angelo squeezed his eyes. Of course, none of this made sense.

"Was that before or after you visited with Jarrett's former colleague?" Wes pressed him.

"We met with Guy and Bobby after we visited Dr. Scott Monroe."

Wes produced the wine bottle and refilled Angelo's glass. "How did you find this guy Monroe?"

Angelo took a sip, set the wineglass on the nightstand. "Wes, I really don't have the strength to go over it all again with you now. Jason and I got hardly any sleep. I haven't eaten. In fact, I shouldn't be drinking wine."

"Poor baby," Wes said. "Would you like me to fix you something to eat?"

Angelo took no offense. This was not Wes talking. This was the liquor, the exhaustion, the goddamn grief. He had come here to say good-bye, not rehash the long series of events that led up to this moment. Now was not the time for talk. Cooler, sober heads would prevail. He needed to get back to the hotel. "Listen," Angelo said. "I'm going to head out, but I don't want to leave like this. Are you going to be all right?"

Wes leveled his eyes at him. "That's right. I forgot. You're skipping town now that Detective Town has solved the No Angels Wept murders." *Stage 3: Accusations of abandonment.*

"I'm not skipping town." Angelo stood up. Momentarily, he felt light-headed.

"Then what would you call it?"

The reunion was veering into uncharted territories. All three stages were morphing into one. Angelo had to intervene, but he had to tread lightly. "I'm thinking of Jason. Most of all, I'm thinking of myself and my psychological safety."

"Psychological safety my ass," Wes spat. "You know what you are?"

Angelo braced himself for Wes's displaced anger, his grief, his pain.

"You're weak," Wes said with such venom Angelo winced. "You've been weak from the very beginning. Rocky said so, but I told her to give you a chance. As usual, she was right. She said the only reason you came to Los Angeles was to absolve yourself of any wrongdoing in Mia Garcia's death. That's why you agreed to an interview with the patron saint of the invisible LGBTQ+ community. You thought if you could portray yourself in a positive light, then you would be forgiven."

Angelo could not tear his eyes away from Wes's face, his teeth bared in a sneering, wet smile.

"Did you really think you could manipulate the narrative?" Wes asked. "The truth always comes out. Rocky wasn't going to annihilate you. She knew you would annihilate yourself given the chance. You have no idea how lucky you were that N.A.W. killed his third victim the same day you were going to be on *A Thorny Mess*."

A blizzard of despair and guilt buried Angelo. He tottered backward, stumbling over bottles and debris. Thoughts of Mia Garcia raced like tires spinning on ice. Not an inch of progress, no matter how fast the tires spun. He collapsed on the floor. Wes's accusation was chilling for its accuracy. He had come to Los Angeles as an act of contrition for his part in Mia Garcia's death. That was the source of his persistent panic. The source of his sickness that had been triggered by his obsession with the No Angels Wept murders.

"Take my hand." Wes hovered. "Let me help you up."

Angelo scrutinized his hand, then his face: Cold. Callused. Fish-belly white. *Who is this person?* He wanted to refuse Wes's help, but he knew he couldn't stand up on his own. *This is not the Wes I know. This is the booze talking. The booze and whatever else Wes took to deal with the loss of Fitz.*

Surprisingly, Wes hoisted Angelo to his feet like he was lifting a ragdoll. He maneuvered Angelo to the bed, though he didn't want to lie down. He wanted to leave. He wanted to go back to the hotel. To be with Jason. *I need Jason.*

"I should go." Angelo felt weary. He rebuked himself for having drank wine. *Clearer, sober heads would prevail*, but like Wes said, he had been weak. He felt appalled with himself and at his body for betraying him.

"Go?" Wes scoffed. "You're not going anywhere until you tell me what this Dr. Monroe had to say." Angelo felt impatient, but he sat on the bed. Resting his head against the headboard, waiting for the light-headedness to pass. Like a burglar realizing the homeowners had returned, Angelo plotted his escape. Wes grabbed Angelo's knee. It felt harsh, impatient. "Tell me."

Take three deep breaths. Serenity now.

Angelo couldn't look at him. He knew if he turned to look at Wes now, at his dilated pupils, his fish-belly cheeks oily with sweat, he'd have to ask him: *Why are you so drunk and high. Like, really high!*

"Angelo, what the fuck. Are you even listening to me?"

Astonished, Angelo had never heard Wes raise his voice.

Take three deep breaths. Serenity now.

Clearing his throat, he explained how he identified Monroe from the *LA Times* article, the online search that provided his office address, and the ruse about a mutual patient from the Parallax Institute that piqued Monroe's interest. Wes listened, the tension in his face diminishing like Angelo's explanation was having a sobering effect.

"He even gave us a demonstration of his suicide word association test."

This last part seemed not to interest Wes. "Don't you think it's strange that Bobby Town called you right after your meeting with Dr. Monroe?"

Lucky, maybe. Or maybe just strange.

"Can you give me Guy Cleveland's contact info?" Wes asked. "I'd like to speak with him. Maybe he's ready to talk on-air with Rocky."

"Where is Rocky?" Angelo sat upright. "I'd like to say good-bye before I leave."

"I told you," Wes said tersely. "She's sleeping."

With mounting unease, Angelo stood, wincing. His ankle flared. Glancing down to examine it he saw a tiny cut in his white sock, dappled with blood drops. Had he cut himself falling on the bedroom floor, rife with debris and bottles? "Well then, I'm going to head out. Tell her I said good-bye."

"Whatever." Wes rose from the bed too. "Don't leave without taking your clothes." He staggered toward the closet, gripping the doorknob, stabilizing himself as if he might fall. "You know." Wes turned back to leer at Angelo. "If Jason hadn't shown up, I might not have been able to control myself around you." At this, Wes laughed as if he'd never heard anything so funny.

Angelo felt his cheeks heat with blood. "I'd better get back to the hotel. You know how cops can be. Don't want to worry Jason."

These desperate words didn't seem to register with Wes. "I can't tell you how many times I thought about what it would be like…you and me."

Angelo had never seen Wes like this before. Laughing, teeth glistening, swaying in the grip of intoxication. *It was a mistake coming here. Take the clothes, say good-bye, and leave this house before this situation escalates beyond any hope of reconciliation.*

"What's the matter? You look scared." Wes stared pointedly at him. His expression shifted as he cocked his head to one side.

"Me?" Angelo chuckled. "Scared of what?"

Inwardly, Angelo *was* scared now, adding to the list of the myriad feelings he was experiencing. He had to get past Wes. He had to get out of this house. Outside, where it was raining. He wanted to feel the rain on his face. That would calm him.

"Good." Wes swung open the closet door and began scanning the interior for Angelo's clothes when suddenly, Angelo's vision telescoped. The stack of games on the top shelf: Monopoly. Parcheesi. Life. Scrabble.

Scrabble!

Falling into a dark chasm, a sensation something around him was collapsing on him like an avalanche or an explosion, the realization that he had been buried alive. In the darkened room, the rain pattering on the window, he observed Wes's physical reaction. Stiff, frozen, as if he, too, had seen Scrabble and made the same connection. "I know what you're thinking. Wes owns Scrabble too."

"I wasn't thinking that." In Wes's spare room, trapped like a fly beating against a shut window, Angelo was unable to bluff.

Wes pulled Scrabble from the stack of games and set it down on the bed like a child opening a birthday gift. "Hey, why don't you show me how you figured out the anagrams."

This seemed unexpectedly painful as a stubbed toe. "I really need to get back to the hotel. Jason will worry."

"Really?" Wes laughed sarcastically. "Is he blowing up your phone? I don't think so." Wes appeared excited as he opened the box and dumped the tiles on the bed.

Angelo smiled bleakly. "I'm sorry, but I don't have time for this right now."

Wes ran his hand through his hair and smiled an unsettling smile. "Okay, I understand." And now, Wes appeared hurt, crestfallen.

"I'm sorry, Wes."

"You know," Wes said, "I'm sorry you bothered to come here, I mean that with all sincerity. Your being here, your standing in my house, reminds me that we're no closer to solving this mystery now than we were last week."

Angelo observed Wes, sitting on the floor, flipping Scabble tiles on the bed to spell, NO ANGELS WEPT.

"You know," Wes said, sounding defeated. "I can't help but feel somewhat responsible for Fitz's death."

Angelo was surprised by this pronouncement. Certainly it wasn't true. On many levels he understood his pain, his grief, and his frustration. Angelo could even tolerate the displaced anger, but he knew by staying and wading through the mire of this mucky conversation, there was no telling where it would lead. At the same time, Angelo pitied him. It couldn't end like this, not with Wes drunk and playing with Scrabble tiles with the evidence board right behind him. There was still so much unanswered, but he thought back to his meetings with Dr. Monroe and Bobby Town. Had he found all the answers he needed and was finished—for now?

"Fitz's death was not your fault."

Wes stood up to face the evidence board. "Such senseless murders. Fitz didn't deserve to be the scapegoat."

Angelo frowned, recalling his own frustration with Town's neatly buttoned-up ending to the No Angels Wept murders and the media's alacrity to accept it. It was as if all of Los Angeles had been waiting for a plausible ending, and now they had it.

"Jesus Christ," Wes shouted. "I fucking can't believe Fitz is dead!"

This eruption of anger came on so fast. Angelo toyed with whether or not to embrace Wes, thank him for all that he had done for him, and wish him the best. Good-bye. Quick peck on the cheek as he hurried out the front door. *Give my love to Rocky.*

But Wes continued to incoherently babble about Fitz. Angelo was momentarily distracted by the Scrabble lid, at the letters that spelled NO ANGELS WEPT, then at the back of Wes's head as his fingers gripped a clump of sun-kissed hair, still babbling, now sobbing again. Angelo's eyes flitted one last time to the photos of the three dead men: Keith Knight, Gabriel Menendez, and Trevon "Blaze" Bolden. He shook his head in slow emphasis of this tragedy. *There's nothing more I can do. It's time for me to go.* Turning to walk away, a little light-headed, a little lost, ready to leave this house for the last time, his eyes traveled across the room and landed on Wes's university diploma.

MICHIGAN STATE UNIVERSITY
has conferred upon
Weston Plagen

It was overwhelming. The rueful clarity, the audacity, and the fact that it had been staring him in the face the entire time. What made him assume Wes's name was Wesley when in fact it had been Weston all along? He had made that assumption on his own. Angelo recalled the first time Wes emailed him. He had looked him up on LinkedIn. Had he noticed then? Wes's full name was Weston Plagen, not Wesley Plagen. Of course, he wouldn't have cared either way. Had he known the significance then, he would have been a genius or a psychic because standing in Wes's spare bedroom he saw as if illuminated like neon that the letters in Weston Plagen's name when rearranged spelled: NO ANGELS WEPT.

A roar of blood rushed to his ears, ringing as if a blast had been detonated. In a parallel world contiguous with this one, separated by the sheerest membrane, a courageous Angelo would overcome Wes. Take him by surprise. Punch and beat and push him to the ground. But no. He was entranced in a kind of spell the real-world Angelo didn't know how to break.

All Angelo could think was that he had misjudged Wes's kindness, his affable demeanor, all the personality traits that would have enabled him access to those young men, and now, he had to make a choice. He could either play along or he could run for his life. But Angelo's feet were welded to the floor. He experienced numbness ascending his legs. His stiff body was uncooperative, not wanting to fight back or flee. The walls of the small room began to close in. Hot, damp, his mouth felt scorched, his tongue swollen. His entire body began to shrink in terror. Every muscle clenched.

Wes's blabbering caused him to retch. Wes attempted to clear his throat, but he had aspirated some vomit. *He's choking. Make your move now.*

Fighting a wave of nausea—it had to be the stifling room or the wine or the overwhelming anxiety—Angelo looked down at the nightstand. *The wine!*

And then it struck him as quick and sharp as a snake bite; Wes had spiked his wine. Angelo wasn't simply experiencing a panic attack. Wes had drugged him! *Wes is trying to kill me. That's why he lured me here.*

As Wes coughed and gagged, Angelo understood he was hopelessly trapped. Soon, whatever it was Wes had put in his wine would take effect since Angelo had downed nearly half the glass. What was happening to him and all around him was occurring beyond his volition. A nightmare from which he could not wake. Teetering now, Angelo's body felt leaden, numb, and small. Shrinking like Alice after she consumed the 'Drink Me' potion, Angelo's vision tunneled.

Glaring at Angelo, Wes's fish-belly white cheeks had turned scarlet. He bent forward heaving, retching, spitting. Angelo, in an eyes-opened trance, had no idea why he hadn't seized this moment, fled from Wes's house, or locked himself inside the bathroom to call for help. Why was he simply standing there?

Suddenly, there was a rustling noise coming from the other room.

The unexpected distraction shook Angelo. Abruptly, the spell had been broken. Sober and gulping air, his chest tightness eased. In that instant, he knew what he had to do. He hurled himself toward Wes, pushing hard against his chest. Antagonized by the unexpected strike, Wes, still choking, gagging, raised his hands to his neck. Angelo pushed past him and bolted out of the room. Running for the door, he crashed into a wrought iron magazine rack. Stumbling over it, heart pounding, he stared at the front door, willing it not to be locked. Surely, Wes was right behind him.

"Angelo!"

Hurling himself against the door, Angelo nearly tumbled down the steps.

"Jesus Christ!" a voice shouted behind him. "What's going on?"

Angelo wasted no time. Sun streaked through the dark clouds as he ran down the walkway to the curb. He scrambled into the street, running as fast as his legs would take him. Unaware if Wes or anyone else was behind him. He kept running and never looked back.

CHAPTER TWENTY-ONE

It was with the acute sense that he had narrowly escaped death Angelo found himself hiding behind a row of shrubs, panting, sweating, his heart galloping inside his chest. Angelo stabbed his index finger toward the back of his mouth, gagging, heaving until he made himself vomit. His eyes pooled with thick, burning tears. The fresh sting of snot in his nostrils smelled like chlorine. He sat on the ground, head against the bushes, sighing with relief, which turned quickly into terror.

He dialed Jason's number, but there was no signal. He had to think, ignoring the unease that puddled around him, setting off a cascade of dry heaves he could not control. *Three deep breaths. Serenity now.* The rain had let up, the sun sitting overhead, flooding him with bright rays. Still the air was wet. If only it were dark. He needed to be in the shadows.

Wes is the No Angels Wept Killer?

His mind spun, attempting to piece together everything he had learned in the past twenty-four hours. Their N.A.W. investigation had taken a sharp left with the introduction of Reverend James Jarrett and the Seven Spirits Church. Had it been Wes's plan all along? A ruse to throw him off? What were the chances Wes knew Mabel Knight was a member of the Seven Spirits Church? She had been so forthcoming about her religious beliefs every time Angelo had spoken with her.

Unfortunately, Fitz had paid the ultimate price. Angelo wondered if Fitz had been collateral damage…or had Wes planted the evidence in her truck himself? Either way, the homophobic Town had nabbed his killer and closed the case while Wes escaped scrutiny. That was, until now. After speaking with Bobby, Angelo had convinced himself the No Angels Wept Killer was Keith Knight's mystery man, but he had been wrong. It had been Wes all along.

Suddenly Angelo was aware of a dull thrum. It was the rumbling of a car engine, growing louder. Rocky's matte black Dodge Charger. He had awakened the beast. The car paused just on the other side of the row of shrubs. Angelo shook his head, confused. He had no idea what to do. He had no idea where to go.

When the car rambled on, Angelo heaved a thankful breath. Once it became quiet, Angelo stood up, dusting the dirt off his jeans. He rubbed ruefully at his ankle, where the blood had dried it had now become itchy. The car had driven a safe distance away, still moving slowly as if taking in every inch in search of its prey.

He took out his phone and walked until a second bar illuminated. Again, he dialed Jason's number. This time it went straight to voicemail. It wasn't like Jason not to answer his phone. *Maybe he's in the shower? Maybe he fell asleep? Maybe he silenced the ringer?*

He proceeded to walk, not sure where he was going, maintaining a keen eye open for the Charger. He tried Jason again. And again, it went straight to voicemail. The pull of dread tightened around his throat, suffocating him. *Where could Jason be?*

Jason had asked for Bobby Town's number. He wanted to check on Guy after assembling the letters from NO ANGELS WEPT into SPLEEN TO GNAW. Guy had told Jason he was from a small town in Indiana called Gnaw Bone. That much Angelo remembered, but this was before Angelo figured out Wes was behind the murders.

"This is ridiculous!" he said out loud.

If Wes was the No Angels Wept Killer that would mean Angelo had been his pawn all along. Luring him to

Los Angeles by enticing him with the prospect of telling his story about Mia Garcia's murder, in his own words.

That's the story I want you to tell.

Wes had assured him he wasn't interested in the salacious version the media had jumped on. The morbid tale of the ambitious woman buried alive in the concrete coffin. But why had Wes chosen Angelo?

You're weak. You've been weak from the very beginning.

Wes's harrowing accusations a short while earlier rang true now. It made sense. Wes had chosen him for all the same reasons Demetre had. Except Wes knew that Angelo's involvement in Mia Garcia's death had left him struggling with panic attacks, crushing guilt, and a desperate yearning for redemption. He saw it clearly now, just as Wes had all those weeks ago. To think Wes had wormed his way into Angelo's mind, gaining his trust on those long calls where Angelo bared his soul. What a fool he had been, believing Wes was his friend when all along he was using him just like Demetre had used him. Sizing him up, casting him as the pathetic, weak-minded doctor who believed if he solved the No Angels Wept murders he would be free from his residual guilt. It hadn't been a coincidence that the third murder coincided with Angelo's arrival in Los Angeles. It had been Wes's plan from the start. The parallels that existed between Wes and Demetre, between Fitz and Mia, seemed so obvious now.

Fuck!

Angelo called Jason's number again, his shoulders pulling up to his ears, his throat getting tight, holding his breath, and not realizing it until the third ring when the call went to voicemail and he was suddenly gasping. "Jason, it's me. Where are you? Call me right away. Wes is the No Angels Wept Killer."

Up ahead, Rocky's black Charger approached, the engine revving, grunting. The tailpipe spitting, popping. A menacing sight that made Angelo freeze. He locked eyes with the driver. His blood ran cold. Wes wasn't behind the wheel. Rocky was! Suddenly, the car accelerated. Angelo turned and ran, a limping trot, like someone playing hop-scotch. He fled across the street, distraught, terrorized, his ankle throbbing, nearly colliding with the Charger as he ran toward Wes's house. He knew there was only one way to escape. He cut to the right of the house and descended the canyon trail. But it was steep. He broke into a gallop, clomping and bucking like a bronco. His feet kicked up dirt, forming a dusty cloud around him. Halfway down the trail, he turned around and saw them at the top of the hill, Wes and Rocky, watching him.

"Angelo, stop!"

His head was whirling from all the revelations. His eyes were burning from the all the dust; Angelo choked on it. Though he tried to slow down, digging his heels into the dirt threw off his center of gravity. Angelo lost control and toppled forward, somersaulting once, twice, before colliding with a tree. Flat on his back, he lay there for several seconds before taking stock. No broken bones, no dislocated limbs, alert, awake and oriented times three. Except for his ankle, which he had lacerated in Wes's house and was now swollen and tender, everything else seemed fine.

Standing up, he began to hobble down the path. He dialed Jason's number. Again, it went directly to voicemail. Next, he called Bobby Town. "Have you heard from Jason?"

"Your Jason?" Bobby replied. "No. Why? Is everything all right?"

Angelo's heart was pounding. "Listen, if Jason calls, please tell him to call me right away."

"Where are you?"

"I'm heading back to the hotel," he explained. "I went to say good-bye to Wes and Rocky." He paused here to consider whether he should confide in Bobby, ask him for help, but decided against it. "Anyway, I gotta go. Are you still at Guy's house?"

"No, I left."

"Bobby, you need to do me a favor. Call Guy. See if Jason is there. He might have gone back to check on him."

A long pause followed. A muffled exchange of words. "Why would Jason need to check on Guy?"

"I can't explain now. Please, please call Guy or text me his number!" He paused, listening, but oddly, Bobby had hung up or they had gotten disconnected. Angelo couldn't be sure which.

He shoved the phone in his back pocket and continued down the trail. His ankle was throbbing, but after limping a few yards, he had to slow down. Catch his breath. His mind swerved from guilty consternation to frenzied disbelief. He trudged forward, wondering now as the dust literally settled around him, what role Rocky played in all this. She had been in Wes's house the entire time. *Did Rocky help Wes kill those three young men?* He had always held an underlying suspicion toward her, but he had never imagined that she was actually involved in murders.

Despite this outrageous revelation, something was wrong. He felt a gnawing agitation in his gut, some deep pulsation breaking through like an aneurysm ready to burst. Angelo forced himself to keep moving despite the ankle pain. And then, staring off to the left, he saw cars. Pulling out his cellphone again, thank God he had reception, Angelo contacted an Uber driver. Standing at the corner of Laurel Canyon Boulevard and Dehougne Street, he waited for his ride. When the car arrived a short while later, Angelo fell into the back seat. Only when the car pulled onto the freeway did Angelo realize he was holding his breath.

The ding of his cellphone rattled him.

It was a text from Wes:

I fucked up. Drank 2 much. Please forgive me! Call me. PLZ!

Instead of responding, Angelo dialed Jason's number. Again, it went straight to voicemail. *Jason must have gone to the gym or for a walk or fallen asleep.* He needed to believe this so that the panic wouldn't consume him.

Twenty minutes later, his worst fear was realized once he opened their hotel room door. No one was there. He called out for Jason, ducking into the bathroom. *Calm down. No good will come from panicking.* Angelo sat on the bed. Head between his knees, gulping air. *Three deep breaths. Serenity now.* And then came the horrifying realization that Wes and Rocky might be on their way to his hotel at this very minute. He stood up and paced. *Where could Jason be?* Had he stumbled upon a clue they had somehow overlooked?

And there it was. The Scrabble tiles on the desk told him everything he needed to know.

SOS

In the center of the Scrabble board, sat the wooden heart Jason had secreted inside Angelo's luggage. The scroll inside the heart's hole still had the line from Angelo's favorite poem by E. E. Cummings. On the back, Jason had written a message:

I'm doing this for our family.

Angelo dropped his face in his hands. *Jason, why?*

Once Angelo had left the hotel, Jason seized the opportunity to investigate Savior of Saints before returning to New York. Of course he had. Jason had too much pride to shrink away from a fight. Angelo had meant what he'd said to Bobby and Guy, that Jarrett had crossed a line having gone after Jason in New York, and that now it was personal. Little did he realize at the time that Jason was considering a visit to Savior of Saints on his own. Saying good-bye to Wes and Rocky gave Jason the perfect opportunity.

Wiping away his tears, Angelo fought the urge to crumble. There was no time for that. Jason needed him. He knew this with a degree of certainty he had never experienced before. He knew this to be a fact more than he had ever believed anything in his entire life.

Staring at the letter O, Angelo imagined he was gazing down the throat of a beast. Jagged teeth, fetid breath, which gave way not to a simple darkness, but something far more threatening he had to confront. The final tunnel he had to explore.

◆◆◆

The sign for Savior of Saints marked the entrance to a long driveway that, past its initial transverse of trees, opened onto a large clearing. There, the monotone structure with three spires that reached toward the heavens barely pierced the massing storm clouds in the afternoon sky.

"Crazy weather we're having," the Uber driver said. "It never rains in California."

"Just my luck."

Angelo got out by the front entrance. As he climbed the stairs to the stained glass and bleached-wood double doors, he willed his features to relax. He had tried Jason's phone twice during the car ride, but as expected, it went straight to voicemail each time. Being direct was his plan. Ask to speak with Dr. Reverend James Jarrett—a bold and somewhat ridiculous plan—was the only one he could come up with in the car.

Just as he reached the landing, the door swung open. A slender and ebullient Black man in his early sixties greeted him. "Welcome," he gushed. "I'm Gates."

"Nice to meet you," Angelo replied. "I hope you don't mind me dropping by without an appointment. I've heard so much about Savior of Saints. I had to come visit before I returned to New York." Then, turning to glance at the grounds, "It's so beautiful." In the distance, Angelo spotted Jason's rental car. As he considered this, he felt Gates's hand constrict imperceptibly around his.

"Reverend Jarrett had a hand in the design. He's a remarkably talented man, but I gather you're aware of his reputation?" Gates said merrily, as if no one who'd actually met Jarrett would disagree.

"He certainly has an impressive record," Angelo said. "Would it be possible to meet him?"

"Thought I'd give you a tour first," Gates suggested. "Then we can see if the reverend is available."

Angelo glanced back one last time, convincing himself that was Jason's rental car, though the dark clouds overhead cast just enough doubt. He couldn't be sure.

Gates led Angelo into the stony, minimalist entrance that opened into a soaring vast space with triangular windows reaching all the way to the pointed ceiling. The scent of incense was overpowering. Beyond the entrance, Gates led Angelo down a long corridor of polished granite walls, which might have seemed claustrophobic if not for the lanterns hanging overhead, bathing the white marble floor in yellow light. The hallway opened to an outdoor cobblestone, circular courtyard. Mature landscaping and manicured lawns provided areas for private prayer or meditation.

The courtyard appeared to be the central hub; a cross of four separate pathways. Just beyond the courtyard they walked straight into a great room with cathedral ceilings. A gold starburst insignia on the back wall of the red-carpeted altar had a central white circle bearing overlapping letters, SOS.

"This is the chapel, of course," Gates whispered humbly.

"Chapel?" Angelo mocked. "More like St. Patrick's Cathedral."

Gates laughed out loud. An unbridled laugh that echoed like the sound of wild-fluttering wings of a flock rising in panic above them, desperate to escape. Almost immediately, he clamped his hand over his mouth. "The complex," Gates explained, "had been designed initially as a research institute. Later, it was renovated to accommodate the reverend's weekend sermons, and, of course, house homeless youth."

They returned to the courtyard where, on the right, Gates gestured to a long path that led to a one-story building with large windows. Though Gates didn't venture to visit this area, Angelo clearly saw the assortment of young men milling about, wearing matching sweatpants and T-shirts—all bearing the SOS logo—and showing no interest in them. The interior appeared divided into an entertainment section on one side with several comfy sofas, and on the other side was an area that appeared to be a cafeteria with a series of foldout tables.

Tree-filtered light dappled Angelo's cheeks as he gazed out the window. He glimpsed a view of the mountains just beyond the building. *This had to be where Jarrett led the study patients through the Frame exercise.* It was just as the LA reporter described.

"Is this more than you expected?" Gates asked. His hands clasped behind his back like he was browsing for antiques.

How could Angelo explain he hoped to find a stuffy dormitory crammed with metal bunkbeds. Boys chained to the headboards. Instead, he said, "It's a lot to take in."

"You know, Dr. Perrotta," Gates said philosophically, "each boy is treated with the utmost care."

Angelo's mouth gaped. "How did you know my…?"

"We anticipated your arrival, of course," Gates cut in. "You'll want answers. I'm sure." Gates paused, tilting his chin upward as if he caught a whiff of something pleasant, "Why else would you be here?"

"Does that make you the welcome wagon?" Angelo asked, now hearing the faint sound of choral music.

Gates shot him an odd look. "All are welcome here."

Angelo shouldn't have been surprised they had been expecting him. Jason's rental car was parked outside. They had to know it would only be a matter of time before Angelo came looking for him.

Where is Jason? Angelo's mind raced. His heart pounding as he followed Gates down the final path where the marble floor gave way to a red, plush carpet. "Savior of Saints incorporates a number of disciplines to realize a common objective for these homeless youth," Gates continued unprompted. "You would be very mistaken if you thought of us solely as a homeless shelter. What we provide here is a luxury these boys would not be afforded, out there, in the cold, harsh world."

Angelo snorted. "I didn't know forced conversion therapy was a luxury."

Gates paused, shaking his head. "I'm surprised to hear you say that. You're a man of science, and a Catholic."

"Former Catholic."

"I stand corrected," Gates muttered. "Still, isn't there a small part of you that misses the church?"

"Miss what?" Angelo quipped. "The guilt? The shame?"

They continued in silence until Gates paused outside a large door. "Here we are." Inside, they were met by a prim woman with silver hair pulled back into a tight chignon. She rose from behind her small desk to greet them. "This is Claire." Gates motioned to the etiolate woman who extended her hand for Angelo to shake. "Claire, may I introduce Dr. Perrotta."

Claire's aqua eyes flared with the urgency of someone meeting a dignitary. "Spirits on high."

"Is the reverend available?" Gates asked.

"I believe so." Claire giggled as though they had rehearsed this exchange. "So, Dr. Perrotta, what do you think of Savior of Saints?"

Angelo, tired of all this irrelevant conviviality, was anxious to move on. "As I was telling Gates, it's a lot to take in."

Claire stared at him thoughtfully, her face wearing an expression of strained enthusiasm. Angelo assumed his answer wasn't what she hoped to hear.

"Welcome, Dr. Perrotta." The booming voice caught Angelo's immediate attention. Tall, bespectacled, with a white goatee and no hair stood a pleasant appearing man. Goose bumps crept up Angelo's legs, he recognized Jarrett from his television commercial. Appearing more like a professor than a reverend, Jarrett wore creased tan slacks, an oxford shirt, a blue blazer, and tasseled loafers. "Come in."

Angelo approached him with his hand extended. Jarrett's grip felt tentative. Unexpected since Jarrett was a towering presence. Big shoulders, thick neck, his appearance an amalgam of a former varsity quarterback and chess club president.

"Have a seat." Jarrett gestured to a leather wingback chair situated in front of an enormous mahogany desk. The office was absurdly large. A sufficient size for a New York studio apartment. Dark, wood-paneled walls. Floor-to-ceiling bookcases. A Persian rug stretched toward a seating area on the far side of the room. By the window stood a telescope made of brass and wood. "Claire, please fetch us some coffee and whatever you call those sweet things."

"Petit fours," Claire said. "Cream and sugar, Dr. Perrotta?"

"Black, please."

Jarrett closed the door and stared at Angelo for several awkward moments. Angelo's blood ran cold. He broke his gaze and sat down at the desk that was so polished it glared.

Nestled in the wingback chair, Angelo found himself drawn again to the telescope, which seemed out of place among the bookcases, the landscape paintings, and the Persian rug. "You seem fascinated with it," Jarrett said.

Angelo's cellphone dinged. It was another text from Wes:

At ur hotel. Where R U? Plz call me!

He shoved his phone back in his pocket. "I'm sorry. What were you saying?"

"My telescope," Jarrett continued. "You seem fascinated by it."

Of course, Angelo knew Jarrett was toying with him. He suspected Jason must have sat in this chair a short while ago, having this same insipid conversation. Jason, being Jason, of course would have cut to the chase, confronted Jarrett with what he knew. Angelo wondered if Jason was being detained in some office nearby, waiting for him to arrive so that Jarrett could have Town haul them off together. Though Angelo was becoming antsy, he knew Jarrett was a narcissist, and like most narcissists, knew Jarrett would be amenable to talking about himself. "Are you a star gazer?"

"Sometimes when I'm working on a sermon, I take a break and view the constellations. It helps provide me with clarity if I'm stuck."

Angelo stood up and walked toward the telescope. He didn't touch it though he was tempted to have a look. "Did it provide you with clarity after the Parallax Institute scandal?"

Jarrett offered an unwavering stare. It lasted several long seconds before he stood up. "My grandfather, Llewyn Jarrett, was a mathematician and astronomer. He gifted me that telescope and showed me how to calculate the moon's distance from the Earth."

Angelo goggled his eyes. "Fascinating."

"You could say I owe a great deal of my career to him." Jarrett walked over and stood next to the telescope like he was posing for a portrait. "It's quite brilliant really." Angelo noticed the way he lit up and came to life, like someone had dropped a quarter in an old jukebox. "The lunar parallax is the shift caused by viewing the same object from two different vantage points. Try this exercise with me."

Angelo was reluctant. He itched to ask about Jason. "Don't go to any trouble."

"I insist." Jarrett picked up a gold letter opener from his desk and held it up. "Now, stare at this and close your right eye." Angelo huffed but complied. "Now alternate by blinking your left eye, then your right, your left eye again and then your right." Angelo blinked back and forth. "See the subtle changes in the letter opener's position in my hand?"

"Your grandfather was a genius," he replied indignantly.

Jarrett laughed. "Hipparchus gets all the credit. He measured the moon's distance in the second century BC. I was so impressed with the implications of parallax that I used it in my research. By looking at disease from two different vantage points, I theorized ways to treat how the brain processes memories stored in the amygdala. I suppose you could say the amygdala is my moon."

Alas, the point emerges. Listening to Jarrett, Angelo recalled those lofty intellectual conversations among senior attendings during his residency. He always found the cadence of their arguments to be insidiously enjoyable. Trouble here was Jarrett was defending his rationale for experimenting on nonconsenting, young gay men. "You know homosexuality isn't a disease," Angelo said, barely hiding his contempt. "I hardly think masquerading a, quote, *cure* for homosexuality based on your right-wing religious ideology, not science, isn't something to be proud of. Your research career is littered with failure, sir."

Claire entered the room, silencing them. She held a silver tray with a blue and green bone china tea set and four white and yellow petit fours arranged on a plate. When she met Jarrett's gaze, her hands began to tremble. He walked over and took the tray from her. "Thank you, Claire."

"Spirits on high." She offered a quick nod and exited the room.

Jarrett picked up a petit four and plopped it wholly in his mouth. "Delicious," he said, chewing. "You should try one."

"No, thank you," Angelo said, an unwise bitter edge to his voice.

Jarrett's jovial expression, the one he had maintained until now, turned grim. "Every advance in modern science has been met with failure and skepticism," Jarrett went on, swept up once again in his own nostalgia. "Throughout my career I have dedicated decades to mapping the neural circuitry responsible for memories. Although my methods with regard to post-traumatic stress disorder were unsuccessful, those men very well may have killed themselves despite my interventions. I don't view them as a failure necessarily. Innovative drug development and bold behavioral frameworks take years to perfect. Trial and error. Failure is inevitable, but I believe we are now on the brink of a major medical success."

"A major medical success!" Angelo stared with incredulity. "Stop referring to conversion therapy as a medical treatment. What you're doing is unethical! What you did to those veterans was inhumane, and after those tragic murders and suicides, you would have thought that would have ended your career. But just the opposite. You started a ministry and began a covert operation, imprisoning vulnerable gay boys so you could experiment on them."

Jarrett appeared unfettered. "You've been given a tour." He reached for a second pastry and dropped it in his mouth. "Where are these prisoners?"

Angelo managed a sarcastic grunt. "I'm not stupid. Of course you had your manservant, Gates, show me around to prove just that but I know they're here. I can feel it."

Jarrett's gracious demeanor slipped away as completely as if a rag had wiped it from his face. He leaned forward, solemn. "The far left would have you believe that people are born a certain way, but upon closer examination, gay men suffer far more than the rest of us. Depression, anxiety, post-traumatic stress disorder, substance and alcohol abuse, HIV"—Jarrett winced with distaste—"and suicide. The list goes on and on. Wouldn't you rather spend your time working with leaders to help fix this problem?"

"Being gay is not a problem for you to fix," Angelo shouted. "If you and whomever you represent only left us alone, we wouldn't feel so marginalized and stigmatized. It's people like you who make people like me suffer. You must give up this obsessive compulsion to fix gay people and turn them into something they're not."

And then it hit Angelo with such stunning clarity he could hardly speak. *Fixed!* That was the word Bobby Town had used to describe Keith Knight's mystery man. The boy who was ousted from his grandparents' house because he hadn't *fixed* his problem. The boy who grew up to become a man with a high-profile career. The same one whose life would be ruined if their affair became public.

"We are part of a necessary result," Jarrett explained with chilling equanimity. "We are a business, naturally, but the soul of our endeavor is to help preserve the purity of our society." Jarrett reached for the cup, sipping tea, pinky up, appearing smug as if he has said enough to make his case, but then reconsidered, adding, "I care about my research. I always have. In fact, I have put my work above anything else. I don't expect adulation, or even recognition. I only ask to be left alone to do what I have been called to do. Won't you let me tell you more about the science before you judge us?"

Angelo swallowed hard to suppress the urge to snap. It was a dangerous mistake coming here. Seeing the same object from two different vantage points had emboldened Jarrett's radical Christian agenda to snuff out homosexuality because LGBTQ+ people conflicted with his religious beliefs. A parallax of epic proportions laid bare the enormous chasm that existed between people like Jarrett and the LGBTQ+ community.

Despite the undeniable weirdness of Savior of Saints, despite its reprehensible ideology, there seemed nothing overtly wrong with what Angelo had witnessed. He had not found a shard of evidence linking these cavernous, echoey halls to imprisoned, homeless gay youth or outrageous psychiatric experimentation. Only a sad, vindictive self-hating homosexual who resorted to the lowest form of depravity to fix the problem in others he was unable to fix in himself.

Yet, something still nagged at Angelo. *Where is Jason?* He had to break free to search for him alone. Nothing else mattered, not even Wes Plagen.

"I apologize for my outburst." Angelo went to sit down. "I would like to learn more about your work."

Jarrett smiled at him. "Good."

Angelo reached for the teacup. "The petit fours look delicious."

"Try one," Jarrett said. "They're lemon."

Angelo's hand hovered over the plate. "Dr. Jarrett, may I use the restroom to wash my hands?"

Jarrett studied him. "Yes, I'll show you where it is." The telephone rang. The blinking red light made Jarrett frown. "Huh"—he seemed disturbed by it—"I think this may be important."

"I'll wait outside so you can answer it in private."

"Thank you," Jarrett said, edging toward the phone. "Claire will show you to the restroom. We can discuss the work we're doing here once you return." Just as Angelo closed the door behind him, Jarrett picked up immediately. His carefully modulated tone turned annoyed. "What is it, Gates?"

To his surprise, Claire was not at her desk. He slipped quietly out of the office. In the carpeted hallway, Angelo decided not to retrace his steps. Instead, he ventured into areas Gates had not shown him. The corridor beyond Jarrett's office extended for several yards, flanked with doors on either side. Angelo forced himself to keep going, his footsteps a metronome for his breathing. A left. Then a right. He tried mentally to grab hold of the number of turns he had taken, but his mounting fear prevented him from retaining anything.

What the hell am I looking for exactly? He went on and on. By now, he was entirely disoriented, having lost track of the number of rights and lefts he had taken. *Where am I going?* But he refused to stop. He had to find Jason.

The carpet gave way to concrete. The corridor extending in front of him narrowed. It constricted to less than four feet wide. A darkened hallway with no windows or doors. Up ahead, he was able to discern a red glow. A metal door appeared in the distance. Overhead, a red light glared, reflecting the metal's sheen.

After a deep breath, he yanked the lever. It was unlocked. Inside, the room was dark. He ran his hand along the wall until he found a switch. The fluorescent light blinked on, revealing a small stockroom. His eyes scanned the interior. Rows of metal shelves stacked with binders labeled with six-digit identifiers. He stepped inside the room. And then, off to his left, he saw them. Pill bottles labeled PLX.

Angelo took out his cellphone and snapped a few photos. He reached for one of the binders. Inside, he found pages of transcribed interviews with young men, medical summaries of their psychological interventions, and surveys reporting adverse events related to study drug PLX. He noticed the word "disrupter" scrawled across the faces of a several boys. *Disrupter of what?* At any rate, this was far worse than he had ever imagined. Dr. Reverend James Jarrett, despite being investigated, continued his research but had moved on from veterans to homeless gay men. What better way to avoid the scrutiny of the FDA than to operate under the veil of religion.

Mumbled voices sent a spider of panic crawling up Angelo's back. He looked to his left and then his right. His body frozen in horror as the voices grew nearer. Angelo closed the door and leaned against it, breathless. He couldn't go back the way he had come. This room was located at the end of a hall.

He was trapped!

Chapter Twenty-Two

Angelo struggled to regain his composure. He closed his eyes, imagining what would happen once they discovered him. What could he say? With no other choice, Angelo decided to call for help. Even if he was caught, the police would have a record of the conversation. As he dialed, Angelo saw it. A small black door just beyond the last row of shelves. It had a single porthole, the kind Angelo equated with a restaurant kitchen. Quickly, he crossed the room, listening to the ringing of his phone. "911. What is your emergency?" But the door neither opened when he pulled it nor budged when pushed. "Hello? 911. What is your emergency?"

"Hello," Angelo said in a hushed voice. "My name is Dr. Angelo Perrotta. Please send the police to Savior of Saints. My life is in danger." Peering through the circular window, he saw that on the other side wasn't another room but a space roughly the size of a closet. On the right side, a single unmarked button glowed.

It was an elevator, the old-fashioned kind.

Even as the operator questioned Angelo, he took a deep breath. The door slid open easily, and he stepped inside. Angelo pressed the button, and the elevator began its descent. "Are you there?" the operator asked, but her voice cut out. The connection lost. Peering through the circular window, Angelo watched as the stockroom door flung open.

Seconds later, the closet-sized booth jolted to a halt. He pressed his ear against his phone, but the line had gone dead. Wherever the elevator had taken him, there was no reception. Quietly, and slowly, he slid the door open just a crack. White walls. Fluorescent lights. Linoleum tile. Two figures in white lab coats quickly passed his field of vision, speaking loudly to one another. The elevator, it seemed, opened into a hallway. He listened for approaching footfalls or voices. Once he was certain the hallway was quiet, he stepped out of the elevator. He could make out the sounds of chatter and foot traffic coming from the direction where the man and woman in lab coats were headed moments earlier. Willing himself to keep searching for Jason, Angelo started walking in the opposite direction.

His ankle began to throb again, but he ignored it. Instead, he concentrated on the sound his sneakers made on the linoleum floor. *What is this place? Some underground office?* The hallway opened into a large room. Tables. Chairs. A vending machine. On the far side, a coat rack with white lab coats stood adjacent to a large metal door. This must be the actual entrance, Angelo thought. There had to be a main elevator just beyond that door. It seemed unlikely the workers entered this underground lair through that small elevator he had just used.

Angelo donned a lab coat and proceeded back down the hall. He hoped that by wearing it he could move about the others unnoticed or, if noticed, could he claim to be new? But who was he kidding? People conducting illegal human experiments wouldn't just have temps sent over from some employment agency. Still, a weak disguise seemed better than none. The hall opened into a large workstation. People in lab coats were seated in front of computers, wearing headsets. Everyone seemed captivated, watching interviews with young male subjects. No one seemed to notice him.

As the initial fear of discovery subsided, he progressed through the room. Another hall, flanked by a dozen glass suites, displayed people in lab coats actively interviewing boys. Each room had a one-way mirror. Electrodes were fixed to the boys' temples. Telemetry monitors measured their pulse and blood pressure. A second displayed their brain waves. The workers seemed to be asking the boys questions and cataloguing the responses on their laptops. Except that these boys were somehow…not right he discovered, looking from face to face. They had vacant expressions and dulled eyes. When they looked at him, he saw they had no real curiosity about who he was. It was as if they were real, but not real.

Only one boy glanced up at Angelo, eyes wide, like a hostage pleading for help. Angelo staggered back a step or two, but he quickly moved on, fearing this boy would draw unwanted attention. It came to Angelo clearly that whatever happened here with the veterans all those many months ago had deviated to an extreme far away from any semblance of humanity in medical research. There was nothing altruistic or humanitarian happening here. Only undiluted evil.

He continued down the corridor. Peering into the final glass suite, Angelo caught his breath. Slowly, like waking up from a nightmare, unsure if what he was seeing was real, Angelo felt hairs stir at the nape of his neck with the incomprehensible sensation that his worst suspicions were true. Jason sat slumped in a wheelchair.

Frantically, Angelo pushed at the door. It swung open, and he dropped to his knees. "Jason, thank God!" But there was hardly any response from him. When Angelo held Jason's face, he detected unfocused eyes under heavy lids. "What did they do to you?"

Once the initial shock wore off, Angelo reacted immediately. He had to get Jason out of there. Attempting to push a wheelchair with an unconscious man weighing a hundred and eighty pounds was far from easy, especially with a sprained ankle, but Angelo rallied every bit of strength he had and threw himself against the chair. Slowly, it began to roll forward.

Back in the hallway, Angelo was faced with a new problem. How was he going to get past the workers? There was no other choice but to wheel Jason in the other direction even though he had no idea what disaster awaited him.

"Don't worry," Angelo said. "I'll get us out of here."

He proceeded tentatively, slowly, he could feel his flimsy determination falling away, replaced by fear. Then he heard a groggy voice call his name.

"Yes, Jason. It's me. I'm going to get us out of here."

Angelo began pushing faster, building momentum. Sweat streaked down his back. He turned a corner, and that's when his eyes lit up. A door appeared at the end of the hall. A door with a porthole just like the one he found in the stockroom upstairs. *Thank God. It's an elevator!*

"Hang on. We're nearly there."

Jason mumbled incoherently. Angelo ran faster, fighting through the lightning bolt of pain shooting through his ankle. Too fast. Unable to slow down in time, the chair crashed against the door. It swung open! A light blinded Angelo. He lost his grip. The chair rolled ahead, and he fell to the ground. When Angelo lifted his head, his entire body went numb.

What the hell?

Like a mouse in a maze, Angelo was trapped.

"Thank you for delivering the subject."

Subject? Angelo was still attempting to digest the word as he sat up. Surveying the room, he found himself momentarily unable to comprehend who they were at first, and there was some strange comfort in that, as if not being able to identify them was a kind of camouflage to hide in. He steeped in silence for a moment, mouth tight. Jarrett reached out his hand. "Let me help you." Oddly, James Jarrett had changed his outfit. Now he wore a white cassock with gold filigree-trimmed cuffs. Behind Jarrett, stood Gates and Dr. Scott Monroe.

"Monroe!" Angelo barely managed to say. "I thought—"

"You thought I had wisely distanced myself from Dr. Jarrett," he said without making eye contact. "I had to, publicly, that is. I needed to maintain my license."

A dawning broke in Angelo's mind when he thought back to his visit with Monroe earlier. On the shelf behind his desk, Angelo remembered a family photo taken on a cruise ship. The life preserver with the letters SOS. Now Angelo wondered if that photo had been taken on an actual cruise or if it was a prop to pose with at a Savior of Saints fundraiser.

Angelo struggled to his feet. He threw his arms possessively around Jason's chest. "What a performance, Dr. Monroe." The snideness evident in Angelo's tone. "You should really consider a career in acting."

Now it made sense. After Jarrett's license had been revoked, he still needed someone to oversee the research. Someone with a license to practice medicine. How else could they continue the clinical development of Parallax?

"Fortunately, Dr. Monroe called us after you paid him a visit this morning," Jarrett said. "We sensed you and your… *friend* weren't deterred by Detective Town even after Fitz Ranchin had been named the murderer. So, we activated Plan B."

"Plan B?" Angelo repeated incredulously.

This gruesome triumvirate assembled before him, staring at him with a mix of pity and condescension, did not deter him. Angelo shook himself from his thoughts. With every bit of strength he had, Angelo grabbed the wheelchair handles and backed out of the room. But it was blocked. Angelo backed into something. Not something, he realized quickly. Someone. There was a person blocking the doorway. Turning around, Angelo could hardly believe his eyes. "There you are!" Detective Town grinned. "We've been looking for you."

The next few actions happened so swiftly; Angelo was stunned. Town seized him, pulling him away from the wheelchair. "Get your hands off me!" Angelo shouted, shedding the lab coat to free himself from Town's vise-like grip. Angelo stumbled to the ground. Frantically, he tried to wriggle away, but Town dropped his massive frame on Angelo's body, knocking the wind out of him.

"That's enough of that." Town pinned him like a wrestler.

"Get off me." But Angelo was too winded to fight back. He relented under the crushing weight of Town's massive body on his. Once he caught his breath, Angelo discovered they had transferred Jason to a stretcher. It was then Angelo realized this wasn't a conference room or a room where they conducted patient interviews. This was a fully operational treatment room.

As Monroe strapped Jason's semiconscious body to the stretcher, Angelo noted the intravenous pole, the monitors, and a tray with gleaming surgical instruments: scalpels, scissors, four syringes, and a cranial saw!

"What are you going to do to him?" Angelo demanded. Town wedged his knee in between Angelo's shoulder blades. He let out a yelp of pain. The crack of a blood pressure cuff caught Angelo's attention. Muffled conversations. Sounds that seemed to have been plucked and crumpled, strewn haphazardly around so that it took a few seconds for Angelo to realize they were prepping Jason for a procedure. "Whatever you're planning on doing," he warned, "don't do it. Remember, he's a cop!"

"Funny, so am I." Town had Angelo's cheek pressed against the floor.

Jarrett's tasseled loafers stopped inches away from Angelo's face. "My work isn't simply about hypnosis and the Frame," Jarrett said. "In developing the program, we began with healthy adult volunteers. Men, like yourself, who wished not to be gay."

"Those men are nothing like me," Angelo spat. "I love being gay. You hear that, Jarrett? I love dick!"

Jarrett bristled. From anyone else, Angelo saw, such behavior would not have been tolerated. "Like you, I told those men they were *not* gay. They suffered from some childhood trauma. Something they had no memory of, which caused them to become confused."

"Jesus Christ," Angelo wailed under the intense weight of Town's body. "Have you lost your mind? Seriously, it's like your brain is stuck in 1950."

Jarrett appeared momentarily stunned. He held out his hand. "Give me your phone please."

"I lost it."

Jarrett nodded at Town who proceeded to pat Angelo down until he confiscated his cellphone. "Thank you, Detective." Jarrett began pacing. "I had limited success with these men. Then one evening, while I was viewing the constellations, I realized, perhaps these men were too old. Their brains too mature for me to rewire their amygdalae. So, I had to go back to square one. That meant completely revamping my scientific approach."

The floor felt like ice against Angelo's cheek as Town crammed his face against it. The stab of Town's knee, pressing into Angelo's back like an ice pick. Angelo kept his eyes on Jarrett, and then it hit him. "I suppose that meant younger brains," he managed to say. "Young, gay brains."

"Precisely." Jarrett motioned for Town to let up. Once freed, Angelo rolled onto his side, moaning with relief. "What a shame. You seem to understand the profundity of what we are doing here. What an apt pupil you would have made."

"You're a lunatic," Angelo shrieked. He struggled to rise on his haunches. "A closeted, gay, lunatic."

Gates turned to look at Monroe, lost for words.

Jarrett's face went slack. "Me? A closeted homosexual."

Then, the old man began to chuckle. Soon Gates and Monroe joined in. "I'm afraid you're confused."

"No." Angelo rose to his feet. "I'm not confused. You're a closeted, self-hating homosexual. A boy born from rape. A boy whose grandparents threw him out because he couldn't *fix* his homosexual *problem*."

This time Gates and Monroe protested vehemently, but Jarrett raised a hand to silence them. "Dr. Perrotta, trust me. You are confused."

"Don't try to deny it," Angelo gritted. "You were carrying on an affair with Keith Knight. Admit it!"

"Who do you think you're talking to," Town sneered. He grabbed Angelo's shoulders and spun him around, drawing back his fist. Angelo braced himself for the impact.

"Enough!" Jarrett's voice echoed with such intensity Jason began to stir suddenly, groaning and muttering something that sounded like Angelo's name. "That's enough, Robert."

A writhing sense of bewilderment wrapped itself around Angelo like a python, squeezing the breath out of him with excruciating defeat. He badly wanted to believe Jarrett was Keith's mystery man because then he could imagine Keith's frustration with keeping their relationship a secret. How long before that frustration turned to anger and spite and threats to go public. Living in fear of Keith's retaliation, Angelo reasoned how Jarrett could be driven to murder. And driven to murder again and again to make it look like a serial killer was targeting gay sex workers, to cover up the secret affair that threatened Jarrett's work. But the look on Jarrett's face when confronted with this theory said it all. Angelo had jumped to the wrong conclusion too quickly because he didn't want to accept Wes Plagen was the killer.

"As I recall," Jarrett began. "Keith Knight grew up in a madhouse with a mother addicted to heroin. Prostituting herself in front of her impressionable young son. It's no wonder Keith began using drugs and selling his body like his mother. Keith's brain was as traumatized as any veteran returning from the War in Afghanistan."

As Jarrett spoke, Angelo also noticed uneasily that Monroe had applied leads to Jason's bare chest and to both his temples. A monitor displayed his blood pressure and heart rate. A smaller one showed undulating green brain waves. "Angelo?" Jason called out groggily. "What's going on?"

"I'm right here, Jason," Angelo cried. "Monroe, stop what you're doing!"

Without acknowledging either, Monroe picked up a syringe and injected a clear fluid into Jason's left deltoid. Angelo lurched forward, but Town subdued him. The effect was instantaneous. Jason stared back at Angelo, wide-eyed, frightened, until slowly, his lids grew heavy. His gaze unfocused. Then, Jason was unconscious again.

"No!" Angelo attempted to break free, but Town overpowered him. He collapsed, dangling from his grip like a marionette. "Let me go!"

"Don't worry," Jarrett said. "He's not dead. You should be grateful. Midazolam has wonderfully relaxing side effects with the additional benefit of short-term amnesia." Angelo glared at Jarrett, who stared back at him blankly, though for a moment, Angelo swore he caught a gleam of amusement in his blue eyes. "Dr. Monroe, keep that man sedated."

Angelo's mind short-circuited, eyes madly searching, both spellbound and attempting to form some rational conclusion as to what was going to happen next.

"If only you had gone back to New York," said a familiar voice with pissed-off indignation. "All of this could have been avoided."

Angelo didn't respond, silenced by the shock that standing in the doorway was Bobby Town. There was something so inherently menacing about him. Even though he was shorter and frailer than Angelo, he loomed in the doorway, poised in the bright fluorescent light behind him. A figure moving fluidly, dreamily toward him, wraithlike. Angelo squeezed his eyes to see if this image of Bobby would disappear once he opened them again. But when he did, Bobby hovered over him, grinning.

"What are you doing here?" Angelo asked.

"He belongs here." Jarrett smiled proudly. He reached out his hand, beckoning the boy. Bobby walked toward Jarrett, sweeping past Angelo like he was stepping over dog excrement. "I'm so happy you decided to join us." Jarrett wrapped his arm across Bobby's narrow shoulders. "Dr. Perrotta, behold, living proof my assumptions were correct."

Angelo was lost. The words had a disorienting effect like he'd been drinking or drugged, and for one absurd moment he thought Bobby and Jarrett might burst out laughing, that this was all part of a vicious prank, and that they would return to Jarrett's office to retell this story over coffee and petit fours.

But as the disorienting effect wore off, Angelo experienced an unnerving sense of vertigo. It was like falling into a dark well, anticipating the impact of the floor rushing to meet him, but instead falling, body akimbo, colliding against cobblestone walls, which raked and tore and sliced his flesh until his spinning body had been battered beyond recognition.

Seeing Bobby standing next to Jarrett, the facts crystallized in Angelo's mind. "Oh my God. They converted you?"

"Not at all." Jarrett's voice was brimming with pride. "There was nothing to convert him from. Robert Jr. had been traumatized as a child. Like his father, he grew up without a mother. She died prematurely like his father's mother, but unlike his father, Bobby had no grandparents to help his busy father raise him."

Angelo turned back to stare at Detective Town, who

had turned conspicuously silent. A strange passivity had overtaken him. Town looked stricken, slightly infuriated, which made Angelo wonder if he had gotten it all wrong after speaking with Bobby about Keith's mystery man. Suddenly, it overwhelmed him. The cumulative shock of this revelation. His thoughts shattered like a mirror, the fragmented pieces reflected the fractured features of Keith Knight's mystery man.

"I should have figured it out sooner," Angelo muttered to Bobby. "When we were at Guy Cleveland's house. You said you didn't know who Keith Knight's mystery man was, and yet, you knew so much about his past. Didn't you, Bobby?"

The veins in Detective Town's forehead pulsed with such intensity, Angelo thought they might burst. "Shut your mouth!"

Calmly, Jarrett intervened. "Robert, control yourself. All will be handled in due time." Like a true narcissist, Jarrett steered the conversation back to him. "As I was saying, all I had to do was rewire Bobby's amygdala and return it to its pre-traumatized state. The result, as you can see, is perfection."

"Spirits on high," Gates and Monroe declared in unison.

"We couldn't be prouder," Jarrett said magnanimously. "Isn't that right, Detective Town?"

"Damn right."

Jarrett pulled away, admiring Bobby like he was something he had created. A sculpture. "To commemorate this occasion, I would like Robert Jr. to administer the Parallax infusion."

"To whom?" Angelo asked, but out of the corner of his eyes, he saw movement. Monroe had just hung a bag on the intravenous pole labeled PLX.

"Who do you think?" Town snorted. "You and your"—he extended his arm and allowed his wrist to flop—"little friend over there."

"Why are you doing this?" Angelo yelled at Jarrett.

The old man removed his spectacles, rubbing his eyes with his thumb and forefinger. "It all comes down to research and the greater good. Why waste the opportunity to learn from perfectly healthy specimens."

"Specimens!"

Specimens. The word formed an eddy in a sulcus of Angelo's brain, churning and spinning, until finally he understood. The plan wasn't simply to get rid of Jason and Angelo, but to expose them to an infusion of Parallax and dissect their brains like frogs in a high school biology class.

"I can't say that I didn't anticipate it would come to this," Jarrett opined, pacing about the room with a satisfied, proprietorial air and losing himself in contemplation. "All these years. It was only a matter of time before it all blew up again. The first time occurred after that *LA Times* article." Angelo was too fixated on Jason, on Monroe, and on Gates to listen as Jarrett lectured. At one point he heard him say, "You see, the Seven Spirits congregation had enough power to influence the *LA Times* to retract that absurd story and fire that incompetent reporter. The news of his suicide barely raised an eyebrow. Isn't that right, Detective Town?"

"No one cared."

"That's not entirely accurate," Jarrett corrected him. "Rocky Thorn cared. She cared a lot." Walking toward Bobby, Jarrett set his hand on the boy's shoulder. "It was Robert Jr. who advised us on how best to approach Ms. Thorn. I'm the first to admit I know little about social media, but Robert Jr. made it clear that if Ms. Thorn were to end up like the *LA Times* reporter, her…what did you call them?"

"Thorny Messes."

"That's right." Jarrett grimaced. "Odd name if you ask me. It was Robert Jr. who stated emphatically that Ms. Thorn's *Thorny* Messes would never accept her death as a suicide."

"So, you threatened her and her family," Angelo said. "That's how you got her to back off."

"If only it were that easy," Jarrett replied with a chuckle. "Once again, it was Robert Jr. who advised us that Ms. Thorn would never stop investigating our research unless she had something more sensational to occupy her time."

The attention embarrassed Bobby. He stared at the ground, squeezing his eyes, tight-lipped. It got Angelo wondering if he wasn't used to flattery or if he was experiencing regret.

When Angelo first met Bobby, he appeared nervous, someone too afraid to speak, but he later figured out that it must have been Bobby who called in to the radio show, offering breadcrumbs so they investigated RentAGuy, the Seven Spirits Church, and of course, the Parallax Institute. Striking fear and pain in Rocky's heart by taunting her with Blake's poem, "The Sick Rose." Every detail thought out and executed brilliantly. Even down to Bobby luring him and Jason to Guy Cleveland's house, where he stumbled upon the Scrabble game. One final staged play to spark an idea in Angelo's mind? It seemed so obvious to him now; Monroe had planted the seed and Bobby had watered the soil. Angelo had played right into their hands.

"Robert Jr. came up with the idea of a serial killer targeting prostitutes." Jarrett spoke like a grandfather recalling the events of a long-ago holiday. "No Angels Wept," Jarrett said with slow emphasis. "Genius."

"Spirits on high," Gates added with deep reverence.

"Nice work, Bobby." Angelo flashed him a contemptuous glare. "Serial killer who preys on gay sex workers. What a great idea. You knew Rocky would care even when no one else would."

"They got what they deserved if you ask me," Detective Town hissed, wrenching his arm tightly around Angelo's neck.

"Proves my point," Angelo struggled to say, realizing he was gasping for air.

Jarrett took over the narrative again. "The Seven Spirits Church is based on the Book of Revelation 5. To best honor the passages, there are seven council members. Five of which are in this very room. The other two oversee the New York chapter. We have taken an oath to cleanse the spirit of men who wish to be closer to God."

"Spirits on high," everyone chimed in. Except Bobby, Angelo noticed.

Hearing about the New York chapter confirmed Jason's suspicions that they were behind the injury that took him off the case. But there was something else. Angelo recalled the part about Revelation 5. The scroll was sealed seven times, symbolizing the judgement of God on sin and wickedness. *Does Jarrett think he's God?* In the passage, the elders reassured John that there is only One who can take the scroll. *Is Bobby the One?*

Angelo shook his head. "While you're patting each other on the back, let me remind you that I'm a physician, and my boyfriend is a New York City police officer. Once Rocky learns we're missing, she will make it her mission to find out what happened to us. You may have escaped the Thorny Messes once. You won't be so lucky a second time. It's not like you can whip up a new serial killer. May I remind you…you killed *Fitz* in the second act."

"We don't have to whip up a new killer," Town said, his sour breath cloying in Angelo's ear. "We have you to thank for that."

"That's very true," Jarrett said. "Bobby will testify that he spoke with you earlier, that you figured out No Angels Wept was an anagram that spelled Weston Plagen, and after you visited Plagen, neither you nor Officer Murphy were ever seen again."

If Wes had been the intended scapegoat all along, how did Fitz get caught up in this tangled mess?

"My son figured everything out," Town chuckled.

"That's correct," Jarrett said. "Robert Jr. even thought to befriend Guy Cleveland after Keith Knight's death."

Angelo smiled sadly at Bobby. "I should have guessed that too. Is that how you found Gabriel Menendez and Trevon Bolden? Cherry-picking them from RentAGuy profiles to fit your anagram." Angelo attempted to pull Town's arm from around his throat. "I bet the Seven Spirits Church owns the LLC that bought RentAGuy, right?"

Bobby took a shaky breath. It seemed to Angelo that he was somehow getting through to him.

"Hey Bobby!" Angelo taunted. "I'm guessing when we first met at Café '50s, it wasn't a coincidence."

Town exploded with laughter. "Coincidence? No, Doc. I called Bobby the minute you sat down for lunch."

Angelo laughed patronizingly. "Ha, ha, guess the joke's on me. And for shits and giggles, what's the significance behind spacing the murders three months apart?"

Jarrett stepped in once again. "Three is the divine number that signifies the Father, the Son, and the Holy Spirit."

"How fitting," Angelo mocked. "Can, you ask He-Man behind me to back off? It's not like I can get very far." Jarrett gestured for Town to ease up. Angelo wriggled his neck, feeling the blood rushing back into his head. He hadn't realized how tight Town's choke hold had been. "Well, since we're in the mood for truth telling, can someone tell me why you abandoned the chosen one's brilliant plan to pin the murders on Wes and framed Fitz instead?"

Jarrett bristled. "That was never part of the plan." He shot Town a look of rebuke.

"Oh, I get it now," Angelo said as though a scrim had been lifted. He turned to face Town head-on. "You're the one that planted the evidence in Fitz's cooler because she knew the truth. You silenced Keith, but Fitz suspected the truth about you and Keith Knight. She may not have had proof, but she didn't need it. Right, Detective? You were worried that Fitz might slip and tell Rocky."

"Shut your fucking mouth!" Town roared.

"But what you didn't know about Fitz was that she would never betray Keith's confidence. Maybe if you knew that, she'd still be alive." Every word Angelo uttered seemed to wrench loose the next, until he pieced it all together only for it to come tumbling out of his mouth like a landslide. "No Angels Wept wasn't the calling card of a serial killer. It was a conspiracy to throw off Rocky Thorn and her Thorny Messes perpetrated by a father and son team. Bobby picked the victims, and his closeted *Daddy* knocked them off!"

Charging toward Angelo, Town pushed him to the ground, squeezing his throat until he nearly passed out.

"Robert!" Jarrett shouted. "Stop this at once."

Bobby and Jarrett pulled Town off him. Gasping and coughing, Angelo grabbed Bobby's ankle. "Listen to me. There is nothing wrong with you. Don't listen to these assholes. You're not a loser. You hear me? You're not a loser!"

Bobby appeared anxious, resuming his concentrating stare at the ground.

"It's them," Angelo insisted. "They're the losers. Not you."

"That's enough," Jarrett shouted. "Dr. Perrotta, I won't allow your disruptive behavior to affect these proceedings. Disrupters are punished here."

"Spirits on high," Gates and Monroe replied.

Disrupters? Angelo recalled that word scrawled over the faces of several boys he discovered in those binders kept in the stockroom upstairs.

"Clearly, you don't see how your traumatized childhood has informed your lifestyle choices," Jarrett said to Angelo, "but I do."

"What childhood trauma?" he argued. "I grew up in a loving, supportive home."

Jarrett scoffed. "I suppose that scar on your cheek is the result of a loving, supportive father."

Angelo flinched inwardly, running his finger along the scar.

What wrenched Angelo was the banality of this evil, the snarky, condescending, matter-of-factness with which these men spoke of gay people in this subterranean lab filled with a cast of characters—mad doctors, a crooked detective, the solicitous butler—exercising their insanely focused will.

And poor Bobby. He was far from a Parallax success. More like the innocent gay boy turned deranged architect of a plot. A plot that resulted in the murder of Keith Knight to misdirect Rocky Thorn and protect his father's secret relationship with him. But then again, Bobby wasn't so innocent. He had a choice, and when it came time for him to choose, he decided to befriend Guy Cleveland in order to access RentAGuy profiles, then picked Gabriel Menendez and Trevon "Blaze" Bolden because they fit an anagram that would pin the murders on Weston Plagen.

But what needled at Angelo like a blister on his heel was that the Bobby he had met at Guy Cleveland's house appeared to be going through something physiological. The anxiety, the watery eyes and runny nose had Angelo wondering if he had taken drugs or was withdrawing from them. Even now, Angelo thought Bobby seemed jittery and impatient as Jarrett escorted him to the stretcher to observe Monroe. Angelo watched with heart-wrenching panic, helpless that he was unable to protect his beloved. Swiftly and adeptly, Monroe inserted an intravenous catheter in Jason's left antecubital just above the splint. Jarrett nodded his approval, but just as Monroe was about to hand over the infusion for Bobby to administer, Jarrett's cellphone rang.

He turned away to answer it. "What is it?" Angelo saw the rage, a deep, consuming rage, cross his features, distorting them. He hung up and spoke directly to Town. "We're needed back at the office."

Angelo looked at Bobby, who was rubbing his shoulder as if his arm had fallen asleep.

"Mr. Gates," Jarrett spoke with restraint. "There's been a change in plans. I'm leaving you in charge. Monroe, keep that man sedated. We'll return as soon as possible."

Once Jarrett and Detective Town exited the room, Angelo's skin tingled with excitement. *What if Jarrett was called back to his office because the police had arrived?* That would explain why he had asked Detective Town to accompany him. But this celebratory moment was fleeting once Angelo heard Bobby ask Monroe, "What if he wakes up?"

"He's not going to wake up, and if he does, I'll take care of it." Monroe motioned to the tray beside the telemetry monitor where three syringes full of sedation were laid out.

Bobby shot Angelo a furtive glance. The gleam in his eyes was unnerving. "I wonder if we should give one to Dr. Perrotta. Just to be safe? We don't know how long they'll be."

Gates leaned forward to whisper in Monroe's ear. They glanced at Angelo as if they were considering Bobby's suggestion. "Dr. Perrotta," Gates called out. "Why don't you have a seat."

"I'm good," Angelo responded.

Monroe picked up a syringe. He and Gates came at him from opposite sides. Angelo hesitated, uncertain exactly what to do. Two against one. The odds, he knew, were not in his favor.

"Now guys." Angelo forced a smile. "Let's think this through."

As Monroe grew closer, he raised the syringe and popped off the protective cover. Angelo caught the glint of the three-inch needle and began taking step after step backward. Just a few feet behind them, Angelo noticed Bobby approaching him too. Angelo weighed his options. Bobby was shorter, skinnier. One-on-one, Angelo knew he could take him. As for Gates, he didn't take his age for granted. Angelo knew many men in their sixties who could run circles around guys half their age. Besides, he looked fit under that corduroy blazer. Not the petit four eating type. As for Monroe, the dad bod said it all, but again, Angelo reminded himself of the odds; he was no match for the three of them at once.

"There's nowhere to go," Gates said soothingly. "Don't make this more difficult on yourself than it has to be."

"Listen to him," Bobby urged. "It'll be over soon."

Angelo was backed against the wall. He watched as Monroe prepped the syringe. A spray of liquid spurt from the needle. Gates reached to restrain Angelo. In that moment, he didn't know where to look. It was then Angelo caught the glint of something metal in Bobby's hand. He, too, held a syringe. "I seriously think one will do the trick," Angelo kidded nervously.

Gates whirled around, visibly nonplussed, but then he saw the syringe in Bobby's hand. Arm raised above his head. Thumb cocked over the plunger. "Mr. Town?" Gates asked in confusion. "What do you think you're—" With determination and confidence Angelo hadn't seen Bobby display before, he thrust the needle into Monroe's neck.

"What the fuck!" Shocked, Monroe stumbled backward, falling to the floor.

Gates spun around just as Bobby popped off the protective cover from a second syringe. Angelo watched in amazement as Bobby chased after the man, inserting the needle down to the hub in the back of Gate's neck. The man stumbled forward, dropped to his knees, and slumped to one side.

An uneasy quiet filled the room except for the fading groans from Gates and Monroe.

"Come on." Bobby pulled Angelo's arm. He tripped over Monroe as Bobby led him to the stretcher where Jason lay unconscious. Angelo was still speechless as Bobby began removing the leads, the blood pressure cuff, and the intravenous catheter. *What just happened?*

"We have to hurry," Bobby shouted.

Angelo was confused, even as Bobby disengaged the wheel locks and began maneuvering the stretcher toward the door. Angelo couldn't be sure this wasn't a trap, it wasn't likely as Bobby had just assaulted Gates and Monroe with sedation, but he still didn't trust him. All Angelo knew was that he had narrowly escaped harm and whether or not Bobby had good intentions, he had at least bought them time.

Angelo snapped to attention, assisting Bobby as they crossed the threshold. With a glance back into the room, Angelo saw Monroe reaching for the wall alarm. In a split second, the white gleaming corridor exploded in fiery red lights. Its shrill pulsating trill sent a corkscrew of panic into Angelo's back.

"Angelo!" Bobby shouted. "Push!"

They barreled down the hall, bumping into the walls as they accelerated. Behind them, Angelo heard the unmistakable blast of doors being flung open, the indistinguishable sounds of shouting, and the Clydesdale clopping of feet running toward them. They rounded a corner and never looked back.

"Why are you helping me?" Angelo asked, breathless.

Bobby's face was drenched in sweat. "Does it matter?"

They ran alongside the stretcher for several minutes, turning left and right so many times, Angelo could not conceive the magnitude of this underground lab. Finally, Bobby stopped in front of an arched wooden door in what appeared to be a vacant area of the lab. "We're here," Bobby said, panting.

Pulling on the lever, the door creaked open. The tunnel extending in front of them was black. Only a few feet of brick wall was visible before cutting out into a darkness so absolute and deafening it looked as if it opened into an unfinished world, a gateway to another dimension that felt far more threatening than the hell from which they had just escaped. "Use the light from your cellphone," Bobby instructed Angelo.

"They took it from me," Angelo explained. "You mean to tell me there are no lights in this tunnel?"

"They shut off the power in the afternoon." Bobby handed over his cellphone. "This tunnel leads to the off-site dormitory. You can escape from there."

"What about you?"

Bobby shook his head. "There's something I need to do first."

Staring into the darkness, the decaying brick walls seemed to constrict around Angelo like a throat. "I can't do this," he said. "You don't understand."

"No, you don't understand. In a few minutes, armed guards will be here. This is your only chance to escape."

"But I have a fear of tunnels," Angelo began to explain. "Come with us. It's not safe for you here either."

Bobby stood in the blinking crimson hallway. A calm had come over his features. "I'm not afraid anymore. I know I'm not a loser. Guy helped me understand that. I stopped taking Parallax because of him, and I'm very sorry for the part I played in the deaths of those three boys, and for not telling you the truth earlier. I have a chance to make it right now."

Grabbing the door handle, Bobby wished Angelo good luck before he closed the door with a thud that echoed around him.

Angelo and Jason were now sealed in a coffin.

Chapter Twenty-Three

The corridor smelled musty. The air was frigid. Taking a deep breath, the dankness filled Angelo's nostrils. He pulled the stretcher deeper into the hallway. Jason stirred. "Don't worry," Angelo said shakily. "I'm going to get us out of here."

Angelo groped his way back to the door, but it wouldn't budge. Bobby must have locked it. Pressed against the door, his labored breathing echoed all around him. He turned on the cellphone light and held it over his head. The white light trembled out before him. The redbrick walls were crumbling, the ceiling low with thick veins of green mold.

I can't do this! No way!

A chill inched down his spine. The dark corridor shrank and moaned as his eyes followed the trembling white light, which disturbed him even more than the plunging darkness. Squinting into the bleakness, Angelo felt himself shrinking. Paralyzed with mounting fear there was someone else in that hall with him. Watching. Waiting. He could not move his feet. The pulse of pain from his ankle reminded Angelo he had sprained it.

Three deep breaths. Serenity now.

Angelo laughed out loud, realizing the absurdity of following this mindfulness exercise all these months. And for what? As if an app could have prepared him for this.

He took a moment to recalibrate his mind, to assure himself he was alone with Jason and whatever it was that brought on his panic was simply a narrative he had concocted in his head. Rationalizing this situation did little to allay his anxiety. His eyes were stinging, and he was drenched in sweat. He could hardly think. Was it his imagination or was it actually getting hotter in here? Fighting a wave of nausea—it had to be the heat—he grabbed ahold of the stretcher. As his mind spun, suddenly he was aware of the faint crunch of footsteps on the other side of the door.

What are you waiting for?

Beyond him, in the dark, was what he and Jason came here to learn, and now that they were finally here, together, it rested on Angelo's shoulders to expose the truth. Angelo planted his eyes on the tunnel ahead. Now was the time to face his fear. Here, in the dark, was the true test of his courage. It was right there. Waiting for him. Even if he couldn't see it.

Go. Now!

Angelo willed his feet to move. Knees buckling under the weight of each step, he inched forward. A shadow loomed to his right. Angelo froze, horrified. But it was his mind playing tricks on him again. Taking a few steps more, he told himself not to look back. Just keep taking step after step.

Don't think about where you're going. Think about what you're leaving behind.

The stretcher clattered against the stone floor. The vibrations jarred Jason, who spoke incoherently. The childlike blabbering comforted Angelo. He tried to rationalize that his fear was unfounded, that it was purely a machination of his guilt, and that if he made it to the end of this tunnel, he would have conquered it. As he considered this, Angelo wondered with a new onset of panic how long exactly this tunnel was. He took three more steps before stopping again. Catching his breath, he tried not to gulp the fetid air.

You can do this. You can do this.

The tunnel curved to the right like a ribbon. Angelo pulled on the stretcher, fumbling and tripping on the stones beneath his feet. With every misstep, his ankle crackled with exquisite tenderness.

No. I can't do this. I'm sorry. I can't!

Angelo crouched down, waiting to be discovered. Failing miserably at protecting Jason and failing miserably as a human being. He waited, his heart pounding, hearing the faint sound of gurgling. He recognized it immediately. The stench of vomit followed. Jason was vomiting. He could make out the silhouette of his profile, gagging and lurching. He recognized the pattern and could hardly believe it.

Jason must be having a reaction to the sedation.

Angelo scrambled to his feet. He turned Jason's head to the side to allow the flow of vomit. Jason's skin felt cold, clammy. His thready pulse told Angelo Jason may have aspirated. This situation was growing more dire by the second. The next few moments happened quickly; Angelo was hardly aware of his actions. He held up the cellphone light with one hand and summoning the remaining scraps of strength he had left, pulled the stretcher with the other. He was trying to see where he was going but it was too dark even with the light.

The corridor seemed to constrict with every step. He kept his eyes not on the floor but on the brick walls, using them as a guide. Counting each brick he passed. The counting kept him tethered to the world, to the reality of this situation, because the darkness was so total it became physical, like a curtain.

The only thing that propelled him forward was knowing he was moving in the right direction. Each step was one step farther away from Savior of Saints. Buoyed by faith, the off-site dormitory was his only hope for escape. His priorities had changed. Jason's life was at stake now. If they were trapped here, he could possibly die.

Angelo moved faster, every now and then he checked on Jason. Forcing himself to move forward, faster, though his legs were throbbing with exhaustion, his ankle shifting under the weight of every step.

An unexpected explosion shook the ground beneath them. Jason mumbled his name.

"I'm right here." Angelo was thankful the explosion had roused Jason awake, though it had rattled him with a new layer of fear. For a moment, he believed Town and his men had burst through the arched door and were right behind them, but smoke began to drift into Angelo's nostrils, choking him. When he turned back, he detected a flickering red glow.

After a split second's hesitation, Angelo was clambering forward, dragging the stretcher across the bumpy, stone floor. Fumbling forward in the darkness, the unknown reality of where they were headed seemed to swell exponentially in magnitude. Angelo was concerned that as much as he had uncovered about Savior of Saints, he still didn't see the full picture. Some missing truth had yet to be revealed. Perhaps it was waiting for them at the other end of this tunnel. And yet, this one remaining question that exhausted and depleted him like a fever that wouldn't break was about to be answered.

Up ahead, he made out the outline of a door. Angelo experienced a rush of excitement. But what if they had fumbled all this way in the dark only to discover the end was tied up in nothing?

He grabbed the latch and heaved on it. The arched wood door creaked like a yawning lion. The corridor just on the other side was dim. The walls covered in grimy, jade subway tile. Angelo locked the stretcher wheels. Jason was still groggy, coming in and out of consciousness. He was breathing normally, his pulse reedy but regular. "We made it." Angelo kissed Jason's forehead. "We made it, my love."

Once he secured the stretcher, Angelo grabbed the latch and pulled the door shut behind them. He waited for his eyes to adjust to the dimly lit hallway. A few feet ahead, Angelo found a locked metal door. He pounded loudly until he heard someone on the other side stir. Waiting for the door to open, Angelo heard a distant rumbling overhead, as if animals were stampeding in terror. The walls of the hallway vibrated. Dust came loose from the ceiling, showering the ground with debris. But then the noise was gone, the hallway turned quiet, and Angelo was left wondering if his anxiety was playing tricks on him again.

He paused, listening, hearing nothing until the metal door unlocked. A man wearing green scrubs stared expectantly at Angelo. He had the battered face of a gargoyle, and no neck. "Who are you?"

With bravado, if not confidence, Angelo said, "It's an emergency"—he pointed at the stretcher—"this man needs help."

"Why'd you bring him here?" The man stepped back to shut the door on Angelo, but he slammed his hand against it.

"You don't understand. I'm in charge. You will assist me in getting this man to safety."

Was that me shouting?

Angelo barged past him. "What's going on in here?"

"Wait a minute," the man said nervously. Just then, the ground beneath them shook. "What was that?"

Angelo ignored him, focusing on the extremely cold temperature inside the windowless room. Immediately, his entire body shivered. He found the switch and turned on the light. The boys scrambled to their feet, anxiously forming three single file lines as if this was a drill. He counted ten of them. They stared blankly ahead. Many refused to meet Angelo's gaze. Rows of metal bunk beds crammed the small room. In the upper left-hand corner, Angelo detected a video camera. In the opposite corner, a thirteen-inch television played a black and white war film.

It was worse than anything he could have possibly imagined. The anteroom of hell.

I found them.

Angelo rubbed his eyes, trying to contain his anger. He took a deep breath and resumed the pretense. For now, he had to get Jason and these boys to safety. "Gentlemen, I'm Dr. Perrotta," he explained in a voice meant to instill authority. "This is an actual emergency. We're going to evacuate this room." Angelo walked past boy after boy, inspecting each one to ensure none of them were in desperate need of medical attention themselves. A punky blond in the rear wore a tag pinned to his sweatshirt. It read, DISRUPTER. "What's this?" he asked, but the boy stared back in confused alarm.

"Hey, you!" Angelo called the man who had opened the door. "What's your name?"

"Rick."

"Rick," he said. "What does this mean?"

He stepped closer, squinting at the label. "That means this one's a troublemaker. Here, troublemakers lose privileges."

"Troublemaker, huh?" Angelo recalled earlier Jarrett had referred to his disruptive behavior and wondered what cruel punishment he had managed to escape. "And what privileges did he lose?"

"Bed privileges." He pointed toward the back of the room where two rumpled mats were laid out on the floor. "Disrupters sleep there."

"There's more than one?" Angelo noticed a second boy. He had choppy, dark hair and freckles concentrated over the bridge of his nose and both cheeks. Like the other young man, a tag was pinned to his sweatshirt with the word, DISRUPTER, scrawled across it. "You two stay with me," Angelo said. "As for the rest of you, again, this is not a drill. Follow Rick. He will lead you outside. I will explain everything once we're assembled safely and everyone is accounted for."

"What's the emergency?" Rick asked.

Angelo cleared his throat. "There's no time for explanations. Now get these boys out of here." Rick jerked his head toward the hallway. "What about the man on the stretcher?"

"I'll take care of him."

The boys followed Rick out of the room in a single file line. Once the room had been evacuated, Angelo focused on the two disrupters. "I need you to help me with a patient. You think you can do that?"

They remained silent, nodding their assent. "Good." Angelo paused to glare at the tags pinned to their sweatshirts. Angrily, he snatched them off. "You won't be needing these anymore."

Angelo recalled his brief time with that therapist who introduced him to SRNiTY. Looking back, it occurred to him he didn't need an app to free him from his panic attacks, but something she said suddenly made sense.

"Gentlemen, remember this," he said. "Call in the forces of peace, otherwise the forces of doom will line up against you. Remember, the world is cruel and illogical. Happy endings are only a matter of framing. Look for opportunities by *disrupting* norms. Understand?"

The boys offered each other befuddled shrugs. Angelo didn't care. He knew one day they would look back on this moment and recall the day Dr. Perrotta had told them there was nothing wrong with challenging the status quo.

In the hallway, Angelo discovered that Rick had already led the boys outside. Leaning over the stretcher, Angelo whispered Jason's name. His eyes blinked open. "Thank God," Angelo breathed, reaching for his hand.

"Where am I?" Jason groaned though his voice was hoarse.

Lifting Jason's head, Angelo cradled it to his chest. "Don't worry. You're safe."

Angelo closed his eyes, allowing the relief to wash over him. He had to soak it in, allowing it to cover him like a warm bath, so that Jason would feel safe in his arms. But they weren't safe yet. "Gentlemen," Angelo said to the two young men waiting nearby. "I need you to help me wheel this stretcher outside. Do you know the way?" He was flooded with adrenaline; he didn't recognize the sound of his own voice. Without further instructions, the boys gripped the stretcher and began wheeling it down the grimy, jade hall.

The three of them managed to roll the stretcher the short distance to where the hallway led to a concrete staircase. Rick was waiting for them along with two other boys. "Figured you could use a few extra hands," he said. Together, they lifted the stretcher and carried Jason up the stairs.

"Hey," Jason whispered to Angelo. "Thank you for saving my life." He smiled, and Angelo felt as if the rising sun had found him in that dark hallway.

Outside, they entered the din of pandemonium. Across a field, Savior of Saints was on fire. Two fire trucks were parked in front of the building. Firefighters were attempting to control the blaze. Hoses sprayed water as the flames lapped at the building like serpent tongues. Standing behind three police cars that had formed a cordon, men and women in lab coats watched in horror. A pair of EMS workers were loading a stretcher onto an ambulance. Angelo recognized Claire, an oxygen mask affixed to her face. Ash stained her perfectly coiffed platinum hair.

"I don't believe it," Rick said. Angelo noted his eyes were fixed on the burning building. "God knows what would have happened had you not come for us, Doctor."

Angelo instructed Rick to lead the boys across the field while he stayed behind with Jason. "Gentlemen," Angelo said to the disrupters. "Let's get this man medical attention." The boys positioned themselves on either side of the stretcher like centaurs. Angelo leaned forward and kissed Jason lightly on the lips, but his knees buckled. The weight of the events of the past twenty-four hours had finally caught up with him. He rallied himself, not wanting to show any weakness now that he had these boys' attention. "Everyone," he said. "Follow me."

They marched like a rebellion across the field. Fierce gusts of wind coiled and writhed with black smoke. Occasionally, a pop of embers showered the dark night like fireworks. The black wind hissed punitively in Angelo's ears, the moon lighting their way. Angelo wouldn't let himself believe it, that he had actually escaped that underground tunnel. Conquered his fear.

After walking a few yards, he looked back and saw the dormitory entrance. It looked innocuous, so non-threatening. No hint of the level of hell that lay inside. The chaos of what was happening all around them made Angelo feel like the world was caving in, but at the same time, he hoped that within the rubble of Savior of Saints, a phoenix would emerge.

Angelo held Jason's hand the entire time until a police officer stopped them. "Where did you come from?"

"I'm Dr. Perrotta. These boys were being held in a dormitory just across the field. It's connected to Savior of Saints by an underground tunnel."

"Seriously?"

"This gentleman needs urgent medical attention."

The officer signaled for help. A first responder ran over. With the help of the two boys, they wheeled Jason's stretcher toward an ambulance. "That doctor is my boyfriend," Angelo heard Jason mutter. "I'm going to marry him one day."

Angelo began to follow the first responders, limping, when he heard someone shouting his name. It was Wes, freeing himself from the crowd. "You don't know how happy I am to see you." Tears brightened his eyes. Finally, Angelo gave himself permission to crumble in Wes's arms, sobbing in the crook of his neck. Such welcomed intimacy between two men, like brothers. Wes stepped back. "I'm so sorry," he said, sobbing. "I don't remember everything I said, but I know I was a total asshole. I meant none of it."

Angelo shook his head. It was as if whatever Wes had said to him earlier had ignited within him the ability to overcome everything that had happened at Savior of Saints. "Where's Rocky?"

Wes telescoped his head, glancing uncertainly around. "Hey," he shouted, waving his arm wildly.

Rocky broke free from the crowd, sprinting toward them. She jumped on Angelo, wrapping her legs around his waist. They fell back, laughing. "You fucking asshole." She kissed his face repeatedly. "I thought you were toast."

Wes helped them to their feet. "Where is Jarrett and Detective Town?" Angelo asked.

Wes and Rocky grinned knowingly. "Jarrett's over there." She pointed across the parking lot where the old man sat in the back of a police car. "And our buddy Town is in the other one."

Abruptly, Angelo fell silent, glancing apprehensively between the two police cars. Amid so much, he felt a rush of relief knowing they hadn't wiggled their way out of this situation. At least, not for the moment.

"What about Bobby Town?" Angelo asked.

Wes offered a confused expression. "We didn't even know he was here. Are you sure?"

"Of course, I'm sure!" Angelo experienced a stab of horror like a mother realizing she'd lost her child. "We have to find him. I left him in there."

Angelo's head snapped toward the inferno. Without realizing, he had broken into a sprint, ignoring the heat scorching his cheeks, the pulsation throbbing his ankle, but police were quick to restrain him. "You have to let me in there. Bobby needs help."

Wes and Rocky caught up to him. "He's probably out here somewhere," Wes reasoned. "Maybe he got out the same way you did."

"No!" Angelo's voice trailed off weakly. "I shouldn't have let him go back."

"It's not your fault," Wes said.

The smell of smoke was intense by then. Their faces and everything around them coated with a pale gray powder. Ash strewn everywhere. "What's that?" Rocky gasped. "Up there."

A figure cut across the second story window within the central spire.

An unexpected explosion rocked the building. Underneath their feet, a rumbling began. A tremor growing in intensity. The crowd began to run from the burning building. "It's collapsing," police shouted. "Everyone back up."

Flaming beams splintered off the main building and crashed to the ground. The spire windows blew out. Thick smoke wafted from them like slithering black snakes. The second floor was nearly engulfed in flames. A figure stood up, staring out the central spire window. Angelo was certain it was Bobby Town. They locked eyes. Angelo felt helpless staring up at him.

All the men in that young man's life had failed him, and now Angelo had failed him too. In that split second, Angelo experienced a stab of pain. Bobby's final choice had been his own.

He offered Angelo one final mournful smile before the entire second floor toppled on itself.

Chapter Twenty-four

In the days that followed, Angelo experienced a deep fatigue, but he couldn't sleep. He had the gnawing feeling that Jarrett was still out there somewhere, watching him. He couldn't believe it, he had actually escaped the Seven Spirits council and after running down white hallways in the underground lab and navigating a pitch-black tunnel to the off-site dormitory, he had not only survived, but he had also rescued ten boys and the love of his life.

The first twenty-four hours transpired in a haze. There were parts he had forgotten or missed entirely. Jason was brought to the hospital where doctors monitored him overnight until they were sure the sedation had completely worn off and he had not aspirated, like Angelo had suspected. The hospital administration seemed enthusiastic for Jason to be discharged. It didn't help that Angelo and Jason had become a hot news story. Reporters camped outside the hospital, drawing the unwanted attention of the Thorny Messes, who hoped to spot their patron saint of the invisible LGBTQ+ community.

Wes and Rocky had wisely decided not to visit Jason.

The first thing Angelo and Jason did after he was discharged was to check out of the hotel. The police had asked them to stay in Los Angeles for a few more days. They moved into Wes's spare room but not before Wes dismantled the evidence board. They slept for nearly twelve hours.

When they woke up, Wes shocked them with the news that the police had reopened the investigation into the deaths of Fitz Ranchin and Detective Boniface. What Detective

Town hadn't anticipated was that Fitz had recorded the interrogation on her cellphone. The actual events contradicted Detective Town's story. According to Rocky's sources, the leaked recording indicated that Detective Town had stabbed Detective Boniface first and shot Fitz after. Once they were both dead, he planted evidence from the murdered victims in Fitz's mobile van.

Angelo didn't believe it at first. Like before, he expected the church to use their political influence to fix this problem, but this time, there was too much at stake. Once Savior of Saints burned down and the boys were questioned, there was no arguing that something sinister had been going on. Politicians, the district attorney, and even Detective Town's fellow police officers refused to stand by him, especially after Angelo provided police with his account of what had happened. When questioned, Angelo stated that while being held hostage in the basement of Savior of Saints, he'd witnessed Detective Town admitting to the No Angels Wept murders.

As for Dr. Reverend James Jarrett, he too found he had no friends rushing to stand by him. The fire may have destroyed critical pieces of evidence, but there were too many witnesses willing now to cooperate with police. Two days after Savior of Saints burned down, Dr. Reverend James Jarrett was found hanging in his jail cell.

Three days after the fire, the three amigos were together again, safe, alive, unharmed, and cozied on the sofas in Wes's living room. Angelo told them everything he remembered, beginning with the anagram Bobby had created to pin the murders on Wes. He hadn't consciously chosen to share so much detail. Rocky looked stricken. Wes seemed slightly annoyed he hadn't figured it out first, which made Angelo wonder if it was wise to be so uncensored, but each word he uttered seemed to unburden him like he had been trapped under rubble.

"We seriously thought the two of you were dead." The tone in Wes's voice seemed shucked of all levity.

Rocky had her Doc Martens on Wes's coffee table, cleaning her fingernails with her knife. "I said it once, I'll say it again. You, are a fuckin' rockstar, Dr. Angelo Perrotta."

They drank wine, and Angelo heard their disjointed banter about how he fled from Wes's house, convinced he was running from the No Angels Wept Killer. "I wanted to call the police," Rocky said, "but what was I going to say, my friend believes my producer is a serial killer?"

Angelo and Wes stared at one another for a long while. "I'm sorry I doubted you," Angelo said.

"Please bro," Wes replied. "The lengths Bobby went to—the anagrams and cherry-picking the victims—shit, I would have believed it myself."

Rocky looked lost in thought. Angelo wondered if she was thinking about Fitz. Coming to understand that Town had changed course from the original plan, Rocky had to reconcile her girlfriend had been murdered by a self-loathing homosexual whose religious beliefs had emboldened him to believe he was above the law, killing an innocent trans woman and a fellow detective. Angelo imagined, that for Rocky, Fitz's death must have brought back memories of Rand's suicide decades earlier.

"We drove around for a while looking for you," Wes continued. "Then we decided to head over to your hotel."

"Oh, boy." Rocky sighed. "That was fun."

Wes had already told them the story about how Rocky demanded the hotel manager let them into Angelo's room, explaining he had called her threatening to kill himself, and that she didn't want to contact the police or call an ambulance because he was a famous doctor who had just signed a contract to join a hit daytime talk show. Once inside the hotel room, Rocky and Wes discovered the Scrabble letters arranged to spell SOS on the desk.

"Just so you know..." Rocky aimed her knife at Angelo, "I wouldn't go near that shelter for anyone else in the world."

"Not even for me?" Wes kidded.

"Especially not you."

"Well," Wes continued. "We didn't exactly go there alone."

Rocky and Wes had called the previous lead detective, Hong Lee, and asked him for his help. Still on disability and grieving the loss of his partner, Boniface, Lee had been keeping close tabs on the case through his former partner, who was also providing Rocky with just enough information. Unfortunately, Town suspected Boniface was a mole, and when the time came, he decided to kill two birds with one stone.

"Lee really stepped up," Rocky said, "especially after we told him it had to do with Jarrett and Savior of Saints."

They told Angelo everything, beginning with the police escort to Savior of Saints. It didn't occur to him until halfway through the story that they had arrived with the police just minutes before Jarrett planned to administer the Parallax infusion to Jason. The call Jarrett had received was from Claire, informing them that the police were there to speak with him. Except the police had come because of Rocky, not because Angelo had dialed 911 while trapped in the stockroom. "You should have seen Jarrett's face once he got that call," Angelo explained. "God only knows what would have happened had you not shown up at Savior of Saints." Abruptly, they fell silent. Angelo stood up. "Come here you two."

They group hugged until they started laughing. "The three amigos," Wes said. "Now and forever."

When they sat back down, no one said anything for a moment, speechless. It felt like such relief, talking about what had happened to them, as if doing so enabled them to finally put this grisly series of murders to rest, extract themselves from the Seven Spirits Church, Savior of Saints, the fluorescent lit hallways and dark underground tunnels, once and for all.

Rocky reached over and slapped Wes's thigh. "You have to tell Angelo how Detective Town reacted when he saw us in Jarrett's office."

Wes's head fell back, laughing. "He lost his damn mind. I mean, he would not speak to Detective Lee until Rocky and I stepped outside."

"Fifteen or twenty minutes later," Rocky continued, "we're in the parking lot when all of a sudden, the fucking place lit up like a tinderbox. I've never seen such a thing."

Angelo's thoughts drifted back to Bobby Town. What had life been like for him growing up with such an evil man for a father? He couldn't help but suspect Bobby had gone along with the conversion therapy to make his father happy. What a nightmare it must have been to be induced into hypnosis, drugged, and subjected to the Frame all to make him into something he wasn't. Still, that didn't erase Bobby's direct involvement in the No Angels Wept murders.

Angelo wanted to believe that Guy Cleveland had been a good influence on Bobby. It was clear that Bobby had finally come to his senses, especially after he discontinued taking Parallax. A ship having survived a storm but still lost at sea. Angelo hoped Bobby was able to experience Guy Cleveland's nurturing love before reconciling the role he played in the murders of those three gay men while under Jarrett's influence.

◆◆◆

Jason had woken up from a nap. He crouched behind the sofa and threw his arms over Angelo's shoulders. "What are you three up to?" he asked, nuzzling his chin in the crook of Angelo's neck.

"Day drinking," Wes and Rocky said in unison, and then laughing added, "jinx!"

"Spirits on high," Angelo added.

In the fading daylight, the room took on an ethereal glow; Angelo hardly recognized it. A Van Gogh painting. An air of enchantment surrounded him, indistinguishable conversations, the sound of wineglasses clinking. Angelo wondered, what was it that had brought them together? Certainly, it wasn't only a shared fascination with a serial killer, though that was partly true.

Jason flopped on the sofa with his head in Angelo's lap. Love, Angelo thought, what a fragile vessel, and how desperate he was to protect it as it pitched into the devastating oceans of uncertainty and danger. And now he was watching his love, Jason, laughing at whatever story Rocky had begun to tell. *I'm the luckiest man alive.* He took one last glance around the room, as if to capture this fleeting moment.

Angelo believed his fate had been sealed the moment he accepted Wes's offer to appear on *A Thorny Mess*, and now he had come to realize that in accepting that invitation, he had accepted a fate bigger than he had imagined, something beyond reach. For over a year, Angelo had beat himself up for making mistake after mistake, and now he saw clearly that coming to Los Angeles, he wasn't fleeing his past but seeking freedom from it.

For what seemed like hours, they stayed up drinking and talking, filling empty glasses with wine and empty spaces with memories. What they'd once feared they now let go, taking silent stock of it all now that it was behind them.

Here it was finally. Exactly what Angelo had been praying for: the end.

About The Author

Frank Spinelli is an American born physician. He lives in New York with his incredibly patient husband and their two dogs.

His writing credits include: *The Advocate Guide to Gay Men's Health and Wellness*, *Pee-Shy: A Memoir* and *Perfect Flaw: Angelo Perrotta Mysteries Book One*. He is a contributing author to *Our Naked Lives: Essays from Gay Italian American Men* and *Understanding the Sexual Betrayal of Boys and Men*.

For further information about Frank Spinelli, visit his Web site at www.frankspinelli.com. Follow Frank on Twitter, Facebook and Goodreads.

Acknowledgements

While writing *No Angels Wept*, certain people and experts provided me with insights containing one or more of the following crucial elements: editorial guidance; encouragement when I struggled to proceed; time in which to work; access to an essential area of expertise; publishing advice when it seemed too complicated. I couldn't have completed this book without you.

Huge thanks and gratitude to my publishing team Nicole Kimberling (still a boss), Dianne Thies and Reese Dante. I'd like to thank my fellow writers Felice Stevens and Nick Nolan for answering my endless stream of questions. Big thanks to Dr. Dr. Emily Freeman who taught me everything I know about behavioral science and finally, my husband Chad.

Other Titles by Frank Spinelli

Angelo Perrotta Mysteries

Perfect Flaw (Book One)
No Angels Wept (Book Two)

Non-fiction

The Advocate Guide to Gay Men's Health and Wellness
Pee-Shy: A Memoir
Our Naked Lives: Essays from Gay Italian American Men
Understand the Sexual Betrayal of Boys and Men

Milton Keynes UK
Ingram Content Group UK Ltd.
UKHW041843090224
437425UK00006B/147